.

NIGHT STORM

Catherine
Coulter

NIGHT STORM

WHEELER
PUBLISHING, INC.
ROCKLAND, MA

★ AN AMERICAN COMPANY ★

Published in Large Print by arrangement with Avon Books, a division of the Hearst Corporation in the United States and Canada.

Wheeler Large Print Book Series.

Set in 16 pt. Plantin.

Library of Congress Cataloging-in-Publication Data

Coulter, Catherine.
  Night storm / Catherine Coulter.
    p.(large print) cm.(Wheeler large print book series)
  ISBN 1-56895-558-8
  1. Large type books
I. Title. II. Series
[PS3553.O843N536   1998]
813'.54—dc21   98-006721
                                                      CIP

To Diana Burgos Camp

A lovely young woman
with talent, brains,
a wonderful husband,
and a perfect child, Kaitlyn.

PROLOGUE

Carrick Grange, Northumberland, England
December 1814

Alec touched his lips to his wife's pale forehead, still damp from the sheen of sweat. He straightened over her, feeling the distance between them that could never be crossed. It was too late now, too late to say the words that were choking in his throat. He shook his head. Finally he lifted her arms and crossed them over her chest. Her flesh was cool now.

Still, though, he wouldn't be surprised if Nesta suddenly opened her eyes and looked at him, smiled at him, asked to see their son. She'd wanted a son so badly. His name would have been Harold. After the Saxton king who had fought and lost to William of Normandy.

Alec stared at her, hard, and he thought, *A child wasn't worth your life, Nesta. Oh, God, I never should have filled you with my seed. Open your eyes, Nesta.*

But she didn't move. Her eyes didn't open. His wife of five years was dead. And there was a scrap of humanity in another room that was alive. He couldn't bear to think of it.

"My lord."

At first Alec didn't hear Dr. Richards's low

1

voice. Then, slowly, he turned to look up at his wife's physician, a small man, foppish in his dress and, at this moment, sweating profusely in the hot room, his intricately tied cravat as limp as his hair.

"I am more sorry than I can say, my lord."

Alec touched Nesta's cheek. Her flesh was so soft, and now so cold. He rose and turned. He towered over the physician. He supposed he was doing it purposely. He wanted to intimidate, to make the man afraid of him, to make him tremble in his boots. He'd let his wife die. He looked at the dried blood on the physician's hands and on the sleeves of his black coat and wanted to kill him.

"The child?"

Dr. Richards flinched at the harshness in Baron Sherard's voice, but he said calmly enough, "She is apparently very healthy, my lord."

"Apparently, sir?"

Dr. Richards's eyes lowered. "Yes, my lord. I am truly sorry. I couldn't stop the hemorrhaging. Your wife lost so much blood and she was so weak. There was nothing I could do, nothing medical science can do when this happens. I—"

The baron waved off the physician's words. Three days before, Nesta had been laughing, enjoying herself immensely with her plans for Christmas festivities, despite her enormous bulk, her swollen ankles and the nagging backaches. Now she was dead. He'd not been with her when she'd died. The physician hadn't called him. It had been very sudden, the man had said. So sudden that there hadn't been time. Alec had no

2

more words. He left his wife's bedchamber, not looking back.

"He didn't even get his heir," said the midwife, Mrs. Raffer, as she methodically pulled a sheet over the baroness's head. "Well, a gentleman can find another wife about anywheres, particularly a peacock swell like the baron. He'll get his heir yet. Just see if he don't. But daughters have to be birthed, too, poor little mites, else how could heirs come into the world?"

"Has he yet named the child?"

The midwife shook her head. "He hasn't even visited the babe, not since looking at her right after her birth. She's eating her head off, her wet nurse told me. Well, no telling, is there? Her mama sick and bleeding away her life, and the little scrap healthy as a ruddy stoat."

"The baron was fond of his wife, I believe."

The midwife merely nodded, waiting now to commence her task after the physician, that pompous good-for-nothing fool, took his leave. He felt guilty, as well he should. Hemorrhage! The baroness had been healthy as a brick. But Dr. Richards had encouraged her to eat and she'd gotten too heavy, her color too high, her blood too rich. What with the large child, the birth had taken too long and Dr. Richards had done naught but stand by her bed wringing his hands. Damnable old fool!

Alec Carrick, fifth Baron Sherard, ordered his stallion, Lucifer, saddled. He rode from the stables into the blowing snow. He was bareheaded. He wore only a black cloak.

"He'll catch his death," said Davie, the head stable lad at Carrick Grange.

"He's frightful hurt," said Morton, an underling whose main task was to muck out stalls. "The baroness was a nice lady."

"He has his child," David said.

As if that was the end to it, Morton thought. As if the baron didn't have any feelings, as if he didn't care that his wife lay dead. Morton shivered. It was bloody cold. He shivered again, but at the same time he was thankful. He wasn't, after all, as cold as the poor baroness.

Alec returned to the Grange three hours later. He was, thankfully, numb. He couldn't feel his fingers, he couldn't furrow his brow, nor could he wiggle his eyebrows, and more important, he couldn't feel the pain that was deep inside him. His old butler, Smythe, took one look at him and shooed away the footmen and the two maids. He grasped the baron's arm and led him as he would a child into the dark wood-paneled library, where a blazing fire burned.

He rubbed the baron's icy hands, all the while talking to him, scolding him as if he were a seven-year-old lad again. "Now I'll fetch you a brandy. Just sit down here, that's a good la—just sit. Yes, that's right."

Smythe handed him a brandy and didn't move until the baron had swallowed all of it. "It will be all right, you'll see."

Alec looked up at the worn old face that held kindness and worry. "How can it be all right, Smythe? Nesta's dead."

"I know, my boy, I know. But the grief will

4

pass and you've a daughter now. Don't forget your little daughter."

"I sat down here and listened to her screams. Even when she was exhausted, even when her voice was hoarse and raw, I could hear her. It's so quiet now."

"I know, I know," Smythe said helplessly. "But, my lord, don't forget your little daughter. I've heard her yelling like a little general for her supper. A right proper pair of lungs the little one has."

Alec stared toward the curtained bow windows. "I don't care."

"Now, now—"

"I'm not in danger of becoming a likely candidate for Bedlam, Smythe. You can stop hovering over me." Alec rose from his chair and walked closer to the fire. "My hands are biting now. I suppose that's a good sign." He fell silent, looking down into the flames. "I must write to Arielle and Burke, and tell them that Nesta is dead."

"Shall I fetch you writing materials?"

"No. When I've warmed up, I'll go to the estate room."

"Dinner, my lord?"

"I think not, Smythe." Alec stayed by the fire for another hour. He could flex his hands now and he could furrow his brow in a frown. But on the inside he was still numb.

The earth was so hard. It hadn't crumbled under the grave diggers' shovels. It had broken off in coarse clumps. The men had grunted at the task.

There would be no brilliant roses to place on Nesta's grave. Only snowflakes, soft and white and cold, would blanket her coffin, and then the earth would cover it.

Alec stood silently watching the men shovel the black earth over her coffin. The Devenish-Carrick family burial plot covered the top of a wide ridge overlooking the Spriddlestone Valley. The ornate gravestones were intertwined with ivy, roses, and delphiniums. They were beautiful in the spring and summer, the vibrant colors of the flowers contrasting with the dark green of the ivy. In the winter, the pruned plants looked pitiful. Naked-branched horse chestnuts, poplars, and several weeping willows surrounded the perimeter of the site. The December winds whistled low and harsh through the trees. The Reverend McDermott had finished his eloquent eulogy and he, too, stood silent, waiting. All the Grange servants, the tenant farmers and their families, the shopkeepers from the village of Devenish, and representatives from all the local families were there, standing silently, waiting. For him, Alec realized. He was expected to do something. Tell them all to applaud? Tell them to go home now and get warm? Tell them to leave him alone?

"Alec."

The Reverend McDermott had moved to him and spoken softly.

Alec looked into the old man's faded blue eyes.

"It's beginning to snow hard, Alec. It's time to release the people."

Release them. What a strange way to say it.

Alec merely nodded and stepped back from the grave, a signal. One by one, people came to him, murmured condolences, and moved on. It took a long time, a very long time.

It was bizarre, Alec thought later as he stood alone in his library. The last of the guests had eaten their fill, conversed in subdued voices, and left, thank God. It was bizarre because he simply didn't feel anything. The numbness hadn't left him. It had invaded and stayed. It continued with him during the next three days.

On the third day, Nesta's half sister, Arielle Drummond, and her husband, Burke Drummond, Earl of Ravensworth, arrived at the Grange. Arielle was pale, her eyes red from crying. Burke was stiff and looked as withdrawn as Alec felt. He thanked them most sincerely for coming.

"I'm so sorry we missed the funeral," Arielle said, holding Alec's hand tightly in hers. "There was a snowstorm and we couldn't leave Elgin-Tyne. I'm so sorry, Alec, so sorry." Arielle had thought of Alec Carrick as the Beautiful Baron, a silly name, but apt. Only now he looked gaunt, the flesh of his face pulled tightly over his bones. His brilliant blue eyes, as light as a summer sky when he laughed, or as deep as the North Sea when emotion held him, were now dull, very nearly opaque. Empty. His clothes were immaculate, certainly, but he looked thin. And it seemed to Arielle that he wasn't really with her and Burke. He spoke to them, responded to their questions, accepted their grief, but he wasn't *there*. If Arielle had wondered how Alec had felt about Nesta before, she was left with no doubts now. Perhaps he hadn't loved Nesta with a burning passion, but he'd cared for her very much. She burst into tears at his pain, at her own.

"Is the child well?" Burke asked, holding Arielle close to him.

Alec looked uncertain, shaking his head.

"Your daughter, Alec. Is she well?"

"Oh. I suppose. No one has told me otherwise. Let me call Mrs. MacGraff. She will see to your comfort. Please stay. The storm will probably continue for another week. Nesta's grave is covered with snow now. I'll take you there. I've commissioned a marble gravestone. It isn't yet completed. Ah, here is Mrs. MacGraff. Please don't cry, Arielle. Burke, thank you again for coming."

Arielle got hold of herself sometime later in their bedchamber. "He's in shock," she said to her husband. "And I had to turn into a watering pot. I'm sorry, Burke. Poor Alec. And the child. We must see her. What is her name?"

The child hadn't yet received a name. Alec looked perplexed when Arielle mentioned it to him over dinner that evening. "She must have a name, Alec. She must be christened and soon."

"Is she ill?"

"No, certainly not, but it must be done. Did Nesta decide upon a name for her?"

"Harold."

"And for a girl?"

Alec shook his head.

"Have you any wishes in the matter?"

Alec didn't say anything. He looked thoughtful

8

as he sipped at his wine. The child was alive, well taken care of. God knew, he could hear her yelling her head off. Smythe was right about the strength of her lungs. And now these questions. Who cared? "Hallie," he said finally, shrugging. "Hallie is her name. It's close to Harold. I think Nesta would have liked that."

Still Alec didn't visit his daughter. The day before Arielle and Burke were due to leave Carrick Grange, they broached the subject with their host.

"Arielle and I have discussed this thoroughly, Alec. If it is all right with you, we will take Hallie back to Ravensworth with us."

Alec stared at him. "You want to take the child to Ravensworth? Whyever for?"

"You are a man, Alec. At least I am her aunt. I would care for her and love her, as would Burke. There is nothing for her here, save a nurse to see to her needs. A child needs love, Alec, and care."

He looks bewildered, Arielle thought, staring at her brother-in-law. He doesn't seem to understand.

Alec said slowly, vaguely, "I can't give my child away."

"You have no reason to feel as if you're not behaving responsibly in this," Burke said. "You are a single gentleman, a widower. You wish, do you not, to return to your shipping? To captain one of your own merchant ships again? What is your favorite? Oh, yes, the *Night Dancer.*"

"Yes, a barkentine and a wonderful vessel." Alec nodded, adding, "That is what I told you, isn't it? There is nothing more to do here. It is so very quiet, you know. I don't wish to remain at the Grange much longer. My steward, Arnold Cruisk, is a competent fellow and will handle the Grange business. I trained him. He will send me reports. He can be trusted."

"You can hardly take a babe on board ship with you to God knows where," Arielle said. "She needs stability, Alec, a home, and people to care for her. Burke and I can do that."

"She's part of Nesta, you know."

"Yes, we know."

"I must think about it. It doesn't seem right— to leave my child and . . . well, I will go riding now and think about it."

Arielle wanted to tell him that it was snowing again, but she held her peace. "He needs time," Burke said quietly to her after Alec had left the drawing room. "It is difficult."

That evening while Alec was dressing for dinner, he heard a baby squalling from over-head—sharp, piercing cries that made him jerk about and mangle his cravat. The crying didn't stop; it grew louder. He looked in the mirror, pulled off the cravat, and flung it down. He closed his eyes. What was the matter? Why was the babe crying as if her life were in danger?

"Stop it," he whispered. "For God's sake, be quiet!"

The babe was yelling to bring the Grange down.

Alec couldn't bear it. He strode from his bedchamber down the wide corridor to the stairs that led to the third-floor nursery. It was cold, he thought, as he stomped up the stairs. The babe's crying sounded raw now as he drew closer.

He flung open the nursery door. There was Mrs. MacGraff, his damned housekeeper, holding the babe, rocking her, trying to quiet her.

"Where the hell is the wet nurse?"

Mrs. MacGraff whirled about. "Oh, my lord, Nan had to return to her home. Her own child is ill and her family . . . well, it's a very tedious story, actually, but there's no food for Hallie and she's hungry."

Alec cut her off peremptorily. "Give her to me. Go downstairs and tell Smythe to have Nan fetched immediately. Have her bring her child back here to the Grange. For God's sake, go!"

Alec took his daughter. For an instant he was terrified. She was so tiny. Her cries were so loud that his ears hurt. Her small body was convulsed with yells. He knew enough to support her neck. He didn't want to, but at last he forced himself to look at her, really look. Her face was screwed up and blotched red. She had a thick head of pale blond hair. Exactly the color of his hair when he'd been little, so his mother had fondly told him many times.

He said softly, "Hush, little one, it's all right. You'll eat soon enough."

The baby stopped a moment on hearing the strange deep voice and opened her vague eyes very wide, looking toward the sound. Her eyes were the color of the North Sea during a wild storm. Dark, dark blue, and deep. Just like his.

"No," Alec said. He held the squirming body away from him. "No."

The small body heaved and strained against the unaccustomed hands. Alec held her away from him until he couldn't bear it. He gave it up then and drew his daughter to his shoulder, crooning meaningless words and sounds over and over, softly, again and again. To his astonishment, she hiccuped several times, stuffed her fist into her mouth, and put her head on his shoulder. Her small body shuddered again, then grew quiet. For an instant he was terrified again, that she was dead. But no, she'd fallen asleep. He was holding her and she was asleep. Alec looked blankly around him. What was he to do now?

He eased down into a rocking chair that faced the fireplace. He pulled a wool shawl over Hallie and began to rock.

He lulled himself to sleep. Nan and Mrs. MacGraff stood in the open doorway and stared.

" 'Tis amazing," said Mrs. MacGraff. "His lordship hasn't been up here before."

Nan held her own child against her milk-swelled breasts. She hurt. "I must feed Hallie," she said.

Alec awoke at the low sound of women's voices. He turned to look at Nan. "She's asleep," he said simply. "I've been rocking her."

Nan blurted out, "She looks just like you! I wondered, but I didn't—" She broke off, appalled at herself.

Alec rose, waking Hallie as he did so. She reared back against his hand, stared vaguely up at him, and bellowed. Alec grinned. "She needs you, Nan."

He watched Nan lay down her own child, then

12

take Hallie from him with competent hands. "After the babe is asleep, I want to speak to you. Ask Mrs. MacGraff to show you to the library."

He nodded to the two women and left the nursery. His step was light, his shoulders squared. He at last felt something that wasn't pain.

1

**Aboard the Barkentine *Night Dancer*
Near Chesapeake Bay
October 1819**

Alec Carrick stood on the deck near the *Dancer's* wheel, half his attention on the beating canvas of the square-rigged foremast, and half on his small daughter, who was sitting cross-legged in the middle of a huge circle of coiled hemp on the quarterdeck, practicing her knots. From his position, she looked to be perfecting her clove hitches. She never took on a new task, or in this case, went on to a new knot, until she'd gotten the previous knot just exactly to her liking. He recalled she'd spent upwards of two days on her rolling hitch before Ticknor, the *Night Dancer's* second mate, a young man of twenty-three who hailed from Yorkshire and blushed like a school-girl at any jest, had finally talked her around, saying, "Now, now, Miss Hallie, 'tis enough. Ye've got it, aye, ye have. We don't want yer fingers to be callused as a snail's, now do we? We'll show yer papa, an' jes' see if he don't say it's perfect."

And Alec had praised the rolling hitch. God forbid snail calluses.

Hallie was dressed like any of his sailors in a red-and-white-striped guernsey and blue denim

15

dungarees. And, like his sailors', they fitted her small body like a glove, flaring out at the feet so that, in theory, she could easily roll them up to wash the deck or shinny up the rigging. She was wearing a straw tarpaulin hat, its broad brim giving a decent runoff of drizzle when it rained, and tar and oil keeping it black and waterproof. Most important, it protected Hallie's face from the sun. She was fair-complexioned and it worried Alec, until he'd managed to convince her never to remove her hat during the daylight hours on deck. He'd told her that he didn't want her to be the first four-year-old with weathered leather skin like old Punko's, the sailmaker.

Hallie had raised her blue eyes to his face and said, "Papa, really, I'm very nearly five now."

"Sorry," he'd said, and pulled the hat almost to her eyebrows. "If you're nearly five, that makes me a very old man. I'll be thirty-two not too long after you're five."

Hallie studied him with intense scrutiny. She shook her head. "No, you're not old, Papa. I agree with Miss Blanchard. You're beautiful. I don't know much about Greek coins, like Miss Blanchard must, but even Mrs. Swindel sometimes just stares at you."

"Miss Blanchard," Alec repeated in a thin, stunned voice, disregarding the rest of his daughter's confidences.

"She was here once, don't you remember? Last May, when we were in London. You brought her here to visit. She was laughing and telling you how beautiful you were and how she wanted to

16

do things to you, and you told her that her bottom was equally something to behold and that—"

"All right, that's enough," Alec said, quickly closing his hand over his daughter's mouth. He saw Ticknor staring at him, his hand over his own mouth to keep in his chuckles. "Quite enough." He felt a large dose of guilt and an insane urge to laugh. He remembered that afternoon some five months before. He'd thought Hallie was with Mrs. Swindel, her nanny, in their London town house, so when Eileen Blanchard had begged to visit one of his ships, he'd brought her. He groaned to himself. At least he hadn't made love to her. Hallie might just have walked in on them and asked for an explanation in that calm, quite curious little voice of hers.

Alec grinned toward his daughter. Hallie was precocious, something of a handful, very serious, so beautiful he sometimes felt tears sting his eyes just looking at her, and she was his. A gift from a God who had forgiven him his rantings, his *frozenness*, and his initial bitterness.

Hallie, now, was also barefoot, her small feet as brown and tough as any of the sailors'. Her toes were wiggling to the beat of Pippin's sea chantey, a funny tale of a captain who managed to lose his ship and all his booty to the devil because he was too stupid to understand that a pitchfork and a tail were something out of the ordinary. Pippin was Alec's cabin boy on board ship and his valet-in-training on land, a bright lad of fifteen whose mother had left him on the steps of St. Paul's, a lad who worshipped him and adored Hallie.

Alec looked up at the foremast. The wind was northwesterly and steady. They were drifting leeward. "Mr. Pitts, bring her in a bit," he called to his first mate, Abel Pitts, who had been with him for six years and knew a ship's ways as well as he knew his captain's ways.

"Aye, Capt'n," Abel called back. "I was looking at that bloody albatross. He's leading us a merry chase and it ain't close-hauled he wants to be!"

Alec grinned and looked out over the horizon. The albatross, its wing span a good fifteen feet, was dipping and churning, racing back to the barkentine, then sheering off again. It was a beautiful early October day, the sun heavy and bright, the sky a rich blue and dotted with the whitest of clouds, the ocean calm, the waves gentle and rolling. They would reach Chesapeake Bay by morning if the wind held, and he would be visiting Mr. James Paxton in Baltimore after they'd navigated the one hundred and fifty miles of bay to reach the inner basin. He'd see Mr. James Paxton or his son, Mr. Eugene Paxton, he amended to himself.

Mr. Pitts called out, "There's Clegg, Capt'n. He's got your lunch ready. And Miss Hallie's."

Alec nodded and waved to Clegg, as wide in the beam as he was tall and blessed with the sunniest nature of anyone aboard the ship. Alec made his way to his daughter. She was concentrating so intently at first she didn't see him. He merely waited, content to marvel at the splendid little creature he'd produced. She was so different

18

from him and from Nesta. "Hallie," he said quietly so as not to startle her.

Hallie looked up and gave him a wonderful smile. "Papa, look." She thrust the knot under his nose. "What do you think? Your *honest* opinion, Papa. I can take it."

"Why, I do believe it's the best square knot I've ever seen."

"Papa! It's not a square knot, it's a clove hitch!"

"Hmm. I believe you're right. Let me study it a bit more over lunch. You hungry, pumpkin?"

Hallie jumped to her feet and rubbed her palms on her pant legs. "I could eat a sea dragon."

"Lord, I hope not. Just think of all those scales catching between your teeth."

Hallie scampered through the hatch and down the companionway to his cabin and followed him inside. It was a spacious cabin despite the fact that the ceiling was but two inches taller than Alec. It was airy with the two stern windows and rather elegant with the fastened-down table, wide bunk, and desk of finely carved mahogany. The port wall held bookshelves filled with nautical books, naval histories, charts, London newspapers, and copies of every issue of the *British Nautical Almanac,* as well as Hallie's readers and grammars. There was a connecting door between this cabin and Hallie's. Hers was much smaller but it didn't matter, for she usually only slept there. She even played in Alec's cabin in the evenings. It was rare that he was apart from his daughter. "Sit down, Hallie. What do we have, Clegg?"

19

"Fresh cod, Capt'n. Ollie caught a good dozen this morning. Boiled potatoes to keep Miss Hallie as healthy as a little sea rat, and the last of the string beans. Thank the good Lord we'll reach port tomorrow, else the little lady here would be chewing her teeth off with salt horse."

Alec fancied that the captain's table was always better when Hallie was aboard. He realized that she hadn't washed her hands, but then again, he hadn't washed his either. He watched her eat, slowly and intently, as she did most things. He waited, knowing that after a half-dozen well-chewed bites, she'd want to talk, or rather, hear him talk.

Just before the seventh bite, she said, "Tell me about the Baltimore clippers, Papa."

They'd been through this several times before, but Hallie never tired of hearing about the clippers. Alec swallowed a bite of cod and took a sip of wine. "Well, it's just as I told you, pumpkin. The Baltimore clipper is really a two-masted schooner. It's sleek and fast because it can sail so close to the wind. Its masts are a good fifteen feet taller than our barkentine's. And the clippers are small, you'll remember, not usually more than one hundred feet long with wide uncluttered decks. And they sit real close to the waterline."

Hallie was sitting forward now, her elbows on the table, her chin propped up on her hands. "That's right, Papa. She isn't much good in the North Atlantic, where there are a lot of storms. Waves would wash right over her decks and the winds would tear down her masts. But she can maneuver quickly, so no frigate or brig or snow or bark can catch her."

"That's right. She's lightly built and can duck and hide and race and turn faster than the albatross. Our English Navy holds a deep hatred for the Baltimore clipper, and with good reason. The American privateers, a Captain Boyle in particular, humiliated our fellows during the war. Eat your lunch, Hallie."

Hallie managed one bite. "Do they hate us in return, Papa? We're English, after all."

"Hopefully not as much anymore, but don't expect the Baltimoreans to welcome us with open arms, pumpkin. I told you once that they managed to keep our British troops out of their city, but the Washingtonians failed. They've got quite a rivalry there themselves."

"They'll welcome you, Papa. The gentlemen like you because you're so witty and smart. And the ladies will follow you about because you're so beautiful and charming."

"Eat your lunch, Hallie."

Alec insisted that she have an afternoon nap, and after he'd endured the ritual complaints from his daughter and finally gotten her to stretch out on her bunk, her favorite blanket pulled up to her chin, he returned to his cabin, sat down at his mahogany desk, and withdrew the letter from the top drawer.

Dear Lord Sherard: (he read)
My father tells me he met you some three years ago in New York. He has followed your career in shipping and is impressed with

21

your acumen and skills. (More impressed with my ready guineas, Alec thought.)

To refresh your memory, my father and I own a shipyard here in Baltimore and we have built the most stalwart Baltimore clipper schooners to sail the seas for the past twenty years. I am not bragging, my lord. It is true. However, since the end of the war, as you probably know, there has been a severe economic setback, not only in ship building but in our major exports of tobacco, flour, and even cotton. It is all mixed up with the New Englanders and their damnable demands for higher and higher tariffs.

In any case, my father knows of your reputation and would like to meet with you regarding a possible partnership between us. The Baltimore clipper, as you know, is the most efficient vessel for the Caribbean trade, and our clipper schooners are the very best. I ask that you will consider a merger or partnership between us. I hope you will come to Baltimore soon. My father is unable to travel to England at this time. Yours, etc.,

Eugene Paxton
Paxton Shipyard
Fells Point, Maryland

The letter was dated two and a half months earlier, in August. Alec was interested. He was, in fact, more than interested. The letter from Paxton's son had greatly simplified the current economic problems facing the United States. Indeed, the Paxton shipyard was probably in deep financial trouble. Perhaps he could do better than a partnership; perhaps he could buy controlling interest in the shipyard. He'd wanted to build his own ships for several years now. He'd wanted to be the major force in the Caribbean trade, and with Baltimore clippers in his fleet, he could become exactly that. His current fleet included the ship he himself sailed—the barkentine *Night Dancer*—two brigs, one schooner, and a snow. To see a Baltimore clipper maneuver in the smooth clear water of the Caribbean would be nothing less than sheer pleasure. With its speed and ability to sail close-hauled, it could beat any other vessel of the day. It was limited, he knew, to the mild climates because of the very construction that made it so fast, and would most probably lose at least one mast in a North Atlantic storm. But it didn't matter. He didn't need any more vessels to dare the unpredictable northern seas, or the Cape, for that matter.

If he wasn't mistaken, and he didn't think he was, there were undercurrents of desperation in Paxton's letter. So much the better. He would have the upper hand in the negotiations.

He folded the letter and slipped it into the desk drawer. He leaned back in his chair. It was at times like this when he thought not about the empire he wanted to build, but rather about the life he led and the life his small daughter led with him. It was irregular, to say the least. But he'd be damned if he'd ever leave her to be raised by someone else, even her aunt Arielle and uncle

Burke, who now had two little boys of their own. If Hallie was different from other girls her age, well, so be it. It wasn't important. And on the occasions when he thought about the life Hallie led with him, Alec also thought about Nesta and what she would have felt about it. He experienced the time-faded pain at Nesta's memory. It wasn't a deep pain anymore, just a gentle sadness for what had been and what had passed. His last visit to his childhood home, Carrick Grange, had been the past February. From there he and Hallie had traveled to France, Spain, and Italy. He'd even taken her to Gibraltar, where she'd dined with the English governor, Sir Nigel Darlington.

With him and Hallie had come Mrs. Swindel, her starchy nanny, whose sharp tongue intimidated just about everyone except Dr. Pruitt, Alec's physician. There was a romance brewing there, if Alec's nose was sniffing aright. Well, it wouldn't matter if Mrs. Swindel left his employ. Hallie didn't really need her anymore. She was becoming quite grown up. Except, he amended silently to himself with a grimace, when Hallie didn't want to go to bed or have her bath in the big copper tub or have all the tangles brushed out of her thick hair. She always wailed, whined, and carried on like a deprived orphan.

He remembered Hallie's comments about Eileen Blanchard. Lord, that had been an experience! Eileen had quite calmly slipped her hand into his breeches and fondled him, all in the dim companionway where any of his crew could have come at any time. He'd been without a woman now for several months. It was calmer without the inevitable scenes, but it was also more lonely. And he was randy. Always randy. He supposed he should remarry, but finding the right lady to be Hallie's mother was a task that boggled his mind. A lady who would mother a nearly five-year-old who was a sailor? A little girl who'd worn petticoats and skirts perhaps a total of six times in her life? And who was quite vocal in her dislike of such fibberish things? No, he couldn't picture such a lady, nor did he really want to. He didn't want to remarry. Ever.

Alec looked up to see Hallie rubbing her fists in her eyes, standing in the open doorway between their cabins. He smiled at her and opened his arms. She walked to him and allowed him to lift her into his lap. She curled up against him and resumed her nap.

Genny Paxton wasn't having it, not a bit of it, and she said so, not mincing matters.

"You've done a poor job, Minter, and it must be redone. Now."

Minter complained and whined, but Genny stood firm.

The new clipper, one hundred and eight feet long, with her rigged two topsails, would be the pride of the Paxton shipyard. But not with sloppy work on the mizzen peak halyard.

Minter shot her a dirty look, sneering as was his habit but silently of course, about her dressing like a man and striding about on board the boats and climbing up the rigging, showing off her woman's legs and hips. It was disgraceful, and if she were his wife, he wouldn't allow it. He'd give

25

her what for, perhaps slap her into obedience. Giving a man orders! Still, a man had to eat, damn and blast. He began reworking the halyard.

Genny nodded, saying nothing more. She had a very good notion what went on in Minter's excuse for a brain, but she wouldn't fire him. He was good at his job so long as there was someone about to check his work.

She thought again, as she did several times a day, of the precarious future. And of the letter she'd sent to that English lord some months before and the short reply she'd received, simply stating that he would be coming to Baltimore sometime in October. Well, it was October. Where the devil was he anyway?

Genny walked slowly about the clipper, speaking to some of the men, nodding to others, all in all doing what her father used to do. She finally went belowdecks to see to the wood-working in the captain's cabin. Mimms, the interior worker, was eating his lunch on deck, so Genny was alone. She sat at the magnificent desk, leaned back, and propped her head against her arms. Please, God, she prayed quietly, let this English lord be interested in us. She knew he was quite wealthy; her father had said so.

She had met very few Englishmen and no English aristocracy. She'd heard that they were normally quite worthless creatures—fops, they were called in London—and were interested only in the cut of their coats and the number of intricate folds in their cravats and the number of women they could mount as mistresses. If this English lord were interested, if he did buy into

26

the Paxton shipbuilding business, Genny didn't doubt that she could keep control. Her father trusted her judgment; surely he would back her on anything she wished to do.

She sighed and straightened. The ship would be finished within two weeks. They didn't yet have a buyer. If one didn't appear soon, the ship-yard would have to be closed. It was that simple and that final. Mr. Truman of The Bank of the United States would have to deal with their credi-tors. She couldn't abide the thought, nor could she abide Mr. Jenks, a man with a leering eye, an old wife, and a patronizing manner.

And this clipper was a beauty. She herself could sail it to the Caribbean, trade flour and cotton for the rum and molasses, and make a fine profit. She'd simply have to talk her father into becoming a merchant as well as a builder. And then he'd have to talk Mr. Truman into lending them the money until Miss Genny the Captain returned from the Caribbean. That would make Mr. Truman sneer, she thought. And all the rest of Baltimore as well. It wasn't fair that she was Genny and not Eugene. She looked up to see Mimms in the doorway.

"There's a fellow topside who wants to talk to Mr. Eugene Paxton or your pa, Mr. James Paxton."

"Do you know who he is, Mimms?"

"Bloody fellow's English." Mimms spat.

He was here! Her hands shook with sudden excitement. "I'll go up and see him, Mimms."

"Who's this Eugene?"

"Never mind." Genny tucked her thick-braided hair under a woolen knit cap, bloused up her shirt to hide her figure, and strode over to the narrow mirror propped up against the wall above the commode. She saw a tanned face that looked pleasant enough and, she hoped, manly enough. She picked up the mirror and managed to see the rest of herself in it. She looked like a male, no doubt about that. She put the mirror back, looked up, and saw Mimms staring at her from the cabin doorway. He just shook his head.

Genny said nothing. She brushed past him, her head held high.

2

Alec stood on the deck of the Baltimore clipper and marveled at the sharp raking bow, the long run aft, the tall, thin masts, and the exquisite workmanship of the low freeboard. The sails were of fine canvas, the rigging of sturdy hemp, the woodwork the finest oak he'd ever seen anywhere. Set out of the water, the sharp dead rise looked nearly like a V, different from other contemporary boats whose sides were nearly straight down, their bottoms almost flat. The Baltimore clipper could slice sharp and clean as a knife through the water, leaving all behind in her narrow wake.

Men were seated about the deck eating their lunch, one eye on their food and one eye on him, a stranger. He was dressed informally, at least by his own standards, in black boots polished by

Pippin to a high gloss, tight-fitting buckskin trousers, a white linen shirt open at the collar, and a loose-fitting jacket of light brown. He was bare-headed. And he was getting quite impatient to meet Mr. Eugene Paxton.

"He's a swell," said Minter, sneering toward the elegant gentleman.

"And a damned Britisher," said another. "Thinks he owns the world, he does."

"Don't he know we pulled his tail off just a couple of years ago? They got short memories, they do."

Mimms took a big bite of his sardine sandwich and grunted. "He'll give Miss Eugenia fits."

"With her dressing like a man?" Minter said. "I doubt that!"

Mimms, an enormous man who was tougher than a strip of cowhide, just gave him one of his looks, which Minter correctly translated as *Keep your mouth shut or you'll swallow your teeth.*

Alec heard the low buzz of the men's conversation and accurately assumed that he was the subject of too many of their sentences and what they said wasn't at all complimentary to him. Where was this damned Paxton?

"Lord Sherard?"

The voice was low and mellow and youthful. Alec turned slowly to face a slender young gentleman—he couldn't have been more than eighteen years old, for God's sake—who was wearing clothes that hung on him, a woolen cap pulled nearly to his eyebrows.

"Yes, I'm Lord Sherard," Alec said easily, and

29

advanced toward the young man, his hand outstretched.

Genny couldn't believe her eyes. She certainly hadn't counted on anything like this. She was staring, but she couldn't help herself. Never in all her twenty-three years had she seen such a man. No man who looked like he did should exist outside the pages of Mrs. Mallory's romances. He was very tall, with a proud bearing, wide shoulders, hair that shone minted gold in the bright sunlight, and eyes so deep a blue that it nearly hurt her to look at him. His face was tanned, his features perfectly sculpted, bones and planes and angles all complementing one another, arranged to perfection as if by an artist's hand. And his body was as delightful as any woman could imagine or dream about. No paunch for this man, and she knew that he would never become like other successful men who grew complacent both in their intellects and in their bodies. He was gloriously made, not an ounce of fat on that wonderful body, lean but fully filled out, too . . . oh, she was having mental fits trying to do him silent justice. Damn him, he shouldn't exist. He was undoubtedly dangerous to any female between the ages of sixteen and eighty. He was undoubtedly not a fop, not affecting any excesses in his clothing, fine as they were. He was undoubtedly magnificent. Then he smiled and she swallowed painfully. His teeth were glistening white and straight, and that smile should have the highest tariff in the world on it. She was terrified of him.

"You're Eugene Paxton?"

Genny gave him her hand, feeling that deep voice wash over her. "Yes, I am. It's October. I'm glad you finally came."

He took her hand and looked down at her. And he knew in that instant that this Eugene was in reality a Eugenia.

Alec knew women, knew how they felt down to the fragile bones in their wrists, and he wondered just who this girl was trying to fool. Not a man who knew anything about women, that was certain. But for whatever dim-witted reason, she fully expected to fool him, evidently. So be it. Alec occasionally made snap decisions, and most of them he'd never regretted. He would have to see about this one. He looked forward to being amused, at the very least. Perhaps even fascinated, if the fates were kind.

He looked away from her. "Well, Mr. Paxton, you're right. It is October. I was much admiring your shipyard as well as your clipper. When will she be finished, do you think?"

He heard her give a relieved sigh at what she thought was her successful deception, and kept all sarcastic comments to himself. He would like to study her as closely as she'd studied him. There would be time.

"Two weeks, my lord."

"Do call me Alec," he said easily, turning that devastating smile on her again. "And I'll call you Eugene. I fancy we're going to become well acquainted."

Not *that* well acquainted, Genny thought, and swallowed. "All right, my—Alec. Shall I show you about the yard?"

31

"Actually, I've already shown myself about. As I said, you appear to have an efficient operation and skilled men. However, it would be a problem, I would imagine, to try to continue without sufficient capital."

"That's plain speaking, my lord."

"You wrote to me, Mr. Paxton. You are in financial difficulties, not I. Now, what I should like to do is finish my tour of this clipper, then meet with your esteemed father."

"I assure you, Alec, that I am well versed in all my father's business. Both of us will be negotiating with you."

"You will? Hmm." He walked to the railing to lightly rub his fingers over the highly polished wood. He saw her shadow shorten, saw her finally shrug and come to him. He wanted to pull that silly woolen cap off her head and see what color her hair was. Her brows were dark and finely arched, her eyes a dark, dark green.

He turned suddenly, taking her off guard. "How old are you, Eugene?"

"Why, I'm twenty-three."

"Odd, I thought you younger. Your absence of beard," he added, grinning down at her.

"Oh, well, you see, the gentlemen in the Paxton family aren't terribly hairy."

"You're from a long line of hairless men?"

"I wouldn't put it quite so baldly."

He laughed and nodded. Twenty-three, he thought, a veritable spinster. Was she Paxton's only child? She looked to be in charge of the building of this clipper. He looked at her more closely and saw that her dark green eyes held

32

even darker golden flecks around the irises. Very nice eyes, very expressive, and quite narrowed at the moment. As for her hair, he simply couldn't tell anything about it, what with that absurd cap. Her man's clothes were shapeless enough to prevent an accurate assessment of her female charms, all save for her legs and hips. No hiding the fact that her legs were long and, from Alec's guess, reasonably slender and well shaped. Her hips were boyish and firm, her stride graceful but without a single swaying motion.

And here she was, a woman, running a shipyard. "What will you name her?"

Genny looked about, her look of pride palpable. "*Pegasus*, I think, if Father agrees. She'll be the fastest ship in the sea and the most beautiful. Have you ever sailed a Baltimore clipper schooner, Alec?"

"Not yet. The ship I brought here is a barkentine, *Night Dancer*, and I have as well two brigs, a schooner—a three-masted staysail—and a snow, all of them fast vessels, but not nearly as fast as this beauty will be."

"I would agree that they are capable boats," Genny said, all condescension, but with a grin.

Alec liked that grin. It was unexpected and impish and quite contrary to the stiff, severe young man she'd introduced him to.

"Thank you, Eugene. I will be honest with you. I want as huge a share of the Caribbean trade as I can manage, and thus, Baltimore clippers are what I need and want. Now, when do I have the pleasure of meeting with your father?"

That made her bristle and he saw that she was

33

keeping her tongue behind her teeth with some difficulty. After a few moments she managed to say calmly enough, "I told you that both of us would be negotiating with you, not just my father."

Not likely, he thought, wondering how much baiting it would take to mow her down and make her reveal the woman, breasts and all. One could only try. "You are too young to be negotiating something so important."

"I am twenty-three, and you, my lord, aren't much older."

"I, Eugene, am thirty-one. A venerable age, one to demand respect, particularly from green 'uns like you."

There was that grin again, impish and quite enticing. He was going about his baiting all wrong. Doing himself in, as a matter of fact.

"There is a big difference, however," he continued after a moment. "I have money and you haven't a sou. I can't believe that your father would want his fate held solely in your hands."

Alec fancied he could see a bit of steam rising. "My father trusts me not to be taken advantage of, sir. I have much experience and—"

"Experience? You? Really, my dear boy, I imagine that you are still very much a virgin youth."

That did it. She hopped right through the hoop. Her face turned bright red—an incredible red, really—and her mouth was open to yell at him, only he'd taken her off guard too completely and she didn't know what to say. So she stared at him. He laughed.

34

And that, unremarkably, enabled her to bring herself back together in a semblance of order. "I wasn't aware that my sexual prowess was at issue here, Lord Sherard."

"My dear young man, sexual prowess is always the issue. Surely such things are the same here as they are in England or in Spain or in Brazil?"

How the devil would she know? Did he mean that men jested about sex all the time, everywhere? "Very well," she said, bowing to what must be true, and if it were true, then she, who was a he, must appear to be like all the others.

"Very well, what? You have experience?"

"Quite a bit! But it is none of your concern. Gentlemen—American gentlemen, at least—don't speak about ladies to other men, or about their conquests."

"Conquests? How quaintly put. I wonder, what is a lady? A female who doesn't enjoy men? No, I haven't phrased that correctly. A lady most certainly enjoys a man's attention, being showered with compliments and presents and jewels. But his body? I don't know. What do you think?"

How had this happened? They were aboard a clipper, for God's sake, out of the water, her men sitting around them, eating their lunches, and she was a he in this man's eyes. He was beyond her experience and, in addition, he was the most arrogant, most forward man she'd ever met. But he thought she was a man, too. She shook her head. This was going too far. She was getting in too deep.

Up went her chin. "A lady, my lord, at least an American lady, is one who speaks of appropriate things and enjoys things when they're appropriate."

Alec laughed at that but missed the sight of her impish grin.

"Ah, then you mean that a lady, an *American* lady, doesn't speak of enjoying men, but simply does so after she's managed to drag the poor fellow to the minister?"

"No! That isn't it at all. You are misunderstanding apurpose, my lord. A lady isn't at all like a man."

That was an understatement, Alec thought. "Too true. Ladies, in my experience, are far more sly than men, far more cunning, and because they determine when the man can have what he wants, they exercise unbelievable power. That, my dear young man, is why men allow themselves to be leg-shackled."

"Why, that is absurd! Ladies have no power at all . . . they . . . well, I don't know. You must stop talking like this . . . you're a stranger here and sex is hardly a topic to be bantered about as if we were old acquaintances—" She stopped. Blathering, that was what she was doing, and all because he'd flustered her so badly.

"Back to being formal again, I see."

Genny saw that Minter was giving her his patented sneering, leering look. She prayed that none of the men could overhear this strange conversation. "Would you like to see the captain's cabin, sir? It's nearly finished and we can be more private."

"If you wish." And he thought: Would an

American lady invite a stranger down to be private with her? "Is your father below?"

"No, my father is at home. Please follow me, my lord."

Alec did, his eyes on her hips. Nice, he thought. He saw his hands on her hips, caressing her, and felt his sex swell. How much longer would she insist on this charade?

The cabin was exquisitely done and was roomy enough even for him. Indeed, it was larger than his cabin in the *Night Dancer,* but there was no adjoining door. "There is a cabin next to this one?"

"Certainly. It is to be the first mate's."

Or his daughter's. "Now this is a man's desk," he said, running his fingertips lightly over the polished mahogany. "Yes, a man would be quite comfortable here. I should like to meet the fellow who designed the desk."

"I designed it."

"Really? And you are so young a man. Scarce a man, I should say. Well, it's difficult to know sometimes, isn't it? I shouldn't have thought that you . . . well, do you still wish to negotiate with me, Eugene?" Alec sat down and leaned comfortably back in the chair, a very comfortable chair big enough for him.

Genny was looking at him. Did he suspect that she wasn't as male as she purported? No, he would have said something, surely. "Yes, and with my father, of course. It is his shipyard."

"True. You wouldn't want to be unreasonable or take all the glory. And as his son, you are his heir and thus have some say in the matter."

37

"That's correct."

"Shall I come to dine with you and your father this evening? You have sisters? A mother?"

Genny's eyes glazed over. What to do? Oh, dear, she would have to speak to her father. Oh, goodness, she couldn't be Eugene at home, with her hair falling all about her face. She gave in gracefully even as her mind raced to formulate a strategy. "Certainly. Seven o'clock? And yes, I do have a sister, but my mother died a long time ago."

"I'm sorry," Alec said, rising. "Seven o'clock will be fine. I look forward to meeting this sister. Now, Mr. Eugene, I would like to see the rest of the clipper."

The Paxton butler, Moses, a black man of immense dignity, ushered Alec into the drawing room. There, an older gentleman and a young lady awaited him. Moses merely said, "Suh," to Alec, then bowed himself out.

Genny had prepared herself, truly she had, only not enough. Alec Carrick dressed informally was one thing, but Alec Carrick in evening garb was enough to make any female lose what little sense she had left. He should be outlawed. No man should be allowed to dress like that, looking as he did. The unremitting black broken only by the white linen and white cravat at his throat made him look like the royalest of royal princes, the most proverbial of knights in shining armor. He was incredibly handsome, his golden hair brushed and gleaming in the candlelight, his blue eyes so vivid and sparkling, so very *alive,* that she just wanted to stand there and stare at him forever. At least forever.

"You shouldn't be allowed in polite company."

"I beg your pardon?"

"Forgive me, I was just reciting Latin declensions.

My name is Genny, my lord. Genny, as derived from Virginia, you know, and this is my father, Mr. James Paxton."

Alec ignored Genny—from Virginia—for the moment and took Mr. Paxton's hand. "It is a pleasure to see you again, sir. Three years or very nearly?"

"That is so. We met in New York at the Waddels. A damned ball or something equally as obnoxious. Someone mentioned that you were married. How is your wife?"

Wife?

"She died five years ago."

"Oh, dear, I'm very sorry. Well, as I recall from that ball, you were interested in returning to your home in England.

"I did. There was business to attend to. However, I spend less and less time in England now. No more than four or five months out of the year."

"You prefer sailing the seas?"

"That and meeting different people, visiting new places. Why, just this morning I had the pleasure of meeting your charming son, Eugene, and—"

"Here is a sherry, my lord, and for you, Father."

"Thank you, Miss Paxton. Now, where was I?"

Alec heard a very feminine, very nervous giggle from behind him. He kept his attention on Mr. Paxton, who had remained seated, which meant that his health probably wasn't very good. He looked to be about sixty, with a full head of white hair. Alec saw the daughter/son in the father. The green eyes, the high cheekbones, the squarish jaw. A handsome man, a formidable man. And there was a distinct twinkle in his eyes. What was going on here? Obviously the father and daughter were together in their charade. Well, who was he to quibble? Alec slowly turned to face Eugene/Virginia.

"You are the famous sister Eugene told me about today?"

"My brother was complimentary? I have difficulty imagining gallantry from Eugene." She thrust out her hand and he took it. "I am Genny Paxton, Lord Sherard. Eugene was called to our uncle's house outside of Baltimore. My mother's older brother. He's ill and Eugene is his heir. He had to go to him. He sends you his regrets."

"Since you take his place, I shan't repine."

"I take my brother's place? I am just a silly female, my lord. I know nothing of ships or halyards or—"

"Clove hitches?"

"Is that in a recipe?"

"Or topgallant bulwarks?"

"Is that some sort of English hat?"

"Exactly. I knew you weren't all that ignorant."

"But I'm just a—"

"I know. Just a female." Except, he thought, you can't hide that impish grin, my dear girl. He looked at her closely. She wasn't dressed like a silly female. Indeed, her gown wasn't at all low-cut to show a gentleman her breasts, nor was it in the first stare of fashion. The color—a pale cream—wasn't really that flattering to her, but it wasn't too bad either. But his practiced masculine eye told him that she'd lowered the neckline, for the lace had been cut and stitched down. She wasn't much of a seamstress either. The lace was sewn crooked and parts were clumped together. He didn't dwell on that lack, however. He could see the curve of her white breasts, see the slender lines of her to her narrow waist. But it was her hair that drew him. Thick, rich sable hair that was braided into a coronet atop her head with long tendrils curling down her neck. Her face wasn't beautiful, he'd grant the objective part of him that much. He'd known a score of other women whose beauty left one nearly in tears. But her face had something he found far more compelling: character, a good deal of it. And determination. That chin of hers—like her father's—was stubborn as the very devil. He wondered about her temper. How would she fight? Would she let go and swear and yell? Alec drew himself up short. This was absurd. He was here to buy, hopefully, a shipyard that built Baltimore clippers, not to moon over some ridiculous female who lowered her neckline at night and played at being her brother during the day and couldn't pull it off, at least not with him.

41

He was staring at her, and Genny felt as if her breasts were on display. What a fool she'd been to succumb to female vanity and lower the gown. She fought the insane desire to cover her breasts with her hands. She didn't have big breasts that drove the gentlemen wild, like Susan Varnet or Mrs. Laura Salmon. She'd been a fool. There was no way she could compete with him. He was the most beautiful man imaginable and she was far from the most acceptable of ladies. Still, she wondered what he was thinking while he looked at her.

Moses appeared in the drawing room doorway.

"Mr. Paxton, suh, dinnah is served."

James Paxton levered himself slowly to his feet. Alec immediately was at his side. "No need, my boy. It's my damned heart, you know. I just can't flit about like I used to do. Everything's slow and easy and irks the hell out of me, but one must survive, you know. You take Genny's arm and lead her on. Moses, come here!"

"I wonder," Alec said, looking down at Miss Paxton as she led him toward the Paxton dining room.

"Wonder what, sir?"

"How much alike you and your brother are. No, I take that back. Mr. Eugene Paxton seems a very serious fellow, and very naive, I think, despite his advanced twenty-three years. By the way, how old are you?"

"One doesn't inquire after a lady's age."

"Does one not? Perhaps if the lady were long in the tooth, it wouldn't be . . . well, enough of that. Now, about Eugene. Other than being on

42

the serious side, your brother is, I also believe, something of a budding rake. He quite embarrassed me with all his talk about things sexual. It's just that he doesn't know how to go about it. Do you think I should take him under my, er, wing and give him some worldly advice?"

Genny wanted to smack his beautiful face. She, Eugene, was a budding rake? How could he intimate such a thing when it was he who had made references to all the raking . . . ? "That, sir, I think Eugene would much appreciate. He perhaps isn't all that experienced, though he would never admit such a thing to me. I believe, though, that such matters should be discussed between gentlemen."

"No ladies involved?"

"Exactly. Won't you be seated there, sir, on my father's right? Now, Moses, what has Lannie prepared for our guest?"

"We'll begin with some calf's-head soup, Miss Genny."

"What an awesome concept."

"It's quite tasty," Genny said, trying not to grin. "Truly."

"Veal cutlets garnished with French beans, followed by stewed rump of beef with turnips and carrots."

"That sounds more appetizing."

"It is Lannie, our cook's, specialty, at least the veal part."

"Well, if the calf's head doesn't kill me, I shall begin Mr. Eugene's education on the morrow. Do you think he will have returned from his uncle's bedside?"

"It is likely."

"Ah, a simple indisposition and not a terminal illness?"

"Just a slight unhealthy condition."

"Excellent. Eugene won't be fatigued, then. I have a fancy he will enjoy what I have in mind for him."

Genny wanted desperately to demand what it was. Alec Carrick, Baron Sherard, looked wicked. She held her tongue and took a sip of calf's-head soup.

3

The dinner was delicious. Alec, replete, sat back in his chair, a delicate crystal wineglass held in his long fingers.

"I can't interest you in some currant dumplings, my lord?"

"No, Miss Paxton, you cannot." He said nothing more, just looked at her expectantly.

Genny was puzzled. Perhaps he wanted some sponge cake.

Finally, James Paxton cleared his throat and said gently to his daughter, "Genny, my dear, would you like to leave the gentlemen to their port?"

Alec was hard pressed not to laugh aloud. She looked at first bewildered, then surprised, and finally quite thin-lipped. This, obviously, wasn't what she was used to. "But I—"

44

"We will see you quite soon, Miss Paxton," Alec said, and his tone was as patronizing as an English vicar's to a pickpocket. "Your father and I have business to discuss, and someone as pretty as you would be bored very quickly."

If she'd had nails in her mouth, Alec thought, she would have spit them. There was no sway to her hips when she flounced out of the dining room.

Mr. James Paxton had been studying Lord Sherard throughout the meal. He was quite pleased with what he saw. He'd remembered the young baron as being thoughtful, intelligent, and far too handsome for his own good. He was older now, still thoughtful and intelligent, and if the glazed sheen in his independent daughter's eyes was any indication, he was even more handsome now than he had been three years earlier. He'd never seen Genny look at a man like that. It both alarmed him and relieved him. But Alec Carrick was treating her with good-natured bonhomie, when he wasn't teasing her or baiting her. If James wasn't mistaken, the baron did not see her as a woman. Well, it was her own fault. When she'd come home this afternoon, dressed in her men's clothes, loudly bemoaning fate, he'd just laughed at her.

"You've done yourself in, Genny. Face it and end it. Don't try to fool a man like Baron Sherard."

"There is nothing to fooling him," she said, snapping her fingers. "Truly, Father. Besides, there's no choice. Eugene must be Virginia tonight."

45

James Paxton simply didn't know what Baron Sherard thought, either about the shipyard or about his son/daughter. He motioned for Moses to pour the port, then dismissed him. "I don't smoke the things, but would you care for a cheroot, my lord?"

Alec shook his head. "No, I've always thought smoking a filthy habit, just as bad as taking snuff."

"Ah, for some good snuff," said James. "Well, my boy, now that it is just the two of us, it's time to get down to business."

Alec nodded. "I will be honest with you, sir. I am very impressed, not only with your operation but with the *Pegasus*. Your son gave me a thorough tour. I have seen your American clipper schooners many times, I know of their reputation during the war, and I would like to acquire the Paxton shipyard and build my own. I want to control a goodly share of the Caribbean trade."

James Paxton looked thoughtfully into his port glass. "Acquire? I don't think that is what I wish. Incidentally, there is another—his name is Porter Jenks—and he also is interested in an outright purchase of the shipyard. He hails from New York. The only thing, though, he wants to build slavers."

Alec started. "What is your opinion of that, sir?"

"Aside from the fact that bringing in slaves to sell is illegal, there is of course a good deal of money to be made doing it. Most men involved would readily agree that profits far outweigh the risks. Also, if one has his own ship, the profit would be even greater. It is already a common practice, and more ships are being built to accommodate the trade every year. However, I would prefer to buy and sell more benign stuff, such as rum and molasses and flour and cotton, and not worry about how many black men and women are dying in the holds of my ships. But facts are facts. It's big business and will only become bigger."

"Your Southern states will guarantee that."

"That's quite true. Another thing, Porter Jenks wants to marry Genny. She's turned him down, of course, but the fellow's a persistent sort. I shouldn't doubt that he'll be visiting again very soon."

Interesting, Alec thought. "Your tone says the fellow's a bounder. He's also dangerous?"

James was on the point of saying that his feeling was that Jenks wanted to marry Genny just to get his hands on the shipyard, but he stopped himself in time. He'd momentarily forgotten about his supposed son, Eugene. He cursed his daughter silently. He didn't like having his hands tied like this, damn her stubborn hide, nor did he like deception.

"A bounder? Yes, he is, and yes, Jenks is dangerous. If you and I come to an agreement, do you intend to live here in Baltimore?"

"I'm not yet altogether certain. I don't know your city. I don't imagine that Englishmen are very popular here, though."

"As the Baron Sherard, a gentleman of wealth and title, you will be offered the key to the city,"

47

James said and shook his head at the vagaries of society. "Don't doubt it, young man."

"Your son, Eugene, told me that both of you wished to negotiate with me." Alec grinned and James wondered at it. Had he guessed? No, surely not. He would have said something to Eugene's father. And Genny had been so certain she'd fooled him.

"True. Pity the lad's gone for the evening." As he spoke, James looked closely at the baron.

"Yes, indeed. My thought exactly." Alec raised his glass of port. "A toast, sir. To a mutually beneficial agreement between us. And to your very interesting daughter."

"Hear, hear," said James, who was thinking that it was an odd thing for the baron to say about Genny.

An hour later, Genny sat on the edge of her father's bed, her hand resting on one of his. But one candle was lit next to his bed. He looked pale, she thought, and felt something tighten inside her. She recognized it as fear. "You're awfully tired. Are you ready to sleep?"

"Very nearly, love. Before I do, tell me what you think of Baron Sherard."

Genny grew still. Finally she said quietly, "He is so very beautiful and charming, it is difficult to really *see* to the real man beneath. I would say he appears to be honorable, but it is too soon for me to be certain."

"He is honest, that I do know. I have made inquiries, ever since you sent him that letter during the summer."

"To whom?"

"Don't act so surprised, Genny. To acquaintances in Boston and New York. He and his wife lived in Boston for several years. I was rather surprised that he was married. I wouldn't have thought he was a man to be domesticated, particularly at such a young age. Not that the ladies don't swoon all over him, of course, but the baron likes to be on the go, to explore, to be seeing new places, meeting new people, doing different things. At any rate, that was the general opinion of him in Boston. That, and he was a man to be trusted, both his word and his opinions. A 'sound thinker,' that was what Thomas Adams wrote about him. However, I want to get to know him better, then decide for myself."

"Why didn't you tell me this before?"

James patted his daughter's hand. A woman's hand, he thought, lifting the slender fingers. He felt a callus on her third finger. "I didn't want to. I wanted you to form your own opinion of him."

"How did his wife die, I wonder?"

"Perhaps you can ask him."

Genny suddenly slammed her fist against her thigh, then winced. "This is horrible, Father, and you know it. Genny Paxton can't know what Eugene Paxton does, and vice versa. I am in danger of imminent sinking. Do you know that he lied to me about Eugene? He said the most outrageous things, called Eugene too serious, naive, with the aspirations of a budding rake. Can you believe that?"

"I don't suppose you're going to deny that you enjoyed yourself, my love. I am pleased."

Genny arched a fine eyebrow at him. "Baron Sherard isn't a bore and that's all I have to say about him. When will you continue negotiations with him?"

James lowered his eyes to the blue velvet counterpane. He was tired, very tired. He silently cursed his body for betraying him. There was still so much to be done. "We'll begin serious negotiations soon. He wishes to visit Baltimore, attend society functions—that sort of thing—see if he wishes to live here."

"Oh."

"Eugene needs to disappear, Genny."

"Not yet, Father, please. He treats Eugene differently. He takes him more seriously. You know how men feel about women who want to do things, to know things. I can just imagine how he would treat me if he knew that I—a woman— was running the shipyard."

Her lips thinned again as she remembered how he'd so neatly sent her from the dining room— to leave the gentlemen to the important matters. Still, she had the impression that he'd just been baiting her apurpose. Genny didn't quite know how to analyze that, so she didn't try.

"He'll find out soon enough, Genny. Wouldn't you rather tell him yourself?"

"All right, but not quite yet." He was going to begin Eugene's education on the morrow. Genny was excited about that.

She leaned down and kissed his cheek. "Good night, Father. Please sleep well."

"Think about what I've said, love."

★　★　★

50

On the *Night Dancer*, Alec was leaning down to kiss Hallie's forehead.

"Papa?"

"Go back to sleep, pumpkin. It's late now."

She did, curling up into a ball, and Alec tucked the blankets more closely around her. He rose and walked quietly through the adjoining door into his own cabin. He always left that door ajar in case his daughter woke during the night.

He undressed, carefully folding his clothes and laying them atop his sea chest, as was his wont, knowing that Pippin would see to each item of clothing on the morrow. The *Night Dancer* rocked gently at her moorings. The bay waters of the inner harbor were calm, the night clear. He lay on his bed, pulling a single sheet over himself. He was randy, painfully so, and he hated it. It was distracting and he disliked being distracted. It certainly hadn't anything to do with that silly chit, Genny Paxton. The girl, or rather early spinster, wasn't even more than passably pretty. She was also too tall for his taste, her legs going on far too long. But her breasts, beautiful full breasts, on display through the crookedly sewn-on lace . . . He shook his head at himself and wished he could have Ticknor, his second mate, turn on the deck pump and hose him down with cold bay water.

He needed a woman. He'd see to it tomorrow night. He also needed to see about finding a house and installing Hallie and Mrs. Swindel there. He wouldn't bring a woman to the ship with Hallie aboard. A lot to accomplish quickly just to relieve his male needs. He disliked going with a whore

51

to her lodgings. Too many men were relieved of their purses and their lives by doing that. Also, he had no wish to catch the pox. No, he wanted something more formal. A mistress. He could find a suitable female and install her as his mistress in a nice house somewhere in Baltimore. That would solve all of his problems.

He would begin Eugene Paxton's education in eight hours. He grinned into the darkness, aware that for the first time in many a long month he was looking forward to being with another person, a female person, who wasn't a mistress because she was playing at being a man.

He found himself wondering about those long legs of hers. Perhaps they really weren't too long after all.

Genny's long legs were back in her breeches, her very loose breeches. She'd braided her hair tightly, wound it about her head, and pulled the woolen cap over it. When she stepped back to look in her cheval mirror, she was pleased. She looked very male. Tough and aggressive. Yes, completely a male. The baron would never guess; unfortunately, everyone else already knew that she was Eugenia and eccentric, but there was nothing she could do about that save hope that people said nothing to the baron until she did. She gave herself a cocky salute, turned, looked at her bottom—no doubt that was a male bottom— then left her bedchamber.

Her father was eating his breakfast in the small dining room just off the kitchen. He looked well rested, his color appeared good, and she breathed a sigh of relief. His health worried her since he'd had that heart seizure the year before. She'd tried to spare him, to take over the day-to-day chores at the shipyard. Most of the men now accepted her. Those exceptions like Minter she could handle.

"Good morning, Father."

"Genny—Eugene! Well, how fine you look. And so much like your mother."

He always told her that when she dressed in her men's clothes. Whenever she was in a gown, she was the very image of him. She grinned, leaned over, and kissed his cheek.

"You'll meet a bad end, Father. Now, I haven't time to eat. I'm expecting the baron at the shipyard."

Her cheeks were flushed, James noted. How very interesting this was. "Lannie made you some of her special sausage patties and biscuits."

"No, not today. I'll be home, perhaps, for lunch. Or perhaps not. I don't know."

And with that definitive assurance, she flitted out of the room. A very unmanly flit. James stared after his daughter. No man would be caught dead walking like that. She was the picture of a woman who felt touched by magic, a woman who was feeling buoyant, happy. All because she was taken with Alec Carrick. His daughter, who had scorned first the boys, then the men, of her acquaintance, with no hesitation and great wit. "I've no time for the nodcocks," she'd said more times than he wished to remember. "They're silly or conceited or they want to kiss me and pull me behind the bushes."

Well, to be honest, James thought, that was a pretty good description of men in general, at least the last part. But the approach varied greatly. He wondered what the baron's approach was. He took a bite of dry toast, chewed slowly, then stopped cold. He stared at the portrait of his grandfather that hung on the opposite wall, the old gentleman beaming down upon him, his peruke thick with rolled curls, his complexion florid, if one were being nice about it. "I'll be damned," he said softly, and took another bite of his toast. "I wonder . . . I do wonder."

There was a problem, of course. James knew that the instant the ladies of Baltimore took one look at Alec Carrick, he would be chased, hunted unmercifully, and otherwise pursued until . . . Alec Carrick had been a widower for five years now. He hadn't succumbed. James didn't imagine that English ladies found the baron any less enticing than the American ladies undoubtedly would. The baron must have learned all the tactics of the unsuccessfully hunted male. He had to be very elusive, as smart as the devil to evade all the female machinations tossed his way.

It would bear profound thought. James called out, "Moses!"

"Yes, suh."

"Ah, there you are. Have Andrews fetch the carriage. I have some visits to pay."

"Yes, suh."

The October morning was bright and cool, a light breeze in the air. Genny looked toward Fort McHenry, still shrouded in morning fog, a grim

54

reminder to all Englishmen—Alec Carrick included—that the Americans, particularly the Baltimoreans, weren't to be trifled with. Genny drew a deep breath of the crisp air and stared humming. She was walking to the shipyard, as was her habit. She stopped and looked up at the large painted sign: PAXTON SHIPYARD. She wished it said "Paxton and Daughter," then laughed at the thought. If her brother, Vincent, had lived, it would have been "Paxton and Son," of that she had no doubt. The world wasn't fair. She was barely tolerated by the other shipbuilders and that only because her father was so well liked and respected. They saw her as an eccentric, a spinster lady who dressed like a man but still didn't act on her own. No, even she followed her father's orders. It was a man's world and it infuriated her.

But it was too beautiful a day to be infuriated. And she, Eugene Paxton, was to begin her education as a rake from Lord Sherard. Her step speeded up.

She reached the Paxton shipyard on Fells Point early. The men hadn't started working yet. She saw only Mimms and he was sitting on the deck, a piece of particularly fine cherry wood in his large hands.

She greeted him and pointed to the hunk of wood.

" 'Twill be the cover for the captain's chamber pot."

"Oh," Genny said. "I'm sure the captain—whoever that will be—will be most appreciative."

"He'd better be," said Mimms, and spat. "No splinters in his butt."

Genny fiddled a moment with a handful of bolts made to fasten the planking to the hull's frame beneath the water.

"What about this English lord?" Mimms said, not taking his eyes off the cherry wood.

"English what? Oh, him. He should be visiting us again today, Mimms. Now I think I'll go below. I've got some work to do on the books."

Genny had moved many of the company ledgers to the *Pegasus,* down to the captain's cabin. That way she could oversee the work and do her own bookkeeping at the same place. It saved time.

She had just stepped through the open hatch, her foot raised, when she heard the words "Good morning. Eugene?"

She jerked about at the sound of that deep, smooth voice and nearly took her foot off, catching it in the open latching of the hatch.

"Watch out!"

She felt her arm grasped and she was pulled upright, her foot jerking free. She wasn't hurt; she was, however, exceedingly humiliated. "Thank you," she said, not looking up at what she was certain would be a mocking look on his beautiful face.

"Not at all." She was released.

"Good morning, Alec. I was sorry to miss you last night." She looked up then and he was smiling down at her, but she didn't see any baiting in his expression.

"Your sister was a fine substitute. You must face reality, Eugene. You really weren't missed."

"Oh, Virginia. She's nice enough, I suppose."

"Well . . . yes, she's all right. But now to more important matters. I would like to see some of the shipyard ledgers."

More important matters! Genny stepped through the hatch and stomped down the stairway. She said over her shoulder, her voice testy, "You didn't like my sister? You can be honest, you know. Genny sometimes is a twit."

"Honesty it is. She is amusing, particularly her stitchery."

"Her what?"

"Her stitchery. Do you know that she actually cut and sewed down the lace on the bodice of her gown? Not very well sewn, I might add. You'd assume a female would be adept with a needle, but your sister? I guess not. I wanted to tell her that a new gown, one in the current style, would not be remiss, but I am a polite fellow, you know, and didn't say a thing."

"Yes, I am beginning to see you for what you are."

She turned away with those words and entered the captain's cabin. He'd noticed her stitching! She felt another, even larger wave of humiliation wash over her. Well, she'd asked for it, for honesty—the damnable man! Alec was on her heels, smiling at the back of her woolen cap.

Genny continued, not looking back at him. "She, ah, is known for her charm. Did you find her so?"

"Charm? She's something of a forward piece,

57

Eugene, probably because she's a spinster and has had no husband to control her. She definitely needs a man—a strong man—to give her guidance and to buy her some new gowns. Aren't your American gentlemen interested?"

"Certainly. She's had scores of gentlemen after her for years!"

"Years . . . yes, it would be many, many years, wouldn't it?"

"Well, yes. Anyway, she's very particular. None of them have pleased her sufficiently."

"I'm certain the shipyard has pleased the gentlemen, however."

Genny wanted to cosh him on his head. She wanted to kick him between his legs and bring him low, the result of such a kick, her father had assured her some five years before when he'd taught her to protect herself.

"Won't you sit down at the desk? That's right. Here are all the primary ledgers. She isn't one of your frivolous females whose thoughts are all on flirtations and new clothes and the like. No, Genny's serious."

Alec sat. "Serious? Your sister? My dear boy, I must beg to differ with you. She assured me that she was quite silly, and I must say that I am in agreement with her. Serious!"

Genny had forgotten saying that. He had the same powerful retention of her great-aunt Millicent, who'd never forgotten a single sin Genny had committed from the age of three months. "She was making sport with you, Alec. Teasing, that's all."

"Was she, now. Hmm. I will say that she does

have beautiful hair. Do you have the same shade, Eugene?"

She felt a spurt of warmth at his compliment. It was silly, really, to feel so wonderful after all the other things he'd said. She said quickly, "Oh, no, my hair's not nearly so lustrous or so rich a color as hers. Now, Alec, here are the ledgers. I will show you how I do the entries so you will get the idea of how we run things. In this ledger"—she opened it, smoothing down the pages—"I show the dollars I pay for building materials and to whom, and the terms if I wish not to pay for more than a thirty-day period. Did she really strike you as being a silly girl?"

"Not precisely a girl, Eugene, at her age. Even though you're doubtless a doting brother, you must admit that she's very nearly past her last prayers. How old is she anyway?"

"She's only twenty-two." It was only a small, only a very little, one-year lie.

"I should have guessed older. Oh, well . . . Now, who is Mr. Mickelson? Ah, yes, I see. He supplies most of your timbers. For the price you're paying, it must be excellent quality. No, I should have placed her at around twenty-five or so. But one can rarely tell with a woman, can one? I suppose it was the way she was dressed. The, er, lack of fashion made her look older, I suppose."

"I can't agree with you. Her gowns are really quite adequate. Yes, the timbers are of excellent quality, and Mickelson is reliable. As you will note, he is carrying considerable debt for us, which is why we must come to some sort of mutually agreeable arrangement very soon. That, or I must find a buyer for the *Pegasus*. Do you think you would find her pretty if she were better dressed?"

"It's a possibility. One can't be certain until one sees the final result. Now, just consider this, Eugene. You're paying Mickelson a thirteen percent interest on monies owed after . . . what is it? Yes, after twenty days of completion. You're tying yourself in too tightly. In other words, you give yourself very little time to sell a ship by the time all the outstanding monies are due. Anything would be an improvement, particularly a gown that doesn't come to her earlobes and consequently get stitched down and badly, at that."

"Of course, even with a new gown, my sister would still have the same face and the same manners."

Alec turned and smiled up at Eugene. "Sorry, my dear boy, but there it is. You've struck the nail on the head, hit the target dead center, tacked through your spit into the wind—"

"You've made your point! And made it and made it!"

"True. Now, these are the weekly wages for your sailmakers?"

"The wages are much deserved, so don't go on about how I'm doubtless being taken advantage of because I'm so young! I—my sister has a very nice face and her manners are all that are charming."

"True. Excellent."

"Really? You mean it?"

"Yes, the wages you're paying are just excellent. I was studying the workmanship on the mizzen lower topsail sheet yesterday. I would say that you've done quite well there."

Genny jerked the ledger away and slammed it shut.

Alec arched a perfect eyebrow. "I beg your pardon, dear boy?"

"I am not your dear boy. You are only eight years my senior, not my grandfather."

"True. It is just that you seem so very . . . well, unworldly, I suppose, what with your virginal hairless self. But I did promise to begin your education, didn't I? Should you like that, Eugene?"

She stared at him. She would like it more than anything. But not as Eugene. She definitely wanted to be Eugenia. She nodded, running her tongue over her lower lip. "Yes, I should like that."

"All right, then. Give me back the ledgers. I do understand your system, truly. You run along and see to your business and I'll study your book-keeping. Your education will begin this evening. I will fetch you at your house at eight o'clock."

4

"You're a fine figure of a man."

Genny simply stared at him. Alec Carrick, Baron Sherard, was the fine figure, not she.

61

Indeed, he was an incredible figure in his black evening clothes and glossy black boots, his black satin cloak swirling about his ankles as he walked. "I—well, thank you. Fine despite my hairlessness?"

"It's dark. One can't really be sure. A lady would give you the benefit of the doubt. Of course, you'd have to remove that hat of yours. Shall I do that for you now?" Alec reached over, his hand outstretched, but fear of discovery made Genny's reflexes fast as a snake's. She ducked away, laughing, her hand pressed on the crown of her hat. "No, no, my hat is very much a part of me. I'll keep it on, thank you!"

"Do you wear that damned hat with the ladies present? With your ladies in bed?"

"Of course not!"

That, he knew well enough, was most certainly the truth. When would she end this absurd charade? He was determined that end it would, and tonight. If he had to push all the way, he would.

The evening was cool and clear, a half-moon shining down on Baltimore. The always unpredictable Baltimore weather was, for once, quite pleasant.

"Fort McHenry is right over there," Genny said, pointing.

"I know."

"You Britishers quite failed in your attempt to take Baltimore five years ago. Turned tail and sailed off, back to your bloody little island."

"That's true. You Baltimoreans were certainly more hardy than your neighbors in Washington."

He was a frustrating man, no doubt about it. "Don't you even want to argue just a bit about that?"

"If you don't mind, I'd rather think about what we're going to do this evening."

"But of course you won't tell me."

"Not yet."

Alec and Eugene had turned off Charles Street onto North West Street, which became Saratoga. As they neared Howard Street, the neat houses soon gave way to the more flamboyant structures. They passed The Golden Horse Inn with its remarkable white-painted facade, then The Black Bear. The inhabitants also became more flamboyant, louder, more raucous. As they walked past The Maypole, Genny slewed her head just a bit to look inside. It was bright and noisy and she saw several women, scantily garbed, hovering over gentlemen who sat at tables, drinks in front of them, cards in their hands.

"You like taverns, Eugene?"

"Not always, but perhaps sometimes. Don't you?"

"No, not overly. I find them far too, ah, common for my tastes."

"They offend your aristocratic sensibilities, do they?"

"Don't be impertinent, my boy."

"Where are we going? I didn't think you knew Baltimore. You're strolling about as if you were born here."

Alec gave Genny an amused look as he turned the corner into Dutch Alley. "Don't you trust me to begin your education properly?"

Genny looked at him consideringly. "I don't know. Where are we going?"

Someplace that will make you bring this nonsense to an end, my dear Eugenia. Someplace that will make even you turn pale in your breeches and run for cover.

"My dear boy," Alec said, all kind condescension, ready to fire his cannons, "when in a new city a man immediately learns where he may find the best women."

"Find the best women! You make it sound like finding the best fish market! The best haberdashery! A—a commodity, nothing more."

"Certainly women are a commodity. You sound as if you don't know their uses. What else are they good for save bearing a man's children once he must marry and provide heirs? One must be practical, Eugene. A good woman in your bed at night and you're in a much better frame of mind the entire next day."

"That's completely . . . well, un-Christian."

Alec burst into laughter, he couldn't help himself. "Not at all. The biggest women haters are in the church. Did you know that for the longest time our ancestor churchmen debated whether or not women even had souls?"

"You're making that up."

"Not at all. I'm only reporting to you something I was lectured on at Oxford."

"Oxford," Genny said, her voice unknowingly wistful. "How I should like to go to a place like Oxford or Cambridge."

"Why don't you? You're a bit long in the tooth,

64

I'll admit that, but nevertheless, your father could get you enrolled in Oxford. He's rich enough."

That shut her up. The wistful look vanished from her eyes and he knew she wanted to scream at him that *a female can't go to your touted male colleges!*

He continued smoothly, harking back. "Unless the man is a pederast, he has no choice but to find himself a woman to relieve him."

"What's a pederast?"

"A man who prefers other men, or boys, to women."

The look she gave him was so wonderfully horrified that he very nearly gave all away. He managed to swallow down his laugh as she shook her head, looking away from him. Then she stopped dead in her tracks. "You don't mean we're going to a brothel? No, of course not. You wouldn't consider taking—"

She looked ready to crack, so he pushed a bit more, saying earnestly, "Only the best brothel Baltimore has to offer. Madam Lorraine's. You're looking a bit green, Eugene. Haven't I got it right? Isn't it the best? Am I misinformed? Mr. Gwenn told me that he wouldn't go to—"

"Mr. Gwenn? Mr. David Gwenn?"

"Yes."

Genny wished there were a sidewalk so it could split beneath her feet and swallow her. David Gwenn was a friend of her father's and she'd been dangled on his knee as a child. His wife was a sweet, motherly woman who always had a kind word for Genny. The idea was disgusting. "It's the best," she said between gritted teeth. She truthfully had no idea at all who Madam Lorraine was.

"Good," Alec said, and resumed his brisk pace. "Your education begins with Madam Lorraine. I did consider how I would go about improving matters for you, Eugene. And this is the place to start. If you like, I can watch you, er, perform and perhaps give you pointers on your technique— What's the matter? No, don't say it. Oh, hell! You're a damned virgin, aren't you, Eugene? You don't yet have a technique."

Genny knew she had to stop it. Now, before it was too late. Before she made a complete and utter fool of herself in a damned brothel. More than that, it was quite possible that a gentleman there would recognize her, despite her garb, for many men of Baltimore would have seen her thus clothed many times before if they'd visited the Paxton shipyard. Then her reputation, whatever that was at present, would be well and truly gone to hell. She opened her mouth. She had to stop it—now. She turned to face Alec, only to find that her blood was boiling in an instant at his look—his baiting, eyebrow-arched, patronizing look. She wanted to howl at the moon and kick him, so that Madam Lorraine's brothel would only be an academic exercise.

But what came out of her mouth was, "Of course I have a technique! I'm not a virgin. Just because I'm not hairy doesn't mean I'm not experienced."

Still not enough, Alec thought. God, she was stubborn. He shook his head, grinning down at her. "Odd, I would have thought you'd never even kissed a girl. Well, I suppose you Americans handle things differently than we English."

"Yes, we do." Actually, she was thinking, he was so handsome, his body so wonderfully constructed, that he couldn't possibly have need of a technique, whatever that was. He'd probably tell a woman he wanted to kiss her and she'd stand on her tiptoes and purse her lips without hesitation. "What do you English do?"

Alec gave two passing men a nod and slowed his pace. "My father, my sainted father, gave me a wonderful present for my fourteenth birthday. He took me to his mistress in London and she, my dear Eugene, taught me all about men and women and what they can do to each other to bring pleasure. Her name was Lolly, as I recall. A wonderful woman, younger than you are, dear boy, but then, of course, she was definitely an older women to my tender fourteen years."

"What happened?"

"Do you really want to know?"

"Of course." The instant the words were out of her mouth, Genny realized she'd horrified herself yet again. Alec was giving her an odd look, but she was thinking about her education and what she'd expected from him.

How far should he go in this? Alec wondered yet again. Why wouldn't the damned chit just give it up now? Would she let him get inside the brothel? Would she run the risk of being recognized? He had a feeling that her men's clothes were an everyday occurrence and that most of the people of Baltimore were familiar with the eccentric Miss Paxton. But discovery at a brothel could ruin her. Damn, he didn't know what to do. He'd been certain she would have folded her tent a good ten minutes ago, and he could have scolded her, put her soundly in her place, and seen her back home, to her virginal bed. Should he tell her about Lolly and his night with her? A youngish lady who aped men? He decided he'd let her do the stopping. He felt outrageous. So be it. "Well," he said with lazy remembrance, "she first taught me all about my body. I, being a randy young boy, couldn't contain myself, but she didn't mind. She let me explode without recrimination—three times, as I recall. Then she began my education. Would you care for specifics, Eugene?"

"I believe that is sufficient. Thank you. You were fourteen years old?" What did he mean that he'd exploded three times?

The horror in her voice made him laugh. "Yes, my father apologized to me for waiting so long. He was a diplomat and traveled quite a bit, you see. He hadn't realized that his son was so sexually, er, advanced. But it all worked out. I still see Lolly occasionally. A wonderful woman. Ah, here we are. Madam Lorraine's."

Genny stopped and stared at the drab three-story red brick building with its modest brown trimming. It was wide and tall, the fourth floor a mansard roof with dormer windows. There was discreet lighting from the shuttered windows. There was no raucous laughter or loud music. It looked like a preacher's house. Genny had walked past it many times in the past, never even wondering who lived there, never questioning anything. She closed her eyes for a moment, knowing she should speak now and get it over with. She should tell him that Eugene was Eugenia and watch him look at her with new eyes. But the new eyes, she was certain, would be filled with disgust at the very least and with full-blown abhorrence at the most. Or, even worse, he might think her as loose as the girls inside that house.

What to do?

The decision was taken out of her hands, at least for the moment. A small opening appeared at eye level on the front door. "Yes?"

A man's voice, low and quiet.

"Alec Carrick and party."

"Ah, Baron Sherard. Welcome, sir. Come in, come in."

Alec turned to her. He said very seriously, "Would you like to, Eugene? Do you want to go inside?"

Genny didn't hear the underlying concern in his voice, the seriousness. She heard only the challenge.

What if she were recognized?

What was she supposed to do if one of Madam Lorraine's girls came over to her? She closed her eyes, knowing she'd gone too far, knowing that she was the biggest imbecile in Baltimore, knowing that the very arrogant man standing next to her saw too much, yet not enough, knew too much, yet not enough. What to do?

"You know, my dear boy," Alec said after watching her facial maneuvers for several moments. "Madam Lorraine has this observation room, from what I understand."

Genny looked at him blankly.

He continued patiently. "A man doesn't necessarily have to participate, you know. Some men prefer to watch others, for example. They gain their pleasure that way. Or in your case, it could be a preliminary, er, introduction. You could pick up a few pointers on things."

"I don't know."

Alec had never heard such a reed-thin little voice. Dammit, he wanted her to end her ludicrous performance. His eyes narrowed. Did she want this? Did she really want to see men having sex with whores? Was she tired of being a youngish lady, with all the restrictions that entailed? Was she using him?

The door opened and a large, muscular, blond-haired giant stood there towering over both of them, his thick arms crossed over his chest.

"Just a moment," Alec said. He put his hand on Genny's arm and pulled her into the shadows beside the walkway. "Well? What will it be?"

Genny drew herself up. He was pushing, damn him. Well, she could push, too. "I want to see your technique." Take that, you bounder! He wouldn't strip knowing she was looking at him, not this proud, arrogant man.

Alec stared at her. "You what?"

"I want to see you and your touted technique. I'll watch you from this observation room of yours."

For some odd reason, Alec felt a spurt of lust so powerful he very nearly pulled off her ridiculous hat and jerked her against him, wanting to press her hard against his suddenly swollen member.

"You win," he said at last.

"I win what?"

"Come along and you'll see soon enough."

Oh, God, Genny thought. He wasn't backing down. She would have sworn that . . . It hadn't worked. Talk about being left in the lurch, and a lurch of her own creation.

Alec left her to speak quietly to the giant. The man nodded, not the least surprised by his words. What had he said? Genny wondered. Her palms were sweating. Her heart was pounding. She was more terrified and excited than she'd been in her entire life. The thought of seeing him naked, seeing all of him, kissing him . . . No, he would be kissing another woman, a whore. She didn't want to see him naked with another woman. She'd kill the other woman first.

"Eugene, come along."

Genny stared at him. Slowly, she walked to him. Neither of them said another word. They didn't enter the main salon but bypassed it down a long, narrow corridor. At the end of the corridor were stairs that wound back toward the front of the house. They followed the blond giant up the stairs. Genny heard music; she heard both men's and women's laughter. She didn't look at the closed doors.

The giant stopped. Genny saw money change hands, saw the huge man nod. He looked at her for a very long moment, then left. Alec said easily, "You, my dear boy, go in there. It is the observation room. I will be beyond the glass, doing my damnedest to show you an excellent technique."

He sounded curt, angry. She looked up at him, saw that his brilliant blue eyes were blazing and yet, strangely enough, quite cold. She shivered. "You don't want to do this, do you?"

"Why not? I haven't had a woman in over a month. I might have to take her twice, however, to give you an idea of how one should treat a woman." He was speaking quickly, making jerking slashing motions with his hands. His anger flowed from him and she felt herself drawing back. Was he angry with her, Eugene? That made no sense. The brothel was his idea, not hers. Well, it was too bad. She turned away, opened the door, and slipped inside.

Alec stood there in that damned dim corridor. This was absurd. He had no intention of going into the room beyond, stripping off his clothes, parading about naked, then plowing a whore for Miss Eugenia's edification. He saw another man, older, slender, gray-haired, leading one of Madam Lorraine's girls, a petite blonde with large breasts and full round hips. He pulled back. Let this man give Eugenia her education. He'd provide the commentary. Yes, that was what he would do. Smiling evilly, Alec quietly slipped into the observation room. It was lit by a small branch of candles, nothing more. There was a comfortable settee and three chairs, all facing a curtained wall, opposite the door. On a sideboard were drinks and various edibles. Eugenia was sitting stiff as a statue on the settee, her legs together,

her hat still firmly on her head, staring like a lackwit at the curtained wall.

Alec said nothing, simply waited. Several minutes passed. Enough time, he thought, for the man to begin his performance.

He walked to the curtain and pulled the cord. He heard a gasp from behind him but didn't acknowledge her. Once the curtain was open, he turned and strode to the settee and sat down beside Eugenia.

"I changed my mind," he said, not looking at her. "Watch now and learn."

The large window gave into another bed-chamber, complete with a huge red-canopied bed, a red velvet settee, and a commode with a pitcher and basin atop it. There was even a scarlet carpet on the floor. It was ghastly, laughable, and like an alien world to Genny.

Genny stared at the man. He was just standing there, a very young girl standing in front of him. He was slowly stroking her breasts, pulling her gown down until her breasts popped out. He leaned down and took one of her nipples into his mouth.

Genny stared.

"Her breasts are quite large for so small a girl. Too large, I think. However, they're well shaped, don't you think? A pity they'll hang down to her waist in a couple of years. This kind of work is hard on a woman's body. Now, her nipples are the largest I've seen in a long time. Do you like large nipples on a woman?"

"I—I don't know."

"The color is nice. A very dark pink."

73

Genny was staring at those breasts, mute.

"Ah, now our gentleman wants the attention. After all, he's the one paying the money. She'll undress him. She does it quite well, don't you think? You'll notice how her hands touch him continuously. Would you like a drink?"

Genny shook her head, not moving. She couldn't believe she was sitting here, beside a man, watching two people do such intimate things to each other. She saw the blond girl's hand stroke the man's stomach, then move downward until she was gripping him, and Genny saw the swollen flesh pushing against his breeches, against the girl's hand.

"I did promise a commentary, didn't I? All right, men like to have women hold them and caress them with their hands. And their mouths. I'm certain our lady will show us all her pleasure tricks. Ah, now he wants to see her. I myself prefer a woman naked before I undress. Do you?"

"I—I don't know."

Alec shot her a look but didn't say anything.

The man was now wearing only his breeches. He was pale-skinned, rather thin, his breastbone prominent. He wasn't ill-looking, but he was old enough to be Genny's father. The blond girl was younger than Genny.

The man sat down on the bed and motioned to the girl to undress.

Genny heard herself say in a faraway voice, "How can they do that in front of us? They don't know we're watching, do they?"

"Certainly. Some men enjoy putting on a show. I am not one of them. Now watch. She's

74

freed her breasts completely. Ah, yes, her nipples are quite spectacular. I think I've changed my mind. I think her nipples are too dark. I really prefer a lighter color, more pink if you—"

"Yes! I understand!"

This had to stop, for God's sake. But she sat there, frozen, pinned by her own curiosity.

"Ah, she isn't a natural blonde. I didn't think she was, but still, her woman's hair is nicely curved at the base of her belly, nearly a perfect triangle. Her legs are well shaped, but a bit short for my liking."

Genny watched the girl prance toward the sitting man, her hands on her hips, her look provocative. She came to a stop not two feet in front of him. She arched her back, brought her hands down to between her thighs. She began to move her hips, showing herself to him in a practiced manner.

Genny sucked in her breath.

Alec smiled mirthlessly. He was watching her profile. So you are shocked, are you, Eugenia? All you have to do is tell me to stop this and I will. Suddenly the man reached out his hand, grabbed the girl by her arm, and pulled her to him.

"Oh, no!"

Alec grabbed Genny's arm and held her still. "Hush!"

"He's hurting her!"

"He's not. Be quiet!"

Genny stared, horrified, as the man pushed his hand between the girl's legs. He was working her, hard, but the girl didn't look to be in pain. Indeed she swayed and twisted, rocking her torso, playing with her breasts, pushing them upward, her eyes closed and her blond hair falling down her back like a golden waterfall.

"That is for our benefit. He's not hurting her. It's an act, nothing more."

Then the man pushed her back. The girl dropped gracefully to her knees between his spread legs. She unfastened the buttons of his pants and he raised himself as she pulled his clothing down to his ankles.

Genny saw his man's flesh spring up, thin and red and bobbing up and down. It was awful. The girl's hands were stroking up the man's thighs, then between his legs. The man leaned back on the bed, his eyes closed, his hands on the girl's head, pulling her forward. She lowered her head and took his member in her mouth, drawing him in deep.

Genny gagged as she jumped to her feet, her eyes fastened on the scene. "No," she whispered, so horrified and repelled, she felt her stomach roil. "Oh, no, it's . . . No!" She was clutching her throat, and Alec knew she was picturing the man's member in her own mouth. But before he could react, before he could call a halt to this very bad comedy, Genny was across the small room. He whirled about, saw her jerk open the door and dash through. He heard her boots on the stairs.

"Genny!" he called after her. He took one final look at the sex melodrama in the next room and saw the man open his mouth, his hands fisted tightly at his sides as he exploded in the girl's mouth. "Oh, damn," Alec said, and went after her. Even dressed as a man, she could get into trouble. Damn her silly eyes. Why had she dragged it out this far?

Why had he?

It wasn't well done of him. He was a gentleman and he'd taken a lady to a brothel to watch nothing less than a lewd display . . . it was very badly done of him. Why had he pushed her so far?

He didn't know. He wasn't certain he wanted to know.

Had she never seen a man's rod before? Evidently not.

Well, she'd gotten her comeuppance. She'd gotten her lesson and probably more of an education than she'd bargained for. Perhaps not the one she'd wanted, but Alec doubted that she would play the man with quite so much insouciant relish anymore. He saw again her mouth working silently, her hand on her throat.

He ran up Howard Street. He saw her ahead of him and slowed. He saw her stop and lean against a brick column. Her shoulders were heaving. He saw her lean over and vomit. She dropped to her knees and Alec, sighing, went to her.

Genny felt his hands on her shoulders, steadying her. There was nothing more to come up. Dry heaves racked her. She wanted to die. More than that, she wanted to kill. Him.

Alec wished he had a flask of brandy in his cloak but he didn't. He handed her his handkerchief. "Wipe your mouth," he said, his voice remote.

She did. She didn't rise, simply stayed where she was, looking into the bushes, wishing Moses would appear and the bush would burn, her with it.

Alec looked up and down the street, heard some men coming, and grasped her under her arms, pulling her to her feet. "I'd just as soon not be found with a puking boy in the middle of Baltimore."

"I'm not puking. Not anymore."

"Thank God for small favors."

He supported her to the next corner. "Stay here. Don't move. Don't consider doing anything more than breathing."

With those orders, he went into The Golden Horse. He returned with a bottle of whiskey. "Here, drink a healthy swig."

Genny looked at the bottle. She'd never drunk whiskey in her life. But her mouth tasted awful. She tilted the bottle up and downed a goodly amount. She jerked the bottle away, gasping for breath. "My stomach's burning up," she whispered, then started to wheeze. Her eyes watered. Alec grabbed the bottle and watched her. She was bent double, holding her stomach, trying to breathe. He felt not a moment's pity.

This damned little chit was responsible for this. Not he. Well, he was, in a sense, but . . .

Two men went by, drunk as toads, paying them not a bit of attention.

"Better?"

"Hmm," she said, her voice a croak. "How do you drink that stuff? It's deadly."

"Do you feel better?"

"By that do you mean do I want to retch again? No, I don't." She looked at him with glowing dislike. "I suppose I should thank you."

"You didn't get very far with your education."

She shuddered and he gave her a glittering smile. "Didn't you appreciate the man's approach, the way he fondled her breasts, the way he stuck first one finger, then two, then his whole fist, into—"

"Stop it! That was disgusting and degrading! How would the man have reacted if she had done it to him?"

He laughed, deeply. She gaped at him. "It's done, my dear boy. Believe me, it's done."

"But that's not possible. Men don't—" Her voice dropped off like a stone from a cliff.

"Men very much like women taking them into their mouths. Did you have a good chance to see how she worked him before you lost your nerve and ran out?"

It was too much. Genny turned stiffly and walked quickly down Howard Street. She never wanted to see Alec Carrick again. She'd done herself in, she admitted it freely, but if he hadn't been so absolutely outrageous, baiting her as he had . . .

"I do believe I've had enough," she heard him say from behind her, his voice more angry than she'd ever heard it. Enough what? she wondered, and speeded up. She felt his hand on her arm, jerking her back.

"It really is enough!" he said between his teeth. "Now, Miss Eugenia Paxton, I'd like to know just how the hell you talked your father into letting you play at being a man!"

He pulled off her hat.

5

Genny didn't move. She felt oddly calm, as if the waves of fate had washed over her, leaving her quite clean and quite drowned. It was odd how other things floated through her mind at that moment, bizarre things. She felt her thick braid slowly uncoiling down her neck like a snake. She felt cool night air on her sweaty forehead. It was wonderful to have that damnably hot hat off.

"Well?"

"Hello," she said, still staring off at that bush, wishing it would magically catch fire and consume her. She wasn't about to look at him, to see the distaste, the anger, the contempt for her in his eyes.

"Miss Eugenia Paxton, I presume?"

"Yes. You presume with great perception." She turned away, still not looking at him, and strode down the street.

"Stop, Genny! Damn you, come back here!"

She speeded up, breaking into a dead run. She felt herself jerked back, a strong hand encircling her upper arm.

"Let me go, you cretin!" The anger came spurting out, full blown, ready to erupt all over the enemy. Anger at herself because he'd been the one to find her out and she hadn't been the one to do the telling. When he didn't immediately release her, Genny reared back, lifted her knee, and drove it upward toward his groin. Alec, a dirty fighter from his boyhood years at Eton, neatly turned in time, but the full power of her knee against his thigh made him realize that she would very nearly have unmanned him had that knee of hers connected with his manhood. "You damned—"

Her fist went into his belly, hard. He grunted, sucking in his breath.

"Let me go!"

He jerked her tightly against him, then managed to gasp, "That hurt."

"I'll do more than that if you don't let me go!"

Alec held on, raised the nearly full whiskey bottle in his other hand, and poured its contents over her head. She yowled, struggling fiercely.

"Hold still, damn you! I'm not about to let a youngish lady walk alone in this city at night. I am a gentleman even though you aren't. Now, calm down."

Genny stood there, whiskey dripping off her nose, smelling as vile as any drunk lolling near the wharf on the lower end of Frederick Street. "I hate you." Her voice was low, calm as the very devil, and he felt his own anger growing to new heights.

"You listen to me, you absurd female. You're not going anywhere until I get some answers. None of this was my idea—well, the brothel was, but only to make you admit to your stupid charade. I haven't the foggiest notion why you

81

decided I was blind enough, callow enough, to believe you were a man for longer than the briefest instant. Why did you ever begin it with me?"

Genny looked at his long fingers still wrapped around her upper arm. She'd show lovely green bruises in a couple of hours. "You knew quickly that I wasn't a Eugene?"

His hand that was holding the now empty whiskey bottle slashed through the air. "Don't be stupid. Of course I knew. You have a woman's hands, a woman's face, a woman's breasts a—"

"That's quite enough!"

"Well, to my eye, there was no question. You were lucky that your workers didn't give you away, but again, it didn't matter. I simply didn't understand why you were doing it. I was amused at first; even meeting your *sister* was mildly invigorating. But then it was annoying when you persisted in your deception. I decided to bring it to an end this evening. Thus the brothel."

"You succeeded admirably."

"Yes, I did. I much prefer straightforward dealing. I don't like playing silly games."

"Oh? Just what do you call tonight?"

"All right, so I wasn't straightforward with you tonight. You did get educated, though, didn't you?"

"Go to hell."

"A young lady, even one rather long in the tooth, doesn't speak like that."

"Go to hell, damn your eyes!"

He laughed. "You look like a drunken spaniel standing there with whiskey running down your nose, your hair in a tangle, spouting curses at me.

If I were your husband, my dear girl, I would beat your bottom for speaking to me thusly."

"Husband! That's a nightmare of a thought! You're a pig, a callow imbecile, an arrogant bastard, a—"

"Let's get back to the subject, shall we? I want to know why you paraded your butt in front of me in a man's breeches."

She said coldly, her eyes on his silver waistcoat buttons, "You would have snickered and scoffed at a business letter from a Miss Eugenia Paxton. You men take only yourselves seriously. If a woman does something well that you touted specimens believe to be only your domain, you sneer at her, treat her horribly, insult her. As you so clearly said, a woman isn't good for anything other than sex and bearing your children when you finally have to marry. I wasn't about to be ignored, or worse, laughed at."

"Why didn't your father write to me?"

"He didn't want to."

"Ah. So you went behind his back."

"I told him right after I sent the letter to England. He hadn't realized how grave our situation was, what with his bad health and all. I told him we needed capital and you were the one to provide it. I also assured him it was quite likely that you were one of those ridiculous English fops who had no interest in anything save the knots in their cravats and the pomade for their hair. Thus we would be able to retain control and continue doing things as we wished."

"You were really quite wrong."

"I wasn't wrong about you being a pig."

83

"Your conversation is as boring as watching you puke up your toes."

Genny sucked in her breath. "Let me go. I wish to return home. You've had your sport."

"You stink like an Edinburgh brewery. I can't imagine what your father will say. Or what tale you'll spin him."

"He'll hopefully be asleep. I shan't tell him a thing, you may be sure of that."

"Then I'll tell him."

"No!" She stared up at him. "You wouldn't."

"Perhaps not the brothel part, since I do carry a bit of blame there, but I shall tell him that we had a short evening out and that you finally ended your charade and that we had a violent argument and the only way to make you see reason, and not destroy my manhood, was for me to pour whiskey over your head."

"Will you let me go now?"

"All right. Just don't move."

She turned, very slowly so he wouldn't grab her again. "Can we start walking?"

He nodded and shortened his step to match hers.

"What will you do now?"

"About what?"

"Don't be obtuse! You're not stupid."

"No, and I haven't made up my mind. I really think I overdid it on the whiskey."

She ignored that last. "Will you at least speak to my father? Will you at least consider doing business with us?"

"Doing business with a chit who dresses like a man?"

She stiffened up like a poker, but surprisingly, at least to Alec, she held her temper. "I have to dress that way at the shipyard. It's difficult to climb over things in skirts. Too, when I wear skirts, the men look at me differently. I want them to see me as their boss, not a fancy piece, not as a—a commodity, the way you look at women. I suppose I've done it for so long that I don't even think about it."

"Are you known as the eccentric Miss Paxton?"

"I don't know what people say about me. Father's friends are used to me and don't much notice, I don't think. I don't go out much."

"You're twenty-three?"

"Yes. A spinster, long in the tooth, past my last prayers, an ape leader—"

"That's an impressive list. I didn't realize that young women were castigated so very early in their lives if they'd failed to find a husband. Did you fail?"

"Fail? A husband?" There was such distaste in her voice that Alec felt his blood begin to boil again.

"I wouldn't let a man with courting on his tiny mind get near me. All of you are little tyrants who expect women to be your slaves, to titter at your inane wit, to praise you when you manage to conclude some business satisfactorily, to—"

"That is really quite a catalog and more than enough."

"—to bow and scrape. All of you want a big dowry so you can waste it away on your own insignificant, selfish pleasures. No, thank you!"

Alec grinned. "Most of that treatment sounds rather nice to me, all except your tyrant part."

"You were married! I'll bet your wife would have agreed to that."

"Actually, I don't think Nesta would have agreed with you at all."

His voice was perfectly pleasant, but Genny, her ears sharp where he was concerned, heard something deep and raw. "I'm sorry, I shouldn't have brought her up."

"No. Now, I'll make you a bargain, Eugenia."

"Everyone calls me Genny."

"The same as your sister, Genny?"

She said nothing, frowning at the deep hole in the walkway just ahead of them, right in front of the Union Bank.

"All right, Genny. You may still call me Alec. Hadn't you ever before seen a naked man?"

"You're shameless! How can you bring that up now?"

"Just to get you enraged. You're almost amusing, you know, when you sputter and turn pink."

"He was disgusting and old enough to be my father—"

"A pity, true. Your first sight of a naked man should have been someone young and virile."

"Like you, I suppose. As I recall, I asked you to do the demonstrating, but you were too much the coward."

"Actually, you're right, that and the fact that I wanted to see your face when I made my comments on the performances. I really couldn't see myself taking a whore with you watching. He

86

was your first naked man, wasn't he, and with a girl who was wonderfully young, probably younger than you. That's the way of the world, Genny," he added for a bit more bait.

"It's as I said. All of you are pigs and tyrants and selfish bastards."

"I didn't say I agreed with it."

"Nor did you say that you disagreed with it!"

He waved that away and said, stroking his fingers over his jaw, "Now, what the devil are we going to do?"

Mary Abercrombie of Hanover Street was one of the leading mantuamakers in Baltimore, or rather her sister was, Abigail Abercrombie. Mary was her sister's assistant, even though she liked to tout her own talents to anyone who would listen. Mary did know the dressmaking business well, knew from the age of nine years old how to pander to wealthy ladies, and knew when a lamb for the fleecing walked through the door, a lamb whose day gown was not only five years out of date but too small in the bosom and too short in the hem.

Genny stood in the middle of the Abercrombie salon, staring about her at the various headless mannequins draped with beautiful fabrics. She hadn't been to a mantuamaker since her eighteenth year. She was relieved that, for the moment at least, no other customers were in the shop.

Miss Mary was pleased also, for her sister, Abigail, was lying down upstairs with one of her headaches. Mary gave her a winning smile, and her marvelous memory clicked into place. "Why, it's Miss Eugenia Paxton! How charming to see you again, my dear. How is your dear father?"

Genny was amazed that the woman remembered her. She, on the other hand, couldn't recall having ever set eyes on the mantuamaker before. "Miss Abercrombie? Yes, well, my father is fine. I am here to buy several gowns. A ball gown, I think, and two or three day dresses. I, well, I need your advice."

Mary Abercrombie wanted to dance, she wanted to sing. At last she could prove to her sister that she, too, could choose materials, and select proper patterns for customers. Thank the heavens that the young lady was well-looking, her figure quite slender, wonderfully proportioned, actually.

Mary pulled out bolt after bolt of beautiful material—satins, silks, the softest muslins, confiding in Genny that just because a fabric was from France and had an excessively long French name, that didn't mean it was any better quality than a similar fabric from Italy. Genny agreed with this outflowing of confidences. She was quickly buried under mountains of information. She was just as quickly intimidated. At last, she threw up her hands, saying, "Miss Abercrombie, I leave myself in your capable hands. Mine aren't at all good at this sort of thing. Please, select the materials for me and the patterns."

Mary was beyond being delighted. She wanted to hug Miss Paxton. She managed to restrain herself, for two customers walked into the salon. She quickly bundled Genny out of the shop, telling her to return in three days. She drew a deep breath of vindication when one of the ladies asked for Miss *Abigail*. Well, Mary thought, she'd show them, her sister included. She would be the one to select materials and fit Miss Paxton. In no time her name would be the one on all the ladies' lips. She rubbed her hands together, smiled very politely at the women, and went upstairs to fetch her sister.

When Genny emerged from the salon, it was with a ferocious headache and a feeling of inadequacy that she, a female after all, didn't have the slightest notion of how to choose fabrics or styles for herself. Even if she did have the choice of whether or not to have a fashion sense, she decided it wasn't worth it. Being a female wasn't worth it. It was annoying, it was tiring, it was painful. She absently rubbed her hip where one of Miss Mary's pins had found its mark.

At least she would have new gowns. And since Miss Abercrombie was one of the best mantua-makers in Baltimore, she should look top-o'-the-trees.

Alec was coming to dinner tonight. She turned into Charles Street and quickened her pace. Thank goodness she had one other gown that was presentable for evening wear. It was a pale green round dress of soft crepe decorated with two broad rows of embroidered white flowers with green leaves, one at the hemline and one a foot higher. It was a gown for a girl of eighteen, not a woman of twenty-three, but at least there wasn't any lace on the neckline to tack down and draw attention to itself. The center of the bosom was already fastened down with a black jet clasp. She owned but one pair of gloves, which were soiled, and one still-nice pair of slippers. Unfortunately, they were black.

It wasn't important. There was no earthly reason that she should even care what she looked like.

Alec Carrick, Baron Sherard, was only a man, and an Englishman at that. He was a beautiful man and she imagined that he was well aware of it, even though she hadn't noticed signs of overweening conceit in him up to now. What had his wife been like? As beautiful as he was? Had they competed in beauty? She pictured him and a faceless woman seated side by side in front of dressing table mirrors, talking of powders and hairstyles, and she laughed.

At the sudden crack of thunder, Genny looked up. The Baltimore weather, perverse at best, was now fully prepared to dump gallons of water on her head. To mix with the remnants of any leftover whiskey, she thought, frowning up at the suddenly dark sky. It had been clear just three hours before. Baltimore! She gritted her teeth and hurried her step. By the time she reached home, she was soaked to the skin, her bonnet limp, her hair hanging in long wet ropes down her back, her boots squashing on her feet.

Moses opened the door to her, opened his eyes wide, and tisk-tisked. He scolded her all the way to the foot of the stairs.

"Moses, please, it's just water, nothing more dire. I'll go dry off immediately."

"The English gentleman is with your pa—"

"Good afternoon, or good early evening, as you wish. Don't you ever believe in taking a carriage?"

It needed but this. Genny turned slowly at the sound of that incredibly wonderful male voice and stared at an impeccably dressed Baron Sherard. He was the epitome of fashion yet completely unfoppish in his pale brown coat of superfine and snug-fitting breeches of a darker brown. His cravat was tied simply and so very white that— She cut off her thinking. Who the devil cared how he looked? Goodness, he could have a tear under his armpit for all she cared.

"My God, it is a female. At least I think it is. Perhaps she's drowned, but no, she is walking. That is a skirt, most certainly. And a bonnet on the head? Amazing. Nothing like a dead brown plume to frame a sodden little face."

Still she remained silent. She shouldn't feel ashamed or embarrassed. It was her house and he was early. She didn't care a whit what he thought of her. Let him have his fun mocking her. She lifted her chin. "I am going to change now," she said and marched up the stairs.

He chuckled behind her. "You're leaving a trail of water wide enough to float a canoe."

"At least you'll not have to sail in it!" The instant the words were out of her mouth, her eyes very nearly crossed. He was laughing now, and she speeded up, grabbing her skirt higher, dashing to the head of the stairs.

Alec watched until she rounded the corner at the top of the stairs. He shook his head, turning.

"Suh."

Alec looked up to see the Paxton butler

regarding him with something of a pained look in his eyes. "Was I too rough on her, Moses? She needs laughter and teasing, you know. She's most damnably serious."

"I know, suh. Miss Genny's been that way since her father done dropped down sick last year."

"She was different before?"

"Yes, suh. Miss Genny was bright and happy and always teasing me and Gracie and Lannie."

"Who is Gracie?"

"She's our handy maid, I calls her, a nice li'l gal who's been ill herself with a chest complaint. She sees to Miss Genny and tells us all what to do. She's nearly well now. You'll meet her soon." Moses didn't seem to mind this, because he chuckled. He added quickly, "But now, suh, so much trouble, always trouble." He shook his head mournfully and walked away toward the kitchen.

Alec felt a stab of guilt. He didn't like it. He had been teasing her, nothing more, nothing evil or malicious, certainly nothing to make Moses look as if he were going to attend a funeral. He returned to the drawing room.

He liked the Paxton house, particularly the drawing room, or parlor, as the Baltimoreans called it. It was a large, square room with high molded ceilings painted cream, making the room airy and light. The walls were papered in light blue; the floor was bare oak with only two small round pale blue carpets. Classical furniture, most of it made in the Chippendale style in mahogany inlaid with satinwood, was arranged in small groupings around the perimeter of the room. The middle was bare, making one feel free and unencumbered. On either side of the fireplace were two highly indented spaces, each holding a tall vase of dried flowers. The effect was charming. Alec wondered how the drawing room at Carrick Grange would look with this kind of furnishings in its sixteenth-century confines.

He imagined he'd be cursed by his long-ago ancestors if he essayed one modern piece of furniture.

"That was Genny?" asked James Paxton.

"Yes, sir, and soaked clear through. Doesn't she ever take a carriage?"

"No, the girl's always been a walker. Strong as a horse she is. And, too, the Baltimore weather always leaves one guessing." James Paxton paused a moment, running his fingers over the pale-blue-and-cream-striped satin on the settee. "I'm glad Genny told you that she wasn't a lad but rather a lass."

"She didn't precisely tell me, sir."

"Ah, so you pulled her hat off, did you?"

Alec started. "How did you know?"

"That's what I should have done. That ridiculous hat she was wearing belongs to me. But I hadn't worn it for some ten years now. My fingers itched to remove it when she appeared with it last evening." He sighed. "I suppose I shouldn't have allowed her to do it. But she was so serious about it, so anxious that you treat her with respect for her business acumen. Well, what would you have done were you her father?"

He was Hallie's father, and he found himself

wondering what he would do if Hallie took it into her head to dress like a man in, say, fifteen years or so. He had no idea. Would he laugh? Threaten her? Thrash her?

No, none of those things, truth be told. "I probably would give her her head."

"Exactly so. Now, before Genny joins us, I'll ask you, my boy. Are you still interested in becoming a part of the Paxton shipyard, knowing of course that Genny runs it, what with my damned body playing tricks on me the way it has?"

Alec said nothing for several moments. He was staring fixedly at the empty gilt birdcage on a card table. Conduct business—ongoing business—with a woman?

"I've been thinking," James went on. "My health continues to plague me. No, don't interrupt me, just listen. I don't know how much longer I have. My doctor, that querulous old lady, just shakes his bald head and strokes his chin and tells me to take it easy. Does he think I'll take to climbing the rigging of the ships? I do think that I shall murder him before I go to my Maker. But back to business. Genny is my heir. Her brother, Vincent, died some ten years ago, more's the pity, not that I don't appreciate Genny, because she's a trump and a hard worker and bright as the sun. But if I totter into the grave tomorrow, she'll be all alone, no more family. You know as well as I do that no self-respecting gentleman will do business with her."

"Surely all the men who have done business with you over the years would—"

"No, they wouldn't. Men are strange. There's home and hearth and there's business. Two very separate spheres. If you take a woman out of the one—where she is perceived to belong—and toss her into the other, men will be threatened and they'll act against her. Hell, I probably would." He paused a moment, watching Alec look at that absurd birdcage that had belonged to his wife.

"I have a proposition for you, Alec."

At those ominous words, Alec looked at James Paxton straightly. He saw concern, hope, and something else . . . pleading. He didn't like it. He didn't know what James Paxton was going to offer, but he knew that he wouldn't like it. There was no way to keep him quiet, so Alec merely inclined his head and waited.

The ax fell quickly. "The Paxton shipyard will be yours—all yours. All you must do is marry Genny."

Alec straightened, stiff as a rod.

" She's a pretty girl—nay, she's a woman now. It's true she doesn't know much about being female. She doesn't pay any attention to feminine furbelows and the like, but she's kindhearted, smart, and good-humored."

Baron Sherard remained obdurately silent.

James plowed doggedly onward. "You're a baron, my lord. You must have an heir. Genny could provide you with as many children as you wanted."

"What makes you think I don't have an heir?"

James started. "I'm sorry, but I just assumed that you didn't."

Alec sighed. "I don't have an heir, 'tis true.

And I suppose at some point in the future I should beget a male child to carry on the title. But attend me, sir. I have no thought to remarry anytime soon. I loved my first wife, but . . ." He shook his head. "No, I don't wish to be saddled with a wife. Listen, sir, I don't know your daughter. I'm sure that she is all those pleasant things you think she is. Nor does she know me. I daresay that she doesn't even like me."

"That, sir, is quite true."

It was Alec's turn to twist about and see Genny standing in the doorway, stiff as a vicar at an orgy.

Alec rose from his chair. "Genny," he said.

She ignored Alec and nearly shouted at her father, "How dare you! You want to *buy* this man for me? He gets the shipyard and I get *him?* I can't believe you would do that. My own father! You don't even know him. I want the shipyard, Father. It is mine by right, not his! He is a dissolute, conceited fop! Just look at him! Would an American man look like he does?"

"He is the handsomest man I've seen in many a long day," said James Paxton frankly, wondering at this very un-Genny-like outburst. "He can't help being English, Genny."

It was odd, Alec thought: he was standing between the two of them, and yet it was as if he weren't there.

"I wouldn't care if he were Russian! I don't want him. I don't ever want a husband! Ever!"

With that Parthian shot, Genny picked up her skirts and dashed out of the room. Her exit was nearly rendered ignominious. Well used to trousers, she tripped on her hem and tottered, arms flailing, toward a wall table. She caught herself at the last second and managed to topple only a vase. It went crashing to the floor. The noise was obscenely loud. Genny just stood there, staring down at the vase, at the flowers strewn over the floor, at the puddle of water spreading toward the base of the stairs.

Alec dashed to the doorway. "Are you all right?"

"Yes, certainly." Genny dropped to her knees and began picking up the carnations and roses. Without looking up at him, she said, "Will you be staying for dinner?"

"Am I still invited?"

"It is my father's house. Obviously he does what pleases him. I don't care what either of you do." She stood abruptly, dropped the flowers she'd gathered back to the floor, and headed for the front door.

"Where the devil are you going? It's still raining."

She stopped cold. That was true enough. Where could one go after enduring sufficient humiliation and embarrassment to last for a good month?

She turned and smiled at him. "I'm going to the kitchen to see to your meal, my lord. Perhaps I shall simper over the stew. What else should a good hostess do?"

"Shall I tell you? Do you need more education?"

There was fire in her eyes. "Go to the devil!"

Alec watched her struggle not to hit him with

something, turn on her heel, and push through the door to the kitchen. He decided, watching the door slam, that she looked quite nice in a gown, even though it was old and rather short.

6

"Papa?"

Alec turned at the adjoining door and returned to his daughter's bunk. "You're awake, pumpkin? I thought I heard loud snores just a moment ago."

Hallie giggled, rubbed her eyes with her fists, and scooted up on her bunk.

Alec was swaying comfortably with the *Night Dancer*. Even securely docked and in the inner basin, she was dipping back and forth in the storm. He sat down beside Hallie and took her hand. So small and yet so perfect and quite competent for a five-year-old, he thought, staring down at the straight fingers. There were calluses on her thumbs.

"Hallie, should you like to live in a house for a while? A real house, one that doesn't move beneath your feet?"

His daughter looked at him. "Why?"

"Why indeed. I wonder why little girls must always question their fathers. All right. I think we'll be staying in Baltimore for a while. It's silly to keep living aboard ship. Tomorrow you and I can find ourselves a nice house."

"You'll let me pick it?"

"I'm not that far into my dotage, pumpkin. I'll try to find us a house close to the water. Now that I think about it, a house might take a bit of time. At least we'll move to dry land tomorrow."

"All right. It's true that Mrs. Swindel wants terra firma."

"What?"

"That's Latin, Papa. Mrs. Swindel is always talking about it to Dr. Pruitt."

"Ah, thank you."

"Were you with a lady tonight?"

"In a manner of speaking, yes. Actually, the lady was quite furious with me and didn't talk to me much. Her father, however, was most congenial."

"What's her name?"

"Genny. She directs the work at her father's shipyard."

"Why was she mad at you?"

Alec grinned at that. "I provoked her, I suppose. Pushed her over the edge, tapped her shoulder one too many times."

"Is she pretty?"

"Pretty," Alec repeated, frowning toward Hallie's small trousers that were folded over a chairback. He should see to buying the child proper female clothes if they were going to remain for any length of time in Baltimore. He turned his attention back to his present thoughts. "I should say she's pretty, although she doesn't seem to think of herself like that. She dresses like a man, you see—"

"Like me?"

"It's a bit different, Hallie. She doesn't care for men. She doesn't ever want to marry."

"She doesn't like you?" This clearly was a notion that made no sense at all to Alec's greatest fan, and he grinned.

"That's stupid, Papa. All ladies like you." Alec said nothing for the moment to this artless disclosure. From the mouths of five-year-olds, he thought, wondering what would emerge next.

"I don't think I'll like her."

"Well, you'll probably never meet her, so it doesn't matter."

"Why were you making her mad at you? I didn't think you enjoyed mad ladies."

Good question, Alec thought. "I'm not certain," he began. "Perhaps I do it because I'm interested to see what she'll do. She's never boring, that's certain, and she occasionally gives as good as she gets. Now go back to sleep, pumpkin."

"All right, Papa." Hallie tugged at Alec's coat lapels. He leaned down and kissed her nose and her forehead and pulled the covers to her chin.

"Sleep well, love. I'll see you in the morning."

"We'll go buy a house?"

"Perhaps. I have a lot of thinking to do first." He remembered his vow to himself to get himself a mistress, one who would be at his beck and call, one who hadn't been in the trade too long. He doused the candle and left Hallie's small cabin through the adjoining door into his captain's cabin.

The *Night Dancer* was silent. Alec, bored with himself and the small area of his cabin, went on deck. The rain had stopped but the air was still thick with moisture. The deck still rolled gently beneath his feet. There were no stars, not even a hint of a moon to show through the black clouds. They were docked at O'Donnell's Wharf, the *Night Dancer*'s prow sticking out over busy Pratt Street. A frigate was docked to starboard, a clipper brig off to port. The entire inner basin— all the average Baltimorean ever saw of his port— was filled with all kinds of merchant craft: barkentines, schooners, frigates, snows, their tall naked masts listing lazily in the heavy waves of the incoming tide. There were also other strange-looking craft Alec found fascinating, craft built exclusively for Chesapeake Bay. These were clustered all along Smith's Wharf.

Baltimore was truly an inland harbor, Alec thought, staring out toward Fells Point, that hook of land that jutted toward Federal Hill, opposite, forming the entrance to the inner basin. If Alec remembered his reading aright, Baltimore hadn't annexed Fells Point until 1773, a definite advantage because Fells Point was nearer to the mouth of the Patapsco River. In addition it provided deep water and boasted half a dozen shipbuilding yards, the Paxton yard one of them. After the war that made the Americans their own nation, Baltimore had surged ahead of Annapolis in trade and had stayed there.

There was one hundred and ninety-five miles of bay between the Virginia Capes and the mouth of the Susquehanna River, northeast of Baltimore. Despite its length, Chesapeake Bay curved slightly—only two points on the compass was all.

And there were so many rivers flowing into the bay, least of which was the Potomac, upon which the American capital was built. The beautiful Patapsco was Baltimore's river, and Alec wanted to explore it before he left. A man could make his fortune here—in cotton, tobacco, flour—what with all the waterways available to transport his goods and all the water power available to mill his goods.

Alec brought his meandering thoughts back to the present, to his own male needs. First a mistress, he decided. He needed relief and he didn't want to put it off any longer.

What to do about the Paxtons?

A house. He would see his solicitor—no, lawyer, he quickly amended to himself, translating into American—on the morrow. Mr. Daniel Raymond of Chatham Street would assist him and also advise him about the financial soundness of the Paxtons. He leaned his elbows on the smooth railing.

What to do about Genny?

Marriage! He snorted. What a damned fool idea. As if he would ever desire anything—even a small nation—enough to marry again. *She was as horrified as you are.* That provoked a strange reaction, a perverse reaction. He wasn't a toad with missing teeth, for God's sake. He was comely—he knew it, had always known it, and ignored it, for the most part. Women, even when he'd been quite young, had wanted him, and he usually took what they offered returning as much pleasure as he knew. He remembered suddenly meeting Nesta more than ten years before. She'd been in London, a debutante in her first Season. For some reason, inexplicable to him he'd wanted her instantly. He'd wanted her more than he'd ever wanted any girl or woman. It was disconcerting, but it was true. It wasn't that she was the most beautiful girl of that Season, because she wasn't. There was simply something about her that made him so randy he could scarcely walk, much less think rationally.

And he couldn't take her because she was a lady of quality. A gentleman didn't seduce a virgin, a virgin who was also a lady.

Because he was young, because he hadn't really looked into the future at all and decided what it was he wanted to do with his life, he proposed to her, was immediately accepted—he hadn't expected any other reply, for he was quite a good catch—and married her. He took her to Carrick Grange and kept her in his bedchamber for several weeks, giving her pleasure, and teaching her how to pleasure him as well.

And his infatuation and lust for her were over within three months of the marriage. What had remained was friendship, and it proved to be sound.

Then he'd inherited the ships from his American uncle—Mr. Rupert Nevil of Boston. He'd packed up himself and Nesta and off they'd gone. She'd never complained, never argued with him, and had always sweetly given herself to him in bed.

Nesta had been a good sort and he had been very fond of her. When she'd died bearing Hallie, he'd felt so much guilt he'd nearly choked on it, guilt and pain that her child would never know its mother.

Alec shook his head. He didn't much like thinking about old memories. One couldn't ever change the past, and he couldn't seem to make himself change his own thoughts about the past. It was always a futile exercise.

What to do about Genny Paxton? Why didn't she want to marry? He couldn't understand such cynicism. After all, Nesta had never wanted anything more than to be his wife, to follow wherever he led her, to be and to do whatever he wished.

Genny Paxton was too independent and too cocksure. He didn't like her *or* her attitude. At all.

Alec grunted a greeting to Graf Pruitt, his ship's physician. Dour Graf, as Alec thought of him, was remarkably humorless, as lean as a piece of dried beef, and possessed of a full head of curly gray hair. He was Mrs. Swindel's romantic interest, and Alec wondered when the two of them would finally visit the vicar.

"Filthy night," said Graf.

"At least it's not raining. What do you think of Baltimore, Graf?"

"Filthy city."

"What does Mrs. Swindel think of Baltimore?"

"Eleanor wants to stay here, brainless woman."

"I'm sure there are lots of sick people here as well as on board the *Night Dancer* and in England."

"Who cares about Americans? If the whole lot of them rotted, it would suit me just fine. Don't you remember what they did to us just five years ago? Good God, five years ago last month—September thirteenth, I believe it was."

Alec laughed, not bothering to respond to Graf's typical British outrage at losing anything. He couldn't, frankly, imagine Mrs. Swindel with Graf Pruitt. They were too much alike. He imagined that when they were together, undoubtedly criticizing everything around them, there would be a black cloud over their heads.

Alec said finally, "I have wondered upon occasion what we would have done if we had beaten the Americans. Humiliated them for perhaps a year before they tried to beat the hell out of us again?"

"Shot 'em all," said Graf. "Lined 'em up and shot 'em."

"Well, that would undoubtedly have taken a good, long time. I'm going ashore now. You have a passable night, Graf."

"I heard you already were ashore."

Alec cocked a brow at that. Then he just shook his head. Graf Pruitt was an excellent doctor. As for his being a reasonable man in other areas, well, one couldn't expect everything. Alec said nothing, and left the ship.

He went back to Madam Lorraine's, selected a young girl endowed with very green eyes—not quite the same brilliant green as Genny Paxton's—and thick, shining dark brown hair—not quite the rich sable of Genny Paxton's—and took her upstairs. Her name was Oleah and she had such a thick Southern drawl that he could scarcely understand her, not that it mattered, really. She was from Virginia, she told him, Mooresville, Virginia. She used her mouth to devastating effect, enjoying herself when he groaned. Her body was white and soft, and when he came into her in one powerful thrust, she lifted her hips and cried out. Alec didn't leave her until it was near to dawn the following morning. Oleah was deeply asleep and richer for her efforts, and Alec was sated. A reasonable trade.

He snorted at himself. How long would he feel sated? Three days? A week, perhaps; then it would be just as bad as before.

What to do about Genny Paxton?

The following day, Alec moved himself, his daughter, and Mrs. Swindel into the Fountain Inn on German Street. It was of prewar vintage, built back in 1773 around an open court and shaded with now naked-branched beech and poplar trees on which the rooms looked out. It was managed by a John Barney, who disliked Englishmen heartily but adored children more. Hallie kept him polite to Alec and Mrs. Swindel. Pippin hadn't been at all happy about the move until Alec swore to his cabin boy that he would send him all his soiled clothing so he could look after it.

Eleanor Swindel, true to form, found the armoires in her and Hallie's rooms to be much too narrow and they smelled. Alec, picturing dead rats, rushed into his daughter's bedchamber. Yes, smelled, Mrs. Swindel assured him. Smelled of nutmeg, of all the ridiculous things. Like a silly pie—their clothing would smell like food. Hallie giggled and Alec, looking pained, quickly took his leave. He walked to Chatham Street, to Mr. Daniel Raymond's office. There were no homes at present that would be suitable, according to Mr. Raymond, but he'd heard that following the death of General Henry, known to the Baltimoreans as Light-Horse Harry, some months previous, his home might be available shortly, for there was only his widow left. Mr. Raymond would determine if this were indeed true. He also gave Alec his advice on the Paxton shipyard, in great and boring detail.

"As you know, my lord, since the end of the, er, war with you, er, England, our shipbuilders have been depressed. Too many ships around, privateering down, no other nation's ships to plunder and sink, if you will. It will increase again, you may be certain. Some of our shipbuilders are going to Cuba, for example, to build ships for the slave trade, that way avoiding all sorts of, er, interference from the miserable federal men. I— are you interested in the slave trade, my lord?"

After being assured that he wasn't, Mr. Raymond continued on about the price he considered fair for outright purchase, possible terms, and other kinds of partnerships to consider.

When Mr. Raymond finished his soliloquy about the Paxtons, shipyards in general, and specific ways to evade existing laws, he turned immediately to what was undoubtedly his favorite topic. Mr. Raymond was a fussy man of middle years who was fastidiously neat and collected pens from all over the world. He actually turned pink with pleasure when he lifted one to show to Alec. "This one, my lord," he said to a startled Baron Sherard, "is from France. It's a turkey feather but you'd never know it, what with the colors so very unusual. And see here, this newfangled gold nib. Lovely, isn't it? Such a find for me!"

Alec agreed that the pen was a marvel. He wanted to ask if the thing worked, but held his tongue, then directed Mr. Raymond back to the Paxtons, to Mr. James Paxton in particular.

"Ah, yes, Mr. James Paxton. He's a fine man, an excellent head for business, and it's a pity about his health. His doctor isn't too optimistic about him, I understand. As for the shipyard, there is another small clipper near completion, I understand, and it's imperative that a buyer be found quickly."

"Are you aware, Mr. Raymond, that it is Miss Paxton who is directing all the work at the shipyard? That she's giving all the orders to the men?"

Mr. Raymond looked at him as if he'd suddenly started spouting Sumerian. Then he grinned and waved his gold-nibbed pen at Alec. "Oh, no, my lord. Don't jest like that. If it got out, why, no man would even consider—even if shipbuilding weren't depressed, why—"

"It would appear that it has already gotten out. If not, then why hasn't there already been a buyer for the clipper? Depression or no depression, the vessel is exquisitely made, only the finest live oak for her frame, copper-fastened throughout, and her bottom is sheathed with imported red copper.

The interior workmanship is also equally remarkable—Spanish mahogany, you know—"

"Yes, it must have gotten out," Mr. Raymond interrupted, too perturbed by this news to remember his manners. "What you say, my lord, I can't believe it, not really. A woman, directing the work at a shipyard? Surely you must not be correct about that. Mr. James Paxton wouldn't show such a lack of judgment as to allow a young female . . ."

Alec listened to Mr. Raymond carry on. He was thinking about his conversation with James Paxton of the previous evening. He hadn't agreed that men would ostracize Genny just because she was working in what was considered a male preserve. He'd been wrong, dead wrong.

". . . damn, the girl should get herself married and pregnant! It's altogether absurd that she should . . ."

She'd crossed into that other sphere. It wasn't fair; at least Genny didn't think so. Alec wasn't certain what he believed, but he knew now that he would do something. He would buy the shipyard and make Genny a silent partner, perhaps. She would have to understand that businessmen couldn't be allowed to connect her to the building of ships. Perhaps it wasn't fair, but it was the way of the world.

". . . well, I don't know what to advise, my lord. Surely James Paxton can't expect the men of Baltimore to condone such behavior, much less deal with a young female—"

"I understand, Mr. Raymond," Alec said abruptly, cutting off the lawyer, who was now firmly astride his hobbyhorse. He rose. "I shall be finalizing some sort of agreement with Mr. Paxton soon now. I will need your services again at that time." Alec shook Mr. Raymond's hand and left. "For God's sake," he muttered to himself as he walked down Chatham Street, "a turkey feather and a gold nib!"

He immediately made his way to the Paxton house. Like Genny, he walked from Chatham Street to the Paxton house on Charles Street. He paused for a moment in front of the house, remarking to himself that he liked the Georgian architecture which dominated the buildings in Baltimore. The red brick had mellowed with age, but the white-columned portico was, he guessed, painted once every few years. There were green shuttered windows and wings. The entire two-story mansion was shaded by a grove of beeches and tulip poplars. It was a nice home, a comfortable home, with a lovely sloping front yard and a white fence surrounding it.

Moses greeted him and took him upstairs to see Mr. Paxton.

"Miss Paxton is at the shipyard, Moses?"

"Yes, suh. Always leaves early, she does. Lannie frets because Miss Genny never has time to eat her breakfast. Ah, here we are, suh."

The master bedroom was large, nearly a perfect square, with two sets of bay windows in the outside wall. It was furnished with old-fashioned high-backed chairs, a venerable walnut canopied bed set on a dais, and a thick Axminster circular carpet in the middle of the room. James Paxton was seated in an old-fashioned easy chair of polished mahogany, its arms and back padded with a singularly beautiful pale blue brocade, its feet eagle claws.

"My lord, come in, come in. I must say that I expected you, but not this early. Moses, bring tea for his lordship, and some of Lannie's sweet crumpets."

Alec took a stiff-backed armchair and pulled it closer to Mr. Paxton. "I've come about the shipyard," he said without preamble. "I must tell you that I came purposefully when Genny wouldn't be here. I won't dissemble with you, sir. You'll be quite ruined if Genny continues directing the activities there. You were right, sir. The men of this city will never allow themselves to purchase a clipper schooner, no matter how excellently made it is, from a yard run by a young female, as Mr. Raymond kept referring to Genny."

"I know that," said James Paxton, studying his newly filed fingernails. "The problem is what to do about it." He closed his eyes for a moment, leaning his head against the chairback.

"I'll buy the shipyard outright. For sixty thousand American dollars."

James Paxton didn't move, nor did he show any change of expression. He said very quietly, "That would break Genny's heart. She's a hard worker, a more dedicated worker than her brother, Vincent, ever was. She's got a brain, that girl; she understands shipbuilding and she sails well. Not with the expertise of the privateer captains during the war, but still, she captains well. No, it would break her heart. I couldn't do that to her."

"Nonetheless, if she continues directing the work—heart intact—both of you will lose everything. She must be made to see reason."

"And reason is a man running things." James Paxton sighed deeply. "Damned body . . . I was as healthy a specimen as you'd ever expect from a man of fifty-five years, Alec, always on the go, always ready to take on anything and anyone. Then one day I had this awful pain in my chest, and my left arm was quite, quite numb . . . well, I don't mean to carp. Death and dying are just as much a part of life as birth is. But to hurt Genny . . . what to do?"

"Suh, your tea and crumpets."

"Thank you, Moses. Just put everything on that table and pull it over. His lordship will do the pouring."

After Moses had again taken his leave, shooting his master one long worried look that wasn't lost on Alec, James Paxton continued. "I'm sorry, Alec, but the only solution I can see is that everyone be made to think that a man runs the shipyard. And the only way I can accomplish that is for Genny to wed. Just lemon, please. If the man isn't you, then it must be another."

"Like Porter Jenks?"

"No, he's not a nice man. He now runs three slavers—at last count. He refitted three frigates after the war. But clipper schooners are much faster—and speed is of the essence, particularly when a full slaver is trying to escape being captured. As I told you before, it's a very lucrative trade. I can't abide him, and even if I could, Genny wouldn't have a thing to do with him."

"She won't have a thing to do with me either, sir."

James gave the baron a slow, long look. "She would if you wanted her to."

Alec, impatient, and feeling strangely guilty, looked at his crumpet, then set it down and rose to pace up and down the length of the bedroom.

"I won't do it!" he said, spinning on his heel to face his host. "I told you I didn't wish to remarry. I mean it. I'm not a domesticated man. I'm not a sentimental fool, I don't like home and hearth, and—" He broke off, seeing Hallie's smiling face as he'd kissed her good-bye that morning.

His heart swelled whenever he looked at his daughter, even when she was tired or out of sorts and thus whined and carped and was otherwise obnoxious. She was a part of him, of Nesta; in short, she was unique, and he loved her more than anything, anyone. She'd come from home and hearth. He wouldn't mind if he had a dozen Hallies, all of them his. "Damn," he said, and walked to one of the wide bay windows and looked out over a pear and apple orchard.

"There's a ball at the Assembly Room on Friday night. That's the big red brick building on the corner of Fayette and Holliday. I've gotten Genny to agree to attend. I will accompany her."

"She can't attend dressed like she was yesterday!"

"No, true enough. She told me that she'd gone to a mantuamaker, one of the best in Baltimore, she said. She'll be appropriately gowned, I guarantee it. I ask that you attend also. After all, Alec, you need to meet the pillars of our society and this will be a good place to do it. Perhaps you can see Genny in a new light, so to speak, and she you. What do you say?"

Alec said yes in the end. But he was cursing silently all the way back to the Fountain Inn.

A raindrop hit his nose at the corner of Charles and Market streets. Wretched Baltimore weather.

Friday night was bone-chilling, with bulging rain clouds in the dark skies and an intense calm that portended violent winds later. The Paxtons rode in a closed carriage to the Assembly Room. Genny hadn't shown her father her new gown from Miss Mary Abercrombie. She herself wasn't all that certain she liked it, but Miss Mary had assured her that it was the *latest* thing and that she would be much admired and yes, *envied* by the ladies, because *she* Miss Mary, had designed and sewn it for her, lucky girl!

So be it, Genny thought, tugging a bit at the overly low bodice of the royal blue satin gown. She didn't particularly care for the color, thinking as she'd stared in her mirror that it made her look sallow, even though Miss Mary had assured her that she looked a veritable angel. And all the frills and flounces and row after row of white velvet bows made her wince, even though Miss Mary had assured her that plain gowns denoted solid bad taste. And it was the latest style, she said over and over to herself. It was also the only gown that Miss Mary had ready, so there had really been no choice anyway.

She was wearing an old black velvet cloak over the gown. It was shiny with too many wearings over too many years, but it was nighttime and who cared?

Genny hadn't been to the Assembly Room in three years. She'd ignored it, ignored any invitation from local families, until they'd ceased to come. The Assembly Room was her only opportunity to try out her new wings and reintroduce herself into Baltimore society. And let all the businessmen see that she was competent and not a silly twit. She squared her shoulders at the thought and wished yet again, as a competent person, that her breasts weren't so very near to bursting free of the gown.

Her father hadn't gotten an argument from her. Genny knew that to be a success she and her father must mingle with the rich merchants of the city. They must convince everyone that a clipper schooner from the Paxton shipyard was something to be devoutly desired. She could practically hear herself explaining all about the *Pegasus*'s finer points, detailing the lustrous yards of Spanish mahogany. . . . During the past year, neither she nor her father had seen anyone. Now it was time to emerge and tell the world they were alive and well and ready to conduct business. She was attending the ball because she was a good businesswoman. That was all.

"Do you think Baron Sherard will be there tonight?"

The carriage was dark. James Paxton allowed

himself a grin, knowing his daughter couldn't see it and take exception. She wasn't immune to Alec Carrick, no indeed.

"I believe he might show his face. He needs to meet the citizens of Baltimore, after all. What better opportunity?"

"That's true," Genny said, and lapsed once again into silence. Their hired carriage left them on the northeast corner of the street and Genny helped her father to descend. Mr. McElhaney, the master of ceremonies, met them at the door of the Assembly Room, remarked on the dank weather, on Mr. Paxton's seemingly fine health, on the bloom in Genny's cheeks, and then moved them through as another party arrived.

"Phew," Genny said behind her hand. "He always says the same things, doesn't he? I remember the identical conversation three years ago."

She slipped off her velvet cloak, handing it to a footman, and turned to do a small pirouette in front of her father. James Paxton's eyes nearly crossed. He swallowed. He closed his eyes, but the vision was stamped into his brain.

Oh, God, who had done this to his daughter? He wanted to remove her instantly, take her home, rip off that awful thing she was wearing, and make a fire with it, but—oh, God, white velvet bows! Too many to count before becoming ill.

It was too late.

"Why, good evening, Mr. Paxton! And Eugenia! How delightful! And how very . . . ah, interesting you look. Such an endless array of white velvet bows. Excuse me, please."

All that was from Mrs. Lavinia Warfield, wife of the very wealthy and influential Mr. Paul Warfield. James watched her hurry away from them, saw the excited malice in her small eyes, and knew for certain it was too late.

Oh, God. What to do?

"How oddly she behaved, Father," Genny said as she self-consciously fingered one of the bows.

"Yes," James said, trying to stifle the curses that were bubbling up in his mouth. He sighed again. At least Genny had the loveliest hair imaginable. She'd managed to braid it loosely and had wrapped it about the top of her head in a thick coronet, leaving tendrils to snake down the sides of her face and the back of her neck. Beautiful hair, just like her mother's. If only she had her mother's sense of style, her taste in clothing. If only people would just look at her from the neck up.

He had no time to run, no time to adjust his thinking into a sound strategy, no time to tell his daughter that she looked dreadful. They were quickly surrounded by the Murrays, the Pringles, the Winchesters, and the Gaithers. The men were honestly glad to see him; the women, unfortunately, were delighted to see Genny, but not because they wanted to renew any friendships. It had gotten around that Genny wasn't keeping to her woman's place, and the ladies of Baltimore were fully prepared to take revenge.

And Genny, with the awful gown, had given them a wonderful, not-to-be-missed opportunity.

7

"My lord? Baron Sherard?"

Alec turned to smile at the beautiful woman at his left elbow. "Yes, I'm Baron Sherard," he said, taking her hand and bringing it to his lips.

"Ah, how gallant of you, sir! Mr. Daniel Raymond has told everyone about you and, well, you may call me the advance guard, if you wish."

"Truth be told, I'd rather call you something else. What is your name, ma'am?"

"Laura. Laura Salmon. A poor widow. My dear husband exported to the Caribbean, flour primarily. I have heard that you wish to remain and buy the Paxton shipyard. An excellent idea. You could carry my flour for me. I own Salmon's Mill on the Patapsco, you know, just two miles southeast of the city."

"I see. Call me Alec. Would you like to waltz with me?"

Alec hadn't expected a negative answer and indeed, he didn't get one, not from this exquisite piece of femininity who was flirting madly with him. The very beautiful Laura laughed up at him and quickly placed her hand on his arm. Her eyes sparkled. She moistened her lips with her tongue. He had the feeling she also wanted to moisten his lips with her tongue. "Oh, yes, I should love that."

They made a striking couple, the English baron

looking like a prince from a fairy tale and the divine Laura like a princess, in her snow-white gown and glittering array of diamonds. When the dance ended, Laura introduced Alec to many of the local gentlemen, then stood back, wisely, and watched him charm the lot of them. Soon other gentlemen joined the group. Goodness, Laura thought, watching him laugh, watching the way he tilted his head so intently when another was speaking, he was beautiful. She loved the way he used his hands when he talked. And his body—no Englishman, or any other male she'd ever known, had looked like he did—not an ungraceful bone in his body, nor a patch of fat anywhere, not even a whisper. She added to herself that she couldn't be completely certain of that just yet. She could practically feel his warm flesh beneath her searching fingers, his tongue against her lips. She shuddered delicately and decided then and there that she would invite him to be her lover. His golden body would look marvelous stretched over her very pale one, his golden-blond hair contrasting exquisitely with her glossy black hair. Both of them had blue eyes, but hers were dark, dark as midnight, as one of the young puppies who adored her had once said, while the baron's were bright as a summer sky, vivid, alive. He didn't appear to be conceited about his spectacular looks. She found herself praying he wasn't. In her experience, though, men who were at all handsome expected women to do everything for them, just because they deigned to be with them.

They were selfish lovers. Would Alec Carrick be a selfish lover? Laura couldn't wait to find out.

Thank the merciful heavens that her very old, very miserly husband had passed to his new reward the previous spring, leaving her all of his old reward.

The orchestra began another waltz. She watched the gentlemen disperse to find their partners for the dance. Alec, she saw, feeling a wave of disappointment, walked over to speak to James Paxton, who was sitting with some other older men.

Laura looked out onto the smallish dance floor as she tapped her foot to the waltz rhythm. Oh, dear, there was that dreadful Genny Paxton, and Oliver Gwenn—of all things!—had asked her to waltz with him.

Laura shuddered just looking at her. The girl looked altogether dreadful. Who had made that gown for her? And why had Oliver asked her to dance? Or had he? Oliver Gwenn was Laura's current lover and she wouldn't tolerate another female poaching on her preserves, even though Oliver was a very unripe specimen on those preserves.

The music finally came to an end. Couples strolled off the floor, Genny Paxton and Oliver Gwenn included. Laura waited for Oliver to politely yet firmly detach himself from that god-awful apparition. He didn't. He lingered.

The Baltimore Assembly Room reminded Alec of Almack's in London, except for the fact that there were no patronesses sitting on their power, ruling the ton with iron-gloved fists from the large, cold building on King Street. This assembly room was also large, high-ceilinged, square, and airless, since no windows were open. The orchestra was mounted on a dais at the east end of the room. There was an adjoining room with a long table holding a punch bowl and plates heaped with cakes and candies. The punch reminded him of the very weak orgeat at Almack's. At least, unlike at Almack's, the cakes were fresh and tasty, not stale bread and butter.

Alec found that he couldn't take his eyes off Genny. It was so appalling a sight that he felt mesmerized. The first time he'd seen the gown she was wearing he'd nearly choked on his punch. She didn't realize that she looked a mess, bless her styleless eyes. But all the ladies did, and many of the gentlemen. The ladies—young and old alike—made it open season on Genny Paxton.

The gentlemen, he noted, had eyed her, more or less shrugged to each other as if to say: What do you expect? She doesn't know how to be a lady. He saw her now in conversation with a young man whose name, if Alec recalled aright, was Oliver Gwenn. He had also danced the last waltz with her. He looked young; perhaps he and Genny had been childhood friends. That better be the case. Alec hadn't as yet spoken to Genny. He made his way over to her and the young man.

"Good evening, Genny."

"Oh, Alec! Hello, what a surprise."

"Certainly," he said, his voice filled with irony. Did she take him for an utter flat?

She stepped back, allowing him and Oliver Gwenn to chat a bit. She thought it rather gracious of her.

"Genny tells me," Oliver said, "that you are

considering staying in Baltimore and going into business with her and her father."

"It is more than a remote possibility. Have you and Genny known each other long?"

"Since we were both in leading strings," Oliver said, smiling at her.

Genny fingered a white velvet bow. She felt heated in the close room. She also felt a good deal of tension. She didn't understand why the ladies were treating her like a pariah. It made no sense to her. Nor was she imagining it. And now here was Alec, looking as magnificent as a god, making all the ladies salivate with lust. When he finally turned to ask her to dance, Genny wasn't paying him any heed. Her attention had been caught by Laura Salmon, who was waving an imperious hand toward Oliver.

"Oliver," she said, cocking her head to one side. "Does Laura wish to speak to you?"

To her further confusion, Oliver flushed, making him look singularly unattractive. He mumbled something and ambled off toward Laura.

"Whatever is the matter with him?"

"Goodness, you're naive." Alec laughed. "Come along, Genny, let's cut ourselves a wide swath on the dance floor."

"All right. Alec, I haven't danced in three years. I fear I trod on Oliver's toes and will step on yours as well."

"If you do, I'll be stoic, or whine just a bit."

He put his arm around her, quite properly at her middle back, and Genny felt more than a dollop of pleasure at that hand of his touching her. The pleasure was insidious and deep and it was spreading throughout her body. She looked up at his impossibly handsome face and frowned.

"What's the matter?"

"Nothing," she said, her voice sharp. "Oh, dear, I'm sorry."

"I trust you didn't do that on purpose?"

She gave him an impish grin and just shook her head. "Not I, dear sir. Well, what do you think of the ball? Have you met most of our leading citizens? Listened to all of Mr. Raymond's nonsense? Drooled on most of their wives' collective hands? Let them drool over yours? Accepted a dozen assignations?"

"You're endlessly impertinent, Genny. Yes, I've met so many people my weak man's head is spinning." With those words, he whirled her about in a wide circle and she laughed with the excitement of it.

"Oh, you're excellent!"

"Thank you. Now, I don't want to hurt your feelings, but—"

"I always distrust people who begin like that. There is always a *but*."

"Genny—" He drew a deep breath. "Where did you get that gown?"

"Why, from one of the best mantuamakers in all of Baltimore."

"That can't be true. Look around you. Do you see any other lady dressed in such a very loud shade of blue satin? Do you see any other lady sporting so many white velvet bows and so many yards of flounces?"

Genny felt a knot of hurt, then more than a

moment's uncertainty. "There are quite a few bows on the gown. I was thinking that, but Miss Mary Abercrombie assured me that it was just the thing and I was being silly."

"Mary Abercrombie?"

"Yes, there are two Miss Abercrombies. And it is one of the best, Alec. The gown—it truly looks not too well?"

The look in her eyes nearly stopped him. He'd never seen such vulnerability in her before and he didn't like what it did to him. But this couldn't continue. "I'm sorry, Genny, but it is an abomination. Is she making other things for you?"

The look of vulnerability was gone, replaced by a flat, nearly opaque blanking of expression. "Yes, several more gowns. I didn't have many, you know, and all of them are quite old and out of date."

How to proceed? He decided to say nothing more for the moment. He didn't want to hurt her any more, nor did he want to make her angry with him. He whirled her about again and was pleased to hear her laugh.

"Have people been kind to you?"

She cocked her head at him. "Polite enough, I suppose. Most of them are acquaintances or friends of my father."

"How are the ladies treating you?"

She lowered her head. "They are coldly polite, if you know what I mean. I don't understand why. 'Tis true that my father and I haven't been in society for over a year now, but they seem quite pleased to see him."

"Shall I tell you why?"

He got a sour look at that. "You, a stranger? An Englishman? You want to tell me—"

"Yes. Listen to me, Genny. I won't lie to you. You are doing a man's job at the shipyard. You have offended all the ladies by straying outside a lady's defined confines. You have offended and threatened all the gentlemen by aping their dress and dipping your fingers in their pots. Now you are gowned like a"—he shuddered as he took a full look at her—"like a dowd with no style, no taste. They are simply getting their revenge on you, and you've made it exquisitely easy."

Genny said quite calmly, "Are you through with your truths, Baron?"

"Yes, I am, and I'm sorry to make you feel bad, but, Genny—Ouch! You did that on purpose!"

She came down on his foot again, denied herself the pleasure of sending her fist into his belly, and stomped off the dance floor, leaving Baron Sherard standing alone, staring after her and feeling like a fool. If, Alec thought at that moment, he had his hands on her and they were alone, he would jerk up that miserable gown and send the flat of his hand to her buttocks. His hand clenched at the thought. She would have very white buttocks, slender, smooth, and round. He shook his head at himself. Slowly, as if he hadn't a care in the world, as if being stranded by his partner were an accepted course of events, Alec strolled from the dance floor to find himself once again in Laura Salmon's net.

She was at her charming best, alone with him. He decided that he wanted her and smiled his acceptance when she invited him to dine with her the following evening. Then other ladies and gentlemen joined them.

It wasn't Laura who started it, but she certainly gave it her best when it came her turn.

"Would you just look at Genny Paxton! I've never seen such a fright in my whole life." This was from a squint-eyed young lady who was not only overweight but blessed with a doughy complexion.

"Yes, how could her dear father—my father thinks the world of Mr. Paxton—allow her to show herself like that?"

"Gentlemen don't understand fashion," Laura said, smiling at Mrs. Walters, the wife of a very rich ironmonger.

Alec said easily, "I understand that Miss Paxton obtained the gown from a leading mantuamaker in Baltimore."

"Impossible!"

"Absurd!"

"No, from a Miss Abercrombie. She told me so herself."

Laura was shaking her head, but there was a frown pucking her brow. "But Abigail Abercrombie makes all my gowns. She wouldn't ever make such a garment."

Something was wrong here. Abigail? No, Genny had called her Mary.

" 'Tis obvious that Miss Paxton made the gown herself and is now telling tales about it to everyone!"

"She is desperate for a husband, I hear," Laura said, "what with the shipyard doing not at all well. Our English lord perhaps will save her and her father." She gave a very seductive smile to Alec, one that wasn't lost on any female in the group.

"Well," Miss Poerson actually sniffed, "she won't get one looking like that. She's insufferable, what with all her silly airs, pretending she's better than all of us."

"Her gown was made by Miss Abercrombie," Alec said. "Miss Mary Abercrombie."

That drew all the female eyes. "Mary! Oh, goodness, how awful!"

"Miss Paxton was so ignorant to let *Mary* touch her, even get near her?" Miss Poerson laughed and laughed.

"She's pathetic," Laura said. "Both Miss Abercrombie and Miss Paxton. Have a bit of charity for Miss Paxton. How would you like to be in her position, looking as she does? And not even aware that she went to the wrong sister and ended up looking like a . . . a . . ." Laura fanned her hands in front of her, unable to find the proper word.

"I saw her dancing with Oliver," said Mrs. Mayer, a glint of malice in her eyes as she gave Laura a sloe-eyed look. "He didn't seem to mind her . . . lacks."

"He was just being nice. They've known each other forever, after all."

"Close to forever," said a very thin woman with a mustache over her upper lip. "How could she find a husband? Why, she must be at least twenty-five."

"She's twenty-three," Alec said.

"She doesn't look it," Laura said, saw that

Alec was looking a bit stiff, and immediately retired from the fray. This gentleman was not a gossip. "Would you dance with me again, Baron?"

Alec nodded and led her to the dance floor. Later, he accepted James Paxton's invitation to return to their home for some refreshments following the ball.

Once inside, Genny removed her cloak and handed it to Moses.

"Oh, my," Moses said, looking down at his young mistress. "You is the prettiest young lady I ever saw."

Genny suspected him of irony, but saw none in his dark eyes. Her one ally, and he hadn't been around when she'd needed him. Once in the parlor, Alec said to Genny, without preamble, "Did you say your mantuamaker was a Miss Mary Abercrombie?"

"You've already said quite enough, Alec!"

"No," James said, sitting forward in his chair; "not enough has been said. Answer him, Genny."

"Yes!"

"Well, my dear Miss Paxton, you evidently attached yourself to the wrong Abercrombie. According to Mrs. Salmon—"

Genny snorted at the name but Alec ignored her.

"Mrs. Salmon says it's Miss Abigail Abercrombie who is the competent one. You, my dear, got affixed to the wrong rigging and were left to flap in the winds."

Genny sat down. Now she remembered. It was Miss Abigail. "Oh, no," she said and groaned.

"Dump the gown in the grate," said Genny's doting father.

"Now?"

"Don't be impertinent, Genny," Alec said. "Look here, it's a pity you have no, er, taste in clothing, but you do have other things."

"I'm waiting, Baron."

"You have beautiful hair."

"I agree," James said. "And she even arranges it herself, Alec. Very talented, she is."

"All right, Genny," Alec said, giving up the ghost without a whimper, "I'll go with you to see Miss Abercrombie—the right one. We'll cancel your other gowns and have the correct sister make you new ones."

"I wouldn't hurt Miss Mary like that! Not only would she be hurt, she would be humiliated."

"Fine. We'll go to another mantuamaker, then."

"I wouldn't go to church with you, and the good Lord knows that you need it."

"Stop acting like a twit," James said, then closed his mouth until Moses, ears at attention, had left the parlor again.

"I wasn't the one shamelessly flirting with Laura Salmon!"

"Flirting? You call the two dances flirting? My dear girl, you wouldn't know flirting if it smashed you in the nose."

"Well, you were, and she was, flirting with you. I bet you already have an assignation with her, don't you?"

Alec didn't twitch a hair. "That is none of your affair."

Genny snorted again. He was going to see Laura, she knew it, and it made her unaccountably furious. Suddenly her fingers closed around one of the white velvet bows. She ripped it off and flung it into the sluggish fire in the grate.

"Bravo! You only have a couple hundred more to go."

"Oh, do be quiet, Baron!"

Alec thoughtfully stroked his fingers over his chin. "You know, perhaps the gown wouldn't be too bad if you removed all the little extras." He leaned over and grabbed another bow and pulled it off, then another and another. Then he said, "No, I don't think so. That shade of blue—it's beyond all attempts to describe it—makes you look bilious."

Genny scrambled to her feet. "I don't think I want to do business with you, Baron. Why don't you just purchase the *Pegasus?* I'll keep building the ships for you."

"I would be your only customer, you may be certain on that score. Why, no self-respecting merchant in Baltimore would do business with you."

"That's a lie! It's because our business in general is depressed and further because we refuse to build slavers."

James sat back, enjoying himself immensely.

"That, my dear Eugenia, has something to do with it, but mainly it's because you're a female doing a man's work. When and if I buy into the Paxton shipyard, you will bow out, gracefully or otherwise, but you will bow out. I'll not let you destroy the business by continuing to parade about in breeches giving the men orders."

"Father! Tell him to leave—now!" She pulled off two more bows in her agitation. They fell to the floor at her flounce-hemmed feet. Alec picked them up, gave them a disgusted look, and tossed them into the fire.

"Genny, what Alec says, unfortunately, is true. When he says he wants you to bow out, it isn't really what he means."

"Oh?" Alec drawled. "Just what do I really mean?"

"You mean," James said mildly, "that Genny must exercise a bit more restraint, a bit more discretion, a bit more illusion, if you will—and leave the appearances and the selling to the gentlemen."

That, Alec thought, was quite good. Genny's face didn't, however, show even a modicum of appreciation. She said, her voice as cold as the celebrated London January five years before, "We were doing just fine before you arrived, Baron Sherard. You're interfering, overbearing, and opinionated, and your only claim to anything is your beauty."

"My what?"

"Why, your devastating beauty, Baron. Your looks must be the envy of every woman you chance to meet."

"Stop being a fool." He leaned over and ripped off another bow. "If you'll recall, *Mr. Eugene,* before I came you were just about ready to go under, you and your bloody shipyard. The only reason you're not under at this moment is because everyone knows I might be pulling you out of the River Styx. Your memory is also quite inadequate. It was you who wrote to me."

"I was quite wrong. I admit it."

"You were simply unrealistic, thinking like a bloody woman. No man with an ounce of brains would let himself be manipulated by a twit like you, even the most dissolute of English peers. Did she tell you, sir? She hoped I would be a fop, a dandy, eager and willing to allow her to hold the reins of power."

"Yes, she told me. I told her she was wrong. Genny is strongheaded, Alec."

"That may be true," Genny said more calmly to her father, "but I know how to build ships—better than most men—and I wager I can outsail anything you can, Baron."

"A race, Genny? You want to race *me?*"

She laughed at the utter confusion in his voice. "Brawn isn't required to sail a ship, Alec, only brains and experience. I probably equal your experience and as for brains, well, I don't think you're remotely close to me."

"Strongheaded, sir? I should say rather that she is wrongheaded, thoroughly conceited, far too arrogant for her own good, and a termagent. You think to race *me?*" Alec threw back his head and laughed deeply.

Genny ripped off another bow and flung it into his face. He caught it and stared down at it. He shrugged and looked wicked.

"Your gown is looking better and better, Genny," James said, regarding the small pile of bows that lay between her and Alec. The ones in the fireplace were smoking dreadfully, the thick velvet refusing to burn.

"If bilious is considered better," Alec said and laughed again.

"When are you seeing Laura Salmon?"

"Tomorrow night," Alec said, realized abruptly that he'd responded to a question whose answer was none of her business, and wanted to strangle her as well as himself for being a fool. She was quick, took a man off his guard.

"Yes," he added, giving her a drawing look, "the lovely lady has invited me to dine with her."

"I'll just bet that's all you do with her!"

"Genny!"

"I'm sorry, Father. I'm tired. I bid both of you good-night." She quickly made her way to the door. "Good riddance to all Englishmen," she said under her breath, but not far enough under. From the corner of her eye she saw that Alec was merely smiling at her, a condescending smile that made her grit her teeth.

"Genny?"

She turned reluctantly to face her father.

"Alec will accompany you tomorrow to another mantuamaker. Dear child, don't be so stubborn. He's offered, and you must admit he has style and a good fashion sense. Don't bite off your nose, and all that."

"Ten o'clock tomorrow morning?" Alec suggested.

"I, unlike you, Baron, have work to do," Genny said.

"No, you don't. You simply want to go to the

shipyard because it gives you pleasure to parade around like a man. You may go to your room now. Tomorrow, Genny, and don't keep me waiting."

Genny wasn't at the Paxton house at ten o'clock the following morning. She was smiling in triumph as she sat at the intricately carved captain's desk aboard the *Pegasus*. Mimms was putting the finishing touches on the Spanish mahogany frame of the large bunk. The lovely cherry-wood chamber-pot cover was finished and propped against the wall.

It was nearly ten o'clock. Alec would be arriving at her house, pleased with himself, knowing himself to be in charge of her. Oh, how she wished she could see his face. She sighed. Well, no matter. She had a good imagination. She closed her eyes and formed the picture of Moses opening the door to the baron.

"Good morning."

That was Alec's voice, all right.

"Good morning, sir."

"Excellent work, Mimms. You have a fine touch."

"Thank you, sir. The wood is soft as a baby's bottom and so fine."

Something wasn't right. Genny cracked open an eye to see Alec, every beautiful flesh-and-blood inch of him, standing in the captain's cabin, looking intently at Mimms's work.

"You're here," she said. "You're not supposed to be. You're supposed to be—"

"I know where I'm supposed to be," he said

easily, turning to face her. "However, I'm not quite the complete imbecile you think me to be. Are you ready, Miss Paxton?"

She was dressed in her usual garb, only her hair wasn't covered. "No, I'm not. I will not go to a mantuamaker's like this."

"Why not? You appear to have no difficulty going anywhere else in Baltimore dressed like a man."

Mimms was all ears and Genny quickly rose from behind the desk.

The baron was right. Why should she care?

The carriage Alec had hired was waiting beneath the large shipyard sign and was dwarfed by the naked masts of the clipper schooner. Workers paused, eyeing Genny and the baron; she knew it and thrust her chin up. She bounded into the carriage, not allowing Alec to assist her. She waited, angry and tense, as he instructed the driver to take them to Madame Solange's on the corner of Pratt and Smith.

"I asked," Alec said before she could form the question. "That's how I know."

"Why?"

"God knows I don't want to be responsible for your purchasing any more dogfight gowns. Madame Solange has an excellent reputation for her stitchery and her choice in materials; I have good style sense, as your father said. All that's required of you is silent cooperation. And money, of course."

"I've never been with a man before—"

"You're still a virgin? At twenty-three? Goodness, never taken the plunge, huh?"

135

She eyed him coldly. "To go to a mantuamaker's."

"First time for everything, including being with a man."

"I hope your tongue rots off, Baron."

"Don't wish that, Genny. My tongue could do marvelous things to you."

"I suppose this is an Englishman's notion of flirting?"

Alec appeared to ponder that for a while. "No, it's too outrageous for formal, by-the-book flirting, English style."

"Will you be outrageous with Laura Salmon?"

"What an odd name that is. I understand her husband was an old, very rich merchant."

"You didn't answer my question."

"I'm in training to become a barrister. What do you think?"

Genny wanted to kick him.

"Laura will probably have my clothes off me before I can even say two words."

"You are conceited, aren't you?"

"Why don't you come and observe?"

"Oh, God, you're asking for me to do you in, aren't you? A pistol? A rapier?"

"Ah, here we are at last. Do come along, Mr. Eugene. Let's exchange your breeches for a charming chemise and petticoat. Should you like me to pick those items out for you also?"

If looks could kill, he would have lain dead at her feet. She looked down then and saw that she was wearing boots. Alec followed her gaze, shook his head, and chuckled.

"A very frilly chemise with lots of lace. To go

with those boots. A most interesting sight you'd make."

"I'll remove the bloody boots!"

"And the chemise?"

"Go to the devil, Baron."

8

The shopping expedition had gone quite well once Genny had gotten over her initial snit. She'd remained distant and defensive but Alec hadn't been unduly disturbed. He thought of her in the pale yellow silk he'd selected and smiled. He thought of his jest and smiled wider. "Think of this as a nightgown, Genny, your hair brushed out and long, fanned out on a white silk pillow, your breasts and hips framed by the soft silk. A very nice vision, don't you think?" And Genny, undone, embarrassed, and furious, had hissed back at him, "I wear only black and it's cotton! And it's high on my neck and down to my toes!" And he'd retorted in a light voice, "You're a witch virgin? No, I don't think so. You're a little American virgin and thus, my dear, you wear only white, high-necked, white, low-toed white."

Alec grinned again and Laura Salmon, not surprisingly, thought that smile was for her.

"What are you thinking, Alec?"

"Ah, I'm a simple man with a very simple thought," he said, and that, he knew, was true, even though he had no idea why Genny—Mr.

137

Eugene—was the subject of the simple thought. He said, "The dinner was superb. I must tell you that veal cutlets prepared with that very light sauce are just to my taste."

"I will tell my chef," Laura said, glad she'd remembered to say "chef" and not "cook." He was, after all, an English aristocrat, used undoubtedly to French chefs, not cooks. "I've never been to England," she said after a moment.

"London society would welcome you."

"Do you really think so? A provincial with an appalling accent? It's quite Southern, you know."

Alec thought briefly of Oleah and smiled. "Do you forget that you provincials beat out the British but five short years ago?"

"Ah, but war has nothing to do with society."

"Perhaps not."

"Would you care for some oyster patties?"

An aphrodisiac, Alec thought, if he remembered aright. He should tell her that he never had need of an additional anything to make him randy as a mountain goat. Well, he would just have to show her, "No, I think not, Laura."

"Perhaps some damson tarts? They're English, you know."

"Yes, I know, and no, thank you. I'm quite stuffed."

"Do you wish me to leave so you can drink a glass of port? Perhaps smoke a cheroot?"

Alec gave her a very slow smile, one that he knew from experience would act powerfully, and let his eyes wander over her plentiful bosom. She really was quite beautiful. He wondered if she would be a good lover. In his experience, females who were noted for their beauty were selfish, quite selfish indeed. They weren't good lovers; they were cold, as a matter of fact. Well, he would soon know.

"What I should like," he said in all honesty, watching the pulse in her throat, "is to pull that gown of yours to your waist and kiss your breasts."

Laura sucked in her breath, feeling a stab of stark pleasure all the way to her knees.

"Yes?"

Alec pushed back his chair and rose. "Why don't I show you?"

He took her hand and walked beside her up the rather narrow staircase. Her hand was trembling. It pleased him. He stopped and leaned down to kiss her. Her mouth was soft, and immediately open to him. She was experienced. Excellent.

He looked at her for a moment, then cupped her left breast. He could feel her heartbeat, faster now, pounding. He kissed her again as he caressed her nipple through the bodice of her gown.

Then he drew back, took her hand again, and resumed the climb up the stairs.

Laura's bedchamber was large, the ceiling high with wide windows along the entire east wall. There was a sluggish fire in the fireplace. The room was furnished in the classical style, the high bed canopied with ruffled white net, the counterpane white with pink-and-green flowers in circular patterns. The walls were papered in the same colors and patterns. It was a very feminine room and tastefully done. Alec wondered what Genny's bedchamber looked like. Probably a monk's cell, he thought, and snorted.

"Alec."

He brought his wandering mind back to the beautiful woman standing in front of him. He leaned down and kissed her once more, feeling her lean against him. He wondered how long it had been since she'd last had a man, remembered poor Oliver Gwenn, and knew that even if it had been the previous evening, she couldn't have been well pleasured. He would please her.

As he kissed her, his fingers were busy on the fastenings up the back of her gown. He kissed her shoulder as he gently eased the gown away, pushing it to her waist. He stepped back and looked at her.

"Lovely," he said, his eyes on her breasts. "Full and white and a dark pink just as I'd hoped." He cupped his hands. "Perfect for my hands."

He took her in his arms again and nibbled at her earlobe.

It was the unexpected shadow, the shift of dark and light, that caught his attention. He continued his kissing but focused his eyes on the window-pane. Another movement, the shadow shifting, turning. It was a face, its nose pressed against the glass.

It was Genny Paxton.

Alec couldn't at first comprehend what he was seeing. Once he did comprehend, he felt a wave of fury, then, almost immediately, an intense desire to laugh until his stomach hurt. He'd told her, taunted her, to come and watch.

Well, come she had.

How was she hanging on out there?

Damned little twit. He'd teach her a lesson she'd not soon forget. Pushy little virgin. He gently drew Laura back toward the window. He pulled her tightly against him and turned so that her profile and his were to the window. He then eased her back and began to caress her breasts.

Genny stared and swallowed. She felt at once terribly embarrassed, yet at the same time she felt hot and tense and very, very odd. His hands were large, tanned, his fingers beautifully shaped, like the rest of him. She wanted him to touch her breasts. She watched him lean down and take Laura's nipple into his mouth. She heard Laura moan loudly. The thought of him caressing her, then taking her into his mouth . . . Her own breathing accelerated.

This was horrible. She should never have come. She looked over her shoulder, down to the ground some twenty feet below. Her position was precarious at best. She'd climbed limbs up the skinny maple tree and was at this moment hanging on for dear life to a four-inch ledge. She looked again at the couple.

She saw Laura's hand—her small white hand—stroke down Alec's chest, lower and lower, until she was stroking his groin, and Genny saw the bulge in his trousers, and Laura's hand caressing it.

She swallowed again. Oh, dear, what was she doing here? Like some sort of Peeping Tom— she was despicable, that was what she was, watching two people making love.

Alec was stroking Laura's breasts, making her cry out, and then Genny saw his hand pull up Laura's gown and saw Laura's stockinged thigh.

It was too much. She was a thoroughly miserable human being, a weak, jealous, silly woman who had gotten her comeuppance. She jerked back suddenly when Alec stared directly at her. He looked utterly furious.

Her body twisted away from that look and she knew in that instant that she was going to fall. And she did. She grabbed at a skinny maple branch and it bent downward with her weight. But it cracked off about six feet from the ground. Genny landed with a thump in the flower bed, fell back, and struck her head against the brick edging. She thought that without that wonderful branch she could easily have broken a leg. Instead, though, she'd broken her head. She cried out at the pain, then slumped back, everything going black.

She opened her eyes, didn't move for a good minute, then slowly, very slowly, raised her hand to touch her head. There was a stab of pain but it wasn't too bad. She looked up. The windows were still alight from within. Perhaps she'd been wrong. Perhaps she'd just imagined Alec had seen her. How long had she been unconscious? Five minutes? An hour? However many minutes it had been, it was too long. She had to get out of here now, before Alec came out and found her lying like a nitwit in Laura Salmon's primrose flower bed.

She felt thorns from a lone rosebush dig into the back of her knee. She lay there a moment longer, wondering if she was dead, angry with herself that she wasn't, but then as she tried to rise she fell down again.

She rolled over onto her side and came up on her knees. She felt a stab of pain through her ankle and fell sideways again. She felt dirt and dead leaves crunch against her men's clothes. She wanted to cry, then just as quickly told herself not to be an idiot woman. She'd come here of her own free will, climbed that fool tree of her own free will, and watched Alec kissing that dreadful woman's breasts. It was nearly too much. Genny tried to rise again. Unfortunately, there was nothing to steady her and she went ignominiously down again.

She didn't know how much time passed. Enough time for the Americans to beat the British again. Perhaps more.

Please, God, she prayed, please don't let Alec come out here. She continued her prayer, promising a life of rectitude and good works. She even prayed that it was all right for her ankle to be broken if Alec wouldn't find her.

"Well, what have we here? A vagrant, I do believe. A fool, at the very least."

No answer to her fervent prayer. No life of rectitude for her now.

"It's something of a shock to look up from the very pleasant pastime of kissing a woman's breasts to see another female staring at you, her nose pressed to the windowpane. It's more than a shock. It's unbelievable."

Genny didn't look up at him. She surveyed his boots, saying nothing. He didn't sound particularly angry. He sounded rather amused. She didn't know which was worse.

"Well, why don't you say something? Why don't you get up? Did you fall from your illicit perch?"

"Yes, I did. I hit my head and I sprained my ankle."

"Well, you deserve it, though I doubt anything could get through that head of yours, wisdom or sense. I would very much like to leave you here, believe me, but I just might be doing business with your father and it wouldn't do for him to be called to fetch his termagent daughter from Laura Salmon's flower bed."

"Just leave! I wondered if you saw me in the window—and you did! You knew that I'd fallen and yet you continued to . . . well, you kept kissing her and . . . you've taken your precious time. I could have been dead by now."

"Do you think another five minutes might turn the trick?"

"Go away." Genny tried to stand up. She fell against the side of Laura's house. Alec merely watched her, long fingers stroking his jaw.

"That's a start. At this rate you'll be home by tomorrow morning." So she believed that he'd stayed up there and made love to Laura before coming down to see whether or not she was dead.

"Oh, just be quiet!"

"Ah, I'm the one at fault now, am I? I, the miserable man, who did nothing but—"

"I was lying down here unconscious, possibly dead, and you were up there making love to that woman!"

144

"Lower your voice, or that woman just might shoot us for trespassers or toss a pail of slops down on us."

Genny bit her lower lip. Her ankle hurt; her head hurt. She felt enough embarrassment to last her for the next ten years. How could she have been so stupid to come here and spy on him?

"All right. Have it your way. I'm a miserable human being. I'm also cold."

Alec heard her mumbling but couldn't make out her words. He said instead, "How long were you unconscious?"

"I don't know. Long enough certainly for you to do what you wished to do up there."

Alec could have corrected her very insulting misapprehension, but he didn't. Let her think that he'd made love to Laura. Let her think he'd made love to Laura ten times before he'd come down to see if she was dead or not. He'd left Laura almost immediately, frightened to death for Genny even as his fingers itched to find their way around her throat. He'd left both Laura and himself very frustrated, Laura wondering what had happened to her eager new lover. He'd simply told her that he had to return to his ship, that he'd forgotten something extremely important.

"It would give me great pleasure to thrash the devil out of you, but I suppose it is only sporting of me to wait until you have a fighting chance."

Genny said nothing.

The light in Laura's bedchamber went out.

"I mean it, Genny. I'm not feeling at all the gentleman right now; actually, I rarely feel the gentleman where you're concerned. When you're well, I fully intend to thrash you until your bottom is as red as your Baltimore tomatoes."

"You try it and I'll kick you in your—"

He held up a silencing hand. "Enough, Mr. Eugene. Now, let's get out of here before Laura hears us or someone wanders by."

"If you'll just help me home, I'll—"

"Don't be more of a fool than you already are."

He picked her up in his arms. Genny stiffened, then relaxed almost instantly. She'd never in her life been picked up by a man. It was alarming. It was also very interesting. He was strong, very strong. She put tentative arms around his neck. He smelled wonderful. Sandalwood, she thought, but wasn't certain.

"Are you taking me home, Alec?"

"No."

"Where, then?"

"To the *Night Dancer*. It's just over on O'Donnell's Wharf."

"Why?"

"Before I deposit you on your father's doorstep, I wish to ensure that you haven't broken your foot or your head."

"I haven't."

"Hush, Genny."

She did.

The Baltimore weather was cooperating. It was dark, clouds covering the half-moon, but it wasn't raining. They passed sailors, some of them drunk, others looking for a fight, the rest merely wandering about the city.

Genny looked up to see Alec turn onto O'Donnell's Wharf. The bow of a barkentine stretched high over Pratt Street. He walked up the gangplank and spoke quietly to a man on watch. Genny didn't move. She stared straight ahead at nothing.

But not for long. She wanted to look at his ship and she did. She raised her head and looked straight into the very startled eyes of a young man who couldn't be more than fifteen.

"Pippin," Alec said pleasantly to his cabin boy. "Good evening. I have a guest, as you can see. Make sure that no one disturbs us."

"Aye, Capt'n."

It was tricky getting down the hatch, but Alec managed, bumping his head once and Genny's elbow twice. "You made it sound like I was some sort of trollop you were bringing here to do . . . well, loose things to."

He laughed. "You don't look remotely like a trollop. If Pippin didn't know me, he could think I was a bloody pederast. You're dressed like a man, Genny, all the way to your wool hat."

"Oh."

"The good Lord save me from illogical women." He paused, then added, much struck, "My God, I haven't been that redundant in many a month."

Genny ground her teeth.

The ship smelled rich, she thought, inhaling deeply. When he kicked open a cabin door, the deep scent of sandalwood was more in evidence. He stepped into the cabin and shut the door.

"This is lovely."

"Yes, thank you, ma'am." He eased her down on his wide bunk.

Genny immediately tried to sit up. Alec shoved her onto her back. "Lie still. I want to look at your ankle. Actually, I don't want to, but I can't see that I have a lot of choice."

"You could be gracious."

"No, you're wrong. I'm so far from gracious at this moment, I appall even myself. Just be quiet."

Genny closed her mouth. Then she closed her eyes as Alec lifted her right leg. She winced and cried out.

"Sorry. I've got to get the boot off. Hold still."

Genny fisted her hands at her sides and kept her mouth closed. Alec got the boot off and dropped it to the floor. He looked up at her and saw that her face was perfectly white. He softened. He didn't want to, but there didn't seem to be any choice. He sat beside her and said gently, "I'm sorry to hurt you, Genny. It's done now."

"It's all right."

"Liar." She felt his fingertips move across her cheek. Then the mattress shifted as he moved. He pulled off her wool sock. "Since you're wearing men's boots, it's not surprising that your feet smell like men's."

"Just what does that mean?" She opened her eyes and saw him grinning at her.

"Give me a while to come up with something utterly repulsive." She heard him suck in his breath. "You did quite an excellent job on your ankle. It's swelled up like a ripe melon." He

148

touched it and breath hissed out between her teeth.

"Sorry." He rose. "Stay put. I'm going to get some cold water. We'll need to soak your ankle, then wrap it up before I get you home."

After Alec left the cabin, Genny pulled herself up on her elbows. It was a masculine lair, and very much to her taste with all the books and nautical instruments, the neat stacks of papers on the desk, the absence of mess. She saw the door that must give into the next cabin and wondered what was in there. She looked down at her ankle and grimaced.

"I'm a mess," she said aloud.

"True, but what can you expect? You decide you want to be educated, so you climb up the side of Laura Salmon's house and look into her bedchamber. You look at *me*, Genny. I don't like that. How would you feel if someone—man or woman—watched *us*, for example, making love?"

"That's absurd!"

"What is?"

"Why, you and I . . . making . . . it's crazy."

"Do you really think so? No, don't answer that." He wrung out a towel and wrapped it around her swollen ankle. She couldn't distinguish which hurt more, her ankle or the cold from the wet towel. Then numbness set in and it was wonderful.

"Lie still. We'll do that for about fifteen minutes. Then I'll bandage you and take you home. Unfortunately, my ship's physician, Graf Pruitt, is out squiring a very dark-mooded lady about Baltimore."

"Where did he meet this dark-mooded lady?"

"He's known her for a good while. Like Laura Salmon, she's also blessed with a name that raises brows. It's Swindel. How would you like a bit of brandy? Never mind, don't reply. You'll have some."

Genny drank the brandy. It was smooth and French and warmed all the innards she possessed. She took three good gulps, Alec grinning over her.

"Why are you smiling like a village half-wit?"

"You. You gulped brandy and now I'll wager you're feeling not a whit of pain."

"No, I'm not," she said, and it was true.

"Hold still," he said, unwrapped one towel, and applied another one, this one colder and wetter. She sucked in her breath but didn't say anything.

She watched him pull the chair from behind his desk and draw it over to the big bunk. He sat down and crossed his ankles. He folded his arms over his chest and watched Genny down more brandy, a lot more brandy. She looked over at him and gave him a crooked grin.

"Did you really make love to her?"

"I already told you that I did. She exhausted me. She'd quite good and very, very loving."

"I'm loving, too."

Alec couldn't believe those words had come from Miss Eugenia's mouth. Not Eugenia the lippy malehater. This was interesting. Alec knew it was in his character to always push the limits, both of nature and of other people. After all, the worst she could do was throw a damp, cold towel at his face. "What do you mean you're loving?"

"I mean that I live to love and be loved. Don't you?"

"Yes, particularly by a beautiful woman."

"That isn't precisely what I mean, but it will do for now because—"

"I know. Because I'm a man and can't really understand these elusive and ill-defined gradations of feeling and sensibility you women experience."

"That's right. You're also hateful and arrogant—"

"That's quite enough out of you. I've been sitting here wondering what I was going to do to punish you. I think I've got it figured out now."

"Got what figured out?"

"You're a twenty-three-year-old virgin, a very long-in-the-tooth virgin."

Her eyes nearly crossed but she held her tongue, refusing to be drawn into an argument she knew was lost even before she began.

"Have you ever had a climax, Genny?"

Her mouth fell open. A wonderful, very honest reply, and not a word said.

"A climax, my dear girl, is very possibly a series of the most phenomenal feelings a human being can experience. So you've never had a woman's pleasure, have you?"

"I want to go home now."

"Oh, no, Genny. I've quite decided on your punishment. And you'll love it at the same time. Just call me a magician, call me magnificent, a man with a heart of gold."

"I want to go home." She sat up and jerked off the towel. Alec, just as quickly, took the towel from her and tossed it back into the bucket of cold water. He sat down beside her, his hands on her shoulders, holding her down.

"Would you like to know what I'm going to do to you, Eugenia Paxton?"

"No, you wouldn't do that."

"Do what?"

"What it is you're thinking. This climax business. You wouldn't."

"Genny, why did you come to Laura's? Why did you climb up the tree at the side of her house and press your nose against the windowpane in her bedchamber?"

Not a sound.

"You wanted to be educated?"

Not even a whisper of a sound.

"You wanted to see what I would do to a woman, didn't you? Well, I plan to educate you a bit, right now."

Her beautiful, very green eyes became at once blank. "No," she said.

"You'll enjoy it, I promise. Aren't you tired of being a twenty-three-year-old virgin, Genny?"

"I don't want any man to touch me!"

"I'm not just any man, my dear. I'm the man you followed. I'm also the first man who will give you a woman's pleasure."

"You can't."

"Can't what?"

"It doesn't exist. Nothing like that could exist. It's something you wretched men made up to try to make women climb into bed with you!"

Alec laughed. "You're a wit, Genny. I'll watch you eat those silly words later. Ah, since I did make love to Laura, you needn't worry that I'll attack you that way. You will, at least technically, remain a twenty-three-year-old virgin." A pity, he thought as he said those words. He did want to end her virginity once and for all. He did want to come inside her and feel her around him and feel her surprise and watch her eyes widen when he came deep and deeper still, then pulled out of her. He wanted to feel her shudder, hear her cry out when he touched her with his fingers, with his mouth . . .

"What way?"

"What way what? Oh. That I'll come inside you. A man needs time to recuperate, time to get his body as ready as his spirit, time to—"

"I don't want you to do that."

"Do what? You're making no sense."

"To touch me. I want to go home now."

"You're so tipsy, you'd probably fall into the Patapsco. No, you'll stay right here and enjoy yourself. But remember, too, Genny, that this is your punishment for your outrageous behavior."

"What you're planning is far more outrageous, and I won't stand for it, Alec! I won't!"

He tightened his grip on her shoulders. He lowered his head and kissed her. Gently, lightly, on her pursed lips. She tried to struggle away from him, but he was simply too strong. He kissed her and kissed her and couldn't frankly believe it. He very nearly pulled away at the beginning, but he couldn't. He'd kissed many women, and now he was kissing Genny and he loved it and wanted to keep doing it until the day he stuck his spoon in the wall, and it frightened him. But he didn't stop. He wasn't about to stop.

When he finally raised his head and looked down at her, he saw clearly that she was as moved as he was. Her eyes were vague, surprised, and she made a tiny sound in her throat, but he understood and kissed her again.

In the next moment, she struck him against his shoulders with her fists. It didn't particularly hurt him, but it got his attention.

"I want to go home!"

"You're not going home, so be quiet. Now, you were enjoying kissing as much as I was. What's wrong with you? I'll just give you more pleasure."

"I won't be your whore."

"No, you won't. You haven't the talent or the skills for it. You couldn't even make it through an interview stage. When I'm finished with you, Mr. Eugene, you're going to wonder why you ever wanted to ape a man, you'll relish your womanness so much. You'll probably burn all your breeches—"

"And beg you to make me your mistress? Beg you to make love to me? I hate you, Alec Carrick. You're arrogant and cruel—"

"At least I don't follow people around and watch them in the most private and personal activity devised by nature! Enough!"

Alec was angry now and when he kissed her again, he was rough, demanding, and he forced her lips apart. He said into her mouth, "You try to bite me, and it'll go badly for you, my dear."

154

Actually, the feel of his tongue had such a startling effect on every part of Genny's body that biting him would never have occurred to her. Now that he'd reminded her that she should very likely bite him to preserve her honor, she did. Hard.

Alec jerked back, his face flushed with sexual desire and anger. It was a combination he'd never felt before. "Ah, Genny, I'm going to make you very sorry you did that."

"I want to go home now, Alec."

"I suggest you hold still, or you'll end up at home with your men's clothing quite shredded." He calmly began unbuttoning her shirt.

"No!"

"I'll tie you down if I have to, Genny. Then I'll force more brandy down your throat."

"No, you won't, I won't let you, I'll rip your face—"

Alec pulled off his cravat, grabbed her wrists, and tied them together, then jerked her arms over her head. "No!"

He tied the end of the cravat to the headboard of the bunk. "Now, enough is enough. Punishment and education. You both win and lose, Genny. Think of it like that. Also, think of it as the man overcoming the woman, as is his right. Think about me making you submit, making you want to feel passion at my hands. Think about it while I finish making you quite as naked as the day you came into Baltimore."

"I wasn't born in Baltimore!"

He laughed. Genny squirmed as his fingers found the buttons on her breeches, trying to turn her body away from him, but it did no good.

155

"Where were you born? In hell? Did Satan take one look at you and turn pale?"

He pulled her breeches down to her knees.

9

"No," he said slowly, staring down at her, "Satan wouldn't have kicked you out. You're something of a surprise, Eugenia Paxton. Yes, unexpected."

He was holding down her legs with his right arm, and staring at her very white belly and the soft fleece of light chestnut hair covering her woman's mound. He raised his left hand and let it hover. Slowly he lowered his arm, very slowly. He knew Genny was watching his hand, watching his fingers. She hadn't uttered a sound since he'd gotten her breeches around her knees.

He didn't look at her face but kept his eyes on her beautiful woman's flesh. His fingers lightly touched her, then eased away, and he finally splayed them over her flat belly.

"Very nice, Genny. Very nice indeed." A vast understatement, he thought. Without another word, he jerked her pants and underthings down her legs and off her feet. He tossed the clothes to the floor.

"Now the rest. Hmm. I'll just have to let you borrow one of my shirts."

He neatly ripped off her shirt and snipped the straps of her linen chemise. When he peeled it

156

off her, he sat back so he could see the expanse of her from head to toe.

Alec felt very odd. He couldn't remember ever having responded this way before in his adult sexual life. She was just a woman, not even a particularly beautiful woman, but her white body, those full breasts of hers, those very long, sleekly muscled legs . . . He felt himself shudder. He wanted to touch her, taste every inch of her; he wanted to strip off his own clothes and thrust deep inside her and tell her that he . . . that he what, for pity's sake?

It was in that instant that Genny took action. She raised her hips, dug in her heels, and pulled with all her strength against the knots at her wrists. She yanked and jerked and pulled.

It did no good at all.

She cursed, quite fluently, then jerked and yanked again.

"I'm a sailor, Genny. I tie knots well."

"Let me go, Alec Carrick! I won't lie here like this with you staring at me and laughing at me and—"

"Do you hear me laughing?"

"You will because I look like a man and I'm skinny and quite ugly and—"

"You look like *what?* Genny, if you look like a man, I'll turn pederast right this instant." He lifted his hand from her belly and cupped her breast. "You call yourself skinny? Your breasts . . . well, I'm a man with large hands and—no, Genny, you're not skinny."

Her flesh was incredibly soft and her nipples, a very pale pink, were downy as velvet and . . .

157

He felt a moment of guilt and something else. That was it: he didn't like himself terribly much, and oddly enough, it wasn't because he'd tied a lady to his bunk, stripped off her clothes, and planned to teach her pleasure; it was because he'd wanted Laura and he'd touched her breasts and he'd wanted her fiercely until he'd seen Genny at the window and his desire for Laura had died abruptly, like doused embers on a summer grate. He didn't understand it and he didn't like it one bit.

"Nor are you ugly. How could you think that? Don't you have a mirror? Even men use mirrors, you know, so it's quite all right to do so for your charade."

She tugged again at the knots around her wrists. "You know very well that I am a homely little beggar compared with the ladies you're used to!"

"Homely little beggar," he repeated, grinning. "All that? Take it from an old campaigner, Genny—you're about the un-ugliest female I've ever mounted an assault upon."

She chewed his military metaphor over for just a moment, then blurted out, "I saw you kissing Laura's breasts and you touched her there and fondled her."

"True." What else could he say? She wouldn't believe him if he said that it simply wasn't the same thing as touching her. She wouldn't believe him; Lord, he didn't believe himself, even though it was true.

Genny didn't know what to do. The brandy made her feel a trifle hazy in the brain, but not so much that she wasn't aware of every look on Alec's face, every touch of those wonderful fingers of his and . . . She had to stop this. She couldn't very calmly accept being tied down and looked at and touched by a man. "Alec, please, let me go home now. I'm sorry about spying on you and Laura. Truly, I'll never do it again, I promise."

"It's too late, Genny," he said, and his voice was deeper and rougher than she'd ever heard it. "It's far too late for that now. I told you I wouldn't take your virginity. That's a gift a woman gives a man, not one a man takes. But I fully intend to give you a woman's pleasure."

"No! I don't want you to. It's ridiculous! There's no such thing."

"Stupid girl. It will make you very wild, Genny, and you'll be completely mine, completely at my will."

"I don't want to be under your bloody thumb!"

"Too bad." He grinned then, and suddenly jerked off her wool cap and sent it flying toward the pile of her clothes on the floor. He pulled the pins out, then sifted his fingers through her hair and smoothed it over the pillow. "Much nicer. Now no one could confuse you with a man."

"Please untie me, Alec."

"Not on your life, Mr. Eugene. You'd try your best to bring me low. No, I want to keep you like this so I can give you all my attention and not have to worry about you destroying my manhood." As he spoke, he ran his hands over her breasts, caressed her nipples into tautness, then stroked down across her ribs to come to a halt with his hands clasping her waist.

"You're not at all skinny," he said. "Now, just let me shift my position a bit. I want to see all of you, my dear Genny, and the best view is from between your thighs."

She started to struggle at his outrageous words, but it didn't slow him down. He pulled her thighs apart and came between them. "Wider, I think," he said, and pushed out with his legs until her thighs were very wide indeed, her knees bent over his legs.

She closed her eyes. This was awful. No one had ever done anything like this to her. Of course not, you fool! She couldn't help herself. She looked up briefly to see him staring down at her, and she was fully exposed to him, every single inch of her. He was a savage, a barbarian. He should be booted out of the English aristocracy.

"You're lovely," he said, and she felt his fingers, his warm strong fingers, stroking gently over her, then slowly parting her, and she knew he was looking at her. "Very lovely."

"Stop doing that—stop looking at me!"

He raised his head. "Why? I wanted your legs wide apart so I could examine you, so to speak. A man enjoys seeing what he will be getting himself into. Eventually, not this evening. I want that to be perfectly clear."

She yowled, there was no other word for it, Alec thought, grinning at the sound. She was furious—excited, if he didn't miss his experienced guess—and she felt ambivalent about being at his mercy, a circumstance which he was enjoying vastly. Very gently, he slid his finger inside her. He heard her suck in her breath, felt her muscles tighten and clamp around his finger. "You're very small, Genny. Wonderfully small and hot and . . ." His voice trailed off. His finger went deeper, but very slowly. It didn't hurt. It was so incredibly exciting that Genny couldn't think of anything to compare it to. She waited, tense, furious, excited, her hips still, her body wanting . . . wanting.

Alec closed his eyes as his finger finally abutted her maidenhead. He pressed lightly, but the thin membrane held. "Genny," he said. He pulled his finger out very slowly; then he thrust it into her again and she cried out, her hips lifting. He smiled, looking at her face. He could see that she was stunned, and this gave him more pleasure than he could have imagined. Stunned, and now disappointed because he had stopped.

"Your education," he said. Then he lowered his head, allowed his fingers to find her through the fleece of soft hair, and she felt his mouth touching her and she nearly died of the shock of it.

"No!"

"Shush," he said, and his warm breath made her shudder and quake with those same unbelievable feelings that his finger had given her. But this was something she never in her life considered part of what men and women did together. It was personal, no, more than personal; he was kissing and caressing a part of her that she'd really been unaware of. But not anymore.

Oh, goodness, it was incredible.

She felt her hips lifting to his mouth, felt his hands slide beneath her hips to hold her. "Very nice, Genny," he said, and his warm breath once again sent her into pleasurable oblivion. "You taste so sweet, like yourself, and like a woman should."

Genny didn't know what to do. She felt herself giving in. If she were being completely honest with herself, she had already given in, minutes upon minutes before, days before; in fact, the day she'd first laid eyes on him. She felt a throbbing pleasure, ebbing then washing over her with greater and greater strength, right where his mouth was learning her, caressing her, suckling her. She knew she was hot and damp, she could feel herself, and if she weren't so filled with the anticipation of something she couldn't quite yet imagine, but something she knew she'd kill to have, she would have ordered him to stop that moment. Instead, she moaned. Moaned again and arched her back. Her legs trembled, then stiffened.

"That's it, Genny," he murmured, his fingers stroking her. "Relax, let go. Just press yourself up against my mouth. Yes, that's it. You taste wonderful. I can feel your legs tightening, tensing. Just a moment . . . ah, there, do you like that?"

He'd slipped his finger inside her again, pushing until he could go no further.

It was more than enough.

Genny's head fell back against the pillow. She cried out, unable to help herself; tearing, harsh cries. Her thighs tightened and she felt a spasm of such unexpected force that she wondered if she would survive it. The thing was, though, she didn't care. She just wanted those incredible feelings to keep pounding through her, and she cried out again and again.

Alec tried to remain detached. He had her now, she was his, she was doing his bidding, she was bent to his will. He knew that until she died she would remember this night, remember that it was he who gave her this beautiful pleasure. There was no doubt in his mind that he also would remember it until he cocked up his toes. But that wasn't important. She was his, and he wanted more than anything he'd ever wanted in his life to come inside her, now, this very instant, and plunge into her and feel her draw him deep and deeper still until he had filled her with himself and touched her womb. He wanted to spill his seed deep inside her.

His breathing was harsh, rough, growing more so as the spasms of her pleasure gradually lessened. He eased his finger out of her, slowed the caressing of his mouth. Finally, when he felt her calm again, he raised his head and looked at her face.

She was staring at him. Saying not a word, just staring. She looked dazed. He grinned, although it hurt him to grin when he wanted to be a complete and utter ravisher and bury himself inside the woman he'd just pleasured.

Mr. Eugene, I think I've got myself a new sex slave. He would have liked to be that flippant, that arrogantly detached, but the words were only in his mind. "Are you all right, sweetheart?" he said instead.

Still she just stared at him, until finally, in a near whisper, she said, "I don't know. Nothing's as it should be right now or as it was. I don't know."

"Just breathe slowly, very slowly. That's it. Your breasts aren't heaving quite so much now. Yes, your heart's slowing, I can feel it." He raised his hand from her breast. "Better?"

"I don't understand," she said, and her eyes were large and filled with confusion.

"A woman's pleasure, Genny. You experienced your first climax. Sex, that's all. You had quite a lesson tonight."

"I don't understand about you. You didn't . . . I saw Laura's hand go down your belly and touch you and you were big and—"

Ah, the pain her words brought to his groin. He shook his head, hoping to shake away the pain with it. "You're still a virgin. Don't worry. That mythical man you will probably marry someday won't be disappointed in you. He'll rip through your maidenhead with tearful gratitude, I doubt not."

"No."

"No what?"

"No man will ever do that."

He sighed. "You have this habit of saying no so positively to things, thus making me want to do them more than anything. I do recommend, Miss Eugene, that you don't take quite so definite a stand on your maidenhead."

"You've done as you pleased. Now untie me."

Instead, Alec leaned down and kissed her. She tasted herself on his mouth. "Part your lips," he

164

said and she did, just a bit. It didn't occur to her to bite him again. He tasted wonderful. He made her feel wonderful, and she felt the growing ache deep in her belly and said, "Oh."

"Hmm?"

"It's beginning again."

He raised his head, grinned down at her, and lightly ran his fingertips over her jaw. "A randy woman. Do you want me to pleasure you again?"

That earned him a quick denial. "Of course not. I want you to untie me."

"You know, we could spend the rest of the night just experimenting. We could see just how many times your body exploded with your woman's pleasure. There are so many different ways of arriving at the same destination, so to speak. Would you like to be a scientist with me, Genny? Would you like to be my own personal experiment?"

"I'm not some sort of depraved female."

"Not totally depraved. But you've got lots of passion, Miss Paxton, and I think I'd like to see more of it. The look on your face at your climax— a beautiful blend of virginal innocence and deep lust. It warmed my cynical, world-weary blood, I'll tell you."

"Let me go, Alec."

He sighed. "Perhaps I should. Next time, though, I'd like to see your pleasure again and again."

"There won't be a next time."

He looked suddenly very hard and utterly implacable, and she shivered. Yet his voice when he spoke was easy, almost amused. "You think not? Again you're so absolutely certain. You need to know me, Genny, really get to know me. The next time I take you like this, I probably won't even have to tie you down. Now, how is your ankle? Less swollen, I think." He lightly touched his fingers to it and she sucked in her breath. "Still tender. Well, not surprising, considering you tumbled a good twenty feet. If there were divine justice in this world, you would have broken it in three places. Count yourself lucky, my girl. Count yourself more lucky that I didn't mention your outrageous act to Laura. Can you begin to imagine the tale she would—even at this moment—be spreading around Baltimore? Good Lord, it boggles the mind."

That was a kicker, and Genny knew he was more than right. "Will you say anything?"

He gave her that slow, incredibly sexy smile of his, one that guaranteed to serve him any female he wished in the world on his plate. "I'll make you a deal, Miss Paxton. I'll keep my mouth shut—not a word, even to Laura—if you agree to become my mistress. Immediately. What do you think?"

If her wrists had been free, he would have gotten an excellent demonstration of her thoughts on the subject. As it was, she tugged once, as hard as she could, then hissed between her teeth at him, "You said I wasn't skilled enough to be your mistress."

"So I did. I must admit to reevaluating my initial conclusion. You have so much passion, so much enthusiasm. It's very delightful, you know.

It adds a touch of something that is quite beyond excellent skills."

"Someday I will do this to you."

His eyes widened a bit and there was surprise in his voice as he said, "Do you promise?"

That made her swallow, for at that moment she saw him lying on his back, his hands tied above his head with her over him, saw herself taking off all his clothes, then looking at him as he had looked at her, studying him, touching him. It would be something extraordinary. She'd like to do it right now. Still, he was a man, and men didn't like to be under someone else's control, especially if that someone else was a female. "You wouldn't mind? You'd like to be helpless on your back? Knowing I could do whatever I wished to you? Don't say yes, because I wouldn't believe you!"

"If I trusted you, if I knew that you approached me with the same enthusiasm and, ah, reverence and respect that I approached you, then I wouldn't mind at all. I would enjoy it. You know, of course, that the best way to become skilled at something is to practice it over and over again.

"Men don't trust women."

"A truism? Goodness, Genny, when did you begin painting everyone, at least every man, with your twenty-three-year-old tainted brush?"

"Ha! You even agree that any *self-respecting* man wouldn't deal with me and I build excellent ships, and just because I happen to be a woman, which has nothing to do with anything! My brush isn't at all tainted. Now, would you please untie me? I'm cold."

He gave her one last, very long look, beginning at her toes and an eon later ending at her eyebrows. "All right." He untied her wrists, brought them down, and massaged them. Then he pulled a blanket up to her waist. "Your breasts aren't cold."

"You can't know that! They are so."

"Your nipples are quite smooth and soft. If they were cold, they would be puckered and . . . well, you understand now. And your breasts are quite beautiful. They enhance my conversation."

"Your conversation is lewd." She yanked the blanket up to her chin. He looked aggrieved but tolerant.

"Forgive me, but I find your breasts anything but lewd. You shouldn't insult yourself so, Genny."

"You've punished me quite enough, Baron. I want to go home now."

Alec sent a look heavenward. "I give the woman pleasure and she calls it punishment. I compliment her breasts and she calls it lewd of me. A man tries and tries, and still the woman complains."

"I'm not complaining."

"No," he said slowly, looking at her thoughtfully. "No, you're not, are you?"

Moses looked at the baron and then down at the little girl beside him who was holding his hand looking like a miniature image of him.

"Suh! Lord Sherard, do come in, suh, ah, yes and the little lady with you, suh."

"Good morning, Moses."

"Now, who is this little lady here? You find her under a cabbage leaf, suh? Goodness, what a lovely little thing she be."

"This is my daughter, Hallie. Hallie, love, this is Moses. He runs the Paxton household and he does it very well."

Hallie looked at the tall, thin black man. "Your hair looks funny. All springy and stiff and like pepper. Can I touch it?"

"Yes, little lady, you sure can." Alec nodded and Moses scooped Hallie up in his arms. She was regarding him with great seriousness. She touched his hair with very tentative fingers, then more firmly. She tugged just a little. Then she smiled. "That's wonderful, Mr. Moses. I wish my hair felt that nice."

"You're a sweet little 'un," said Moses, "but I bet yore papa likes yore hair just like it is."

"What have we here?"

Alec turned to Mr. James Paxton. "Good morning, sir. I just brought my daughter over to meet everyone. Hallie, my dear, this is Mr. Paxton."

Hallie didn't show any interest in leaving Moses's arms. "Hello, sir. You have a lovely house. Papa says it's George's architecture. It's very different from our houses in England."

"How many houses do you have, young lady?" asked James.

"I don't know. You'll have to ask my papa."

"We have four houses," Alec said.

"Mr. Moses has very nice hair."

"I hadn't noticed before," James said. Then he looked much struck. "I do believe you're right,

169

Hallie. Moses has very substantial hair, yes, indeed."

Moses hugged Hallie, then gave her over to her father. "I'll fetch you some of Lannie's delicious seedling cakes. Would you like that, little 'un?"

"Oh, yes, Mr. Moses, very much."

James smiled at Alec over the child's head. "Have you considered the diplomatic corps for her?"

Alec grinned.

"Papa, what kind of cakes?"

"Lannie's cakes, poppet. Trust Mr. Moses. If he thinks you'll like seedlings, I promise you that you will."

James Paxton was moving very slowly this morning, Alec saw. He didn't like it, he realized, seeing for the first time that the man's health wasn't at all good. He followed him into the parlor, showed Hallie the gilded birdcage, then moved over to sit beside James.

"How are you feeling, sir?"

James smiled. "Age, my boy. It's a miserable thing, but of course being dead would be a good deal worse. I'll live."

"Is Genny here?"

"Yes, strangely enough," James said. "She usually leaves so early. But Moses said something about her spraining her ankle. I can't imagine that that's true, but we'll see. Your daughter is beautiful and she's your exact likeness. Nothing of her mother?"

Alec looked at his daughter, who was now very carefully, very tentatively, running her fingers lightly over the hand-carved perch on the inside of the cage.

"You see her absorbed look? Everything in her is focused on what she's doing. Her mother was like that occasionally. Hallie is just about everything that is important to me," Alec added.

"Did her mother die birthing her?"

"Yes."

"So did my wife. Wretched doctors. You'd think they'd know what to do when something goes wrong and how to stop it. Makes me so mad I could spit. Poor Mary. The years she could have had, we could have had. . . ." James fell silent and in that silence Alec felt the pain, vague and gentle now, but there, always, with him. He looked again at Hallie. Thank God she'd survived.

"Sorry to become a maudlin old fool. Have you come to any decision, Alec?"

"Good morning, Father. Baron."

Alec was aware of a sharp pulling deep inside him at the sound of Genny's voice. She sounded stiff, excessively formal. He smiled to himself as he slowly turned to face her, freely admitting, silently, of course, that he'd brought Hallie with him as a buffer. He wasn't a complete fool, after all.

"Hello, Genny. What's this about a sprained ankle?" Though he sounded concerned to the uninvolved ear, Genny heard the mockery, saw the devilry in his beautiful eyes, and wanted to spit and howl and throw him to the floor and kiss him until he . . . until he what? She was a fool, a great fool and he was here laughing at her, enjoying her discomfort, looking at her, through her clothing, seeing her naked again, knowing her and caressing her. She shivered.

She had to pull herself together. "It's nothing at all. I simply twisted it going up the stairs last evening."

"You should have told me," James said. "I could have gotten you to soak it."

"Soaking is excellent for that kind of injury," Alec said. "However did you manage to hurt yourself on the stairs? Isn't a sprain more likely from a fall, say?"

"No! I didn't fall. Ah, here's Moses with tea and food. What? Who's that?"

At that moment Genny saw Hallie. She stared at the little girl and the little girl stared back at her. Genny kept staring, she couldn't help herself. Hallie was the most beautiful child she'd ever seen. She didn't know children or understand them, or much care for them for that matter, but that solemn little face, why, it was a replica of Alec's . . . he was the child's father. Genny swallowed, thankful that she didn't have to say anything while Moses poured coffee and tea.

"Thank you, Mr. Moses," Hallie said with exquisite politeness as she extended her small hand for a cup of tea.

"You like milk, little 'un?"

"Oh, yes, please, Mr. Moses. These are Lannie's special seedling cakes?"

"They sure is. You just takes what you wishes."

"Thank you."

172

Genny continued to stare. Alec had a child, a little girl, and the little girl was dressed as she was, in boy's clothing.

"Who are you?"

Hallie smiled at the seemingly pretty young man who wasn't. "You aren't a man like Papa," she said. "I don't wear a wool cap on my head unless it's cold."

"I begin to think that I am the only one who believes I ever did look like a man," Genny said and pulled off her wool cap.

"I'm Hallie Carrick. He's my papa. He braids my hair like yours when he wants me to wear my wool cap. Otherwise my hair gets too tangled and Papa says things that I can't say or he'll tan my bottom for me."

This beautiful man braided a little girl's hair?

"You're only supposed to sing my praises, Hallie."

"You're the best papa in the whole world."

"That's better," Alec remarked, "and naturally it's the whole truth. Now, sit down, pumpkin, and drink your tea. I see that Lannie's cakes are sesame seed and lemon. Now, this is Mr. Eugene Paxton when she feels like pulling the wool over my eyes, and then Eugene becomes a Eugenia or a Genny. Genny, my daughter."

"My pleasure, Hallie. May I have some coffee, Moses?"

Moses smiled at her and handed her a fine English bone-china cup.

"Actually," Alec said, the devilry still in his eyes for Genny to see, "I realized that Hallie was in the same situation as you, Genny. She needs a couple of little-girl dresses, underthings, shoes, and stockings. The sorts of things you've heard about, perhaps."

He carried in his pocket a list from Eleanor Swindel, who had told him roundly that breeches on a five-year-old girl were outside of enough. When she'd handed him her list, she'd said, "Outgrown everything she owns. Even these fool breeches are too short on her." Of course she didn't know what to do about the armoire in Hallie's chamber at the Fountain Inn. Smelled like nutmeg and camphor, it did; nasty smell for a little girl. These colonials didn't know a thing about armoires or little girls. This didn't necessarily follow, but Alec wasn't fool enough to go into it with Mrs. Swindel. He'd already endured quite enough with the initial nutmeg controversy.

"So here I am to ask you to accompany us to your mantuamaker. I should imagine that you have something ready, Genny. Would you like to change into something more, er, socially acceptable?"

"My ankle is much too sore for me to go walking into all sorts of shops."

"How odd. You seem to be doing all right. Indeed, I was amazed at your recovery. A fall—did you say *up* the stairs?—isn't to be treated lightly. Shall I take a look at it? I'm known to be something of an expert on ankles."

Genny wanted to spit several colorful invectives in his face. In that instant, she met his eyes and saw herself reflected there and she was naked and on her back, her hands tied above her head, and her back was arched as he caressed her with his mouth and hands.

She swallowed.

"Genny?"

10

"I'm going to the shipyard."

Hallie looked up from her cake. "Shipyard? You're the Genny who works in a shipyard?"

Genny shot Alec a look. "Yes, my father and I own the Paxton shipyard on Fells Point."

She didn't have to wait long to find out what he'd said about her to his daughter. "Oh. You're the lady Papa makes angry."

"That's quite true. He does it well and very quickly."

"Hallie," Alec said quickly, "would you like to, ah, feel Mr. Moses's hair again?"

"Not right now, Papa," she said, all patience then turned her full attention back to Genny. "I asked him why he did that and he said he didn't know. He said he liked to see what you'd do. He said you didn't like men and didn't ever want to marry, and I told him that was impossible, that all the ladies liked him."

"Is that what he tells you?"

Hallie gave her a curious look. "Of course not. I watch and see how people act, you know."

Genny felt like a fool. Taken down by a child.

175

She smiled and offered Hallie another seedling cake.

"I was happy when Papa said you dressed like I do. Now he wants to buy me some frilly dresses. Would he listen to you, Genny?"

"No, never in a century."

"Well, that's all right. Papa's usually right about things. Can I see the shipyard? May I, Papa? I don't want any silly girl's dresses just yet. Please, Papa."

"After chewing me up and spitting me out in front of Genny, you want me to reward you?" Alec threw up his hands.

Hallie turned the force of her papa's beautiful blue eyes back on Genny. "Pippin—he's Papa's cabin boy—he told me all about shipyards. He was an apprentice carter—"

"Caulker?"

"Yes, that's it, a caulker. He was in Liverpool a long time ago. I want to be a caulker and I'll fill every space between the planks and my ship won't leak. Can I watch your caulkers? Do they use twisted hemp? It's called oakum, Pippin told me."

Genny smiled; she couldn't help herself. "Yes, you can watch our caulkers. They'll be starting next week. It's a wonderful sound to hear, and you hear it only at a shipyard."

"Ah, yes," said James. "I miss the ring of the caulker's mallet. Here in Baltimore, Hallie, we use a caulking iron struck with a mallet of mesquite wood. We cover the ends of the mallets with steel. Do you think you're strong enough to join in the caulker's brotherhood?"

"It would have to be a sisterhood," said Alec. "That's just fine. Let me see your muscle."

Hallie showed James her muscle and he looked deeply thoughtful. "As impressive as Baltimore Billie's," he said as he lightly squeezed Hallie's upper arm. "Now, he's a fellow I wouldn't want angry at me."

"And I can be covered with tar," Hallie said with such awed delight that Alec burst out laughing, earning him a wounded look from his daughter.

"Acquit me, pumpkin. You make it sound like the most marvelous of Christmas presents."

Genny found that she was again staring at the little girl. "Where is your mama?" The instant the words were out, Genny gasped. "Oh, never mind, I'm sorry. I forgot. Oh, dear. Another cake, Hallie?"

Hallie said in an unemotional voice, "My mama died a long time ago when I was just born. I don't remember her, but Papa has a picture. She was very pretty. Papa told me she was very sweet and that she didn't like to travel but she did and didn't ever complain about it."

"Do you travel with your papa?" Genny asked.

"Oh, yes. Papa and I go everywhere together. We even had dinner with the governor of Gibraltar. It was last February. Mrs. Swindel hated Gibraltar. She said the Spanish wanted to come in and kill all the English. She said it was full of nasty monkeys who jumped on everybody and scared them into gray hair and gave them the Black Death."

James Paxton laughed, leaned forward, and

patted Hallie's shoulder. "Did you see any nasty monkeys?"

"Oh, yes. I wanted Papa to give me one, but he said a monkey wouldn't be happy on board our ship. He said he'd bring the Black Death on board before he'd bring a monkey."

"I suspect he's right about that," Genny said. She was having difficulty fitting this new man into the Alec-mold she knew. But last night had happened. He had tied her to his bunk, stripped off all her clothes, and touched her . . . Genny jerked. "Just stop it," she said aloud. Then she jumped to her feet, groaned at the pain in her ankle, and promptly sat back down again. To Alec, she said, "Just stop it, do you hear?"

He looked at her, and Genny knew exactly where Hallie got her wounded look; then he shrugged and looked wicked. "What are you thinking about, Genny? Something that happened last evening, perhaps? Your sprained ankle? You really should be more careful. You fell off the side of a house, you said?"

"No! I fell down—up—the stairs."

"Perhaps you could demonstrate. That way all of us could avoid such an injury in the future. A pity that you have no ivy growing next to the stairs you could have caught."

"I must change. I will see you shortly, Hallie."

"I thought you were going to the shipyard," James said.

"Later, Papa. First we'll go buy Hallie some clothes. After lunch we'll go to the shipyard. I'll take her to meet John Furring. He rolls oakum

178

into strand for the caulking," she added to Hallie. "He's an old man and he has wonderful stories."

Hallie gave her a heart-stopping smile. "I should like that. Thank you, Genny."

"Now this is very interesting," James said as he watched his daughter limp from the parlor.

"Hallie, take your *third* slice of cake and go examine the birdcage some more."

"Yes, Papa. You want to talk to Mr. Paxton about business."

"That's right."

"She's a wonderful little girl, Alec."

"Yes, she is, and she never ceases to amaze me. I had no idea she knew anything at all about shipbuilding. So my cabin boy was an apprentice caulker. Now, down to business, sir. Before you were ill, you directly ran the shipyard? You were the master builder?"

"Yes. Genny assisted me, mainly with the bookkeeping. But she knows all the phases quite well, and has since the age of thirteen, I might add. I lofted the plans of the *Pegasus* last winter. When I had my heart seizure, she took over and finished the plans. Has Genny shown you through our warehouse? No? Well, all that's left really is the half-model I built and the lines I laid down. Still, it's Paxton property and you should see it. Also, there's our sail loft on Pratt Street. We've probably eight men finishing sewing the *Pegasus*'s sails right now. It was Genny's decision to rig up the sails in sections. She tells me we're right on schedule, so the last of the sails should be finished by the end of October."

"There's no buyer in sight?"

"No. As I told you, Mr. Donald Boynton commissioned her, paid for initial materials, then went bankrupt. We found out that he lost two ships in the same storm, both of them carrying black slaves. He'd assured me that he didn't want another slaver, but—" James shrugged. "He was a prominent citizen. You know the sort, Alec—outwardly all bluff goodwill and inside, ruthless as a snake. We were running out of our own private funds. In early September, we had to borrow money from the Union Bank to pay the men's salaries and to purchase further materials, or scrap it all. We couldn't do that. It would have meant losing everything. The clipper schooner will be a marvel. It must be built. It will earn great profits in the next five years."

Alec stared down at his clasped hands. "Like my daughter, I should like to see the actual work."

"The sail loft as well? Ah, that's something. The camaraderie warms the cockles of the heart. I'd estimate that the men will sew something close to eleven thousand square feet of canvas, use miles and miles of thread and a good forty pounds of beeswax on it before they've finished."

Alec whistled. His whistle changed in a flash. Genny had limped back into the parlor. She was wearing a simple muslin gown that was too short for her and sported a neckline that came nearly to her earlobes, but it didn't matter. Alec knew now what was beneath that gown. He wanted to see her again. Very soon. All of her. He didn't think she'd agree, but that didn't matter either.

He decided that it was one of his favorite pastimes —to enrage Genny Paxton and then seduce her.

"Are we ready, then?" he asked, standing. To James, he added, "Things will work out satisfactorily, sir. Please don't concern yourself further."

"Well, you know what I want, Alec."

Alec knew and he winced. He wouldn't marry Genny Paxton just to get control of a shipyard.

"I won't let you die like Nesta did! I know now what to do, and nothing will happen to you. Nothing, I swear it!"

"Papa?"

Alec came awake with an abrupt jerk, his heart pounding, and rolled over immediately at the sound of Hallie's scared voice coming from the open adjoining doorway. "Pumpkin? Are you feeling all right? You're not sick?"

"No, Papa. I heard you talking to someone. I was scared that someone was in here and was hurting you. You were yelling, but there's no one here."

So I was, he thought, staring at his small daughter's outline in the dim morning light. He'd been yelling at Genny, a Genny whose belly was swelled with his child.

"It was a dream, Hallie, a nightmare. With Genny."

"I'm cold, Papa."

Alec shook off the bizarre feelings the dream had left and lifted the covers. "Come in with me, pumpkin."

Hallie scooted into bed beside him. Alec was careful to put her on top of the sheet since he slept nude. He bundled her against his chest, kissed her ear, pulled the blankets over them, and settled back to sleep. But it wasn't to be.

"What won't you let happen to Genny, Papa?"

"I dreamed that she was married to me and that she was going to have a baby—your little brother or sister, I guess. She was afraid of childbirth. I was telling her not to be afraid, that I wouldn't let anything happen to her."

"She wouldn't die like Mama did?"

"No. I was promising her that I knew what to do, that I wouldn't let her die."

"Did I kill Mama?"

"No, of course not. Where did you get that idea, Hallie?"

"Well, I came and she died. Mrs. Swindel was talking about it to Dr. Pruitt. She said that some babies were just too big for their mamas."

"That's true, but she didn't mean it was your fault. You could have died, too, Hallie. I couldn't have borne that. At least I have you now."

"Why didn't you save Mama?"

"I was stupid and ignorant then, pumpkin. I didn't know anything about babies and Dr. Richards—he was the doctor with your mama—I don't think he knew any more than I did. I happened to meet a very wise man when we were in northern Africa last year. Do you remember Oran?" At the sleepy nod on his shoulder, he added, "He was an Arab and a physician, and I ended up telling him what had happened to your mother. He told me what to do if ever I was with a woman who was giving birth."

"Is Genny afraid to have a baby?"

"That's what is so strange about my dream. I have no idea if Genny is afraid of having babies or not. I think it's I who am afraid of her dying. Your mama was very special, Hallie, and it hurt a lot when she left us. And I feel guilty because I realize that if I'd only known then what I do now—well, perhaps she would be with us today. But things didn't happen that way. It's true, you know. Your mama was very, very sweet, don't ever forget that."

"But she didn't like to travel like we do."

"No, not really." Alec suspected that in the clear light of day he would regret speaking so frankly to his daughter, but it had always been his practice not to mince matters with her.

"I had fun with Genny. She doesn't know anything about ladies' clothing, Papa. She's not like Mrs. Swindel. Mrs. Swindel has an opinion about everything, and sometimes her opinion's awful. It was strange that Genny didn't know about anything."

"Neither of you did. I felt like the fashion arbiter."

"I like Genny—"

"But?"

"She doesn't know who she is, Papa."

Now that, Alec thought, his body tensing, was a kicker.

"Do you know what you mean by that, pumpkin?"

"She's kind of afraid of you, I think, and you do tease her awfully, but . . . is she going to be my mama?"

Another kicker, Alec thought, still reeling a bit

183

from the initial one. "No," he said. "No, she's not."

"But you dreamed about a baby and you were afraid."

"I know. I don't understand it myself. Now, what did you mean about Genny not knowing who she is?"

"She's afraid, that's all."

"Of me?"

He felt Hallie's head nod again against his shoulder. Well, Genny should be wary of him, at least. He'd done exactly what he'd wanted to with her—well, not everything. He only wished that he'd come inside her, made himself one with her, showed her what it could be like between a man and a woman, showed her what it would be like between the two of them. He snorted at his own foolishness.

"She's real mad at you, too. I think she would like to cosh you on the head."

"True enough. I tend to irritate her."

"How did she hurt her ankle, Papa?"

"She said she fell up the stairs."

Hallie snorted. It sounded just like him, and Alec grinned.

"Did you do something to her?"

"No, I didn't—at least I didn't make her hurt her ankle."

Hallie was silent. She said finally in a sleep-blurred voice, "I'd like some brothers and sisters, Papa. Genny isn't a silly girl, so she wouldn't want me to be silly either. She'd teach me how to build ships, wouldn't she? And she'd like to travel everywhere. I think she'd like to travel even more than you do."

"I suppose that could be true."

"Maybe she wouldn't want to be a mama. Maybe she'd just rather travel and be like you and not have a wife."

But a woman should want a husband and children and a home and hearth, he thought, then stopped, appalled at his line of thinking. He'd never really considered that when he and Nesta had been together, he'd done precisely as he'd pleased and never even considered that Nesta might not want to fit herself in with his plans. She always had, without complaint. He'd been a selfish, arrogant bastard. It wasn't pleasant to see oneself in such a negative light, but he knew it was true. And now here was Genny. But Genny was a stubborn, very irritating female—not at all like Nesta—and she needed to be told what to do, preferably by someone like him. He started to tell his daughter that Genny would do just as he wished her to, when he realized that it would be a stupid thing to say, and further, Hallie was asleep, her breathing even. He listened to her, then fell back to sleep himself.

Alec and Hallie sat at the Paxton dining table, Hallie gowned in a new sprigged muslin dress dotted with blue-and-white flowers, and Genny in a pale peach silk gown that made her skin glow, her hair glisten with gold-and-red lights, and her eyes turn so green that . . . Alec paused in his idiotic catalog of Eugenia Paxton's attributes. She looked all right, nothing really out of the ordinary.

He found that he was staring at her stomach, seeing it swollen with his child, as it had been in his dream.

Genny was laughing, quite unaware that she was pregnant at the moment. She was arranging her silverware to make her point. "Look, Father, Hallie. Alec was standing right beside the stern hatch coaming." She added with a smile to Hallie, "The hatch coaming is a box that covers the hole in the deck that leads belowdecks. It's there to keep the rain out. In any case, the box wasn't yet fastened down, and when Alec turned to ask a question of Mr. Knowles, one of the men who was fitting the rigging overhead dropped a hammer and it landed right here and the coaming jumped and very nearly smashed Alec's foot. I've never seen a man leap so high so quickly and curse so very fluently while he was still in the air."

"Your daughter, sir, is something of a sadist."

"What's that, Papa?"

James said, "A sadist is someone who enjoys the misery of others, like my daughter here."

Hallie giggled. "I should have liked to see that, but Mr. Furring was so nice. Was it really funny? Papa never leaps about or does anything that would make anyone laugh at him. He didn't tell me about the hammer falling."

Alec arched an eyebrow a good inch. "Where the devil did you get that, pumpkin? Of course I do occasional stupid or foolish things."

"No, Papa, you're always so perfect," Hallie said and took a bite of roast partridge.

Genny hooted with laughter. "Hallie, he very

nearly squealed, like a pig. His hair stood on end. His eyes turned yellow. His mouth dropped open and his chin fell to his stomach." Genny stopped, giggling more, then added, "No wonder you're so arrogant, Alec. Why, you've trained your innocent daughter to sing your praises!"

"No," Hallie said in all seriousness, "Papa wouldn't ever do that, Genny. It's just that . . . everyone likes him and admires him, gentlemen of course because he's so smart, but the ladies, well, sometimes I watch them and they stare at him and talk behind their fans about him."

"Eat, Hallie," Alec said. "No more talk or I'll fetch Mrs. Swindel and she'll bring rain to this neighborhood."

"What's this?" James asked, his wineglass halfway to his mouth.

"Mrs. Swindel is not what you would call an optimist. If there is a dark lining to a cloud, she will pounce on it with great relish, and it will dominate her conversation until everyone is either asleep or speaking as gloomily as she is."

"She's the only lady who doesn't fall all over Papa all of the time."

"Hallie, eat! Be quiet or it will go badly for you, I mean it."

"Yes, Papa. Genny doesn't either, but I could be wrong."

"Hallie!" Genny said, very nearly squealing herself. "Mind your papa! Eat!'

"I've been thinking," James said after all parties at his dining table had calmed down. "I know the Fountain Inn is a charming place and that you're also looking for a house. However,

Alec, this house is enormous, mostly empty, and Genny and I would be delighted if you and Hallie and, yes, your Mrs. Swindel would stay with us until you found a house to suit you."

"I could see Mr. Moses every day! Even Gracie is really nice and she gives me currants and apples when Lannie isn't looking. That would be wonderful, Papa."

Alec quickly stuffed a forkful of bread sauce into his daughter's open mouth. "Keep your mouth shut and chew until I tell you to swallow."

Genny was staring at her father. This was the first she'd heard about such an offer. She didn't know how she felt about it. She knew that all her conscious thoughts focused on him and on him touching her and looking at her. Just thinking about it made her face flush and made her feel warm all over. But to live in the same house with him, to know that he was in a bedchamber just down the hall from her, well, it was enough to make . . .

"You may swallow now. Then take another bite. Good girl."

"Don't you agree, my dear?" James asked his daughter. "We have so much room now. You can hire another maid to help Gracie."

"Yes, that's true."

Alec met Genny's eyes across the table. She looked appalled, slightly terrified, and definitely excited. He changed his mind in that instant and knew he was indeed a perverse creature. "If you're certain it wouldn't be too much trouble, sir, Hallie and I would be delighted to come here. As for Mrs. Swindel, I doubt not that she will find doom and gloom from one chamber to the other, but she is good to my daughter and I will contrive to keep her out of your servants' hair."

"Excellent. It's decided, then. Moses! Bring port for the gentlemen. Genny, take Hallie to the parlor and entertain her with stories about your first try at caulking. Lord, Hallie, what a mess she made!"

James sat back and smiled. It was nice to get exactly what one wanted, no doubt about it. Genny looked as if she'd swallowed a prune, but she'd get over it. He wondered how she had really sprained her ankle.

Alec watched Genny take his daughter's hand. He felt that elusive feeling again, a need that he refused to recognize. He needed to see Oleah again. Later this evening. It was lust he felt, nothing loftier than that. He simply had to contrive to remember that, but his fingers curled and warmed with memory. He could *feel* her body clutching around his finger as he'd pushed inside her. Alec swallowed.

Thirty minutes later, he stood for a moment outside the parlor door. It was time to take Hallie back to the Fountain Inn before she fell asleep on the Paxtons' parlor carpet. Moses had helped James up to his room, leaving Alec to his own devices. He paused as he heard Genny speaking. She was saying, "I'll take you gudgeon fishing, but not until April. That's when they're running. . . . Gudgeon? Well, they're a member of the carp family, about five inches long, and their backs are iridescent blue and their bellies are silver. We'll go down the Patapsco River to Relay.

That's several miles south of Baltimore. . . . What? Oh, yes, we clean them, then roll them in cornmeal and fry them in bacon fat. Yum. They're delicious, you'll see."

"Gudgeon?" Alec said as he entered the parlor.

"That's right, Papa. Genny will take me. Would you take Papa, too?" Hallie asked.

"I'll go," he said, "but only if I don't have to clean those gruesome-sounding things."

"Papa likes to fish, but he thinks cleaning them is disgusting."

Alec grinned. No secrets when it came to his daughter. None at all. "Will you tell Genny all my shortcomings?"

"No, Papa, I promise I won't. Oh, a piano!" She'd skipped to the corner of the room to look at the instrument.

"Do you play, Hallie?" Genny asked.

Hallie shook her head wistfully. She very gently and very tentatively touched a finger to middle C.

"It was made in New York by John Geib. My papa bought it for me for my last birthday."

"There's no room on board ship for a piano," Alec said, wondering that he should explain anything to Miss Eugenia Paxton, spinster of Baltimore, hoyden extraordinaire, and a very passionate woman who would, if dreams portended truth, have his child. He shook his head; he was fast becoming a half-wit.

"No, there wouldn't be much room, and think how it would slide about during a storm. I play a little. I would be delighted to teach Hallie."

"That's kind of you, Genny. Should you dislike

it excessively if Hallie and I were to move in here with you?"

"Don't forget the inestimable Mrs. Swindel."

"Answer me, Genny."

Genny looked up at his beautiful face and said truthfully, "I don't want you here. I want you to buy into the shipyard and then leave. If you also bought the *Pegasus,* it would be a help."

She'd succeeded in angering him, and he said coldly, "I'm not about to leave until I take you to bed with me."

"I've already been in your bed!"

Hallie, bless her soul, was intently studying the keyboard. "Yes, you were, but I wasn't inside you."

Genny jumped to her feet, felt her ankle give, and slumped down again. "Stop it, Alec! I won't be your mistress!"

"Possibly not, but I will be the first man to have you, Genny." *And hopefully the last.* Where had that nonsense thought come from? "Would you like to come with me to the ship tonight?"

Genny pulled back her arm, fisted her hand, and heaved toward his jaw. But Alec was faster. He caught her wrist and bore her arm down. He tugged her close to him, and Genny felt the sweet warmth of his breath on her face. "I'll come inside you, Genny, and you'll wrap your legs about my flanks. You'll love it, and you'll be tight and wet and very, very hot for me. Then I'll caress you with my fingers and you'll cry out, Genny, into my mouth, and I'll keep you safe—"

"Papa?"

"A daughter is a wonderful chaperon," Alec

said "Yes, pumpkin?" He didn't release Genny's wrist.

"Genny looks mad."

"She is, but she'll get over it. Now, Hallie, are you ready to leave? Mrs. Swindel is having an evening out with Dr. Pruitt, so I'll be your maid. All right?"

Hallie nodded, but she looked faintly worried.

"It's all right, Hallie," Genny said, tugged again, and Alec released her wrist. "Your papa simply adores teasing me. I'll see you tomorrow morning. As for you, Baron, I challenge you to a race. The *Pegasus* against your *Night Dancer*. To Nassau and back."

"You're crazy and I accept."

11

Genny loved the gentle rolling of the *Pegasus* beneath her feet. As always, she enjoyed the ship finally being in water and out of the yard. It somehow seemed more real then, even though the ship was firmly tied to the dock.

As her father had said of every ship he'd built since Genny could remember, "Well, it's time to launch her. She's not ready for Chesapeake Bay, but she is ready for the Patapsco!" They'd launched the *Pegasus* two days before Alec had arrived. She wished he'd seen that. It was always an exciting, somewhat nerve-racking event. Her father had broken a bottle of black rum over her post, signaling to the men to knock away the wooden braces, or the dogs, as they were called by the initiated, and the *Pegasus* had slid into the water. Every man had cheered loudly.

Then Moses had taken her father home, for he'd been so tired he could scarce walk.

She sighed as she watched one of Boss Lamb's riggers scamper like a monkey in a forest canopy, hoisting up the yards on the foremast's halyards.

It seemed to Genny as if but a moment had passed since her offer of that outrageous wager and Alec's acceptance, but it was more like two days. She hadn't seen a hair of him. She knew he'd gone over the Paxton records with her father and toured the sail loft and the Paxton warehouse with Mr. Furring. She wondered where he was this morning.

She didn't have long to wonder. She looked up and realized that she now was seeing more than a hair of the baron. She was getting the whole man. She watched him come aboard the *Pegasus,* speak to each of the men in his path, comment suitably, she supposed, on the progress of the building. He looked like he belonged here, and that made her unaccountably furious.

Alec saw her glowering at him beneath her ridiculous wool cap, grinned widely in return, and strode over to her, saying without preamble, "What's the wager?"

Genny's chin went up, and she said without pause, "You know full well what it will be."

"Do I, now? Well, it's a foregone conclusion that I shall beat you despite the possible superior speed of the *Pegasus*—"

"Bosh! You know very well that the *Pegasus* has the capability for superior speed. You also know that it's the ma—the woman in command who will determine the winner."

"I know, Genny, I know. All right. If I lose, you will expect me to buy into the shipyard—forty-nine percent, I suspect—but leave all business matters in your white hands, correct?"

"That's right."

"Very well. I agree to that. I also agree to the price your father presented to me yesterday. Surprised you, did I? Here's what I want if I win." As he spoke his eyes were firmly on Genny's breasts. He knew it made her furious and he manufactured the most lecherous look he could manage. Then he paused, quite on purpose, knowing that she was expecting the very worst, but still he waited, seemingly now in rapt study of Boss Lamb and his crew of riggers who were swarming over the clipper, stretching tarred hemp lines until the slender masts were held rigidly in place. Boss Lamb was himself chewing his mustache as he swayed back and forth in the lookout's perch on the fore-topgallant mast, eyeing the set of the masts and feeling the tension in the shrouds. He was a man of few words, one who didn't seem to have a problem dealing directly with a woman. He called Genny lass, even though he wasn't remotely Scottish and she wasn't remotely lasslike. Boss Lamb had eyed Alec with a good deal of speculation, but had said nothing. It turned out, from a remark made by Genny, that Boss Lamb had known James

Paxton since they were both boys. Thus, Alec thought, the reason for his loyalty.

"Well?"

Alec looked back at her. "It's amazing how you can make one little word sound so very shrewish. Ah, look, they've got the heavy rigging set up on the bowsprit. My uncle used to tell me that you tuned a ship just like a guitar . . . a little more tension on the starboard topmast shrouds, slack off on the main-topgallant stay, and on and on."

"Alec, I will cosh you on the head if you don't stop toying with me!"

"But it's so very enjoyable. Toying with you, that is. Why, my hands still curve at the thought of your beautiful breasts filling them and—"

She growled at him. He suspected her fondest hope would be to have a mallet in her hand and swing at his head with it.

"But wait, that's not possible, is it? You were on your back, your arms stretched over your head. A woman's breasts are not at their fullest at such a time and so—"

Genny sent her elbow into his ribs as discreetly as she could. He laughed.

Alec raised a placating hand. "All right. I'll hold my tongue. Behold a serious man." He leaned against the highly polished foredeck railing. "What I want when I win are two things. First, I want you—willingly—in my bed. Second, I want fifty-one percent of the shipyard, and that, my dear Mr. Eugene, means control."

He delighted in the absolutely disbelieving and furious expressions that winged their way across

195

her face. Were they to his first or second demand? Lord, at that moment he wanted to pull her cap off and kiss her until she was silly and weak; he wanted . . . He thought about his several bouts with Oleah the previous night. One would have thought that the girl would have exhausted him. She'd certainly done her best to, but here he was, randy as a mountain goat, for a female dressed like a man, her face scrubbed and shiny under a very weak Baltimore sun, her breeches baggy, and not a hair of her beautiful hair showing from beneath that awful cap of hers.

He cut off that appalling train of thought in short order, saying, "After I take over, I'll even contrive to find you a husband so your time will be filled with those things a woman should be doing. You'll be out of the shipyard business. You'll be out of all these men's hair."

"No! Never! Another thing, Alec, I don't want a husband! Ever, do you hear me? And stop making sport of me. I would never, never allow some idiot man to run my life and tell me what to do."

"Goodness, all that? My, my, you do feel strongly about some things, don't you? Listen to me, Mr. Eugene. Your interference with this shipyard will cease, one way or the other."

"Interference!" This was a shriek, an impassioned one, and it even made him start. "This is *my* shipyard, Alec Carrick, and I will run it and you won't say a word otherwise and—"

"If it remains *your* shipyard, it won't remain. How can you be so blind, Genny? You may have little or no respect for men, but they do run things and it's best you accept that. You don't have to agree with it, but you must see that it is the way things are. You can flutter about behind the scenes, but to continue to ape a man you won't do. Do you understand me?"

Her hands were fisted at her sides. She felt such frustration, such fury at his pigheadedness, that she wanted to choke on it. She managed to say calmly enough, dismissing him, "We will race as soon as the *Pegasus* is finished. That will be a week and a half from now."

"Do you accept the wager?"

Genny gave him a long look. She also gave him an exceedingly cold voice to go with the look as she said, "Go to bed with you? You know, I think I just might, Baron. You men seem to think sex is such a marvelous thing—"

"You should remember; your memory isn't that short or selective. I did give you a woman's pleasure. I will give you that every time you're in bed with me and more, Genny, much, much more."

That gave her only momentary pause. "My, my, Baron, you do seem to believe you're the greatest lover in the civilized world—"

"And the uncivilized as well, I daresay."

She shrugged with dazzling indifference. "Well, why not? I'm a woman, not a silly girl, and I can do precisely as I please. If you wish to brag and posture and proclaim yourself a wonderful lover, who am I to disbelieve you and forgo such an experience? After all, it's not as if I would have to undergo this experiment more than once—"

He interrupted her smoothly, "On the contrary, Genny, 'tis I who will do the undergoing, or performing, if you wish. I, a man, am the one of whom things are expected. A woman by her very, er, nature has but to lie on her back or on her side or come up on her knees . . . well, you know what I mean."

"I don't really want to know what you mean. As I was saying before you rudely interrupted, I don't want to do it more than once. It sounds altogether repellent and unnatural."

Alec laughed. "You won't, you know."

"Won't what?"

"Won't want me to make love to you just once. You'll want me again and again, Genny, and if you like, we can have another wager on that. What do you say?"

"I say, you odious clod, that hell is much too pleasant a place for you!"

"You do that so very well. I applaud you, Mr. Eugene. Yes, I do. I am put soundly in my lowly man's place. Actually, I've changed my mind—"

"You can't!"

"We haven't shaken hands yet, Mr. Eugene. As a man-aper, you must know that a deal isn't a deal until hands are duly shaken."

"What have you changed your mind about?"

"I want you in my bed now. Tonight. I don't want to wait until we return from Nassau."

"Ah, there's Jake—you met him, I believe. He's one of Mr. Furring's men from the sail loft, and he's bringing Hallie with him. I don't want her on board with all the riggers swarming about.

I'll take her belowdecks to see the captain's cabin."

"She'd rather see where the sailors will live."

"I'll show her everything belowdecks. I need to speak to Jake anyway. Hallie can explore while I do."

"When you come back up, Genny, I want an answer."

"You will die young, Baron. It's your fate, and at the hands of a furious woman, I doubt not."

"But not at your hands, my girl. Oh, no, not at your hands."

It wasn't at all coincidental, Alec thought. The moment Genny disappeared belowdecks with Hallie, Boss Lamb climbed down from his terrifyingly high perch. It was as if he'd waited to find Alec alone.

"The masts are the best," Boss Lamb said, and spat chewing tobacco overboard. "America yields some of the best spruce in the world. Makes the best masts and spars, don't you know."

"I read that you keep the masts in dirty backwater so that worms won't bore into them."

"True enough. Those worms are the bane of our existence. You know, of course, that we cover all the oak planing with pitch, then a layer of felt and then a sheathing of thin white pine. Then the hull below the waterline we encase in copper. That stops those wood-boring worms, thank the good Lord."

"Indeed."

"Don't suppose it's much of my business, but I worry, sir, about what will happen to the shipyard. James Paxton is my friend, his daughter, too."

"Yes, Genny told me you'd been a very good friend to them. One of the few men who were willing to work with and for her."

Boss Lamb, a very thin individual of late middle years, appeared to chew that over with his tobacco. "Yes, the lass is smart, really smart about some things. You give her a problem with a pump tube or an anchor or a halyard block, and she'll figure out a solution. But she can't be bluff and crude and, well, one of the men, if you know what I mean. Even if she could, they'd never accept her. And she isn't uncaring and unheeding of insults and slurs, and you can bet one of your English quid that's mostly what she gets. Not just from all the prominent citizens of Baltimore, but also from many of our own men. They look at her like she should be on her back with her legs up and spread. It fair galls them to do what she tells 'em. I can't see it makes much difference meself. Now, if she hadn't a brain, that would be different."

"The way you put it, it seems hardly fair, does it?" Alec, amazed at his comment, shut his mouth very quickly.

"No. Not a bit fair, but that's the way of the world, ain't it? Poor lass. You gonna buy things here? Take over the day-to-day overseeing?"

"There will be some kind of deal. The Paxton shipyard won't go under. We're in the midst of negotiations."

"I feel sorry for the lass." Boss Lamb spat more tobacco over the side. "She ain't cut out for prissing about in some man's house. I can't see her sitting in her parlor pouring tea for all the mealymouthed females."

"Her father didn't raise her right," Alec said. Boss Lamb let that observation slide and Alec continued. "Do you really believe no one would buy the *Pegasus* because Genny built it?"

"That's the right of it, sir. Once that old bugger Boynton went under, the word got out that James wasn't in charge anymore, it was little Genny. That did it, it did. Even now, all your gentlemen sit in their clubs, smoke their cheroots, and make fun of her, the little twit in breeches, I doubt not that they call her. And their wives just add coals to the flames. Jealous matrons, the lot of 'em. All they're good for is shooting out babies and talking about their infernal gowns."

Alec, thinking of Hallie, said, "I'm glad they shoot out babies. The world would soon be an empty place if they didn't."

"Oh, aye, but you know what I mean."

"It sounds to me like a case of cutting off one's nose to spite the face. The clipper is excellently designed and built, after all. Who cares if a troll made it?"

"True, but that's the way of it, ain't it? Everybody got to look down their nose at somebody, and in this case, all the fancy gentlemen got the little lass to look down on and scorn."

"Yes, I suppose you're right. Don't worry, Boss, nothing bad will happen, I swear it."

Alec didn't allow himself to question his promise. He would see to it that the Paxton shipyard continued, and continued successfully. He simply wasn't certain yet just how he would accomplish that, nor was he certain at all what to do with Genny.

It wasn't fair that Genny should be scorned and laughed at. Alec frowned at himself. A lot of things weren't fair in this life, as Boss Lamb had said. What did it matter to him if this was just one in a long series of unfair things? He wasn't a knight to right the wrongs, especially when he wasn't so very certain about what was wrong in this case.

He waited on deck, closely studying all the rigging work. The masts were tall and slender, and not at all perfectly straight up like the masts on other vessels. Her masts were, in fact, more sharply raked than even the masts on other clipper schooners he'd seen. Also, she had a very sharp dead rise, completely unlike his barkentine, whose bottom was nearly flat before rising slowly and gently upward with almost straight sides.

The Baltimore clipper was a vessel he much admired, and he admired it more by the day. He thought of the yards upon yards of sail being sewn in the sail loft and the yards that were already fitted to the rigging. The *Pegasus* would be more heavily canvased than his own barkentine, a vessel a third larger than the clipper, and at the same time very lightly stayed. She'd take the wind head-on, and there would be no heavy weights to drag her back and slow her down.

Unlike his barkentine, the *Pegasus* didn't carry clutter all over her decks. They were bare, broad, not far above the waterline. He could imagine in a storm the waves washing easily over the decks with the freeboard so low. But then again, it was speed that was her hallmark, nothing else. A remarkable feat of design, yes indeed.

Alec came out of his appreciative fog to hear his daughter calling, "Papa! Papa! It's wonderful and very cool in the sail loft, and all the gentlemen sit around telling stories while they stitch the canvas! They use traiang—"

"Triangular," Genny said, laughing.

"Yes, triangular sail needles and palms."

"Palms? Did you bring me a coconut, pumpkin?"

"Not trees, Papa! They're pieces of leather and they fit against your hand—you know, Papa, against your palm—and protect you from the sharp needles."

"Ah, an excellent idea." Alec ruffled his daughter's hair and thanked Jake for taking care of her.

"She's a smart little 'un," Jake said. "Terrible smart. Scares me, it does."

"She doesn't take after her papa," Genny said under her breath, but not under enough for Alec not to hear.

Alec didn't say a word. He looked at Genny. She stared back at him. He finally shrugged, bade his good-byes, and lifted Hallie into his arms.

"Where are we going, Papa?"

"Back to the Fountain Inn for a nice lunch with Mrs. Swindel. I think the owner, Mr. Barney, is enamored with you. Me, he could very easily do without."

"Oh, Papa, Mrs. Swindel hates everything they serve in the dining room. She'll say that the carp tastes like dead turnips—"

"Goodness, how about swordfish, then?"

"I want to meet Mrs. Swindel," said Genny.

"A woman after your own temperament?"

"Can we have dinner with you, Genny?" Alec's ingenuous daughter asked.

"Well, of course, that would be just fine. You suffer through your dead turnips, then I'll have Lannie feed you some live spinach."

"Yeck!" Hallie hollered and laughed and laughed as her father carried her off the *Pegasus*.

Once Alec was on the dock, he turned and said quietly, "I want my answer tonight, Mr. Eugene, otherwise the wager is off. Your time is up."

Genny didn't say a word. She was very aware that Boss Lamb was looking at her, that Jake was standing there, uncertain, and that the lecherous Minter was smirking.

I am your boss, she wanted to yell at them. I'm not some trollop for you to gawk at! "Oh, damnation," she said, and tromped belowdecks to the captain's cabin where she belonged.

When Genny returned from the shipyard in the late afternoon, Alec, Hallie, and the inestimable Mrs. Swindel had moved in.

"Hello," she said, stretching her hand to the older woman, who was standing on the bottom stair. "You're Mrs. Swindel."

"Aye, that I am. And you're, well, you're a young lady, I can tell that much. His lordship said you weren't quite in the common way, and I do believe he just might be right in this case."

And to Genny's astonishment, Mrs. Swindel took her hand and pumped it heartily.

204

"Thank you," she said. "Won't you join us for dinner, ma'am?"

"Certainly not. I'm Hallie's nanny. It wouldn't be proper. Besides, I'm dining with Dr. Pruitt."

"Ah, I see. Well, I hope everything is all right, Mrs. Swindel. Do ask Moses if there is anything you need."

"I asked Gracie, who, if you don't mind my saying so, miss, is something of a weak-willed shadow. She's indecisive and told me that Moses knows everything."

"Gracie hasn't been well," Genny said in automatic defense of a woman who had been with her family since Genny had been seven years old. "She's planning on leaving soon and living with her sister in Annapolis."

"As is proper," said Eleanor Swindel obscurely.

Poor Gracie, Genny thought, watching Mrs. Swindel sweep away. There went a very decisive woman. She looked up to see Gracie Limmer coming into the entry hall from the dining room. Genny smiled at her. "You're feeling better?"

"Much better," Gracie said. "Your company is nice, Miss Genny. That Mrs. Swindel knows what she's about and will take care of things." She drew a deep breath and blurted out, "I told your pa I was leaving tomorrow!"

Genny stared at her, hugged her, and finally wished her well. It wasn't really a shock. She'd been nothing more than a cypher for the past several months. It was time for change. And change was certainly on their doorstep.

"Well done, my lord," Genny heard Mrs.

Swindel say later to a non-present Alec as she walked down the front stairs. She grinned. The eccentric Mrs. Swindel would doubtless prove amusing. And contrary to Genny's experience, this lady seemed to approve of her male-aping hostess.

Genny was smiling when she entered her bedchamber. So I'm not in the common way, am I, Alec? What did that mean?

She disliked herself every minute she was doing it, but by the time Genny emerged from her bedchamber, she was beautifully gowned in a new creation selected by Alec, an evening dress of cream-and-pale-yellow silk with a low rounded neckline and a thin band of pale yellow satin beneath her breasts. She'd brushed her hair and braided it loosely in a coronet atop her head; myriad loose tendrils framed her face and curled down her neck. She was even wearing her mother's amethyst necklace, the stones nearly an opaque purple that for some unknown reason made her eyes a very deep green.

The parlor door was open. She paused, seeing Alec. It wasn't fair, she thought, not wanting to enter the room. He was so beautiful, so absolutely breathtaking, she felt like a ragpicker in comparison. He was wearing evening clothes, all stark black and white, and with his tanned face and golden hair, he looked beyond any man she could even have imagined in a fairy tale. It was many minutes before Genny forced her eyes away from him to his daughter. Hallie, wearing another one of her sprigged muslin gowns, was seated next to James Paxton, chatting about everything she'd seen. Like her father's, Hallie's golden hair had been brushed until it shone, and her eyes glittered that same amazing blue. The child was not only a pleasure to look at, she was also amazingly precocious. Genny supposed it was because she'd been surrounded only by adults for all her five years.

That, or she had her mama's brains.

And her papa's beauty.

Genny forced herself to say brightly as she walked into the parlor, "Good evening. Welcome to our home, Hallie, Baron."

Alec whistled softly. "Good heavens, Mr. Eugene," he said as he took her hand in his, "I believe you're nearly as lovely in clothes as out of them."

"Hush!"

"What, Papa?"

"Genny is just welcoming me, pumpkin. I know how to dress you, Genny, no doubt about that. And undress you," he added, pitching his voice very low. Without pause, Alec said to James, "What do you think, sir? Is she not a newly hatched Venus, a veritable goddess of Baltimore?"

James was markedly silent, just looking at his daughter. He said in an almost stunned voice, "I hadn't realized how very much you looked like your dear mama. Beautiful, Genny, just beautiful."

"Well, Papa, I have it on the best authority that I'm not in the common way."

"What does that mean?" Hallie asked.

"It means," Alec said, not taking his eyes off

Genny, "that Miss Eugenia Paxton isn't a copy of all the other young ladies of this city. She is an original."

Why did he have to sound so admiring? Well, it was a lie, that was it. He just wanted her in his bed so he could rid her of her virginity.

Unfortunately, she also wanted him to rid her of her virginity. Genny blanched at her own undeniable wish. She'd never even thought all that much about sexual things until Alec had arrived. He made her aware, just looking at him, aware of every inch of her body, of her breasts, of that secret place between her thighs. Alec was looking at her now, and there was no serious expression in his beautiful eyes; there was only amusement and devilry and a big dollop of wickedness. He knew what she was thinking.

She jutted up her chin and tried for a smile that a very polite hostess would offer when faced with awful guests. "I believe dinner is ready."

"Mr. Moses," Hallie said, running up to the butler and holding out her arms.

Moses picked her up and said, "What a purty little 'un you are, Miss Hallie. That's a nice dress, yep, it sure is. Yore pa picked it out for you?"

"Oh, yes, and Genny's, too."

Alec supposed he should tell his daughter that one didn't jump into a butler's arms, but he saw the pleasure in the old man's eyes and the open delight on Hallie's face. He heard her tell Moses about her day. "Oh, yes, Moses, Mrs. Swindel did say dead turnips! And Genny said she'd serve us live spinach. What did Lannie say about that?"

Moses, bless his heart, laughed with Hallie.

Alec turned to James, ignoring Genny. "Sir?" He offered his arm, which James thankfully took. Genny quickly moved to take his other arm.

"So bloody tired," James said, then quickly added to his daughter, "A long, very busy day, Genny, that's all."

James shouldn't have come down to dinner, Alec thought, but kept his mouth shut.

It was midnight. The house was quiet and Alec was sitting up in his bed reading a boring treatise by Edmund Burke. It was a chilly evening, and a sluggish fire still burned in the grate.

He put the book down, sighed, and leaned back against the pillowed headboard. Life had become complicated. Very suddenly and, he knew, irrevocably complicated by a single female who wasn't even English.

He never should have come to Baltimore in answer to Mr. Eugene Paxton's letter. He'd been a fool, and now he was caught up in their lives and they in his and he could see no way out of it. Nor did he think he wanted out.

What he wanted was Genny. He wanted her more than he'd ever wanted a woman in his adult life. He'd hoped it was just a case of lust. He could have dealt with that quite easily. But it wasn't. He accepted it. It didn't make any sense to him, but nonetheless, it was true. He kept seeing her belly swelled with his child. Damn, he hadn't wanted that, not after Nesta had died; he hadn't wanted hearth and home and being domesticated and sitting in his parlor at night, being tied down and deadened with time.

He shook his head against the pillows. He hadn't wanted it but now he did, curse her green eyes. And now, of all the crazy things, it was Genny—the perverse female—who loathed the notion of home and hearth, of a husband who would dominate her and tell her what to do. No, she wanted to remain free—but the silly little twit wasn't free; any man with a brain could see that. She wanted to create, to build, to accomplish, to travel and see things that most folk could only dream about.

That just wasn't right. It wasn't the natural order of things. It was the woman's place to domesticate the man, not vice versa. At the same time, he could most unfortunately, see himself in the same parlor with Genny, see them talking, arguing, oh, yes, lots of arguing and then making love. He could see their children, and a life that was built around one place, and that place would hold meaning and friends and ties that would be too dear to ever break.

He didn't turn his head when he heard his bedchamber door quietly open. He simply stared straight ahead and waited, his heart pounding, his body taut with anticipation.

"Alec."

"Hello, Genny. You came. I hoped you would."

"Yes. I saw—can't you face me?"

He turned his head on the pillows and smiled at her. She was in her nightgown, a tentlike white cotton affair that covered her toes and came to her chin.

"You look like a vestal virgin. A rather long-in-the-tooth vestal virgin, but who am I to quibble?"

Genny heard his jest, but she was too nervous to even acknowledge it. She'd convinced herself that Bedlam was the place for her. But she was also determined. Very set in her path. Alec wouldn't remain in Baltimore, not a man like the baron. Soon he would be gone, and she would have lost her chance to learn about physical things between a man and a woman. She couldn't imagine wanting any other man to even look at her after Alec.

"You escaped this evening without telling me your decision. I'm glad you are delivering it in person."

"I want you to make love to me."

"Ah. I thought perhaps you wanted me to give you a cup of tea." He saw her wildly dilated eyes and quickly retrenched. He lifted the covers, just a bit. "Come here, Genny."

He was nude and his member was hard and swelled and throbbing.

Genny walked slowly to the bed and stopped. She ran her tongue over her very dry lower lip. "Alec, can I see you?"

"You mean my body?"

"Yes. I've never seen a man before."

"Do you want me to get up and parade about in front of you, or can we simply do things naturally?"

"What do you mean by naturally?"

"Come here and let's talk about it."

Genny looked at that lifted cover. She knew if she climbed into bed with him, it would be all

211

over. "Do you want me to take off my night-gown?"

She sounded scared to death. "Not yet. I want to do it, in the natural course of things. Come here, Genny."

12

Her hands fluttered and she stalled, her eyes on that lifted sheet.

"Would you like to sit here?" He lowered the sheet and patted the spot beside him. "We could talk, if you like, perhaps about the harems in Constantinople or the way Muslim women cover their bodies and their faces when they're out in public."

He sounded amused, bloody well amused and patronizing, and she wished she had the aplomb to blight him with a word or a snort or something.

Instead, she sat beside him, her hands folded primly in her lap, her bare feet not quite reaching the floor. She felt like a child, and worse, a fool. She shouldn't have come. She'd lost her mind, her perspective, and all in the hope of losing her virginity.

"I don't want to talk about those things."

"What would you suggest?"

She raised her eyes and looked at him. "Would you really cancel the wager if I don't let you make love to me?"

"Naturally. I said I would, didn't I?"

212

She swallowed.

"It's always much easier to plan to do things than to carry through with them, isn't it, Mr. Eugene?"

"I was really quite convinced when I came in here," Genny said, her eyes now trained on the white pillow just above his right shoulder, which was quite bare, as was his chest. She wanted to look at him, look her fill—a good fifty years would probably do it—and touch him and kiss him. She drew in her breath.

"All right. I'm ready now."

He grinned at her, but it hurt to grin, his member hurt, his groin nearly cramped, and something deep inside him pinched and prodded and ached and yet, at the same time, something very sweet and infinitely satisfying filled him.

"You don't have to, Genny."

She stared at him, full face. "What? You don't want me now? You think I'm not . . . well, not alluring? I know you think my nightgown is stuffy and dowdy, but I don't have another, one like I'm certain Laura Salmon would have."

"Yes, you're alluring—where did you dredge up that word? And no, your nightgown suits you." He chuckled, but she was too nervous to quibble. She pleated the cotton.

"No, my dear, it's just that I have belatedly realized that I am a gentleman, and a gentleman does not bed the daughter of a man he esteems and in whose house he is a guest."

"That makes you sound very noble, Alec, but it's not true. You're not the one doing the seducing. I am." And she flung herself across his chest, grabbed his shoulders, and kissed him, missing the first time, but landing close to his mouth the second time.

Alec was laughing, catching her arms in his hands, trying to keep her off him, but the instant her mouth touched his, he knew he wasn't long to remain a logical adult male. She was soft and sweet. "Genny," he said into her mouth, and felt her at once tense with excitement against him.

He filled his hands with her soft hair, stroked her back, never releasing her mouth. Her lips were pursed like those of a virgin schoolgirl, which in a sense she was, but he didn't mind. He envisioned the next fifty years with that soft mouth of hers against his and he deepened the pressure. Slowly, very slowly, he pulled the hair back from her face and gently pushed her away. She was above him, looking down into his face, her eyes wide and filled with surprise and delight, and now disappointment.

"Please, Alec."

"No, love. I'm sorry. I really meant what I said. I can't do that to your father. He trusts me. And I, I hope, am not yet lost of all honor. Shall I give you pleasure? Yes, that's what we'll do. Come here."

Genny knew what that pleasure would be, but at the same time, it meant her being naked and him looking at her and making her wild, all the while he was watching and detached, and she didn't want that, not this time.

She felt his fingers unfastening the buttons on her nightgown. She wanted to tell him to stop, but all she could manage was to place her hand over his. He smiled at her. "Easy, Genny."

Her gown gaped open and he parted it, baring her breasts. "Lovely." Alec sat up in bed and drew her over his lap. She lay against the crook of his right arm, naked to the waist, and he couldn't seem to get enough of her and that was just looking. Slowly, very slowly, he let his forefinger touch her nipple. He closed his eyes at the feel of her, only to open them as she gasped.

"Oh, dear."

"That's wonderful, isn't it? Give me your hand. I want you to feel yourself."

Genny felt him raise her hand, felt him gently lower her hand to her breast. She felt her nipple. "I just feel like me."

He chuckled, and caressed her again. To his delight and her near undoing, she moaned.

"It's all right, Genny. You're supposed to enjoy what I do to you. Your responsibility is always to tell me what pleases you."

"I want to touch you."

That elusive satisfying ache came through him again at her unexpected words. "All right."

Genny splayed her fingers and let her hand glide over his chest and shoulders. His chest was covered with golden hair and his flesh was firm, the deep muscles rippling beneath her fingers. "No man could be like you," she said, and he believed her and reveled in the honest wonder in her voice, the erotic sweetness of her touch.

He leaned down and kissed her again. His hand cupped her breast, lifting it, pressing inward to feel her heartbeat. He pushed her back again

215

against his arm, then moved his hand downward, coming to rest just below her waist, on her white belly.

She was shuddering and her kiss was suspended, all feeling focused below her waist, just below where his fingertips were. "Alec," she said, and he knew that she wanted, that she hurt, not as much as he did, but enough, quite enough.

"All right," he said, and his fingers tangled in her hair and he watched her face as he found her. "Soft, Genny, you're so very soft." Her eyes widened on his face as his fingers began a gentle rhythm.

"That feels wonderful, doesn't it? As much as a man loves to come inside a woman—for that's where he can find more pleasure than he deserves—you hide your feelings here, Genny. A small, quite hidden little treasure that can make you beautifully wild. Remember the other night, Genny? Remember how you cried out and moved against me and then everything shattered and you lost yourself and your body took over?"

"I remember," she said, astounded that words still existed in her mind.

"Now, I want to caress you with my mouth. You want that, don't you?"

"No, Alec, you can't possibly do that—why . . . oh, please, please . . ."

She was trembling, her hips bucking slightly against his caressing fingers.

"It's not that I—" Alec would never remember what it was he'd wanted to say to her, for at that moment, he heard Moses yelling, "Oh,

God! Miss Genny! Baron! Oh, God, come quick! Oh . . ."

Alec lifted Genny off his lap. "Quickly, Genny!" He was out of bed, shrugging into his dressing gown. He heard Genny behind him, pulling down her gown, fastening the buttons.

A loud pounding came on the bedchamber door; then Moses threw it open, stumbling in. "Hurry, suh! It's the master! Oh, God, Miss Genny—"

Alec pushed past him and down the corridor to the master suite, Genny at his heels. He paused for an instant, then went into the bedchamber. There was one candle lit by the bed. Alec saw immediately that James Paxton was dead.

He stood beside him, feeling the pain of surprise, the pain of James's passing. His eyes were closed, the expression on his face peaceful. He'd died in his sleep, an easy death. Alec leaned down and gently laid his fingertips against his throat. There was nothing, of course.

"Papa?"

"He's gone, Genny. I'm sorry." Alec turned to see Moses standing at the foot of the bed, staring at his dead master.

"I come to see him, suh. I don't usually do that, but something just kept naggin' at me and I came. He was so tired tonight and it worried me. I came. He was dead."

Genny moved around Alec and sat beside her father. She took his hand and brought it to her lips.

"His heart, Genny. Doubtless it was his heart. He died in his sleep, an easy death."

"Yes," she said, still looking down at her father's face.

"Papa?"

Alec whirled about to see Hallie standing in the doorway, dressed only in her nightgown, her feet bare, her model barkentine under her left arm.

"Just a moment, Hallie. Moses, have his doctor fetched. He'll know what's to be done."

"Yes, suh."

"I'll be right back, Genny. Let me see to Hallie." Alec picked his daughter up in his arms and carried her out of the bedchamber.

Genny said very softly, "I'm sorry, Papa, truly sorry. Alec said it was easy for you. I hope it was. I love you so much. There's no one for me now. I wasn't even here when you died. I was sprawled on a man's lap, his fingers on my body, and you were dying, alone."

The words were soft, blurred, but Alec heard. He paused, not moving. He watched Genny lean down and lay her face against James's chest. She didn't cry, just lay there.

He left her alone.

James Paxton's funeral was attended by over a hundred Baltimoreans from every rung of society, from out-of-work sailors to the Gwenns, the Warfields, the Winchesters, and even Laura Salmon. The weather didn't cooperate. It was cold and drizzly, not even a hint of warmth or sun. Alec stood beside Genny, his hand under her elbow, though she didn't need his support. She didn't move, merely stared straight ahead, her back rigid, seemingly oblivious of everyone there.

Alec hadn't allowed Hallie to come. She didn't really understand what had happened, only that Mr. Paxton had gone to Heaven, just like her mama had. She and Mrs. Swindel had remained at the Paxton house.

That was something else he had to decide about, Alec thought as he forced his attention back to the Reverend Murray, minister of Saint Paul's Episcopal Church. He was a gaunt man, his face lined from years and years of the harsh sun. He was articulate, his eulogy moving. He'd known James Paxton, he said in his slow, well-modulated voice, since the two of them had been boys, fishing off North Point. He recalled James's part in the growth of Baltimore; the completion of his first Baltimore clipper schooner, *The Galileo*, in 1785; his stand against the British in September of 1814, during the Battle of Baltimore. He'd been at Fort McHenry during the shelling, encouraging the men to keep calm. He'd been a quiet hero, a man he, the Reverend Murray, had been proud to know. He was survived by his fine daughter, Eugenia Paxton. Amen.

Genny didn't move during the eulogy. Alec wished she'd do something, anything, to show she was thinking, feeling. Anything. He saw Laura Salmon looking at him and forced a slight smile.

After the ceremony, he stood beside Genny as she accepted condolences from the dozens upon dozens of people. And he remembered that long-ago day, nearly five years ago, when he'd stood accepting condolences, in shock, wondering at the use of it all.

He took Genny back to the house and stood beside her again while people came to eat and speak in lowered voices and offer more endless condolences. She was calm, self-possessed. She wasn't there. He wondered if he'd acted the same after Nesta's funeral.

Oddly enough, it was Mrs. Swindel who had taken over. Gracie Limmer had remained, for another week, she'd said, but she gave over all responsibility to Mrs. Swindel. Lannie had prepared enough food for fully half of Baltimore. It was late in the afternoon by the time the last of the guests had taken their leave.

All except for Mr. Daniel Raymond.

"If it is all right with you, Miss Genny, I should like to read you your father's will."

Alec was on the point of protesting that it could wait, but Genny simply nodded, turned on her heel, and walked toward the small library on the east side of the house.

"Would you come, too, my lord?"

Alec looked his surprise. "It can't possibly concern me, Mr. Raymond."

"It does, my lord. You see—"

"Very well. Say what you will, but say it in front of Miss Paxton."

Genny watched Daniel Raymond walk into the library, Alec just behind him. What was Alec doing here? It really didn't matter, not now. Nothing seeming to matter. She motioned him to sit at her father's desk.

"Miss Paxton," Daniel Raymond said as he sat down, "your father made a new will."

"I beg your pardon?"

"A new will, Miss Paxton. Just five days ago."

"I don't understand—"

"Tell us what's in the will," Alec interrupted.

Why did he sound so angry? Genny wondered, looking at his set face for a moment before turning back to Mr. Raymond.

"Very well, my lord. There are bequests to the servants, the largest being five hundred dollars to Moses and three hundred dollars to Mrs. Limmer. As you know, Miss Paxton, Moses is a slave. Mr. Paxton stipulated that upon his death Moses be manumitted. Your father assumed that Moses could continue his employment in this household." Mr. Raymond paused, and Alec thought he was girding his loins for an unpleasant task. Alec knew, he just knew what it would be. Damn James Paxton!

"Miss Paxton, your father wanted it made perfectly clear to you that what he was doing was in your best interest. You are alone, without other family, without male protection. He loved you, ma'am, and he was looking to your future, a secure future."

"Yes," said Genny, and nothing more.

Dear God, Alec thought, looking at her pale face, she sounded not a whit interested.

Mr. Raymond cleared his throat, then sent an agonized look toward Alec. "Mr. James Paxton leaves the Paxton shipyard to Alec Carrick, Baron Sherard, if he weds you within thirty days of his death. If Baron Sherard refuses, or if you, Miss

221

Paxton, refuse, then the shipyard is to be sold to anyone other than Baron Sherard, and you will receive the selling price.''

Genny just looked at him.

''You see, Miss Paxton,'' Mr. Raymond added, sounding rather desperate now, ''your father knew you couldn't continue to run the shipyard. He knew you would lose everything if you did. He wanted only to protect you. He didn't want you to know poverty.''

''Thank you, Mr. Raymond. I understand perfectly now.'' Genny rose as she spoke, then extended her hand to the hapless lawyer. He shook it out of habit.

''Don't you have any questions, Miss Paxton?''

She shook her head and walked out of the room, not even glancing at Alec. She looked awful in the black bombazine gown. It made her sallow, and the gown itself was too short. Alec hated it.

''My lord, surely you have questions—''

Alec felt defeated, angry, and ready for a fight. He reined himself in. It wasn't the lawyer's fault, after all. ''The man I would have to ask is dead, Mr. Raymond. Please leave a copy of the will so that I may go over it myself. Thank you for coming, sir. Oh, incidentally, I do have a question. Is the thirty days from the date of Mr. Paxton's death or from the date of his funeral?''

Mr. Raymond consulted the finely scripted pages. ''From the date of his death, my lord.''

''So we now have twenty-seven days. Thank you again, Mr. Raymond. I'll show you out.''

Nearly five years had passed since Nesta's death. Five years during which Alec hadn't once considered taking a wife again, at least not seriously. He remembered Maria Cordova Sanchez in Madrid, a very wealthy contessa and a widow, if he remembered aright, and how she'd bedded with him with great enthusiasm, showing him skills that he hadn't ever before experienced, then cooed and exclaimed over Hallie until the little girl, barely more than a baby at the time, had proceeded to vomit on her best gown. Alec grinned at the memory. Maria hadn't cooed again.

No, he hadn't wanted to marry the contessa. He hadn't wanted to marry anyone.

What was he to do about Genny? James had written his will in such a way to make Alec feel responsible as the devil, at the very least. He'd recognized that Genny couldn't inherit the shipyard; that if she did, it would be lost within months. He'd given it to Alec on the proverbial platter, the shipyard and a very unwilling daughter.

What was he to do? Genny seemed like a phantom, locked away from him, from everyone, since her father had died. He winced now, remembering her broken confession to her already dead father. Genny's guilt must exceed anything imaginable. He felt very sorry about his role in it, but it had happened—she had been in his bed—and there was nothing that could change that.

Why not marry her? He laughed at himself. A man was forcing his hand, a man from the grave, yet Alec wasn't particularly upset about it. He decided to speak to Hallie.

He found his daughter in her bedchamber on the second floor in the east wing. Hallie, an independent and self-sufficient little person, was sitting cross-legged on the floor, busy with her model ships.

"Hallie," he said quietly so as not to startle her.

She looked up and gave him one of her wise looks. "Hello, Papa. Is Genny all right? She's so pale and sad."

"She's fine, pumpkin." He sat down on the floor beside his daughter and picked up a ship, a brigantine actually, with fourteen guns.

"She's French, Papa, the *Eglantine*. She sank off Gibraltar in 1804."

"That's right," Alec said absently. He set the brigantine down. "Hallie, I'd like to speak to you about Genny."

His daughter cocked her head to one side.

She was so smart, his daughter. "I heard Mr. Paxton's will today. He's made things rather complicated, but basically, he wants me to marry Genny. She has no one left, you know, no family at all. I wanted to know what you thought about the idea."

"Do you have to marry Genny?"

He shook his head.

"Good," Hallie said, then picked up a model of an English frigate, *The Halcyon*.

"Good what?"

"Well, if you felt like you were being forced to marry Genny, that wouldn't be good. You have to want to marry her."

"Do you want me to marry her?"

"I like Genny. Will she give me little brothers and sisters?"

"It is very likely. I should want to."

"She feels awful bad right now, Papa."

"I know, Hallie, I know. We have to help her. Make her feel better."

"Do you think she'd like to see my collection?"

"I think it would please her mightily."

Alec ate alone in the Paxton dining room. It was as if he were now the owner, sitting in regal splendor, and it felt odd. Moses was standing deferentially by the door leading to the kitchen, ready to fetch anything Alec wished to have.

Genny, he'd been told, had requested a tray in her room. Alec took a bite of jugged hare. It wasn't bad. A bit too peppery, but not at all bad. He placed his fork beside his knife on the plate. He wasn't hungry. Nor, he thought, eyeing the wine, was he thirsty.

"Did Miss Genny have her dinner, Moses?"

"Yes, suh. Lannie took a tray up to her."

"I'll see to her shortly." Alec sighed. "We've got a problem, Moses."

"Yes, suh. Miss Genny, suh, well, she's tough, but her pa, he was all she had. It hit her hard, suh."

"I know. I think I'll see her now. If you hear crashing plates—no, never mind, Moses."

"Yes, suh."

Alec stopped in front of Genny's bedchamber five minutes later. He raised his hand to knock, then lowered it. She was crying. He could hear the muffled sobs, and the sound made his insides twist up. She hadn't cried since her father had died, at least not that he knew of. It was time that she did. But he found that he couldn't turn around and leave. Quietly, he opened the door and stepped into the room. There was but one branch of candles lit on the mantelpiece, leaving most of the room in shadows. Alec didn't move for a moment, adjusting his eyes to the dim light.

Genny was sitting in the window seat, her knees drawn up to her chest, her face pressed against her thighs. Her shoulders were shaking. He walked quietly to her. He laid his hand on her shoulder.

"Genny."

She jerked up. "Get out, Alec. Now. Leave me alone."

"No, I don't think so. Is there any room for me here? I believe there is." He pressed against her until there was enough room to sit beside her. "Now, I see you didn't eat your dinner."

"I don't like jugged hare."

Alec took a handkerchief from his pocket. He lifted her chin with his fingers and dabbed her eyes.

"What do you want?"

He continued with his task, not answering. She grabbed his wrist and pulled his hand away. "Go away, Alec. I never want to see you again."

"Listen to me, Genny." He broke off immediately at the deep pain in her eyes. It was too much because it brought back memories of those days after Nesta had died. Alec drew her into his arms and pressed her head into his shoulder. "I'm sorry, love. I know it hurts. God, I know."

His gentleness undid her. Genny wept, quietly,

steadily. Alec kept talking to her, saying nonsense words really, wanting her to cry, to get her pain and grief outside herself. It had taken him months simply because he hadn't.

He continued to hold her when her crying ceased. He stroked his hands up and down her back, still murmuring to her. From one moment to the next, she changed from a woman who needed his comfort to a woman who needed him as a man.

She raised her face and looked at him. Her eyes fell to his mouth and her lips parted slightly. Alec lost control in that instant. He kissed her, hard, his tongue probing, savaging her soft mouth. She didn't stiffen, she didn't draw back, she opened her mouth and willingly accepted his tongue. Her complete yielding to him and his demands gentled him immediately. "Ah, Genny," he said, his breath warm in her mouth.

She pressed her breasts against him, her arms going around his back. "Please, Alec."

He controlled himself. It was difficult, but he knew that this time, her first time, he must not ravish her, he must not take her too quickly. And he was going to take her, he knew that, he accepted it, even though he also realized her yielding was for all the wrong reasons. As for his motives, they didn't bear scrutiny. But it didn't matter. He'd set his course and she was aiding him in achieving what he knew was right, for him, for both of them.

To his surprise, she was moving frantically against him, like a wanton lover, and he rose to his feet, bringing her with him, and she rubbed her belly against him and he thought he would explode with lust. He cupped her buttocks and lifted her, rubbing her against his swelled member, listening to her gasps, feeling her breath, hot and fast, on his face.

It was wrong, this urgency of hers, but it didn't stop him. She wanted to reaffirm that she lived, and he understood that. Suddenly she lowered her arm and slipped her hand between their bodies. He felt her fingers slide over him, then curve around him. "Oh, God," he said and he moaned, thrusting his hips forward, wanting her to caress him. And she did until he knew he would spill his seed.

He jerked away from her, breathing hard, and lifted her off her feet, carrying her to her bed. He dropped her onto her back, quickly strode to her bedchamber door, and closed it. He stripped off his clothes as he returned to her. Genny came up onto her elbows. She was staring at him as he jerked off his shirt, as he pulled off his boots. He was wearing only his breeches now and she wanted to see him, wanted that more than anything she'd ever wanted in her life.

Alec looked up at that moment and stilled, his fingers on the buttons of his breeches. Her eyes were huge, her body utterly quiet. "Take off your clothes, Genny."

"I want to see you."

"All right. You will." He smiled then and stripped off his breeches. He straightened and let her look her fill. He glanced down to see his member hard and thrust forward. He ached. He pictured her white legs, widely parted; he saw himself coming into her, then thrusting with all his strength, filling her completely. He cleared his throat. "I'm just a man, Genny."

"You're . . . more than I could ever imagine a man . . . being."

"Thank you. Now it's your turn."

He moved to the bed and his hands were all over her. He ripped her gown, ripped her underthings. By the time she was naked, her legs parted, him over her, she was so wild that she was panting. "Please, Alec, oh, God, please . . ."

But he was wise enough, experienced enough, to slow down. He came down beside her and began to weave a sexual spell. "Do you know what I'm going to do to you?"

"Yes. You're going to stick that . . . thing inside me, but I don't see how that will work and I'm afraid, but not enough that I don't want you to do it."

Alec hadn't quite counted on that reply from her. "That thing is my sex or my member or my phallus. There are many terms from which to choose. I can provide you with a whole list in the morning. You'll hold me, Genny, you're made to do that, but the first time I come into you it will hurt a bit. Then never again."

She rolled over to face him and wrapped her arms about his chest. "I want to be a woman now, Alec."

It was her last lucid thought, her last sensible words. He touched her breast, then stroked his hands down her back to her buttocks, and she was lost. Genny didn't realize that she'd become wild, responding with unexpected passion to a man her first time, but Alec did. It was wonderful. He kissed her, feeling her tongue now, and it made him nearly as wild as she was.

His fingers found her and she was wet and hot and when his fingers pressed downward and inside her, she cried out, her back arching. My God, he thought, staring down into her face, she was ready to climax. Quickly, he came between her legs, bending her knees, and said, "Genny, look at me. I want to see your face when I come inside you."

She looked at him, and all the wild urgency she felt was mirrored in her eyes. He was between her legs, his hands holding them wide apart. She felt him pressing against her, and he was huge and hard, and she felt a twinge of fear and swallowed.

"It's all right. Don't be afraid of me." His fingers were parting her then, widening her for himself, and then she felt his member come into her and without realizing it, she lifted her hips, offering herself more fully to him. He groaned, closing his eyes for a moment, and arched his back.

"Genny," he said, his voice deep and hoarse and raw, and he plunged forward, the small membrane holding him back for but an instant before ripping, and she cried out. "Hold still," he said, trying to mind that order himself, but he knew he was the first man to have her and it was a heady thing and she was so soft and giving. He drew a deep steadying breath and eased down over her, forcing himself to hold perfectly still.

"Are you all right?"

She looked up at his beautiful face, now rigid

with the control he was exerting over himself. She touched his cheek, his lips, his nose. She tilted her hips back a bit and he slid in further. "I could never have imagined anything like this. You're so deep in my body. Isn't that odd the way that works?"

"Yes," he said, reared back, and pulled nearly out of her. "Yes," he said again and thrust his full length into her, touching her womb.

Genny felt pain and rawness, but then she felt his fingers coming between their bodies to find her and caress her. And she moved against his fingers. When he told her to hug her legs around his flanks, she obeyed him. She felt him come deeper into her and then his fingers found his rhythm and she knew that everything would be different now. She was dissolving into someone different, a Genny she didn't yet know or understand. She just knew she was no longer Genny Paxton, that young woman who'd lived within herself, sufficient unto herself, a young woman no man had ever touched in any way.

But Alec touched her.

She screamed, her body flying out of control, and she looked up at his face and saw him staring down at her, surprise in his eyes, then heard his hoarse groans. He was driving into her savagely and she welcomed it and his fingers and she didn't want it to stop, ever.

He was deep inside her. He felt his seed deep within her and her virgin's blood but he didn't move. He couldn't. He managed finally to come up onto his elbows.

Her eyes were closed, her lashes long and damp on her cheeks. She looked to be asleep.

He said very quietly, "Marry me, Genny."

13

Genny wasn't asleep. She was stunned at what had just passed between them. She couldn't even focus on his softly spoken words.

"What did you say, Alec?"

He paused, not wanting to repeat himself, because he suddenly realized it was too soon and Genny was too vulnerable and he . . . well, he didn't know what he wanted or what he was going to do. No, that wasn't precisely true, but still, he shouldn't rush his fences. He leaned down to kiss the tip of her nose, then said easily, "It was nothing really, just nonsense. I was commenting on how you were holding me inside you so tightly I want to ravage you again. What do you think?"

"You did your commenting in a remarkably short number of words the first time."

He chuckled, but it sounded a bit strained to her ears. She sighed, saying, "Oh, I don't want to be rational again. I just want to stay like this for a very long time—sort of weak and easy and soft in the head—"

"And everywhere else as well."

She shifted beneath him and he filled her again, hard and wanting her. It was odd the way she affected him. "Soft and tight around me, that's what you are, Genny. Am I also crushing you?"

She shook her head, unable to respond to his words.

"Won't you look at me? Since I'm your first man, Genny, I need to be reassured that I pleasured you sufficiently."

She opened her eyes at that bit of nonsense. "I don't know what's sufficient and what isn't."

"Well, you screamed and bucked and dug your nails into my back, into my shoulders. I think you even bit my mouth—"

"You were sufficient."

"Good. I don't think I want to be *exceedingly* sufficient, otherwise you might have killed me with your ardor. I'm glad you're seeing things the way they're meant to be seen." He moved slightly within her. "Does that hurt you?"

"No. Perhaps a little."

He moved again, just a little bit, drawing back, then pushing very slowly forward, feeling her muscles tighten and convulse around him. He closed his eyes at the intense sensation and held himself still.

Genny said in a thoughtful voice, "Well, I've done it once and nothing awful happened. Did you know that young girls are told again and again that they should never, ever allow a man to touch them, and if they allow liberties of any kind, the consequences would make their hair fall out. Or something equally repulsive. I think my hair's still on my head."

He grinned down at her. "Yes, it is, but it's a bit sweaty now from all your exertions."

"Well, that's a bit embarrassing but hardly a dire consequence. Thank you, Alec. I'm beginning to feel like a very smart woman of science who's succeeded wonderfully in her experiment. I've solved a mystery. I'm free now."

Her words, meant to cloak her feelings, succeeded admirably, and he was angered beyond all reason. So she'd just used him, had she? Not cared about him, merely wanted his man's body for her own bloody female purposes? He gritted his teeth against showing her his anger and his growing sense of injustice. What surprised him, however, was that his anger translated directly into his sex, and without saying a word, without more thought, he was pushing into her again, rhythmically and deeply.

"Alec!"

"Well, I haven't solved the mystery yet. Open your legs wider, Genny, and push up against me. Yes, that's it."

"But I don't want this, you . . . ah, Alec!"

"That's right, don't think, just feel."

Genny tried to keep her moans to herself and she succeeded for about three seconds. Then she was wrapping her legs around his flanks. He lifted her buttocks in his hands and worked her against him. What he was doing to her, what he was saying to her, were incredibly erotic, but she didn't want to succumb to him again, to lose all sense of self. It was frightening to become lost in another person, to give oneself over, to be swirled away by feelings that were beyond logic and command. "Do you know how many ways I can take you, Genny? How many ways I can pleasure you until you're yelling? This is the time-honored way, you on your beautiful back, your legs up and wide apart for me. But you'll see. I'll turn you on your stomach and lift your hips and then come into you from the back . . . it's so deep that way, Genny, and I'll hold your breasts in my hands at the same time." He groaned and she wondered if he was reacting as strongly to his own words as she was. "Feel how you're closing so tightly around me . . . yes, bring your legs up higher. Yes, yes."

Suddenly, without warning, her jerked out of her. She cried out, her hands tugging at his shoulders to bring him back into her, but he was gone. Just as suddenly, his arms hooked around her thighs and he lifted her. She saw his intent expression before he lowered his head and found her and caressed her with his mouth, stabbing his tongue into her, circling her, nipping her, and she found the pleasure so beyond anything she could have imagined that it was nearly pain, but she didn't want him to stop. She was crying now, her head twisting back and forth on the tangled sheets, her fists striking against the bed at her sides, her back arching, and still he pushed her, drew back, pushed her again.

"Alec, oh, please . . . Alec!" He quickly replaced his mouth with his fingers so he could watch her face as she climaxed. It was beyond anything he could have imagined, the expressions on her face. He'd brought her to this. He'd made her spin out of herself. He'd made her lose all control and become precisely what it was he wanted. Before the feelings faded, he came down into her, thrusting deep.

Experiment, hell.

Ridiculous woman. She was his now. And that was that.

He'd made up his mind.

She was asleep this time, an exhausted sleep. Alec gently eased down beside her and straightened the blankets over them.

"Silly woman," he said, and kissed her forehead. He brought her over to lie on her side, her head upon his shoulder. Her hair cascaded over his chest, thick and soft. "This is where you belong and I'll thank you not to forget it."

Genny moaned softly in her sleep.

He kissed her again. He settled himself then, closing his eyes. He remembered refusing to make love to her that night the previous week because of his honor and her father. He wondered if she'd take him to task over that. The truth of the matter was that he'd made love to her, in part, for her father; at least that sounded plausible to a sated man's brain. She had to marry him now.

He hoped he'd gotten her with child.

She had to realize that what he'd done was what her father had wanted. Had James known that Alec would force her hand like this? Probably; the man had been very perceptive. He'd also known that Alec wanted his daughter.

Alec sighed.

The next conscious thought he had sent him into nearly blind panic.

"Papa?"

He jerked up, his sleep-fogged brain clearing miraculously when he saw Hallie standing in the doorway. He should have locked the door. Damn. It was hard, but he managed to get hold of himself, to dredge up a welcoming smile.

He'd never let Hallie know that she was the last person he wanted to see at this particular time.

"Good morning, pumpkin. Isn't it awfully early for you to be wandering around the halls?"

"I don't know. I woke up, so it can't be too early. There's a little bit of sun out, Papa. Why are you cuddling Genny?"

The Genny in question stirred, sighed, stretched, and opened her eyes upon a five-year-old girl standing in her room, a model ship—a frigate, if she wasn't mistaken—under her arm.

Genny groaned and buried her head under Alec's arm.

"Don't be a coward. Come here, Hallie. It's cold. Oh, and shut the door, if you please."

"Oh, no," Genny groaned again, burrowing deeper.

"Why are you cuddling Genny? Why is she making funny noises and buried under you?"

"Good morning, Hallie," Genny said, poking her head up. But she couldn't straighten. She was quite naked. She clutched the cover to her throat and tried to scoot up in the bed. Alec, however, had other ideas. He tightened his arm around her and she couldn't move.

"I sometimes sleep with Papa," Hallie said,

and continued looking at them in that very accepting, very unblinking way.

"There's probably still some room, pumpkin. Come here. Genny won't mind and she'll help keep you warm."

"Oh, no," Genny groaned yet again, completely routed.

Hallie carefully set her frigate on the night table, then climbed onto the bed. She crawled in between Genny and Alec. Alec kept himself and Genny covered with a sheet and arranged Hallie on top.

"Settle in, love. There, quite good."

He pulled the covers over all of them, then lay on his back, his right arm outstretched, Hallie's head resting on his shoulder and Genny's resting in the crook of his elbow.

"This is nice," Hallie announced. "Genny's as warm as you are, Papa."

"Oh, no," Genny moaned.

"Why did you come into Genny's room, Hallie?"

"I went to your room first, Papa, but you weren't there. I knew you liked Genny, so I came here."

Alec chuckled. "Genny, if you moan one more time, I'll be very disappointed in you."

"Will I get a little brother or sister now?"

Genny didn't moan. She gasped.

Alec said easily, "We'll see, pumpkin. These things take time, you know. But I'll keep trying. Do you think you can get along with Genny all right?"

Hallie was thoughtfully silent. Finally she said,

"I like her a lot more than that lady, Miss Chadwick, who was always telling me what a sweet little plum I was. She was horrid, Papa, but you liked her so much I didn't say anything."

Alec said over Hallie's head to Genny, "This infant's idea of not saying anything in order to protect her poor papa's sensibilities was to pour a very dismal-tasting punch into Miss Chadwick's slippers. The lady had removed them after a particularly zealous waltz, you see, and when she did, Hallie struck."

"She yelled," Hallie said with great pleasure. "And her face turned quite an ugly red. A Chinese red, Papa said. He was laughing, but that was later."

"Did you really like this Miss Chadwick?"

Alec heard acrimony, he knew it, and it pleased him inordinately. "She was quite a, er, enthusiastic partner. I had no intention of marrying her, however."

"You just sail from port to port finding compatible partners, all of them willing, even standing in a line, waiting for you to hand out your favors."

"Hmm, an interesting concept. I told you I'm just a man, Genny. I haven't all that many favors to hand out at any one time. And this time, well—in Baltimore I was far more fortunate. I found a more-than-compatible mistress to bestow my many favors upon. I just might also have found myself a wife. I'm pleased with the outcome."

"Your daughter is lying between us, all ears, I doubt not."

"Hallie, are you asleep?"

239

"No, Papa."

"See, I told you! And you know I can't tell you what I really think of you!"

"Do you love Papa, Genny?"

Genny growled. "I want to cosh him in the head with that frigate of yours, Hallie."

Hallie twisted about to face Genny. She studied her face. "You're very pretty and I like your hair. It's got a lot more colors than mine does—there's red and brown and blond, like mine, and a gold even. And your eyes are quite nice. Papa said they're straight green with no shilly-shallying around. But no woman—even me—well, we can't be as beautiful as Papa, but you are pretty enough for him, I suppose. I don't even try anymore."

"Hallie, you're five years old!"

"She's old, nay, ancient, in the ways of women," Alec said.

"Hallie, when you grow up, all the gentlemen will be following you about, composing poetry to your eyebrows, your earlobes—"

"That's because all their sisters will be after Papa."

Unbidden, Hallie's words conjured up a vision of Genny married to Alec, and she was a good fifty years old and there were young girls cooing at Alec, well over fifty, but looking just as he looked right now. Oh, dear. "You mustn't speak like that. You're making him insufferably arrogant and conceited. He's very nearly unbearable now. You mustn't keep telling him how perfect he is."

"He's not perfect, Genny, he always insists that he isn't, but he is a wonderful papa."

"The child makes excellent sense, doesn't she? I am an honest man, Genny, all the way to my toes."

Genny stared up at the ceiling. She realized suddenly that she hadn't really looked at it in years. It was quite plain; indeed, there was a water stain very nearly directly over her bed. The wallpaper that reached the molding had once been a bright blue and yellow. Now it was dull and grayish and incredibly drab. Why hadn't anyone said anything? Didn't the servants think she cared? Evidently not. She said, unwitting amusement lacing her voice, "This is the strangest morning of my life. Here I am lying in my bed with a man, and his little daughter is between us. Surely it must be some sort of aberrant dream brought on by the jugged hare."

"You didn't eat any of the jugged hare."

Hallie giggled. "Mrs. Swindel said I didn't have to eat it. She said it looked like cooked bones. She gave me a big bowl of damson pudding. What did you eat, Papa?"

Alec gave Genny a long look, then said easily, "I kept Lannie happy. I ate my full share of dinner. Now, pumpkin, why don't you go back to your room. Genny and I need to get up, and she doesn't want to while you're in here, and I can't."

"All right," Hallie said. She kissed Genny's cheek, hugged her father's neck, and skipped out of the bedchamber, the frigate under her arm.

Alec didn't wait. He rolled over and put his

arms around Genny, pulling her against him. "Are you all right, love?"

She wished he wouldn't call her that, but it sounded so nice coming from his mouth that she didn't say anything.

She nodded against his shoulder.

He was rubbing his knuckles against her jaw and cheek. "Are you sore?"

Genny realized she was not only sore but very sticky. Alarmed, she bolted upright, grabbing the sheet at the last moment to cover her breasts.

"Oh, dear."

"What?"

She flushed. "Please leave, Alec."

He gave her a long, thoughtful look. "There will be blood on you, Genny. It's from your maidenhead being torn, that's all. And my seed. Is that the problem?"

She turned on him, saying viciously, "You know about everything, don't you, Baron? You know exactly what to do, what to say, to make the frightened little former virgins unfrightened—"

"You may be a former, but you're not at all little. If you let that sheet drop just a bit more, I could point out that your lovely breasts—"

"Be quiet! I don't like you. I think you're very probably a philandering blackguard who is used to having ten different women in your bed a week. Well, I might not be a virgin anymore, but I'm not sorry, because I wanted to know what it was all about. I don't want anything more from you, do you hear me?"

She looked lovely, he thought inconsequentially, staring at her as she squawked out her fury

242

at him. Quite pretty enough for him, as his daughter had told her so seriously. Her hair was a tangled mess around her face and down her back. Her green eyes were somehow even greener, perhaps because her face was so pale. He realized that she'd lost weight since her father's death. Her high cheekbones were more prominent now, more finely sculpted. It made her look fragile and that frightened him. He wanted her tough. Tough but giving, too, when it came to him.

Oh, hell.

"I hear you. You're very nearly yelling."

Genny slammed her fist down on the bed. "Damn you, Baron! I really mean it and—"

"You could be pregnant, Genny. I hope so. It will make you see reason."

She stopped cold in her diatribe. "Pregnant," she repeated, and it didn't sound at all like her voice. This excuse for a voice sounded as thin as a piece of newspaper.

"As in with child. I spilled my seed in you twice. I touched your womb when I climaxed inside you, Genny. Nearly there, so to speak."

Those very calm, drawling words pushed her over the edge. She whirled about, slammed her fist in his jaw, then leaped on him. He fell onto his back and he was laughing, and she straddled him and pounded his chest as hard as she could, yelling at him. Her hair spilled over her shoulders onto his chest, and finally he grabbed her arms and jerked her down.

"You're enchanting and demented," he said,

and kissed her. She tried to bite him and he ended the kiss very quickly.

He held her hands but let her straighten over him. "This, my dear Eugenia, is another way we'll make love. Ah, I see by your crossed eyes that you begin to understand me. You'll do the riding, as it were. Can you imagine how I'll feel thrusting upward into you? But you'll be in control, you know, and you'll move over me and I'll pull you down and kiss your breasts and—"

She jerked off him, rolled to the side of the bed, and yanked the covers up and off. She wrapped herself in them, then turned to face him. She wanted to tell him what she thought of him, but she'd yanked the covers off him as well and he was lying in the middle of her bed, on his back, his legs slightly parted, and he was naked, completely naked. His member was swelled, and she swallowed. His body was so exquisite she wanted to hurl herself on him again and touch him all over and kiss him all over as well. This had to stop. She was becoming beyond demented.

"Oh, dear," Genny said.

He grinned at her, the wretched lout.

Alec came up on his elbows. "Genny, truly, before you run off, listen to me. Surely, even when you were aping a man, you knew you were a woman, and a woman can be gotten with child if she sleeps with a man."

"Sleep, ha!"

"You know what I mean. We had sex, Genny, twice. You could be with child right now, at this very moment, even as we speak—"

244

"Oh, be still. Go away. Please, Alec, I have so much to do now and—"

"Have you so lightly dismissed or forgotten the stipulations in your father's will?"

She became utterly still. Her shoulders rounded, sending her hair tumbling down, veiling her profile from him.

"It won't go away, Genny." His voice had become incredibly gentle. "The month will pass and it will be over for you, and for me. We must talk about it."

He sat up and swung his legs over the edge of the bed. He stretched and she could only stare at the movement of muscles across his back. It was as if he belonged here, in her bed, in her bedchamber.

"I can't right now." Her voice was low and empty-sounding, and he held his peace.

"All right. This afternoon, then. We have only twenty-six days left."

She didn't raise her head. She was thinking blankly, my father is dead and I was romping in bed busily losing my virginity. She felt tears sting the backs of her eyes and swallowed. She said nothing more, merely waited until he had finally left her bedchamber.

"Genny, you've bloody well lost what little brain you had left!"

"No, I haven't. I'm perfectly serious, Alec. Would you care for some more tea?"

He stared at her, bemused, but handed her his teacup. "Let me get this straight. You want to know if I really, truly, honestly want to marry you?"

"That's right. Please tell me the truth, Alec."

"All right. Yes, I want to marry you."

"Even though you've known me only a short time?"

"Yes."

"Even though you've seen me throw up?"

"Your questions become difficult, but yes, despite that."

"Even though I followed you to Laura Salmon's house and climbed up the tree and watched you through her bedchamber window?"

"It becomes more and more difficult, but yes, even after that."

"Do you love me?"

Alec looked into his teacup for a moment, remembering the gypsies who used to visit Carrick Grange when he'd been a boy. One of the old hags read tea leaves. The old hag had thought him a darling little boy and had taught him how to do it. It didn't help him now. He didn't see a thing in the bottom of the cup, rotten or otherwise. "I care about you, Genny," he said finally, his voice low. "I like you. I believe we can make a fine go of marriage."

"You don't love me."

"You seem quite insistent about something I'm not even certain exists. Do you love me, Genny?"

It was obvious his question surprised her. She gave him a lost look that made him want to gather her into his arms and hold her and rock her and protect her from anything that could harm a hair on her head. Genny jumped to her feet and strode to the bow windows that faced the front lawn. He watched her wrap her arms around herself, as if in self-protection.

"Do you, Genny, despite the fact that I took you to a brothel? Despite the fact that I tied you down to my bunk and stripped you and made you scream with pleasure?"

"Now you're insistent," she said, not turning to face him. "Besides, how can one love another when there's been such a short time of acquaintance between them?"

"There's been much more between us. My member, for example. Between us and inside you. We've certainly gone beyond mere acquaintance. I don't like to embarrass you—"

"You much enjoy outraging me and you know it!"

She still hadn't turned and he grinned at her stiff back. "That's true. You're such a satisfactory audience, all arrogance and innocence. An irresistible combination, believe me. We know each other well enough, Genny. I will try to make you happy."

"I don't want to marry. Truly, I'm not being coy, Alec. I want to go places and see things and *experience* different people and watch the way they act and—" She tossed up her hands. "You probably don't understand what I mean."

"Oddly enough, I understand you perfectly. It's just that I've never in my adult life heard a female say she wanted those things. They're the sorts of activities a man pines for—to go places and be doing and acting."

She faced him then. "Men," she said, splaying

her fingers in front of her. "You think only you should have all the fun, all the adventures. Well, I want to have them, too. I don't want to serve up tea in the parlor and have ten children clinging to my skirts while my husband is out traveling the world, seeing new things, learning about new places. I won't have it, do you hear?"

"You're shouting again. Of course I hear you." Alec was remembering what Boss Lamb had said. He supposed he'd thought at the time that Genny could crave a bit of adventure, but this . . . Damn, she sounded just like him. It was unnerving. He'd knocked about the world for a good ten years, first as a married man who'd felt guilty if he left Nesta at home and almost as guilty when he took her with him, and then with the gusto of freedom, thinking nothing of hauling his infant daughter with him from Brazil to Genoa. He didn't crave it so much anymore. When he'd thought of Genny for the past several days, he'd thought of them together in one of his houses, secure and stable.

He cursed to himself, very quietly.

"Well?"

"Well what?"

"Oh, never mind! You're like a lot of men I know, Alec. If they don't like the question, they simply ignore what a woman asks."

"Actually, I was thinking very profound thoughts."

"And what is your conclusion?"

"That we should marry at the end of the week. Sooner, if it's possible."

Genny came away from the window and

walked toward the parlor door. "I'm going to the shipyard."

"That's another thing, Genny. In twenty-six days, if you aren't married to me, you'll lose it."

"Buy the *Pegasus*. It will give me enough capital to build another shipyard."

"You could do that, but I would consider it a vast waste of money. You could build the best shipyard in Baltimore, but you wouldn't succeed. I don't want to go into it anymore. You can't change the way of the world—"

She slammed out of the parlor. He heard her racing up the stairs and knew she was going to her bedchamber to change into her wretched men's clothes. He sighed. It hadn't yet occurred to Genny that his presence in her house—without chaperon—was extremely improper. Unlike Genny, he knew that Baltimore society was chewing over with relish all their supposed activities. Nor were they all that supposed either, he thought. Alec rose slowly and crossed the parlor to the sideboard. He poured himself a brandy and sipped at it slowly. The idea came to him full-blown. He thought it through again and then another time. He set down his brandy snifter.

It was possible that it could work very well.

And it would save Genny's pride. He realized that he didn't want her to feel ground under. That was the way her father's will had made her feel. He would turn it around and she would salvage her pride and he would salvage the shipyard.

He would salvage them.

14

Genny had thought about the fact that Alec and his entourage were living in her house without a chaperon. But she was too drawn into herself to worry much about it. What did it matter anyway? She'd already gone beyond the pale by sleeping with Alec, not that she regretted it. Her father was dead, the shipyard was soon to be sold to someone else—a man, naturally—and she couldn't see that there was anything in her future in any case. Money, she supposed, from the inevitable sale of the Paxton shipyard. She wondered if Porter Jenks had heard about the infamous will. No, no one knew of the particulars. She would say that about Daniel Raymond. He was as close-mouthed as a clam.

What to do about Alec?

Genny spent only two hours at the *Pegasus*. She spoke briefly to Boss Lamb, listening to one of his stories of him and her father back in the old days of Baltimore. He was blowing his nose noisily when she went belowdecks to the captain's cabin. She wanted to cry in peace, alone. She did, then shook herself. Her father wouldn't have wanted her to carry on like a weak fool. She gave herself a headache going over the accounts. Fiddle as she might, the scant dollar amounts on the bottom line didn't vary. There was barely enough money to pay the men on Friday. Then, if there were no buyer for the *Pegasus*— She shook her head. It didn't matter. Whoever bought the shipyard would get the *Pegasus*. It simply didn't matter.

Genny left the shipyard two hours later. She decided to walk home, a goodly distance on any day, but today the sky was bloated with dark rain clouds. There were few folk about as a result. At Pratt Street and Frederick Street she paused for a moment to look at the *Night Dancer,* secure in its moorings on O'Donnell's Wharf. It was a beautiful vessel, not sleek and sharply raked like her Baltimore clipper, but substantial of line and constructed to survive the harshest of winter storms.

Genny put her head down and walked on.

Alec wanted to marry her. What to do?

She knew he didn't love her, but then again, she didn't love him either. She wanted to spend the next fifty years with him, but love? Alec was a man who expected a woman to behave as he and most men deemed proper. Odd how women censored other women if they dared stray out of their predetermined confines. It seemed, indeed, that women were many times more demanding of their own behavior than were men. But men— oh, yes, she knew what kind of woman Alec wanted. Certainly submissive, undoubtedly yielding, never argumentative, and always in frills or in nothing at all. No, Alec wouldn't be a man to tolerate any behavior that didn't fit into his notions of female conduct. The rotter.

What to do?

Alec wanted the shipyard. He wanted the

Pegasus. He got both if he married her, and without spending a sou. She paused, shaking her head. This trail of thinking led nowhere. Alec was already a very rich man—at least she assumed he was. Her father had seemed to think so. If he indeed were, it wouldn't matter if he didn't get his hands on the Paxton shipyard. He could easily deal for another. And he wouldn't have to tie himself to a woman who obviously wasn't in his style.

What if she were pregnant?

Why, she'd be just like Alec and sail the seas with her child, finding adventure after adventure. And her child would be like Hallie—precocious, almost too honest at times, and sweet-natured. Who would be her crew? Blind men who fancied she was a man also? She quickened her pace. It was silly to worry herself about something that couldn't be changed in any case.

"Well, Miss Paxton. You trust the weather, do you?"

Genny turned at the sound of Laura Salmon's voice. "Hello, Mrs. Salmon. I fancy we haven't much more time before the heavens let loose on us."

Laura waved a negligent hand. "Allow me to tell you how very sorry I am about your father, dear. I trust you're feeling better?"

"Yes, I'm quite all right."

"I imagine from the clothing you're wearing that you've been climbing about your father's shipyard again."

"It's my shipyard now, Laura," Genny said,

knowing that that was true, at least for twenty-six more days.

Laura was stylishly gowned in a walking dress of dark green velvet with black velvet braid. On her head she wore a high-crowned bonnet of matching green-and-black velvet. A tall black velvet ostrich feather curved around her cheek. She looked delicious. She looked like a woman should look, the way Alec liked women to appear.

Laura continued with studied nonchalance that wouldn't have fooled her own mother. "I understand that Baron Sherard is staying with you. Most unusual, now, Miss Paxton, given the altered circumstances."

"His daughter is an excellent chaperon." Genny thought of Hallie's entrance this morning and knew she would have routed her father completely had she entered the evening before.

"His daughter! I don't understand. What is—"

"His daughter is a beautiful little girl. She quite manages him, you know, tells him what to do and he does it. Yes, indeed, the baron is quite in her pocket."

"No one told me about her," Laura said more to herself than to Genny. A raindrop landed on her nose at that moment, but she wasn't through and persevered. "I assume the baron is a widower and the child isn't a bastard?"

"He's a widower."

"Ah. Really, dear, he shouldn't be staying there. I thought someone should tell you, a friend with your best interests at heart."

Genny wanted to take Laura's parasol and

wrap it around the widow's beautiful neck. "It doesn't really matter," Genny said.

"You do have something of a reputation for being eccentric, dear, but this is going a bit far. I understand, of course, but others won't. The baron should return to the Fountain Inn. That or purchase a house."

"You should tell him that, Laura. Why don't you come for tea this afternoon? The baron should be there. You can tell him precisely what it is he should and should not be doing."

"So very kind of you, dear. You know, I believe I'll accept your invitation. Yes, I shall. Good day, Miss Paxton."

"Until four o'clock, Mrs. Salmon," Genny said in an equally formal voice. "Don't get wet."

Thirty minutes later Genny informed Alec of his good fortune. She was damp around the collar, but otherwise had beaten the rain. Alec was staring at her, his eyebrows lowering.

"Who's Mrs. Salmon, Genny?" Hallie asked, looking up from a book of children's story rhymes Mrs. Swindel had given her. "That's a very funny name."

"She's a lady who isn't at all a cold fish and she much admires your papa, Hallie. She doesn't want him to do anything that would make him unpopular in Baltimore society."

"She wants Papa," Hallie said with a five-year-old's candor. "I've seen it so many times, Genny. I'll wager she doesn't even hide it well. Yes, Papa, she wants you."

"She's already had him," Genny said, quietly

enough for just Alec to hear, "for what that's worth."

He gave her a slow, very drawing smile.

"A woman will murder you," she said between her teeth.

"Jealous?"

That called for retribution, but Genny wasn't up to it at the moment. She ignored him instead. "Now, Hallie, I must change into more tealike clothing for our visitor. Should you like to assist me?"

Hallie agreed to that request and the two of them left Alec in the parlor to fume alone. He'd returned only a few minutes before Genny. He'd had a busy day and was quite pleased with his progress. He'd looked forward to a quiet afternoon with Genny and his daughter, and to an equally quiet dinner. Now he had to put up with Laura before he could tackle Genny with his proposition.

Alec had always believed that if you were going to do something, you should do it right. And he did. He put up with Laura charmingly. Both Genny and Hallie weren't pleased with the seemingly ardent tea party between the other two members.

"What a dear little girl," Laura said for perhaps the third time, and Hallie stiffened up like a poker once more. After the second time, Hallie had remarked in a low voice to Genny that the fishlady reminded her of Miss Chadwick.

"Thank you," Alec said, "but I rarely think of her as a dear little girl, you know."

"I got the impression that she was older, nearly

grown, but of course, you are far too young for a nearly grown daughter, aren't you, Baron?"

"I suppose it would depend upon all the girls who grew up with him," Genny said. "I've heard stories that would easily make Hallie all of fifteen years old if only the baron had been more persuasive as a boy."

"Miss Paxton, really!"

"She's probably right," Hallie said, earning a scandalized look from Mrs. Salmon. "I didn't know Papa when he was a boy, of course, but I imagine he was just as he is now, only less so then."

Alec was laughing. He picked up a small lemon cake from a platter and tossed it to his daughter. She caught it handily.

"Into your mouth, pumpkin. And keep your more terrifying observations to yourself."

"Yes, Papa."

"Good girl. Sometimes."

Hallie opened her mouth but Alec shook his head. "No, pumpkin. Keep quiet or you'll go to Mrs. Swindel."

"Who is Mrs. Swindel?"

"Our chaperon—"

"Hallie's companion—"

Alec and Genny looked at each other and laughed.

"She is both," Alec said.

Laura toyed with a small scone that oozed strawberry jam over its sides. Finally, or at least that was how Genny saw it, she screwed up her nerve and said, "Miss Paxton, why don't you take the darling child upstairs? I really must speak to the baron in private."

Genny gave Alec a beaming smile. "Why, certainly. Come along, Hallie. No, don't argue. We'll stop by the kitchen and fetch more goodies."

Hallie grabbed her book and dashed to the parlor door. She heard her papa say her name very softly, and immediately turned. "It was nice to meet you, Mrs. Salmon. Good day."

"Such a delightful child," Laura said.

Hallie said with great seriousness, "She'll try, but she won't get him, Genny. Don't worry. Papa's never silly when it comes to serious things, and you're serious."

Genny stopped in the middle of the stairs and stared down at the little girl with the very serene voice.

"It's true." Hallie patted her hand. *Her* hand. "She's very pretty, even beautiful, but don't you see, Papa doesn't like ladies like her. Oh, he'll flatter them, perhaps, if he's in a good humor, maybe even see them in their bedchambers, something all adults seem to do. But he likes ladies who are prettier on the inside. Like you."

"You told me you thought I was pretty."

Hallie nodded, all seriousness. "Yes, that's true, but Mrs. Salmon is quite excapton . . . excepio—"

"Exceptional?"

"Yes, that's right. She wants to be Lady Sherard and she thinks she's beautiful enough to deserve it. Papa isn't fooled ever, you know."

"It doesn't matter to me, Hallie."

Hallie gave her a very tolerant, very long-suffering look, one designed to make Genny feel quite inadequate, which she did. She held steadfast, however.

Genny came to a sudden stop at the top of the stairs. "Hallie, did you . . . no, you couldn't, it's impossible."

"What, Genny?"

"You said your papa went to ladies' bedchambers."

"Of course he does occasionally. Don't be silly, Genny. Papa's a man, after all. And he went to your bedchamber, too. Adults," she added, shrugging, "just do that."

Genny gulped in the face of this timeless wisdom. "Hallie, would you please just be a little girl for the next hour?"

Hallie beamed at her. "Will you read to me? Papa thinks I can already read all the stories, but I can't."

"I would love to."

"Odd as it may sound, you look lovely in black."

"Thank you. Would you care for more mutton cutlets with soubise sauce?"

"I believe not, though they are quite tasty. It is wonderful to have such warm friends as Mrs. Salmon, is it not?"

"Indeed. More bacon-cheek?"

"I don't feel the need, thank you. She invited me to her house tomorrow night."

"Go, by all means. Perhaps some sprouts?"

"They make me bilious, just the thought of

them. Mrs. Salmon is concerned—as a good friend should be—that I am living here with you, a poor, defenseless, long-in-the-tooth maiden lady."

"More hare soup?"

"It's cold now. I assured her that you were far from defenseless, that you wouldn't be poor for over another three weeks, and that I liked your long teeth. Oh, yes, I assured her that you were far from being a maiden."

"Would you like the cold hare soup in your face?"

"Genny, Genny, you normally dish out insults with remarkable verve. What's the matter? You feeling under the weather? The weather is quite nasty, that's true. Or is it that since you've discovered lovemaking, you want more? Well, I suppose I could be convinced to visit you again tonight. Would you wish to try another position, perhaps? Being on your side is nice; you'd like it. Your knees would be bent, your beautiful right leg drawn up toward your chest, and then I would curve around you and—"

A spoonful of peas struck Alec full face.

He laughed. The beast was actually laughing at her.

Then she was gasping, as he tossed a return spoonful of peas into her face. One particularly fat pea landed on her bosom and stayed there.

"Now that is impressive," Alec said, eyeing her breasts. "No, there it goes. Mrs. Salmon has the most excellent pair of breasts it's ever been my privilege to fondle. But wait, didn't you observe her upper endowments also?"

"Yes, I did."

"Before you fell, landing on your wonderful bottom and spraining your equally wonderful ankle?"

"Ah, then, of course, your night of pleasure began. Did you like it when I tied you to my bunk aboard ship, Genny? I assure you that I enjoyed your pleasure immensely. Your outpourings of moans and groans and little breathy gasps pleased me. You're quite lovely, you know; your legs are long and firm and shaped quite acceptably, and your woman's flesh is soft and pink and—"

"Keep still!"

He opened his mouth again and Genny shouted, "Moses! Moses!"

Moses slipped into the dining room with no sound at all. "Yes, ma'am?"

She gave him her best smile. "We're ready for coffee now, I believe."

"I'm not through with my mutton cutlets," Alec said.

"You'll gain flesh. Coffee, please, Moses."

"Suh?"

Genny wanted to yell. Looking to Alec for orders!

"Miss Genny's quite right. It wouldn't do for me to become a fat stoat." *At least not until I've nailed you down, Miss Eugenia,* his look at her clearly said. "Coffee it is. With brandy, please."

"Yes, suh."

Moses left the dining room with as little noise as he'd entered it.

Genny leaned forward. "Would you please stop being outrageous, Alec?"

260

He was serious in an instant. "You haven't been depressed or silent or withdrawn for the past half hour. And you've eaten your dinner."

Genny paused, staring down at her nearly empty plate. He was right. She'd wanted to kill him so much she'd forgotten about her father, the endless pain of the present, her unadmitted jealousy of Laura Salmon, and eaten her dinner. She'd really been quite hungry. She looked up at him. There was no amusement or devilry in his eyes.

"No, Genny. Don't look back right now. You really must look forward. There's no choice for you."

"I don't want to. It's hopeless."

"I don't believe I appreciate being considered hopeless. No, don't argue, just listen for a minute. I'm here to rescue you, Genny. I've already made love to you and you appreciated my efforts in that direction." Alec paused for a moment, then frowned. "As a matter of fact, my body is busily informing me that it's time to become close to you again. I'd like to toss up your skirts right here on the dining table, but—ah, here's Moses with the coffee. A man of questionable timing."

Genny said not a word. She watched Moses glance toward Alec and saw Alec give complete directions with but a nod. It was hopeless even here in her own home. At least her father had left her the house.

"You've the look of a woman going backward again. Would you care for some brandy? No? Well, I insist. You need it. It'll warm up your vitals."

It did. Genny gulped the first drink, felt the brandy steam all the way to her stomach, and coughed. Alec merely sipped his coffee, looking at the portrait of James Paxton's father on the wall above the sideboard. The fellow was bewigged, and his full-cut, whale-boned coat was a heavy purple brocade with heavily braided sleeves. Impressive, that was what he was, but his expression was as cold as the North Sea.

Genny got hold of herself and the brandy. She felt warm and she felt soft. Things were beginning to look less hopeless.

"Now, as I was saying," Alec continued as he poured a bit more coffee and a lot more brandy into her Wedgwood cup, "I want you to look at me as your knight-errant. A brave fellow am I, and you, my dear Miss Eugenia, can be considered in the light of the Holy Grail. Do you like that notion?"

"You're being quite absurd," Genny said, but she wasn't at all serious. The coffee was delicious and so warming, making her tingle to her knees.

"Here's what we're going to do, dear lady. You will marry me on Friday."

That brought Genny's head up. She stared at him. "You're mad, quite mad. You don't love me. You only want the shipyard and the *Pegasus*. Why?"

"Because I want to make love to you for the next forty years, every night, every morning, perhaps after breakfast and before tea, and—"

"That's absurd."

"Your conversation is growing stunted, my dear Eugenia. Now just be quiet. As I said, you'll

262

marry me on Friday. That way the shipyard will be quite safe. Then we'll have our race to Nassau."

"I thought you'd forgotten about that. I had. Why? There's no reason for a wager now. You've got everything."

"I'm not quite the fool you seem to think I am, Genny. You don't want to have anything to do with me—at least you don't see me as likely husband material."

"I don't see any man as husband material! You're all pompous asses, unfair and unkind and—"

"You've covered it quite thoroughly, I think. Knowing the way you feel, I am going to offer you a business proposal. You beat me sailing to and from Nassau, and I'll leave you to your own devices. I will deed ownership of the shipyard over to you. You can run the shipyard, bankrupt it as surely as we're sitting here right now, anything you wish. It won't matter to me, not a bit. I'll buy the *Pegasus* so you'll be able to stay afloat. But you won't have to be saddled with me or my daughter after we return."

"That sounds wonderful. What if by some horrid mistake I don't beat you?"

"Ah, then I shall have my way, Genny, in all things."

"Such as?"

"You will be my wife. You will manage my household. You won't ever again dress like a man. You will bear my children, if God blesses us. You will stay out of my business affairs. You will give up any and all interference in the shipyard."

"You would wish me to die."

That stopped him cold and made his belly cramp with something that resembled guilt, but he rallied. "On the contrary. Regardless of whatever wild fancies you have now, you're still a woman. God knows, you convinced me of that last night. I would like to believe that such a conclusion would lead to your happiness."

She gave him a lost look that brought a temporary return of guilt, then rose to stand beside her chair.

"Do you have any questions? Is there anything you would wish to change or modify?"

She shook her head, saying as she did, "We'll be married before the race, but when I win, you said you'd leave. We would still be married. I don't care about myself, but don't you think you would wish to marry again?"

"No."

The brandy was still warm on her stomach, but there were tears behind her eyes, and her head ached to release them. The tears weren't just for her father, no, they were for . . . She shook her head.

"Good night, Baron."

"What is your answer, Genny?"

She didn't look at him, merely kept her head down. "I will tell you in the morning. Is that all right?"

"Yes, but tomorrow it must be."

Genny walked slowly from the dining room, pulling the door closed behind her. Life had turned excessively strange. A month ago everything was as it should be. But now—what a bloody mess.

Genny awoke slowly, aware to the tips of her toes that she was alive, fully and exquisitely so, her body tingling, a deep ache between her thighs. His large hands were warm and covered so much of her at each long sweep. Her nightgown was around her waist, the buttons unfastened all the way down. His lips were lightly caressing her nipple.

"Alec, what are you . . . ah, yes . . . Alec?"

"Hush, Genny. I'm just here to convince you. Do you like that?" His warm mouth closed again over her nipple and she obligingly arched her back and moaned deep in her throat. She felt his hand slip beneath her nightgown and rest unmoving on her belly, his fingers splayed outward.

"Alec—"

"Yes, Genny? You want me to touch you? Here?" His fingers sifted through her hair to find her. She was wet and swelled; she could feel herself as his fingers caressed her. But how was that possible? She should have been embarrassed and she was, for perhaps a second or two. Then her hips were lifting against his beguiling fingers.

"That's nice, Genny. Do you know how your woman's flesh feels to me? The man who will be your husband? No, don't argue, just feel. You'll have this every day of your life, Genny. I promise you." She moaned, and he kissed her, touching his tongue to hers, feeling her start with surprise, gentling now, slowing himself and her down. He

265

eased his fingers between the soft damp folds and slipped inside her. She was tight around his finger, and he wanted to come into her in that instant so badly he didn't think he could control himself. His member was hard and throbbing and pressing against her thigh. But he wanted her to climax before he came inside her. He wanted to be certain that her pleasure was a conclusion.

"Genny, open your legs wider."

She didn't understand him, she was so far drawn into the vortex of sensation he was creating inside her body.

"Open your legs," he said again, and this time he helped her, pressing her thighs wide so he could come between them. He lay atop her, with his full weight, and kissed her mouth again and again.

"Would you like to discuss philosophy?" he said. "Or perhaps the exploits of Napoleon?"

He was teasing her, but she couldn't think of a single word to retort. "Alec," she managed, although that was all.

"Very nice, love," he said, and began kissing her again. And he knew that finally she was experiencing the inevitability of it, accepting it, perhaps even wanting it. She was trusting him that he would bring her pleasure and that it was what she needed from him, what was good for her. He didn't disappoint her. He eased down her body, kissing her as he went, caressing her with his hands, holding her waist, lifting her hips. When his mouth closed over her, she cried out and then cried out once more.

Alec felt something deep and giving inside him.

It was an elusive feeling, and he sought it out naturally. It was from Genny and it was into himself.

When her back arched tight as a bow, her legs stiffened, he pushed and pushed her until she was pounding his shoulders with her fists. But he didn't let her pleasure fade. He came into her in a single, powerful thrust, lifting her hips high, forcing her thighs wider still. "Match my rhythm," he said, his voice deep and dark as the night.

She did, and little aftershocks of pleasure shot through her. Then he quickened his pace. She was with him. Then suddenly his fingers were between their bodies, fondling her, caressing her, and she cried out, nearly bucking him off her in her frenzy, clutching his shoulders and burying her face against his chest. He met her, and plunged so deep that they were one, and he knew it and accepted it as he spilled his seed, filling her with himself.

It was a moment in time that he never wanted to end.

He became sensible sometime later. He didn't know if five minutes had passed or an hour. He just became aware that Genny was crying softly. He said her name and lifted himself onto his elbows.

15

"Shush, don't cry. What's wrong, love?"

Genny tried to stop the sobs. She hiccuped against his shoulder. He leaned down and nuzzled her throat with his lips.

"I'm so afraid, Alec," she whispered against his cheek.

Alec eased off her and rolled onto his side. "Look at me, Genny."

She turned her head on the pillow to face him. He'd lighted a single candle on the bedside table. He seemed mysterious in the shadows, his face all planes and angles, and his brilliant eyes so dark a blue as to be nearly black. She looked down the column of his throat to his shoulders and the sprinkling of golden hair there. He gently stroked his fingers over her jaw. "Tell me why you're afraid."

It was difficult, so very difficult. She felt a fool. "A month ago I was myself, just myself, and there were worries, certainly, yet everything was as I knew it all my life. Papa was ill, but I was used to that. Then you came.

"I think when I first saw you I thought it would be all over for me. I didn't want it to be, though. You were just so very overwhelming."

"I didn't know you existed a month ago either, Genny. Oh, like you knew of a Baron Sherard, I knew of a Mr. Eugene Paxton, but not you,

Genny. I don't think I realized it was over for me until I held your head while you vomited that memorable night after your headlong flight from the brothel. Are you sorry I came into your life?"

"Yes . . . no. Oh, God, Alec, I don't know!"

"Are you glad I held your head?"

She started to say something, swallowed it, and punched his arm with her fist.

Alec stroked his fingertips over her jaw. So smooth, he thought, and stubborn. "Behold a serious man. Now listen to me. I'm not quite certain either what it is I should be feeling right now—joy, terror, or just plain confusion. But don't be afraid of me, Genny. I'll never hurt you, never."

You do but you don't realize it. Oh, God, what am I to do? A sob broke from her throat and she turned her face away from him.

"No, no, don't cry. You'll make yourself sick. Hush."

He was treating her as if she were Hallie, soothing her as an adult would a child to rid the child of the monsters in the night, stroking her hair, rubbing her back. It galled her and at the same time, oddly, provided some comfort.

"I'm not a child," she said.

He smiled. "That, my dear Genny, I can vouch for personally." He lay his palm on her belly again and began to massage her. "You are so soft," he said and looked down at his long fingers caressing her. He'd always thought a woman's body was fascinating, providing him with endless and delightful explorations. He splayed his fingers, lightly touching her woman's mound. Lord, but

Genny's body ... she was simply more. He couldn't explain it, but it was true. He was beginning to accept that he would never get his fill of her. He found himself simply wanting to touch her, just to know she was there beside him. And now she would be his.

He felt her quickening and smiled lazily, then realized that it wasn't sex he wanted at this moment. He wanted her to talk to him. He forced his hand to still itself.

"We can make a go of it, Genny. All you need to do is trust me in matters other than sexual ones."

"You have no idea if I trust you in sexual things!"

He gave her the most wicked smile imaginable. "My dear innocent, don't you realize that you give yourself completely to me? I tell you to open your thighs wider and you obey me immediately because you know I'll give you pleasure. I've felt you raising your hips to draw me deeper into you. I've heard your cries, watched your face when you climaxed. And you climax beautifully, Genny, freely, with what I've decided to call American abandon. Now, I consider that trusting me in sexual matters. Will you trust me in other matters as well?"

"You're saying you know what's best for me?"

He heard the sharpness in her voice, the underlying bitterness, but didn't allow himself to respond to it. Her father's death was still so close, so painful for her, and her pride, well, her father had gotten her off on the wrong path, encouraging her independence, building her pride beyond what a woman should have, and it just made matters more complicated, more difficult for him. "I was only going to point out that I'm your senior by some years and I'm very fond of you; and let's just say that I do have your best interests at heart."

"But you refuse to acknowledge what *I* consider to be my own best interests."

"Genny, I truly don't believe you do know what's best for yourself right now. I think you're very confused and uncertain about the future, about us. There are so many changes in your life, so many unexpected things you have to deal with. But I know one thing. Your father didn't do justice by you, Genny, letting you play at being a man, roaming about the shipyard, hobnobbing with fellows no lady would admit to her drawing room."

What was the use? she wondered, silent now, her tears firmly set aside. Silly woman's tears. He couldn't begin to understand, and even if he could, he wouldn't approve. There was no hope for it. It was either marry him and accept his wager or allow the shipyard to be sold to a stranger.

She simply couldn't do that.

Was she wrong? Had her father misdirected her? Tried to make her into the son he'd lost?

She wanted to yell that no, she was what she was, and she wasn't wrong, and her father hadn't been wrong either.

She wondered about Hallie. Alec certainly allowed his daughter all the latitude he'd give a son. When Hallie reached a certain age, would he draw her in, force her to learn to sew samplers and wear petticoats? Would he expect her to forget all the freedom she'd enjoyed? Genny wanted to ask him, to demand that he explain his masculine reasoning to her. . . .

But Alec's fingers were moving on her belly again, easing lower, and she felt the anticipation, for she knew the ache would build between her thighs. She wondered how he could so effortlessly make her body respond to a simple movement of his fingers. She wanted to ignore the feelings. She wanted to push him away. He'd come uninvited to her bedchamber and forced himself upon her.

"I don't want you to force me again."

Alec's fingers didn't stop their rhythm at the outrageous words spoken in that stony voice. "Force you? What a cheery thought. That's quite rich, Miss Eugenia. I'll admit to getting things started, so to speak. Just let my fingers caress you for another blink of an eye and you'll be begging me to pleasure you."

She said nothing. The throbbing was becoming more insistent and she squirmed beneath his fingers, unable to help herself. He chuckled and she wanted to scream at him, to throw his damnable beautiful self against the wainscoting.

"Twice a night for forty years. That's more times than I can figure out in my head. You'll wear me out, Genny, but I'll try to keep up with you, I promise."

"I don't want to do this with you again, I . . . ahh . . ." Her voice fell away into a groan.

"That's it, love. Give over to me, Genny, trust

me. I'll protect you, take care of you. It's all right. I'm here now. I'll be here for you always. Will you just believe that?''

She wanted him to be here for her, but she didn't need protection, didn't want a man to tell her what to do and what not to do; she didn't want to be taken care of, like an infant, like a lady, like Laura Salmon. She opened her mouth to tell him that she did believe him, but that she was also quite capable of taking care of herself.

Instead, she moaned, a deep, tearing sound.

She felt him shudder, then move quickly over her. He pushed her thighs wide apart and she parted them wider still; then his mouth was on her, and she knew she was completely open to him, just as he'd told her, and she knew what he would make her feel, wanting those feelings, not caring that tomorrow would come and she would look at herself, at him, in the light of day, and she would have to make a decision that would affect the rest of her life. And his and Hallie's.

She cried out as her climax overtook her. He didn't come into her immediately this time, but gentled his touch, slowing now, his mouth soothing, easing her. When she quieted, he moved her onto her stomach. "Come up on your knees, Genny.''

She felt languid, light-headed, her body still giving small shudders of pleasure. She obeyed him, not wondering what he intended. She trusted him, she thought wearily. He pulled her nightgown over her head and tossed it to the floor. He caressed her hips, easing her toward him, and then he was behind her, parting her,

273

and he came into her very slowly, very gently. Every few moments he stilled. "You're so small and tight, Genny. Am I hurting you? Am I too far inside you?"

His voice sounded strained. He was deep but it didn't hurt, it felt tight and throbbing and she didn't want him to pull back, it was too wonderful.

"No, no," she said, arching her back naturally, drawing him in deeper. "Alec, this is so . . . oh, goodness . . . oh!"

He reached his hands around and cupped her breasts. "You control how deep I come into you, Genny. Move your hips against me when you want more of me."

She did. It came naturally, this business of sex, and it was beyond anything she could have imagined. His fingers stroked over her stomach and found her and he began his caressing rhythm again and she swayed and felt him come so deeply into her that he was a part of her then and she wanted him again, so badly that she couldn't keep the soft cries to herself. Then they weren't soft, they were sharp and dark and raw, and as she cried out, stiffening under him, he climaxed powerfully, his fingers digging into her hips, his head thrown back.

He eased to the side, bringing her with him. He was spooned against her back and legs, kissing her nape through her tangled hair while his hand touched her breast languidly, almost as if he did it because her breast was within his reach and because it pleased him enough to caress it. She tried to sort through things but she was trapped in her own vagrant thoughts, thoughts that were really questions with no answers; at least there were no answers in the dark of the night after she'd been loved twice by a man who wanted to protect her and take care of her. She gave it up and fell asleep with him still deep inside her.

The truth of the matter, Alec thought as he held the weight of her breast in his palm, was that she would remain his wife regardless of the outcome of their race, not that the outcome was in any doubt, of course. He closed his eyes for a moment, feeling again the incredible sensations that had engulfed him when he'd thrust into her, his hands on her hips, her breasts, her belly. He'd wanted all of her, and that wanting just seemed to get more and more powerful, and he now accepted it and silently offered his loyalty and fidelity to her until the day he died. He felt her nipple tighten between his fingers. It was so sweet. Sweet now and easy and slow. But what he'd felt moments before hadn't been sweet, it had been hard and demanding and urgent. And the feel of his seed spurting from his body so deeply into her, and Genny drawing him even deeper, wanting him as he did her . . . He could still hear her cries of pleasure, see her hair rippling down to her waist as she'd arched her back and jerked her hips against him.

If someone had asked him, he would have said with complete certainty that he'd gotten Genny with child tonight. Soon she would want to accept the fact that she was a woman—his woman. She would want to wear her woman's clothes, she would want to bear his children, she would want him to care for her.

She would come to accept what she was meant to be. He would see that it was so.

He thought of Nesta, his wife of five years. Sweet, dear Nesta, to die so very young and all because that fool of a doctor hadn't known what to do. Well, Alec knew now. He'd never let anything happen to Genny. Never.

How could she possibly believe she would ever beat him, even in her Baltimore clipper?

What he didn't understand, what he truly believed was her father's blunder, was Genny's insistence on playing a man's role in life. She would forget that nonsense. He'd see to it.

It was the second of November. Baltimore during the fall could be as beautiful as the Garden of Eden; at least that was what Baltimoreans always told each other and any stranger who would listen. But more often, truth be told, the weather was chilly, threatening to drizzle, the sky a murky gray, just as it was today.

Alec waved to Genny, who was standing on the *Pegasus's* deck, garbed as a man, her legs planted wide apart, hands on hips. Alec felt indulgent; he felt exquisitely tolerant. This would be her final performance in men's clothing. He allowed himself to think that she looked beautiful regardless of her loose breeches, the leather vest that hid the lovely curves of her breasts and the lines of her woman's waist, and that blue wool cap. She met his gaze and smiled, waving back.

She was Eugenia Mary Carrick, Baroness

Sherard, and he rather hoped that she was pregnant. He hadn't asked her. He wasn't certain even if she could know as of yet. She hadn't had her monthly flow, at least since he'd come into her bed, and that had been more than three weeks ago. She hadn't volunteered any information, but he supposed that a lady wasn't accustomed to speaking of such intimate things, even to her husband. Nesta hadn't ever, and Alec had teased her about it, eventually calling her Nonsensical Nesta. Alec felt a lump in his throat at the bittersweet memory. *I've married again, Nesta, after five long years. She's an American—that's a difficult pill to swallow, isn't it?—and an unusual girl. But she'll become just what I need. I know that I'm the man she needs. Hallie is fond of her and she is equally fond of Hallie. You would approve, Nesta, I swear it. Our daughter will be just fine.*

Alec was a husband of two days now.

Odd, but he'd felt no hesitancy, no uncertainty at any point about what he was doing. Perhaps it was because Genny had been such a mass of nameless fears and insecurities, dithering about like a true flighty, featherheaded female, countermanding her own instructions until Mrs. Swindel had simply told her to leave the house and the preparations to her and go finish building her ship. Alec, wisely, had not drawn any verbal conclusions, at first just reassuring Genny as best he could. When that failed, he'd finally told her what to do, told her another time for good measure in a very sharp voice, and she'd obeyed him. But she'd still been nearly incoherent until the Reverend Murray had pronounced them man and wife to the small audience gathered in Saint Paul's Episcopal Church for the ceremony.

It was then, Alec supposed, that she'd realized there was nothing more to decide, that everything was over and done with and all she had to do was simply accept it. Alec had lifted her veil and given her a triumphant grin. Then he'd kissed her, very lightly, very gently. Her dilated eyes didn't worry him now.

Most friends of the Paxton family had seemed genuinely pleased at the union. Relief was probably the uppermost sentiment, Alec amended to himself. Eugenia Paxton was no longer an eccentric young lady to be worried about. She was now an eccentric married lady. She was also a baroness and was considered a very fortunate young woman. He wondered if Genny agreed with the consensus. He also wondered if Genny would have married Oliver Gwenn if he, Alec, hadn't come to Baltimore. Oliver looked more down-in-the-mouth than a rejected suitor, which, Alec knew, he hadn't been—at least Genny hadn't considered him that.

As for Hallie, she'd accepted the marriage, saying little, merely smiling at Genny and taking her hand at odd times, giving her silent encouragement. His five-year-old daughter, the wise old woman. She'd said to him several days before the ceremony, "Papa, I like Genny very much. She'll come about and everything will be all right. When you and she return, we'll be a real family."

And Alec had replied, hugging Hallie close, "Thank you, pumpkin. Just keep your eye on her, all right? We don't want her to bolt at the last minute."

"Genny isn't a filly, Papa!" But Hallie had kept a close watch on her soon-to-be stepmama nonetheless.

Laura Salmon, furious and not invited to the small wedding, busily spread rumors about the baron living at the Paxton house without a proper chaperon. The rumors, of course, didn't go far enough, but Alec enjoyed the fact that no one credited Laura's venom, merely shaking a head at her tantrums.

Alec also made certain that all the gentlemen who counted in Baltimore knew about the wager and knew as well that it represented the final hoorah for Miss Eugenia, that he as her husband was allowing it, and upon their return from Nassau, she would become a woman and a wife and would doubtless entertain them and their wives at dinner parties. The gentlemen chose to regard Alec as a very forward-thinking man; as for Genny, all past sins were to be forgiven and this prank to be indulged because the baron had her under control when all was said and done. The baron had given his blessing to the project. Could they do less?

Had Genny known what every gentleman at her wedding knew, she would have taken her father's old war pistol and shot Alec in the foot.

It was also the only way that Alec could secure a crew for Genny to captain on their race to Nassau. It was he who was really in charge, the sailors doubtless reasoned; the young lady was merely being indulged by her doting new husband.

Alec prayed that none of this reasoning would reach his bride's tender ears.

This morning, both vessels were moored side by side at Fells Point. The water was smooth, calm, with hardly a breath of wind present. But Genny knew that the *Pegasus's* tall masts and equally tall sails would reach those upper winds that were unique to Chesapeake Bay, and her clipper schooner would pass North Point practically before Alec could get his men up the ratlines of the barkentine. It didn't matter, though. His skill and her lack of experience would become clear enough once they were sailing south in the Atlantic. He looked over at her again.

It was time, Genny decided. She cleared her throat and called for the men to gather around her on the quarterdeck.

She looked at the nine faces, only two unknown to her.

"Some of you—Morgan, Phipps, Daniels, Snugger—you've known me since I was no taller than this wheel. I hope you will tell those here who don't know me that I am to be trusted with the *Pegasus* and their lives. I know you wonder at this race. I know you wonder at taking orders from a captain who is also a female. This is true, gentlemen, but I'm a better sailor and a better captain than that damnable Englishman aboard that cumbersome old barkentine over there. We are all Americans. The *Pegasus* is an American vessel. She's a Baltimore clipper, gentlemen, the fastest vessel in the world. As you know, my father designed her. She has the sharpest raking bow ever built; she has the tallest masts for her size of any clipper today. This is her maiden voyage. She'll beat that English excuse for a water-bound log and you'll make it happen. She's lightly stayed and heavily canvased, and the ten of us will handle her to perfection. Just look at her uncluttered decks. No ropes or braces or ties to stumble over. When we reach the Atlantic, you'll see that she'll sail so close to the wind that we'll leave the old barkentine far behind, tacking starbard, then tacking port, covering about three times more ocean than we will and going a third of our distance in the same time.

"I'm proud of the *Pegasus*, for I helped to build her. I'm proud of her because I'm an American and she's an American vessel. Think of this contest as being not between a man and a woman but between an Englishman and an English vessel and an American and a Baltimore clipper!"

To Genny's infinite relief and pleasure, the men looked at one another, Snugger spat toward the barkentine, and they all cheered.

"Remember how five years ago we routed the English from our very city? We'll do it again, this time on the water!"

Wild, frenetic shouts.

"Let's find that wind!"

Alec, who had been watching, blinked at the loud, sustained cheering. What the devil had she said to the men? Had she offered them bribes? He curbed his curiosity, waited for the noise to die down, and called out, "Are you ready, Mr. Eugene?"

"Ready to take the wind from your sails, Baron!"

"After you!"

Alec watched the *Pegasus* pull away from the dock. He heard Genny's calm voice calling out orders.

There was a light breeze on the Patapsco that morning, a disadvantage for Alec's barkentine. However, the clipper, with its higher masts and sails, could take advantage of the stronger winds above the barkentine's reach. Alec's ship would slough its way out to the bay, hopefully gaining enough wind to fill the massive sails and catch up with the clipper on the one-hundred-and-fifty-mile voyage to the Atlantic. But Alec was also a realist. Even the most inexperienced captain in the world would know that real wind wouldn't be there for them until they sailed from the bay into the Atlantic.

He would simply bide his time and he would have a lot of it to bide. It would take them a good nine hours to reach the ocean.

They passed North Point at the mouth of the Patapsco, the place where the British commander had halted for the attack on Baltimore, and turned to starboard into Chesapeake Bay.

There was a sharp wind. Alec grinned.

The *Pegasus* and the *Night Dancer* were very nearly bow to bow as they sailed past Cape Henry and into the Atlantic at six o'clock that evening.

Alec looked over at Genny, gave her a salute and a mock bow.

Genny was so happy that she simply grinned back at him like an idiot.

"The race, gentlemen," she called out, "is on!"

16

Snugger was her first mate. He was short, very hairy, his upper body massive, and his voice so powerful he could be heard over the din of a gale-force storm.

It was Snugger who shouted Genny's orders to the men. It had been Genny's suggestion that Snugger do the shouting. Perhaps, she'd thought, the men would forget and think that the orders came from Snugger, a man and therefore competent, at least more so than she was.

Daniels stood by her side watching the men scamper down the ratlines.

"She's smooth as a pebble skipping on calm water."

"Aye, Capt'n, she is that. Your pa would have been so proud. Of both of you."

He'd called her captain. She felt pleasure wash through her. She did wonder if her father would have been proud of her. Somehow she had her doubts. Ah, but she wished he were here, seeing her, approving of what she was doing.

Genny was in charge and she felt in charge. She turned the wheel over to Daniels, her second mate, saying in her best captain's voice, "Keep her close into the wind, and that wretched bark will begin to look like she's sailing backward."

"Handles like a dream, she does."

Genny grunted. There was a quarter moon overhead. The night sky was clear, the stars glittering down, silvering on the ocean waves. Genny yawned and stretched.

"Your bunk'll feel good this night, Capt'n."

"Yes, it will, Daniels. I'll take the third watch. Have Snugger awaken me at two bells."

"Aye, aye, ma'am."

Genny grinned, squeezed Daniels's brawny arm, and swung about to the open hatch. She took a deep breath as she descended the steps. The *Pegasus* was too new, too fresh, to yet smell of bilge or rats or wet clothing, or, thank God, of male sweat and unwashed male bodies.

The clipper, unlike Alec's bark, was quieter, her timbers not creaking under her own weight as she sloughed through the waves. Since she was lightly stayed, there was no moaning of the rigging to break the silence.

Mine, she thought; the *Pegasus* is mine.

But it wasn't. It belonged to Alec, just as did everything. Even her home now belonged to Alec simply because he was her husband. At least she assumed that was the case, having overheard two gentlemen speaking of their ownership of their wives and all their belongings sometime before.

She would win this race. Alec simply didn't understand that she had sailed since her sixth birthday and had taken command of a clipper when she was fifteen. She remembered the *Bolter* down to its last halyard block. That clipper's design had been ahead of its time, but it didn't compare with the *Pegasus,* a vessel that was truly extraordinary. There was no doubt in her mind that she would leave Alec and his heavy barkentine far behind, and through no lack of ability on his part.

Well, he was stubborn. He would see. She wondered what he would do then. Would he behave like many men she knew in Baltimore and be furious with her because she beat him? Would he really deed the shipyard back to her?

Genny lighted the cabin lantern and fitted it into its slot atop the captain's beautiful mahogany desk. She closed and latched the door and stripped off her damp clothing. She laid out another set of clothing in an orderly fashion, knowing that in an emergency she would need to be on deck in thirty seconds—or less.

She doused the lantern, slipped a flannel nightgown over her head, and stretched out on the bunk. The *Pegasus* was heeling sharply to port, but it was such a constant movement that after a few minutes it wasn't particularly noticeable. One simply leaned into it, or turned into it, as she was doing now. The *Pegasus* was so very smooth, slicing through the waves cleanly, staying high in the water as she'd been built to do.

Why didn't anyone buy her from me? Genny wondered. Why does my being a female make my vessel any less to be valued?

Silly questions with no answers. Alec would probably just shake his head and tell her it was the way of the world and to forget about it. He would forget about it, of course; he was a man, after all. She yawned. The day had been full, the men excited about winning the race, beating those damned Brits. That ploy, she thought now, grinning into the darkness, had been an excellent one. She'd just have to keep them excited, keep Alec and his bark as the enemy, so they wouldn't spend their time mulling over the fact that their captain was a female.

It would take nearly two weeks to reach Nassau. Perhaps less, depending on the winds, and they were nearly always erratic along the eastern seaboard, particularly during the fall months. Just before it became dark she'd seen Alec's barkentine in the distance. Not closing the gap between them, but not dropping back either. She'd wager her last American dollar that his men were already exhausted from tacking all day to maintain as little distance as possible between the two vessels.

Genny closed her eyes and saw Alec. Not the Alec who was captaining the barkentine, but Alec her husband and lover, naked and on top of her, kissing her, caressing her breasts, closing his eyes as he came into her, as if the feelings were so strong he had to. And when he was deep inside her, he would sigh with the pleasure of it before he started moving within her. And she would kiss his throat, his chest, grasp his arms as tightly as she could, feel him plunge deeper and deeper into her, only to withdraw, teasing her, knowing how to drive her distracted. And she'd lift her hips, trying to bring him into her again, and he'd smile down at her and ask her to tell him what it was she wanted. She hadn't told him yet, her mind too overwhelmed with the wildness of the feelings he aroused in her and with the inherent embarrassment of saying aloud to him what it was she was feeling and wanted. But he always knew without her saying a thing, and he knew he was right and it pleased him, she guessed now, this power he held over her.

Genny's eyes flew open. There was a faint line of perspiration on her forehead. Goodness, her body was reacting as if he were here with her. She wanted him. Now. Very much. The intensity of her feelings surprised her. It hadn't been that long since he'd first taught her about passion. But taught her he had. She realized also that she'd never taken the initiative with him. She wondered if a woman was allowed to or expected to. She didn't know. She thought of his member, hard and slick, pressed against her belly, and wondered how he would feel rubbing against her hand . . . or in her mouth. Was it any different than him caressing her and stroking her? She didn't know, but she firmly intended to find out. Both of them should have power over the other. It was only fair. But that made another problem rear its head.

When she won the race what would she do? Leave him? Make him leave her?

She couldn't imagine not being with Alec, couldn't imagine never seeing him again.

Nor could she imagine not working at the shipyard, not sailing, not being responsible, not knowing the triumph of accomplishing something, of seeing her efforts succeed. And Alec would say that she'd know a wonderful sense of accomplishment when she birthed their children.

A mare could birth colts, but not every mare could win a race. It was a rather conceited, very self-important analogy, but Genny liked it. Just as not every woman could build Baltimore clippers.

Well, the truth of the matter was that very few little girls were ever given the opportunity to do anything save play with their dolls and sew samplers. They were educated from their cradles, but not with the kind of education that would make them competent and independent; no, all their education was in how to please a man and how to run a man's house. She'd been lucky that her father had treated her no differently from her brother. Until the will, that cursed will of his.

Life, her father had said once, was a series of compromises, some of them hurting like the very devil, others making you feel like a king, or a queen, in her case. But she doubted that her father could possibly have been considering compromises when it came to a marriage.

Or maybe he had. Was that why he'd written his will the way he had? To force her to compromise?

She shook her head on her pillow. If that was true, then the compromise meant her utter and complete defeat and capitulation.

She fell asleep wondering what Alec was doing, what he was thinking, if he was thinking about her. She slept deeply until Daniels woke her for her watch.

As for her husband, Baron Sherard, he was drinking a snifter of fine French brandy and wishing to heaven he'd never suggested the stupid race.

Damnation and bloody hell. He'd underestimated her. And the wretched clipper. He'd watched nearly openmouthed as the sleek vessel had borne herself so close to the wind that she was nearly head-on, whilst he and his crew had had to tack repeatedly to keep the distance between the two vessels within reason. But she would gain on him. His men simply couldn't spend twenty-four hours a day tacking the bark. It was exhausting work. He drank more brandy. Damnation. She'd win. There was no hope for it.

He was going to lose the race. And he was cursing too much, even though it was mental cursing.

Papa, you told me if I ever said one of those words, you'd cuff my ears!

He got his daughter out of his mind for the moment. If ever there was a situation that called for an outpouring of invective, it was this one.

And she would leave him or request that he take his leave. But he knew he couldn't do that. She was his wife. He couldn't leave her in charge of that shipyard and let her bankrupt herself. And it would happen, there was no doubt about that.

Was she pregnant?

Alec realized he was being not only a pessimist but morose and sullen and a defeatist. He hadn't lost to her yet. If he and his men had to tack the *Night Dancer* a hundred times to the *Pegasus's* one time, he'd do it. He'd do whatever was necessary to beat her. For her own good.

He wondered how his men would feel about that.

The following afternoon it was drizzling. The sky was a cast-iron gray, the waves choppy, the winds more erratic than they'd been just two hours before.

The *Pegasus* wasn't at her best in this kind of weather.

"It is the Atlantic, Genny," Daniels said, forgetting that the ruddy-cheeked girl beside him was also his captain. "It's also late in the season, a bit too late to believe a clipper could sail without incident. You know that. It was your decision to chance running into foul weather."

"Yes, I know. I'd just hoped we'd be lucky and that wonderful northwesterly wind would keep up."

"Maybe the winds will calm and straighten out. If we hold our current distance from the barkentine, there'll be no problem. You just keep thinking about all that sun and calm water in Nassau."

"I'm thinking of little else at this moment." Suddenly a gust of wind whipped off Genny's wool cap. She made a grab for it but was not quick enough. She and Daniels watched it swirl in the winds over the side of the *Pegasus*.

"It's just a mild passing storm, that's all," she said.

Daniels nodded dutifully. He prayed it was so. Truth be told, he didn't like the idea of Miss

Genny—captain or no—being caught in the Atlantic in a gale, particularly not in the *Pegasus*. He knew she was thinking hurricane. It was the season. It was possible. They would be in grave trouble if it were a hurricane. Daniels wasn't all that convinced that the extreme design of the clipper would survive a severe storm, even in relatively protected waters. Mr. Paxton had planned the masts to be more sharply raked than their predecessors, and the stays were more than minimal. With its canvas fully unfurled, the foremast mainsails overlapped the mainmast, making both masts resemble great white isosceles triangles. If they did run directly into a gale, gusting winds of sizable force against those already sharply angled masts would snap them neatly in two and tear the sails to shreds. Also, the freeboard was very low to the water. A storm worth its salt, and the waves would wash over her decks.

Oh, hell, Daniels thought, and watched. There was little else to do. He heard Miss Genny— Lordy, now she was an English baroness!—shout to reef the topsail on both masts. That was a good idea and the perfect time to do it. It wasn't wise even in this wind to add stress to the masts. He heard Snugger with that giant's voice of his bellow out her orders again. This time the men heard and hastened to obey, swarming up the rigging, surefooted.

Daniels licked his left forefinger and held it into the wind. He sniffed the air as it blew off his finger. He cursed softly.

He didn't think the virgin voyage of the *Pegasus* was going to be successful.

"What do you think, Captain?" asked Abel Pitts, Alec's first mate.

"I think," Alec said, his brow furrowed as he tried his best to make out the *Pegasus* in the growing dark, "that this better be a mild autumn storm and over soon, or my bride of four days is in big trouble."

He knew he sounded quite light about the situation, but within he was scared to death. He wasn't all that familiar with sailing in the southern Atlantic in the autumn. He knew there were hurricanes at this time of year. But no, this was just a passing storm, nothing more. He wouldn't worry about it. He looked to his own vessel. The *Night Dancer* was continuing her way through the choppy waves as if naught were occurring out of the ordinary. Her timbers groaned as she plunged deeply into the trough of a wave, her rigging of tarred hemp rope moaned and shrieked like the damned as the wind pulled and whipped at the sails—all the normal sounds Alec was quite used to.

"Where are we, Abel?"

"I reckon we're about one hundred and five miles due north of Cape Hatteras."

"That's the cape off Pamlico Sound? In North Carolina?"

"Aye, Capt'n, and it isn't kind to vessels; it's known to be in treacherous waters. Sailors call it the graveyard of the Atlantic."

"Obviously my wife knows that. She'll keep due east."

"Aye, Capt'n," said Abel and wondered silently. He watched the baron keep looking in the distance and he knew that his lordship would have given just about anything to catch but a glimpse of that clipper schooner.

Abel turned his head and went about his business. The topsails were reefed a bit, the foremast sails and the mizzenmast sails brought in. The wind was picking up. It was nearly dark now. He heard Pippin, the captain's cabin boy, say to Ticknor, the second mate, "I tell you, I don't like it, Tick. The air's thick—you can taste it nearly. I don't like it at all."

Ticknor grunted as he tested the tautness of the forestay. It was tight, humming slightly from stress in the swirling winds.

"Maybe not," said Ticknor. "The capt'n knows what's what. It ain't up to us to stew about it."

"But that's his wife on the clipper, Tick."

"Aye. Did you get a good peep at her?" asked Ticknor.

"I saw her good when his lordship brought her on board weeks ago."

"Here? His lordship brought her on board our vessel? You never told me that."

" 'Tweren't none of your business. He was carrying her, he was, like she was hurt or something."

"Odd," said Ticknor. "She's a lady, you know."

"His lordship wouldn't have married her if she wasn't a lady, baconbrain."

"You know what I mean. She's different. She's captain of that clipper."

"Aye," said Pippin. "That's true enough and we got to beat her or the capt'n will have no peace for all his years."

Alec, in the meanwhile, had given up trying to see in the darkness. He ate what Clegg put in front of him and thanked his cook absently. He studied the charts to Cape Hatteras. With the winds as perverse as they were, they'd be lucky to reach it by midmorning. Would Genny steer the clipper well clear of the cape even if it meant losing time? Of course she would. She wasn't stupid.

But she wanted to beat him, and there was the rub. She probably wanted to beat him more than anything else in the world. He cursed over his slab of beef, now congealed in gravy on his plate. He shoved the plate away and rose. He couldn't stand the cabin or his own thoughts. He stayed on deck until the slashing rain drove him below.

When finally he slept, he dreamed and it was terrifying. Genny was yelling to him, screaming, and he heard the fear in her voice. He was trying to turn to see her, but something was holding him in place. He called her name. Then he saw her, not all of her, just her eyes, and he saw anguish there, so much anguish that his belly cramped viciously. Then it wasn't Genny's eyes, it was someone else's, a stranger's.

Alec woke up with that cramp, a very real one. Something would happen to her, he knew it, and he'd never felt more helpless in his entire life. Except when Nesta had screamed and screamed and died and he'd done nothing because he hadn't known what to do.

Alec rolled out of his bunk and lit the lantern. Eerie shadows danced through the small cabin. He looked out the stern window. It was raining more heavily, thick sheets of rain. Still, nothing to be particularly concerned about. Unless it was the prelude to a hurricane. He jerked on his boots, pulled on his oilskin coat, and went up to the quarterdeck.

Everything was in orderly array.

"Good evening, Capt'n," said Ticknor, who had watch.

Alec nodded. His gut cramps eased. He stopped rubbing his belly. That bloody dream! It had been ghastly. What the devil should he do now?

Where was she?

Genny was watching the waves grow higher and higher. If the storm continued, if it grew stronger, water would wash over the decks. It wouldn't be very pleasant, but on the other hand, it wasn't the end of the world either. The sky was suddenly darker. It was then that she knew, knew deep down, that a hurricane was coming north from the Caribbean. It was the smell of the air, the *feel* of it, really, and something primitive inside her knew what was to come. "I think it's time to think of the present, Snugger."

Snugger wanted to tell her that late autumn westerly gales weren't unexpected. He wanted to tell her they could survive, even in the center of one. It would just be a passing storm, he wanted to say. He had no chance to say anything. Genny gave him her orders and he shouted them out to the crew.

"Starboard a little," she said to Daniels, who had the wheel. "Yes, that's it. Keep her as close-hauled as you can."

"Aye, aye, Capt'n."

"Snugger, tell them to get the fore-topsails in. Set the main top—no, wait! Daniels, quickly, sheer off!"

Daniels sheered off, the wheel spinning in his large hands.

Genny was flung sideways, falling hard, hitting her hip against the mainmast.

"You all right?"

"Yes. Now, believe me, and don't argue. This is a hurricane. We're going to Pamlico Sound, to Ocracoke Island. You know it's got the deepest inlet in the sound. We'll be safe. We'll ride out the hurricane there." She stood a moment, watching the waves crash over the deck. Her hair was whipping into her face, stinging her cheeks, strands going into her mouth. Finally she grabbed the thick mass and began to braid it. When she finished, she realized she had nothing to tie it with. Snugger, without a word, handed her a thin strap of leather. She managed to tie the braid securely, then said, "Shout to the men to be careful. I don't want to lose anyone. Tell them what we're about."

Snugger nodded and bellowed over the wind. "Tell them it's a hurricane."

Snugger did as he was bidden. He turned finally and cleared his throat. "The sound is shallow, treacherous."

"I know that. We'll go around Diamond Shoals into the inlet, then to Ocracoke. It will take us three to four hours, I think, depending on the winds."

Snugger sighed. "It'll be tricky as the devil."

"It's better than drowning out here in the Atlantic. A hurricane would snap the masts in a thrice and waves would wash over us, sending us down in a matter of minutes. You'd better pray that we get to Hatteras in time."

"We'll do a direct bearing," he said and shouted to Daniels to bear to starboard. Even three feet away, he had to shout. The winds were shrill now, like banshees screaming in the dark on All Hallows' Eve.

"I want the barkentine to follow. I don't imagine that his lordship has had too much experience in this part of the world. He must come after us into the inlet."

"He will, I doubt not," Snugger said. "He'll have some help from O'Shay."

Genny turned wide eyes to Snugger. "He took on O'Shay?"

"You have to agree that the man's a wizard when it comes to sailing the straightest, safest course in this hemisphere. He can't help his love of the bottle—he's Irish, after all. Likely the baron won't let him near any whiskey until the voyage is over."

"O'Shay's a wild man."

"Just in a tavern, Miss Genny. Get him on the

deck of a vessel and he turns magic. He says it's the magic of the Irish. Your pa always said it was the magic of the soul."

On the *Night Dancer,* Alec was discussing the situation with his native Baltimorean, Mr. O'Shay, who'd lived locally nearly all his life and spoke with the thickest Irish brogue Alec had ever heard.

"Aye, and sure enough, milord, it's a hurricane we'll have to chill our bones. The lass ahead in the clipper, well, I hope and pray she'll know what's to be done. Her pa always said she was a bright 'un, female or no."

"And that is?"

"If she knows what she's about, she'll sheer off and head direct to Hatteras. Pamlico Sound, sure enough, into the inlet and on to Ocracoke. It's a deep inlet, the only place I'd choose to ride out the storm."

"We need to catch that clipper, O'Shay. If something happens, I want to be there."

"Sure and we'll do it, milord."

Genny had never been so wet in her life. It became natural to be wet and cold, her fingers numb. She'd found another wool cap and flattened it over her braided hair. The wind could flay the flesh off a person's face. She tried to keep her back to it, but the winds switched from the east to the north with no notice and no predictability.

The men were as miserable-looking as she was, but they kept to it, knowing that each of them

298

was responsible and that if they weren't, they could all die. No one wanted to die.

My first voyage out and this is what happens. It isn't fair. It isn't even ironic. It isn't what should have happened.

She drove her fist against her thigh and grimaced.

The wind was howling now, stronger than it had been but a moment before. She judged its speed to be around fifty miles per hour. The clipper made headway only when the wind was behind them; then she shot forward as if from a cannon. Most of the time they were tacking, sheering off again and again, praying, watching the waves wash over the decks.

A damnable hurricane. There was no fairness at all in life.

"We'll be to Hatteras in another hour, I'd say," Daniels said, spitting, thankfully, away from the wind.

It was daylight, the sky a dirty gray, the rain now clearly visible, coming down and whipping about in thick sheets. The wind was bursting behind them and the clipper was making speeds that were unheard of.

"Maybe less if the winds stay where they are," Genny said.

She wanted the winds to hold steady. They would push the barkentine forward as well.

The shrieking was becoming unearthly. Genny shuddered, then resolutely took the wheel from a fatigued Daniels.

"Get us coffee," she shouted.

It was half rain and cold when she got it, but she drank it off in one healthy slug.

When Diamond Shoals came in sight, Genny yelled and pointed. The men turned, saw it, and cheered just as loudly. From behind them, the barkentine shot from the center of the dense black clouds, propelled by the increasing winds at her back.

The men on the barkentine heard the shouts from the clipper, and they yelled back.

Genny had never felt such profound relief in her life.

Which was stupid, given the fact that they had to negotiate the shallow waters of Pamlico Sound to the deep inlet of Ocracoke. She prayed then, a very simple, straightforward prayer.

"Please, God, save Alec and save the *Pegasus.*"

Snugger heard her words and shouted over the winds, "Pray for me, too, if you will, Miss Genny. I'm too sweet and too important to the ladies to feed the fish just yet."

She smiled and added Snugger's name after the clipper's.

The wind was gaining in force. They managed to round Diamond Shoals and head into the inlet. The wind almost tore Genny's oilskin off her back. She clutched it together at her throat between numb, nearly blue fingers.

She turned the wheel back to Daniels. If anyone on the face of the earth could get them to Ocracoke, it was Daniels.

And O'Shay.

Alec held the spyglass to his eye. He could

make out Genny; her cap had blown off and her hair was whipping about her head. He saw her step away from the wheel to be flung to the side by the gale-force wind.

"For God's sake, take care!"

He watched her, his stomach in his throat, as she gracefully grabbed the foremast rigging. She was looking up at one of the sailors who was clutching at the ratlines in a frozen panic.

The wind howled and shrieked. The *Night Dancer* heaved and groaned, her timbers cracking ominously under the strain of the heavy stays topside.

Twenty minutes later the *Night Dancer* rounded Diamond Shoals, lurching sharply to starboard.

"Thank God," Genny whispered. "We'll make it, both of us."

Snugger wasn't so certain. The winds were buffeting the lightly stayed clipper, pushing her toward the treacherous shallows in the sound, flinging her about in the whipping water as if she were naught but a toy. Genny knew exactly what was happening. She shouted orders to the men until she was hoarse.

Snugger never tired of bellowing out what she said.

"Get that main-topmast staysail in! Another reef in the tops'ls!"

The *Pegasus* was rolling and plunging like a mad thing now in the choppy waters of the sound, like a very insubstantial mad thing, Genny thought in growing despair.

"Heave to! It's blowing a full gale now, Capt'n!"

"You're drifting leeward, Daniels! Hold her steady!"

Genny managed to keep half her attention on the barkentine behind them. It was lurching and shuddering, battering her way through the waves, keeping close, keeping steady.

"Man the halyards! Daniels, hard astarboard!"

On and on it went, as both vessels lurched and plunged through the sound toward the inlet. The barkentine gained on the clipper, its greater size and ability to stay firm holding it in good stead.

"Nearly to her," said O'Shay.

"Oh, God, look at the foremast!"

This was from Abel Pitts. Alec stared and stared again. The sails were tightly reefed, the stays and masts looking nearly naked in the stark gray sky.

"The mast just might go," said O'Shay quite unemotionally. "Nothing to do about it. I ain't ever seen a foremast raked so much afore."

"Hell, man, they can steer into the wind and keep out of the crosscurrents."

"Aye, and sure enough, milord, but the sound's too tricky. They've got to hold course, keep right on the line they're going. And pray they get to the deep inlet."

The mighty barkentine plowed through the smashing white waves that flecked the gray sea. Gallons of frigid water sprayed wildly over the quarterdeck. Alec could see the waves completely cover the deck of the clipper. God, Genny, stay safe! Hang on!

But she was in command. She didn't move from her post beside the wheel. He could see her lips move, then vaguely heard a man's awesomely loud voice over the roaring winds.

He'd never been so scared in his life.

This race was supposed to have been a competition with no danger. He'd envisioned waving to Genny in the warm, balmy breezes of Nassau as his barkentine passed her clipper. What a fool he'd been. A damnable race in November. He hadn't realized. But Genny had, he knew it, but she'd wanted to be rid of him so much that she'd said nothing, knowing the danger and disregarding it. Because she'd wanted the shipyard and she hadn't wanted him.

He'd kill her if she survived this.

"I want to board the clipper," he shouted to Abel. "Once we're in the inlet, I want to board her."

"Aye, aye, Capt'n."

17

Genny held her breath watching the barkentine lurch and shudder and roll as the vessel battered its way through the waves toward them.

She shut her eyes then, sending a prayer heavenward. Alec was closing fast now. No matter what happened, at least he would be near her through this.

The *Pegasus* tacked as the wind veered off to starboard. Even as they came about, the clipper was twisted by the howling winds that were mercilessly pulling them leeward.

For many minutes it was pandemonium. Finally the winds shifted once again, dropping off slightly, and the clipper continued toward the deep inlet of Ocracoke Island.

Alec was frozen with fear as he watched.

" 'Tis well and right the lass is, Capt'n," said O'Shay, his cheerful voice making Alec want to throttle him.

"How much farther to the inlet and the island?"

"Nearly there now. See that spit of land and those pine trees and live oaks? A full blower of a hurricane will wash over Ocracoke, but those blasted trees will still be there when it's over."

Alec stared out at the stunted trees and the flat and barren land. He shivered. He wouldn't like to be marooned on that point of miserable land.

Genny wasn't quite certain how they'd accomplished it, but they finally sailed into the deep waters of the Ocracoke inlet.

"Head her directly into the wind," she told Daniels.

The shortened, reefed sails were brought in completely and tied firmly down. She saw one of the men nearly torn off the rigging by the swirling winds and yelled. Of all things, he swiveled about, his legs hooked through the ratlines, and gave her a big grin and a salute, then shimmied down to the deck. The tall masts stood naked above them. Genny gave a thorough look around the clipper. Everything was battened down. There was nothing else to do now but ride out the storm.

The barkentine was drawing nearer. Genny could make Alec out, swathed in oilskins, his head bare. He was pointing, shouting out orders she couldn't understand.

What was he doing?

When she realized that he intended to jump aboard the clipper, she felt as if she'd swallowed fourteen prune pits and all of them were sitting in her belly. Was he insane? It was dangerous, far too dangerous. Oh, God, he was going to do it. If the winds shifted suddenly, they could send the bark into the clipper's side. If the winds increased, they could lurch the bark forward, slamming her into the clipper's bow. The world wasn't make of *if*'s. It was made of *now*'s and of Alec coming to her. Genny kept her mouth shut, watching the bark's progress.

They could die in this storm. It was a thought

that made her furious with herself, but it wouldn't go away. She wanted him here with her.

Nothing mattered but to be with him.

The barkentine was drawing dangerously close. There was a sudden shift in the wind and Genny knew they'd be rammed. She clutched the base of the mainsail, preparing herself. But at the last instant, the bark sheered off. O'Shay was good, Genny saw. He was at the wheel and his fingers were dancing around the spokes and he was magic. She saw Alec, now poised on the railing of the barkentine.

Four of her men were on the deck waiting for his jump.

He leaped into the air. For an endless moment, the wind held him as if he were naught but a plaything; then just as suddenly it propelled him forward. He landed on his feet, his knees bent, then was pushed forward by the wind with great force. The impact didn't faze him, though, for he rolled with it and came up on his feet, a wide smile on his face.

Two sailors bounded toward him and shook his hand. There was cheering from the barkentine. Cheering from her own men. Genny stood there, smiling foolishly at her husband.

O'Shay sheered off, and the barkentine's bow lightly scraped against the clipper's stern. Alec straightened and looked at his bride.

She was safe. He walked to her, bowed in the howling wind, and when he was near, he stopped and held out his arms.

Genny went into his embrace without hesitation.

"You're safe," he said into her wet wool cap. "Thank God you're safe. I couldn't have borne it otherwise."

The feelings were too strong, too new, and thus she said, "You've left O'Shay in command?"

He smiled down at her. "He'll do just fine. I wanted to make certain you were safe." His hands were all over her then, feeling her arms and her shoulders, closing about her face as he kissed her.

She pulled back a bit. "We're as safe as we can be. Anything can happen now, Alec, you know that. We're headed into the wind and our sails are in. There's nothing more to do but ride it out."

It was his turn to be silent for a moment; then, of all things, he smiled again, a wicked, go-to-the-devil smile, and his beautiful eyes became brilliant in the gloomy light. "A race to Nassau, that's all I wanted. And look what you got me into, woman—a damnable hurricane. Genny, I wonder if I should beat you now or later."

"So this god-awful storm is my fault?"

"I suppose not. Let's get out of this wretched rain. You said everything's battened down?"

"Unlike your cumbersome barkentine, sir, my clipper has very little to batten down. Shall we go to the cabin? I'm leaving only three men topside. No need for everyone to be miserable at once." She paused a moment, then continued deliberately. "If the worst happens, there'll be time to come up on deck."

Alec didn't like the sound of that, but there wasn't a thing he could do about it. In all his years of traversing both the Atlantic and the

Pacific, he'd endured his share of storms, but never before had he been in anything like this, in anything that resembled a hurricane of this force. Nothing that could rip his barkentine to pulpy shards. He stopped in his tracks. "You've strapped Daniels to the wheel?"

She nodded. "Who knows how the winds will behave? O'Shay didn't suggest that?"

"Likely he will soon. After you, wife."

But Genny suddenly balked. She'd wanted Alec here with her more than anything, and for a moment she'd forgotten that the *Pegasus* was her responsibility and hers alone. The men who sailed the clipper were also her responsibility. "I'm the captain, Alec. I can't leave Daniels here alone."

"What would you do were you to stay here?"

"Talk to him. Help him get through things. Give him orders if necessary."

Now that, Alec thought, momentarily nonplussed, was a kicker. He said easily, his words blurred by the winds, "Come down with me just for a little while, then, love. Just to change into dry clothes."

Genny nodded. That was fine with her. She wanted to hold him, to reassure herself that he was all right and that he was hers.

In the captain's cabin, Genny lit the lantern, then made certain that it was securely fastened to the desktop. All any vessel needed in a hurricane was a fire. She turned to face her husband. "You took a risk with that jump, Alec. I was never so scared in all my life. You could have broken something."

"Would you have cared?"

She grinned. "A bit, I suppose. After all, you were my valiant knight leaping through gloom to be at my side."

"Actually, I was just concerned about my clipper."

"No one risks dying for a thing, Alec," she said mildly, not to be drawn.

"You're right about that, wife. I didn't hurt a thing, so you can forget it now. I might begin to think you're showing wifely concern, Genny."

"I'd have to shoot you if you'd broken your leg, and I don't happen to have a pistol with me."

He chuckled with her. "Off with those wet clothes."

"What about you?"

He looked thoughtful. "I suppose it's under the covers with me. Will you join me?"

She looked at him as if he'd lost his mind. "Alec, we're in the middle of a hurricane. You want me to get into bed with you?"

"Why not? There's nothing we can do about nature. We'll either die in the next twenty-four hours or we won't."

"You're sounding mighty philosophical about the end of things."

"Shush. Listen, Genny. Where's the wind?"

Dead silence. She felt prickles of apprehension crawl over her flesh.

"We're in the eye of the storm," she whispered into the silence.

"How long will it last?"

"I don't know." She stripped off her oilskins. Alec was out of his clothing in a thrice and under the warm covers of the bunk. They were blessedly dry.

Genny was listening to the absolute silence, standing in the middle of the cabin with but a wet shirt on.

"Genny, come here now—it's cold."

She jumped at his voice, wheeled about to look at him, realized she was nearly naked, and squeaked.

He laughed. "Come here."

She did, quickly, slipping off the shirt and easing in beside him as he lifted the covers for her. "Not long, Alec. I must go topside soon."

Alec drew her against the length of him. He smelled her wool cap and pulled it off her head, tossing it to the floor near the cabin door. "Shall I unbraid your hair for you?"

"No. I'll be going back on deck in a little while. I don't need pounds of hair plastered to my face."

Alec frowned over her head and decided it was best to just come out with it. "Genny, love, you aren't going anywhere until the hurricane is through with us."

"What do you mean? What are you talking about?"

"Just what I said. Be reasonable. I want you here, in this cabin, in this bunk, safe."

She grew as still as the wind. "So that's why you risked your life to leap like a wild man onto my clipper. You didn't want to be with me. You wanted to take over. You didn't trust me—a simple-witted women—to do what is right and proper."

"Yes and no to that," Alec said. He wasn't a

310

fool. She was stiff as a board in his arms. Damnation, why couldn't she be reasonable about things? He didn't want to argue with her. He knew what was right and he intended that it be done. He said as much, his voice calm, reasonable. "I mean what I said. You'll remain in the cabin, safe. I've just commandeered your vessel."

"The devil you have!"

She wrenched away from him, smashing her fist against his shoulder and landing on her bottom on the cabin floor. It was very cold. Genny grabbed for her flannel robe and jerked it over her shoulders. "Stay away from me, Alec!"

He subsided back into the bunk, lying on his side, watching her with narrowed eyes that held absolutely no amusement.

"It's cold," he said, even as he braced himself to keep from being thrown from the bunk. He watched her slide leeward, then catch hold of the desk leg.

"I'll be just fine, thank you." She pulled herself to her feet and jerked the sash tightly about her waist. The clipper lurched to port; she lost her hold and went flying across the cabin. She grabbed the doorknob and steadied herself. She looked back to see if Alec prepared to leap out of the bunk just as he'd leaped from the barkentine.

"Don't you dare move!"

"Genny, I will tell you once more—come here. It's dangerous out there, as you've just seen. I don't want you to fall and hurt yourself."

"Go to the devil, Alec." She turned away, lurching with the clipper, and eased her sore bottom into the desk chair. She pulled it close to the desk, leaned her elbows on the desktop, and stared at him. She steepled her fingers and rested her chin on them. She said slowly, easily, only a trace of fury underlying her words, "I am the captain of this vessel, sir. I wouldn't care if you were President Monroe. It makes less than no difference that you are my husband. It changes nothing."

Alec tamped down firmly on his anger. It burned brightly inside him, but he could control it. He understood her position, at least vaguely, but that wasn't the point. "Please listen to me, wife, for I really have no taste for repetition. I am fully and completely in charge aboard this vessel. It is my responsibility as your husband, as a competent man, to ensure your safety to the best of my abilities. You will remain in this cabin even if I have to tie you to this bunk. Do you understand me, Genny?"

The clipper swayed and plunged, heaving and bucking like an unbroken horse. The two of them scarce noticed.

"We're no longer in the eye of the storm."

"True enough. Would you listen to that wind! Do you understand me, Genny?"

What to do? He was the stronger and could thus enforce his will. It wasn't fair, but railing wouldn't help matters. She fell back on reason.

"It's my vessel, Alec."

"No, it isn't. You have been the captain on sufferance, nothing more. If you wreck her, I will lose a good deal of money."

He'd gone too far with that jab and her fury erupted. She came to her feet, her palms flat on the desktop. "You would take everything from me! I won't let you, Baron Sherard, you damned bloody English clod!" In a flash, she grabbed up dry clothing and rushed to the cabin door. Alec was faster. He caught her arm and jerked her back against him and folded his arms over her breasts.

"Oh, no, Genny, you've had your say and you've tried your best. You lost, my girl, fair and square."

"There's nothing at all fair about any of it. Let me go, Alec. I am the captain. Let me go!"

He didn't release her, but she managed to twist about and kick him in the shin.

The howling of the wind didn't drown out his grunt of pain. Well, she'd gotten him that time. He would have laughed if they weren't struck in a bare protected inlet, headed into the wind, waiting for a hurricane to go about its business and not kill them.

He leaned down and kissed her, hard. Her lips were cold and pursed. He raised his head just as she opened her mouth, not to kiss him back, but to bite him. He grinned down at her, although there was no reflected amusement in his eyes.

Genny was panting, wishing she could kick him higher, in his groin. But he was holding her too tight, too close.

"You just wanted me down here so you could have sex with me. Then like a swaggering male, you'd leave me here and go save the damned world!"

"No, just the damned clipper. And yes, I want to have sex with you. You're my wife. We might not be alive tomorrow. Why not? Perhaps it will soften you, Genny, make you realize that you're really a woman, and that a woman should be giving and yielding and submissive—"

He thought she'd growl in accompaniment to the wind, but she said nothing. He felt a stab of guilt but only briefly, for she managed to send her fist with a goodly amount of strength into his naked belly.

"Enough," he said and dragged her to the bunk. He held her there, stripped off her dressing gown, then lifted her, tossing her onto her back. He came over her hard, knocking the breath out of her. She lay there panting, looking up at him, feeling his hands prying her thighs apart.

"No, Alec, no."

"Why not? You're mine, Genny, this wretched clipper is mine, and we might well die before morning. Why not?"

Unfortunately, whilst he'd given her his declamation, she managed to loosen his grip on her left wrist. She jerked free, bucked upward frantically, smashing her fist into his neck, his shoulder. Alec saw red. He jerked her arms above her head and slammed his body down over hers.

"Does this remind you of another evening, Genny?"

She was staring up at him, mute.

"Does it? Remember, you silly girl, that night aboard my barkentine? I tied your hands over your head and gave you your first dose of woman's pleasure. You went crazy with it. You howled as loud as the wind is howling right now, you loved it so much. Remember how I caressed

314

you with my fingers and then my mouth? Remember how your legs parted for me, wider and wider? And I didn't have to force you to part your thighs, dear one, you were eager to do it. You were eager for whatever I would give you."

The clipper suddenly slammed to starboard. "Jesus," Alec said under his breath. He wanted to punish her, to prove to her that she was his and it was his will that would dominate. But the wild shimmying of the clipper held him still. He knew deep, gut-wrenching fear. He drew an unsteady breath. "I'm going above. You will remain here."

He knew she wouldn't. The moment he swung his legs off the bunk, she bounced up, ready to fight him.

He tied her down again, just as he had that other, long-ago evening. Only this time, he told himself, it was for her own good. It had nothing to do with sex, damn her stubborn hide.

She yelled at him, snarled at him, until he'd securely tied her wrists above her head, her ankles to the posts. He took a moment to look at her lovely body, then pulled all the covers firmly over her. "You'll be warm enough. I'll be down soon to check on you."

"You'll let me drown here!"

He dressed in his sodden clothes, grimacing as he did so, ignoring her foolish words. There was nothing worse than wet clothing.

"Don't do this to me, Alec."

She didn't sound furious, nor was she pleading. She sounded . . . desperate somehow. He turned and frowned at her. "I can't trust you, Genny. I care about you and—"

"And you tied me down to the damned bunk?"

"Yes. You'll be safe here."

"Ha! If we sink, I'll have no chance to save myself and I'll drown like a trapped rat.

She could be right about that, but he didn't think so. "I'm going above to check on Daniels. I'll be back soon. I'll think about it."

And he was gone. At least he'd left the lantern lit.

To think that she'd actually prayed for him to be safe! She was a fool—no, she was much more than a fool. She was an idiot woman and he'd won.

That stark fact drove her into a frenzy. She pulled and tugged and jerked, but the bonds about her wrists stayed firm. Then she forced herself to calm. She took several deep breaths. She listened to the sounds of the clipper. The seasoned oak timbers were creaking slightly as the *Pegasus* turned one way, then the other. The wind was shrieking louder now. The crisis was close.

She had to get free. But calmly, slowly; she had to prove herself more adept than the bonds around her wrists, smarter than the damnable man who'd tied her down.

She set herself to work.

"Daniels? Would you like me to take over for a while?"

"My lord! No, sir, I'm fine. Holding her steady,

sir, with the shifting winds, it's difficult. I'm fine for a while yet."

Alec nodded and looked over at the barkentine. She was plunging and twisting but riding high and steady, as could be expected. While the clipper—but it felt like he was in a toy boat.

The wind whipped about, flipping the clipper to starboard, then to port. The rain lashed down, stinging the men's faces. Freezing sheets of water slammed over the decks.

"She's a good vessel, my lord," Snugger said, struggling against the wind as he came up behind Alec. "Where's the capt'n?"

"She's in the cabin, resting for a moment."

"Ah," said Daniels, and gave Alec a troubled sideways glance.

Suddenly the wind shifted once again, bearing directly against the bow, then just as quickly tore to starboard. Alec heard a loud creaking. Daniels, Snugger, and Alec looked at the foremast.

"Oh, my God!"

The mast was being bent back with such force that the men knew it couldn't hold. There was a great ripping sound, coming from the very bowels of the clipper's belly.

Just then Alec saw the white flash of a man's shirt. He was rushing toward the mast, screaming, "Hank! Hank, I'm coming!"

It didn't occur to Alec to hesitate. He felt the wind grab him, jerk him about, as he raced forward.

"My lord, stop! No!"

It was over in an instant. Genny came through the hatch at the moment the foremast cracked.

It was like the thundering of a loud cannon shot. The mast splintered and sheared nearly in two, coming down with the sails wrapped around it like a huge arrow falling from the heavens.

She screamed as Alec disappeared under the masses of rigging and white canvas.

She heard yelling, but it sounded like blurred whispers in the mouth of the howling, maddened wind. Men were rushing, heads down against the wind, toward the broken mast. It lay crookedly, half of it over the port side of the clipper, a huge splintered gash halfway up its length.

Genny plunged toward the fallen mast, feeling the wind pulling her toward the side, yet through her will alone she kept going, toward Alec.

The whole feel of the clipper changed with the broken mast. Despite the fact that the canvas had been fully furled, it had still added stability to the center of the clipper. Now it was as if the world were spinning wildly, freely, with no center. She heard Daniels cursing, but she didn't look back.

Two men were digging through the masses of wet canvas. There were three men buried there. And Alec was one of them. She heard a moan. It was from Hank. The man who'd tried to save him—Riffer—was dead. She fell to her knees beside Alec, saw the gash in his head, and quickly pulled off her wool cap and pressed it to the wound. He seemed to have escaped other injury.

"Wake up! Wake up, you wretched stubborn Englishman!"

"Let's get him below, Capt'n," said Snugger, lightly touching her shoulder.

"He won't wake up, Snugger."

"I wouldn't either, given the situation we're in now, Capt'n. Come along, now. Cleb, give me a hand. You others, take Hank below and strap him in his hammock. You, Griff, see if you can help him." Snugger paused, staring a moment at Riffer.

Genny brought herself back to her responsibilities. "Riffer's dead. Send him overboard. We'll say prayers for him later, that or we'll join him."

Snugger nodded.

It seemed an eternity to Genny before Alec, stripped and beneath mounds of covers, was safe as he could be in the bunk in the captain's cabin. She sent Snugger back on deck to relieve Daniels. She knew she was acting on instinct now—washing the wound, patting it dry with bascilicum powder. The wound wasn't too deep, not enough for stitches. Satisfied, she ripped off a strip of dry shirt and wrapped it around Alec's head.

Why didn't he wake up?

She kept him warm, covering him with every blanket in the chest. Then she knew she had to go on deck. It was her vessel, her responsibility, and one man had already died. She tied Alec to the bunk as best she could and went topside.

"The winds have risen," Snugger said.

"The sky's as black as the devil," Daniels said and spat into a huge wave that was breaking over the deck.

"Blacker," Genny said. She glanced over to the barkentine and was relieved to see that it was holding as steady as could be expected.

"How's his lordship?"

"I don't know. I tied him to the bunk. He's still unconscious. The wound in his head isn't all that deep. I don't know why he won't wake up."

Snugger recognized strength when he saw it. She was terrified that her husband would die, terrified that they would all feed the fish off Ocracoke Island, but she kept her control, kept her head. In a burst of feeling, he hugged Genny to him. "It'll all go better, you'll see. We'll make it. Yes, we'll make it."

A stupid wager and she'd nearly destroyed the clipper. She looked at the broken mast. It would take hours and a lot of money to repair it. *If* they returned safely to Baltimore.

The hours marched slowly forward.

The winds howled and screamed like banshees from the pit of hell. The waves lifted the clipper high, then brought her down into deep troughs, slinging mountains of freezing water over her decks.

The hours marched.

Genny was staring down at Alec. He was pale his lips bloodless. She touched her fingers to his cheek. "Please," she said softly, "please don't die, Alec. I couldn't bear it, you know."

The hours marched.

It was at four o'clock in the morning when the winds slacked off.

Genny was afraid to say anything. No one said anything. They felt bowed with superstition.

As it grew light, she saw the barkentine, saw a man waving toward them. She waved back. She heard him yell, "We're bloody well alive, ma'am!"

He's English, she thought, and laughed.

Soon Snugger and Daniels were laughing. She heard laughter from Alec's men on the barkentine.

The skies were lighter now, a dull pinkish gray. The wind had fallen sharply. The rains had diminished to a slight drizzle.

"It's over!"

Genny stayed on deck for another half hour. There were orders to be given, tasks to be seen to, repairs to be made. "We'll hold our position here for several more hours until we know the extent of our damage. At least we've got the bark to help us back to Baltimore."

Finally she went below.

Alec was still just as pale and just as unconscious. She quickly untied the rope from around his chest. He was shivering.

Genny didn't hesitate. She stripped off her wet clothes, dried herself, and slipped into bed beside her husband. She drew him to her, rubbing her hands up and down his back, trying to warm him. His big body was shaking.

"Alec, love," she said over and over, rubbing her hands over his body. "Please, come back to me."

He was warming and she felt another wild spurt of triumph. "Alec," she said again, and hugged him to her fiercely. She felt his warm breath against her throat.

He stirred. She came up onto her elbow, not even aware that she was naked and that her breasts were pressed against his chest. "Come now, wake up."

He opened his beautiful eyes and looked up at her. He frowned then and he looked down at her breasts. He still said nothing and looked into her face again.

"This is all very nice," he said at last, his voice low and raw.

She smiled, leaned down, and lightly kissed his mouth.

"Hello. How do you feel?"

"Like the very devil. My head is still on my neck?"

"Yes."

"You're very pretty but your hair is wet."

"To be expected. It will dry soon. We're safe, Alec. The hurricane has changed direction, headed out into the Atlantic, and left us alone. Your bark is fine. We lost one man, however."

He was frowning again. "It's very nice of you to be here in bed with me."

She cocked her eyebrow at him. Did he believe she'd leave him to fend for himself, given the way he'd treated her? "You were shivering from shock," she said with a slight smile. "You needed my warmth."

"Yes, that's a good enough reason, I suppose. I should thank you. Did we make love?"

"I think that should wait for a while. Until you're a bit better."

"All right," he said and closed his eyes. "My head does hurt abominably. I just don't want you to think I don't appreciate your, er, charms. You have beautiful breasts."

Genny looked down at herself. "I don't mean to be immodest, Alec, it's just that—"

"No need to explain. Except for just one thing. As I told you, this is all very nice. However, I would like to know who you are."

18

Genny stared down at him, nonplussed. "What did you say?"

He wanted to explain more fully, but he found that his head hurt too much for him to want to make the effort. He also found that he couldn't. It was too confusing.

"I don't know who you are," he said again, more slowly this time because it hurt his head to say each word.

"You're saying you don't recognize me?"

"That's right." He closed his eyes at her appalled voice and Genny saw the furrows of pain beside his mouth, the pallor of his flesh. *He couldn't remember her? That was insane, impossible!* She lightly touched her fingertips to the bandage around his head. She'd heard from someone a long time ago that blows to the head could produce forgetfulness, but she'd never before seen such a thing. Alec couldn't remember *her?*

This was madness.

Genny felt sudden embarrassment. But she didn't want to leave him. She could feel her body heat going into him. He needed her, and he needed her just as she was, bare-fleshed and pressed against him. She lowered herself a bit more until her breasts were again flattened against his chest. "Alec, listen to me. You're my husband. My name is Genny. I'm your wife."

He grew very still. "My wife? But I wouldn't marry, I know that somehow. . . . Married? I can't imagine marrying, but—" He shook his head, wincing with the pain it brought him. "You called me Alec. Alec what?"

Genny drew a deep breath. "Actually, I couldn't imagine you marrying either. Or me, for that matter. Oh, dear. This is going to be excessively difficult. There's a lot to tell you. First of all, your name is Alec Carrick, fifth Baron Sherard. Next, we just survived a hurricane in a Baltimore clipper schooner."

He considered this and said, "I thought your accent was different. You're an American?"

"Yes, and you're an Englishman. Now, you just lie still and I'll tell you about things."

"All right."

Where to begin? "Well, you came to Baltimore only a month ago to look over my shipyard. My father and I needed a partner, one with money. You thought I was Mr. Eugene Paxton, but I wasn't really, and you realized it almost immediately and took me to a brothel to punish me and make me confess and—"

He moaned. "Did I really do that? Take you to a brothel?"

She grinned down at him. "Yes, you did, that's not the half of it, sir. Then . . ."

Alec fell asleep long before she'd finished her recital. His color was better, she thought, studying his impossibly handsome features. He

324

was breathing easily; his body was warm. She carefully unwound the bandage from his head and examined the wound. The flesh was pink and healthy-looking.

Dull gray light came through the stern windows into the cabin. It was better than rain, that was certain. Genny rebandaged Alec's head, then eased slowly out of the bunk, careful not to disturb her sleeping husband.

My husband of less than a week and he doesn't know who I am.

Life had sometimes been a bit tedious before Alec had come to Baltimore. Now it was nothing but one surprise after another. But this surprise he hadn't intended. It was nearly beyond belief. She couldn't take it all in, even now. What about him? How was he feeling? She couldn't begin to imagine. She did know that he needed her, and that all the rules had changed.

He was breathing deeply and slowly. Healthy sleep. She dressed in dry clothing and went on deck.

"How is Hank?" Genny asked Daniels.

"He'll be up and about in a couple of days. Bruised like a Continental flag, but all right. His lordship?"

"Like Hank, he'll be all right in a couple of days. But there is one thing . . ."

"Yes?"

"He doesn't know who he is, Daniels, or who I am, or anything about the race, the wager—nothing."

"You mean that blow on the head gave him aneri—amosei—"

"Amnesia, I think it's called. That's it. His head was hurting badly, but he's sleeping now."

"My God."

"Yes," said Genny and turned to look at the great splinted mast that lay nearly the length of the deck, then out over the water, its canvas trailing white against the blue of the sea. Its splintered stalk stood six or so feet off the deck, and looked incredibly fragile. "I must stay close to him. Can you imagine not knowing who you are?" She shook her head at her own question and could only begin to imagine the fear that would accompany such a realization.

"What are we going to do?"

"Why, take him back to Baltimore, of course. I need to speak to Alec's first mate and to O'Shay. We'll be able to maneuver a bit, but I want the bark to stay close."

"And the mast?"

Genny looked thoughtfully at the sixty-odd feet of spruce. Her mind went blank for a moment at the notion of the replacement cost. Then she shook her head. "Let the mast remain where it is. Have one of the men crawl out and secure the canvas to the mast so there isn't so much drag. The last thing we want is for the mast to pull the ship over. Also, have it lashed more securely to the railing."

"Aye, aye, Capt'n," said Snugger and grinned at her.

Alec lay in the bunk, not moving, simply staring at the cabin furnishings. He'd memorized them. It was a hell of a lot better than thinking and thinking and trying to figure out who he was, what he'd been. His head hurt.

He was scared. He didn't like to be scared. It wasn't an emotion he was particularly used to. It went to part and parcel with helplessness and that was unacceptable to him. He cursed softly. At least he hadn't forgotten how to do that. He forced himself to concentrate on the carving on the captain's desk. It was intricate, obviously done by a superb craftsman. For an instant, he saw a man sitting cross-legged on the floor, an array of knives and other tools beside him on a flat cloth, and he was carving on this desk. The man was dark and full-bearded. Alec tried desperately to cling to him, but he was gone in the next instant.

Well, it had been something. He would ask Genny about him.

When she walked into the cabin his first words were, "The man who carved this desk, describe him to me."

"He's very dark, middle-aged, I guess you'd say, and he has more hair than half a dozen men."

"Ah."

Genny moved closer and stood staring down at him. He took her hand and pulled her onto the bunk. "I saw him," Alec said. "Just for a moment, but I saw him."

Genny's face lit up. "That's wonderful!" Without thinking about it, she leaned down, clasped his face between her hands, and kissed him soundly. He grew very still. She raised her head and stared at him.

"Genny," he said. He brought her head back

down, holding her with his hand cupped about the nape of her neck.

He kissed her this time, slowly, but she tasted his hunger and responded to it.

"You're my wife," he said into her mouth, his breath warm and sweet from the wine he'd drunk at lunch earlier. "My wife."

But he didn't remember her. It was as if he sensed her restraint, her uncertainty, the strangeness between them. He released her and watched her through troubled eyes as she straightened.

"We're moving slowly, as you can feel, but we are moving. Your bark is staying close. I left the mast where it landed. It isn't too much of a drag on us. Mr. Pitts sent over clothing for you. Actually, it was flung over and landed on deck, thank God. If you would like to dress, I'll help you."

"When do you think we'll be back in Baltimore?"

"At our impressive rate of speed, I'd say another three days. It's very slow going, Alec."

"I have a daughter."

"Yes, you have. Do you remember her name?"

Alec gave her a sour look. "Do you think the blow made me into a village idiot as well as blanking out my memory? I'm not an imbecile, Genny. You told me about Hallie. What does she look like?"

"Like you. In other words, she's incredibly beautiful."

He frowned at her. "Beautiful? I'm a man, Genny. That's absurd."

"No, it's quite true. You are, at least in my humble opinion, the most handsome man God ever made. Well, no, that's not really true. It's more than just my opinion. You see, Alec, you walk down a street and women turn and stare at you. They look hungry."

"That's ridiculous," he said, scowling ferociously. "Give me a mirror."

Genny rose and rummaged through her chest. She found a silver-backed mirror that had been her mother's. She handed it to him silently.

Alec stared at a pale-faced stranger. He didn't know his own face. "Beautiful? Dear God, I have enough stubble for half a dozen men. A desperate need to shave, that's all I can see."

She smiled at him, shaking her head. "I can do that for you, if you like. Also, if you would like to bathe . . ."

"Yes," he said. "I should like that very much. Then you can tell me more about my background."

"I don't know any more than I've already told you, Alec. We've not known each other long, and you know much more about me than I do about you. You're Alec Carrick, Baron Sherard. I know you have a number of homes in England, but you've never told me where they are."

"I see. Yes, I remember now, you mentioned that before."

"And you were married, but your wife—her name was Nesta—she died birthing Hallie."

In that instant, something opened in his mind. It was like a door suddenly swinging wide, and he saw a laughing young woman, her belly swelled with child, and she was saying something to him about presents for their people. Then he saw her lying on her back in bed, and her eyes were open but they were staring, and he knew she was dead. "Oh, God. I just saw her. Nesta, I mean. She was alive and then she was just . . . dead."

Genny heard the anguish in his voice and rushed to sit beside him. She stroked his jaw with her fingertips. "I'm so sorry, Alec. Don't let these things hurt you. You'll remember good things, too, not just bad parts. Remember your image of Mimms? It wasn't bad."

She shaved him, then had a bucket of hot water fetched. He insisted that he could bathe himself. She supposed even a man—a creature who didn't seem to have a modest bone in his body—was reticent with a woman who claimed she was his wife but whom he couldn't remember. So she left him, praying he was strong enough not to fall and break a leg.

When she returned, he was fully dressed, sitting at the desk, studying some papers.

"My, don't you look ready for the Assembly Room."

"Assembly Room? You have those in the colonies?"

"Don't be a snob. Wait, you know there are assembly rooms in England?"

"Yes, I know. I don't know how I know, but I do. You're captaining this vessel?"

"Yes." Unconsciously she raised her chin just a bit, waiting for him to say something, to insist that she wasn't capable, that he would take over now.

But he didn't. He merely sat there, a thoughtful expression on his face. "I imagine that is very unusual," he said finally. "You, a woman, being captain of a vessel."

"I suppose it is, but you needn't worry. I'm quite good."

He gave her a warm smile. "If I married you, I would assume that you are more than good. Superior, I should say."

She said very slowly, simply staring at him, "You don't mind me being your captain?"

"Why should I? You got us through a hurricane, you said. You seem intelligent and well spoken. As for how you are in bed, well, as I said, you have beautiful breasts. For the rest of it, time will tell."

"Time usually does."

They both fell silent, Genny thinking that it was stranger than Alec could possibly imagine. Here he was, not minding at all that she was captain. As if to reflect her thoughts, he said, "This is the oddest thing."

"What is?"

"Sitting here, on board a vessel, not knowing who I am and wondering why I'm not the captain. I know deep down somewhere that I should be."

She said carefully, trying to keep her voice on an even keel, "You were the captain of the barkentine that follows just behind us. It's your vessel, in fact. You own about half a dozen, I believe you told me."

He waved aside her comment. "Yes, I know, but that's not it." He sighed then and absently rubbed at the clean bandage wrapped around his forehead. "Don't mind me. It's just—"

"Don't be absurd, Alec. You're aboard my

clipper and thus my responsibility, and besides, I happen to care about you. I know you must be feeling tip over arse—"

"Tip over what?" A beautiful smile appeared. It was as if the sun had just broken through the clouds to shine on her head.

"It's just a saying."

"Did I catch my modest little wife saying something naughty?"

"Just a bit naughty."

"Shall I punish you? Perhaps bring you across my legs and pull down those ridiculous breeches you're wearing?"

"Alec! Now I see that you simply don't forget some things. You're outrageous and will always be so, memory or no memory."

He leaned his head back, suddenly exhausted.

"Come to bed," she said, her hand lightly on his forearm.

"Will you come with me?"

"Yes."

If he'd had any sexual thoughts in his mind, they disappeared in a thrice. Genny scarce had time to curl up against his side before he was breathing evenly and deeply in sleep.

"I do wonder what I would have done if you had proved amorous," she said aloud to herself, then rose to leave him. "I probably would have delighted in everything you did to me." She shook her head, suddenly bemused. Would he remember how to make love? Remember all the wonderful things he did? She supposed she would see soon enough. She left him. He slept throughout the afternoon.

"North Point, at last," Snugger said with great satisfaction.

"Nearly home," Daniels added.

Alec stood silent, staring toward the city of Baltimore. He looked toward Fort McHenry and a memory flickered briefly. Then he looked toward Fells Point. "The Paxton shipyard is there, isn't it?"

"Yes," said Snugger.

Alec merely nodded and answered a shout from Abel Pitts on the barkentine.

He remembered Nesta—an odd name—and he'd briefly seen a face, a laughing, pretty face. Then he'd seen her dead. Soon he would see his daughter. That was an awesome thought. He needed to ask Genny more about Hallie. He didn't want the child to be frightened of him.

"Hello."

"Hello yourself," he said, turning to face his male-clothed wife. He eyed the wool cap and the loose blouse with its leather vest. "I want to see you in a gown."

"You will."

"This wager. Tell me about it again."

She'd given him the barest outline. It didn't occur to her to lie to him, to twist things to her advantage. "The problem," she finished some minutes later, "is that the conclusion is inconclusive, I guess you'd say. Who is the winner? I think we both are, since we both survived. But what to do? I don't know, Alec. I would prefer—" She broke off, studying her fingernails.

'You would prefer that I deed the shipyard over to you and leave you alone?"

"Yes, no, well, half of that."

"Which half?"

"The shipyard. It's mine. It should stay mine."

"Why did your father make his will to your disadvantage? Were you at odds with him?"

She swallowed. "No, it wasn't like that at all. Oh, I might as well tell you all of it."

He said, very softly, "Did you lie to me?"

"Don't be ridiculous. Now listen to me, we haven't much time before we dock. My father was sick. I was running the shipyard. I was building the *Pegasus*. The problem was that none of the wonderful men of Baltimore would buy her simply because I—a woman—was responsible for building her. Well my father thought I would lose everything if he died. And he cared mightily for you and your daughter. He even invited you and Hallie to come and live with us, which you did. Then he decided that you would make him a fine son-in-law. He willed the shipyard to you with the proviso that you marry me. It was you who came up with the wager—"

"As salve to your pride?"

That was it exactly. "That sounds awfully bald."

"But true. Now, my dear Genny, what the devil are we going to do? If I deed the shipyard over to you, you will lose everything. Even you admit that."

"Perhaps."

"You got us through the hurricane. I think you're a fine captain, despite the weakness of your sex. No, don't draw up on me, I'm just teasing you. Incidentally, what was I doing on the clipper? Why wasn't I captaining my own vessel?"

It was now time for a lie, a wonderful bouncing lie. It came out of her mouth with scarce a pause, her conscience telling her that it was a bit true, a very little bit true. "You thought we were going to drown. You wanted to be with me."

He frowned at that. "But you said I married you only because of the shipyard."

"You did—do—like me, I think."

"Since I don't know myself, I can't be certain, but it seems to me, Genny, that I most certainly wouldn't marry a woman that I simply *liked*."

"You'd also seduced me."

"Good God. I must have enjoyed that. Did you enjoy your seduction?"

Her eyes never left his face. She smiled. "Immensely."

"Were you a virgin?"

"Yes. You called me a long-in-the-tooth virgin."

"So I married you because I'd deflowered you and because of the shipyard?"

"You were quite fond of my father also."

"Captain!"

"Yes, Snugger?" She turned to speak to her first mate. She added to Alec with a pleasant smile, "Excuse me. I must see to things. Just relax, and stop worrying."

But he couldn't, of course.

335

They docked before he had a chance to ask more about his daughter. And there she was, waiting on the wharf with an older woman, gaunt and severe-looking as the devil.

"Papa!"

That was him, he supposed, taking in the child's features and reflecting that they were very much like his own. He waved to her and called out, "Hello, Hallie."

"Did you win?"

"I'll tell you everything soon."

His daughter knew of the blasted wager? Then he saw many people converging on the two vessels, men and women alike. What was he, a local diversion? He simply didn't understand all this interest.

"They're all here to see who won," Genny said, and realized in that moment that she should have told him all of the truth. She sighed. "Just follow my lead, Alec. No one need know that you cracked your head into oblivion. I spoke to Daniels and Snugger. They won't say anything."

"You think not?"

"No, I don't think so, but if they do, we've at least bought some time. I want to get you home and into bed."

His head was aching just a bit, not enough to prevent a lecherous smile from appearing.

She grinned up at him and poked him in the ribs. "There's your daughter. Mrs. Swindel, her companion and nanny, is with her. She's romancing Dr. Pruitt, your ship's doctor. They're both kindhearted, but in their view of the world there's always a black lining to the clouds, even on a sunny day."

She stopped, seeing his brow furrow in concentration and in pain.

Genny had been wrong. No one spoke of the wager. It was the hurricane that held everyone's interest, and how they'd survived it. The crowd marveled at the broken mast on the clipper, some men shaking their heads, saying it proved the design was unsafe, others saying it was stupid to sail in this weather to Nassau. She even heard one of the men say that it was likely her fault that the mast had been broken. There were nods and murmurs of agreement. She stiffened like a poker, the smile on her face a mask.

She watched the gentlemen clap Alec on the back, saw him respond with automatic politeness. The women were equally as outgoing as the men. Genny saw Laura Salmon give Alec a trollop look and ground her teeth.

Well, not really a *trollop* look, she supposed in all fairness, but it was a look of vast female appreciation.

Alec responded with a different kind of politeness; she recognized it and knew it came quite naturally to him, this charming arrogance he adopted with women. When he finally reached his daughter, he simply stared down at her for a moment, then said, "Hallie."

"Papa!" Her arms went up and Alec quickly lifted her and felt her arms go around his neck. She gave him a wet kiss on his cheek and hugged him as hard as she could. "I missed you, Papa. So much, but Genny was with you. When we

337

heard about the hurricane, Mrs. Swindel said you'd be all right. She said you were like a damned cat and—"

"That's quite enough, Miss Hallie," said Eleanor Swindel, gaining two patches of color on her thin cheeks.

"I had Genny to take care of me," Alec said.

Hallie cocked her head to one side in bewilderment.

"What's the matter, Hallie?"

Genny, hearing this exchange, quickly stepped forward. "Hallie doesn't mean anything, do you, pumpkin?"

"I suppose I don't," Hallie said slowly. She kissed her father again and settled in his arms.

"Does this mean that I'm to carry you all the way home?"

"Yes, Papa."

Genny laughed. "I'll have a carriage fetched for us. Just stay here and visit, Alec. All those gentlemen still wish to speak to you."

His daughter, Alec thought, and he hadn't felt the slightest glimmer of recognition. This beautiful child was of his loins, but she could have been anyone's child for all he knew. He felt the small body warm against him. His daughter. He hugged her and Hallie giggled.

"You're home," she said.

But where the devil was home when you had no memory of anything at all?

He tried to keep the paralyzing fear at bay but he couldn't, not indefinitely. His head began to ache again.

"Soon we'll be home," Genny said, and took his hand.

"Tell me all about the hurricane," Hallie said that evening when they were seated at the dining table.

Alec paused, his soup spoon midway to his mouth. "Genny will tell you, Hallie."

Hallie, all unsuspecting, turned to her step-mother. "Were you scared?"

"More than you can imagine. Let me see. We were winning—my clipper, that is—then the storm hit. It was like a hundred winds howling at once, like a band of crazy witches, and all coming at you from different directions. They were so wild and strong that if you weren't careful, they'd just pick you up and toss you over-board. Your papa was very brave. During the hurricane he wanted to come to me, so he brought his barkentine as close as he could and then he jumped to the deck of the clipper."

"Oh, Papa, surely that wasn't very wise!" Hallie then giggled. "But it is very romantic."

Alec just nodded. Genny wished she could cry for him, yell his frustration for him, but she couldn't, of course.

"But you could have been hurt."

Alec spooned down another mouthful of the sweet turtle soup.

"I wasn't," he said shortly.

"Does your head hurt, Alec?" Genny asked.

"No." His voice was curt but he couldn't help it.

"Did you take over the *Pegasus?*"

Alec frowned and Genny quickly said, "Certainly not, Hallie. I was captain of the *Pegasus*. Your father just wanted to be with me. We didn't know if we would survive the hurricane."

"That's odd."

"What is?" Alec asked, bending his attention to his daughter. "Eat your soup," he added.

"That you didn't take over and become the captain. That's not right, Papa."

"Hallie, don't you like the turtle soup?"

"Just a moment, Genny. What do you mean, Hallie?"

"Papa, you're not acting right. You seem different, like you aren't really you, but that's silly—"

"Yes, it is, excessively silly. Eat your soup. Genny and I are both very tired."

Hallie, hurt, retreated to her soup.

Genny said not another word until she asked Moses for the next course.

An hour later, in their bedchamber, Alec said in a very weary voice to Genny, "The child is very bright. I won't be able to fool her for long."

"Don't worry about it now, Alec. You need rest, lots of it. Would you like to see the doctor tomorrow?"

"I don't want to think about tomorrow," he said, and tossed his discarded shirt to a chairback. "I want to think about tonight and making love to my wife."

19

Genny turned slowly to face him. Her fingers, busily unfastening the buttons on her gown, stilled. "You put things baldly," she said, not looking at him above his neck.

"Is that something new or have you known me to do that before?"

"Oh, you're always saying the unexpected, the outrageous. You bait me very easily, for I'm the perfect foil for you."

"You always rise to the bait?" He was unbuttoning his breeches now. It hurt her to look at him. In the candlelight, he was achingly beautiful, all shadows and planes and sinew. She sighed.

"Always."

"Genny, don't—*didn't* you enjoy making love with me?"

"I don't think 'enjoy' is really the right word. Actually, you touch me and I want you madly, wildly. It's very worrisome, particularly since only a short time ago I was a virgin with no thought of not being one."

He gave her a very male smile. "That's nice."

Some things, she thought, a male simply never forgot.

She raised her chin. Tit for tat, she thought. "You also melt when I touch you."

His left brow arched at that. "I don't know if I particularly care for that concept. I prefer being rigid, turgid, hard, all those sorts of things, not melting."

She grinned at him. "Your body is all of those things, but your feelings are soft and warm and wonderful."

He stepped out of his breeches, folded them over the back of a chair, stretched, then looked at her, his eyes smiling lazily at her. She was gazing intently at his groin and he felt his member swell and thrust forward. His head didn't ache now, but his body did. He walked over to her and placed his hands on her shoulders. She looked up at him, though not with wholehearted welcome. She appeared nervous, uncertain. She looked very vulnerable.

"I know this must be extremely difficult for you, Genny. I can't say I blame you if you don't want me to love you. After all, I don't know you and it must seem very strange, very embarrassing, to give yourself to someone who has no real emotional memory of you." She opened her mouth, but he placed his fingertips over her lips. "No, let me finish. This must be said, because it is the truth. I like you, Genny. You told me that I liked you enough to marry you. We will simply have to build on that. My memory will come back and then we will see. All right?"

She wanted to cry, so she swallowed hard, burying her face against his bare shoulder. Her arms went around his back and she hugged herself against him. "I don't want you to leave. I want to be your wife. Forget the wager."

"I was thinking that it *was* perhaps a damned wager. No, I won't leave. Besides, I wouldn't know where to leave to. As much as I may dislike it, I'm rather dependent on you at the moment. Let me ask you a question. Do you like me, Genny?"

"Yes," she said, snuggling closer, her voice muffled. "Of course, I've also wanted to hit you many times in the past."

He grinned and kissed the top of her head. "And did you?"

"Yes. You always grunted, very obligingly, for me."

"I'll try to continue to be obliging. Let me help you off with that gown."

He set her away from him and deftly finished undoing the buttons that marched up the bodice of the gown. He pushed it down and unfastened the tiny satin-covered buttons on her chemise. When she was naked save for her stockings and slippers, he stepped back and looked at her. "I like that. Very much. Let me take off your slippers. But keep the stockings on."

It was hard for her not to try to cover herself, for the simple fact that she was a stranger to him and he looked at her differently, spoke to her differently. Then he cupped her breasts in his hands and she sucked in her breath, closing her eyes.

"Your heart's pounding." He leaned down and took a nipple into his warm mouth.

She gasped and steadied herself, her hands on his shoulders. "Oh, goodness, that's so very—"

He raised his head. "Some things a man doesn't forget. So very what, Genny?"

"Wonderful," she said simply. "You're wonderful."

He began kissing her again, caressing her and kneading her breasts with his hands. "I'm glad you think so, even though I'm not in all likelihood remotely wonderful," he said between nipping kisses. "You're lovely. I can see that I must have quite liked your body."

"I'm glad you do, Alec, but maybe you've forgotten about all those other women in your life. So many beautiful women you attracted. And I'm so very—"

"So very what?" But before she could answer, his hand roved down over her stomach, combing through the soft hair. "Ah. There you are. Soft and wet and swelled. Feel yourself, Genny." Before she could even think to protest, he'd taken her hand and placed her fingers over herself.

"Oh." It was embarrassing and at the same time marvelously exciting.

Then she grasped him in her hand and it was his turn to suck in his breath. He felt incredibly smooth and alive. Her fingertips lightly touched the tip of his sex and she felt a drop of liquid. In the next instant he grabbed her hand, pulling her away.

"I'll explode if you continue doing that." His chest was heaving, his eyes dilated. "Come."

He closed his arms around her hips and lifted her onto the bed. He came down over her and she felt his member against her belly, hard and throbbing and wanting.

He balanced himself up on his elbows. "Now

that I've got you where I want you, answer me. You're so very what?"

She gave him a wild look. "I'm so ordinary!"

"You, ordinary? Silly woman . . . you're, well, let's just see, shall we?"

He reared back, standing beside the bed, staring down at her. He pulled her legs wide apart. His fingers touched her sweet woman's flesh and he probed gently into her, caressing the soft folds, finding her. "Ordinary? You're all soft and pink and very much a woman. That's special, not at all ordinary."

She arched her back, her hips lifting to his fingers.

"Yes," he said, "that's it," and then he lowered his head and his tongue slid over her and he kissed her, nipping, teasing kisses, and she felt his finger ease into her deeply and she cried out, and he stopped immediately. She moaned his name.

"No, not just yet. When you climax, Genny, I want you to scream."

Another thing he hadn't forgotten, she thought vaguely, feeling demented now as he easily took control. He brought her again and again to the edge, then pulled her back. She pounded his shoulders with her fists, and her hips twisted against his steadying hands. He wasn't about to be rushed.

"All right," he said finally, and when he took her into his mouth again, he changed his rhythm and the deepness of his finger and she cried out, loudly, and felt his hand come over her mouth and she tasted herself on his fingers and the fren-

345

zied pleasure went on and on until she thought she'd die from it.

Then he came over her and into her in one long, smooth thrust. She cried out yet again, closed her thighs around his flanks, and met his rhythmic thrusts.

It was incredible. When he reached between their heaving bodies and found her, she spiraled out of control once again and he joined her this time, pouring himself into her, taking her into himself.

"No, you're anything but ordinary."

"How can you possibly know that?"

He frowned and nibbled her ear. "Actually, I was just thinking that it was amazing that I could think at all, much less talk. You have a powerful effect on me, woman. No, you're not at all ordinary. I haven't the foggiest notion why I'm so sure about that, but it's true, I'm certain of it. You scream very nicely. It . . . pleased me."

Alec was Alec; he just didn't realize it. She knew him so well now. She hugged his back, hard.

"You're a very enticing man, Alec."

She felt him growing hard deep inside her. She smiled up at him. "You're certain your head doesn't hurt?"

"No, it's just my—"

"Outrageous, now and forever, I expect."

Genny hadn't ever considered that a woman could climax more than once. Well, perhaps twice. But three times? She was smiling blissfully as she fell asleep.

As for Alec, he was as sated as his wife, but

his head had begun to hurt again. He tucked Genny against him, settling her head against his chest. He kissed the top of her head. No, Genny wasn't ordinary. He rather looked forward to learning all about her.

Had he really taken her to a brothel? To punish her for pretending to be a man around him? He grinned into the darkness. He wished he could remember that. He closed his eyes, willing the damned headache to quiet down. It was some time, however, before he fell asleep.

Genny said brightly, "You've never told me about your houses in England, Hallie."

Hallie looked up from the model eighteen-gun frigate. It was French and had been one of Napoleon's finest. "We mainly go to Carrick Grange when we're home. Papa grew up there and it's a big estate. There's the house in London, of course. We went there once during what Papa and his friends called the Season. There's an abbey in Somerset, near Rotherham Weald, I think. I don't remember the name of it. Papa never told me what a Season was."

Houses with names. Well, they had them here in America, too. Could this not be called Paxton House?

"A Season," Genny said, "is a time of the year when young ladies come out of the schoolroom and find husbands. Where's Carrick Grange?"

"In Northumberland. Our village is called Devenish. It's very isolated. Papa likes it there, but he soon makes everything work smoothly and then he gets bored. He always likes to be doing things and going to new places. I don't know if I'll ever get him to settle down." The little girl sighed and moved the frigate carefully behind a schooner.

"Do you remember when you last visited Carrick Grange?"

Hallie looked up and said matter-of-factly, "Last spring. Why don't you ask Papa?"

"He isn't feeling too well. He's sleeping."

"Has Dr. Pruitt seen him?"

"That might be a fine idea."

"Genny, what's wrong with Papa? He acted funny last night."

How much to keep from her? The child looked worried and uncertain. "He had an accident during the hurricane."

Hallie very carefully set the frigate aside and rose, coming to stand beside Genny's chair. She said nothing, merely waited.

"He saw a man being pushed by the wind toward the foremast and he saw that the foremast was breaking. He rushed forward to save him and the mast broke. He was struck on his head. But he'll be all right, Hallie."

"Did the man live?"

"There were two men, actually. One didn't survive."

"Shall I read to Papa?"

"He might enjoy that. But let him rest for now, Hallie."

It was late that afternoon when Daniel Raymond came to the house. A letter addressed to Baron Sherard had been delivered to him

348

because it was known that he was the baron's American solicitor.

Genny saw to Mr. Raymond's comfort, then looked at the letter. "It appears to be from a London lawyer," she said.

"Yes," he said, and bit into one of Lannie's delicious scones.

Genny fretted, then excused herself for a moment. She didn't want to bother Alec with this, but she realized she had no choice. She was his wife, but that didn't give her the right to read his personal communications. She went to Alec's bedchamber. He was awake, sitting up in a chair, Hallie on his lap. He was leaning back, his eyes closed, and his small daughter was reading to him in a voice filled with high-flown drama.

"Charge away, my hearties, and you'll soon
Know that we're here, impatient for the fight,
Four woman-squadrons, armed from top to toe."

Genny laughed. "What is that, Hallie?"

"It's Lystrea . . . Lostra—"

"Lysistrata," Alec said, not opening his eyes. "You read very well, Hallie. Women warriors? Did I hear aright? Who selected this reading?"

"I did," Hallie said. "Papa said he didn't care."

"I do now," Alec said with some feeling. "Listen to this, Genny. 'We must abstain—each—from the joys of love. How—' "

"Stop, Hallie, you're making me cry!" Genny was hugging her sides with laughter, while Alec was looking completely and utterly appalled. "I gave you this play?"

"Yes, Papa, but it's in a book with a lot of other stories, and I don't think you really noticed."

Alec groaned.

"I'm sorry," Genny said, trying to control her giggles, "but I must interrupt your daughter's dramatic rendering. Mr. Raymond is here, Alec. He's your lawyer in Baltimore. He brought this letter from your solicitor in London."

Genny handed him the letter, then turned immediately to Hallie and offered her a hand. "Would you like a scone, love? Why don't we go downstairs and visit with Mr. Raymond?" Hallie hesitated, her eyes on her father, and Genny added, "Scones with lots of strawberry jam."

That found immediate favor and off they went. Alec read the letter, some two months old now, then read it again, folded it, and replaced it in the envelope. He closed his eyes and leaned his head back.

The headache had returned, only this time he didn't think it was from his injury. He cursed very softly.

"It seems I must leave you after all."

Genny carefully laid down her fork. "The letter?"

He nodded but said nothing more. He seemed abstracted, worried, and she wanted to yell at him to trust her, to confide in her, to treat her like his wife. She quickly amended that silent wish. No, Alec would always want to protect, shelter, and cosset his wife. She wished he'd think of her as his best friend, a person he could trust

350

without hesitation. That hadn't changed either with his loss of memory

Hallie was having her dinner with Mrs. Swindel, a request made by Alec, and thus they were alone in the dining room. Alec had thanked Moses and dismissed him. Genny had perked up. He wanted to be alone with her, to tell her about the letter. But he'd said nothing.

She fiddled now with a piece of warm bread, then tossed it onto her nearly full plate. "Please tell me what has happened, Alec."

"I will have to return to England. That letter was from my man of business in London, a Mr. Jonathan Rafer. It seems that Carrick Grange has burned—on purpose, it would seem. My steward, a man named Arnold Cruisk, was murdered. I must return immediately."

Genny simply stared at him, waiting.

"It's odd, you know. After I had read the letter, I suddenly saw this beautiful old stone castle in my mind. Very old, Genny. If it is Carrick Grange that I saw, at least the stone walls will still be standing. They've been standing forever. A little fire wouldn't bring them down."

Genny said nothing, merely toyed with a tart lemon pudding that was Lannie's specialty.

"I know that you're an American, Genny. I know that you wouldn't want to ever leave your country, or Baltimore for that matter. More importantly, I know how you feel about the shipyard. It's yours. I've given this a great deal of thought. I will deed it over to you on the morrow. Then you may do as you please with it. Just one thing, though. If things don't work out, I don't

351

want you to worry about finances. I will leave instructions with Mr. Tomlinson at the bank. You will have constant and immediate access to any funds you may need."

She stared at him, her lemon pudding forgotten. He was offering her everything, including complete independence. She would never have to worry about anything again. She would never have to give an accounting to another man and wait to be criticized. She would never have to defend herself for being a woman. She would never again have to . . .

But what did all that have to do with her now? Odd, how everything shifted in her mind, how things that she'd considered as important to her survival as breathing suddenly blurred and seemed ridiculous. She was an American, that was true. And the shipyard had been the most . . . She cleared her throat and said her thoughts aloud. "Alec, you're my husband. You are more important to me than my country, than the shipyard, than the *Pegasus*. I will find someone to manage the shipyard. I will find someone to live in this house. We will take Moses with us, if he wishes it. I will see that all my other people are well taken care of. My place is with you, with my husband. When do we sail for London?"

He frowned at her. "I thought these things were of the utmost importance to you. I don't understand. I'm not pleading with you to come with me, Genny. I can deal with matters on my own."

"I know you can, but you have me, so you

don't have to. And, Alec, I can't imagine you pleading with anyone for anything." She gave him a tremulous smile. "The shipyard is important and I will keep informed on it through Mr. Raymond. Did you really mean what you said? You'll deed it to me?"

"Of course, whyever not? I know nothing of it. Since I can't seem to remember, I don't truly understand why your father served you such a turn. If the shipyard was your dowry, let me say that I have no need of money—" He broke off, frowning down at his veal cutlet. "I don't have need of money, do I?"

"No. You're quite sound financially, unless someone has absconded with your funds."

"But I knew I was wealthy," he said thoughtfully. "I wonder how."

She smiled at him, wishing she could bound out of her chair and press his face against her bosom. She wanted to protect him, to cherish him . . . Lord, it was ridiculous. If he were himself, that would be the last thing he'd want. He'd look at her as if she'd lost her mind. He'd tease her mercilessly, then try to toss her skirts over her head and make very thorough love to her.

"It's just a matter of a few more days, Alec."

"It's strange how this amnesia works. I know which fork to use, for example, yet I can't place my solicitor's name with a face. I know how to make love, yet I can't remember making love to any other woman. You're the only woman in my mind now."

Now. And when he remembered? Disappointment, she thought. He'd know disappointment and regret. No, no, Alec was loyal; he was honorable.

"Is there anything pressing to keep us in Baltimore?"

"Just the shipyard. We need a manager. He doesn't have to be someone who knows ship design. My father left three or four, including the *Pegasus*'s design." Genny paused. "You know, Alec, I was just thinking. About the shipyard—you don't have to deed it over to me. We're married. It's ours. I don't need to see my name alone as the owner." Had she really said that? Had she changed so much in so short a time? It was mind-boggling, and a bit frightening. What would happen when he remembered? She tamped down on that thought instantly. He needed her. He needed her trust and her loyalty. It was the least she could give him, this token of her trust.

"It occurs to me that it may prove to your advantage to keep the shipyard in my name," Alec said. "This matter of the men of Baltimore not wanting to do business with you because you're a woman. Well, let them think they're dealing only with a man. A male manager and me. What do you think?"

He was asking her opinion, not telling her what to do. He was serious. She said with but an instant's hesitation, "I think you're very smart, sir." Strange, but it would have nearly killed her to say those words even the day before. The unfairness of it still was clear to her and it still hurt, but it simply no longer mattered all that much to her life.

"We'll see to the repairs on the *Pegasus* tomorrow."

"Yes. Your bark weathered the hurricane with scarce a tremor, big clumsy hulk that she is."

"You're just jealous. Oh, another thing I was thinking about. I don't want to sell the *Pegasus*. I'm a merchant baron, Genny, that's what you told me. There's no reason not to expand my operations to Baltimore. You build ships and I'll sail them to the Caribbean. Flour, tobacco, cotton—we'll make a fortune."

Genny felt excitement flow through her. "Perhaps Mr. Abel Pitts would be willing to stay in Baltimore and captain her. Or should you wish to have an American?" They remained at the dinner table until very late, plans and laughter filling the room.

In bed that night, when Genny lay soft and sated in his arms, she said, "I think you should tell Hallie the truth."

"No."

"She's a very smart, perceptive little girl—"

"Little girl? She's a bloody old woman! The child is frightening, what she understands—"

"Exactly. Right now she's very confused. She knows something isn't right with her papa."

"I'll think about it," Alec said finally, and kissed Genny's ear. She turned her face and gave him her mouth. In but another moment, he was hard against her belly.

"Lie still," she said between light kisses. "All right?"

"Why?"

"Trust me, my lord."

He looked at her askance until she eased down and pushed his legs apart. She came between them and leaned down to kiss his hard belly. He moaned, feeling her fingers close around him. "Genny."

"Yes," she said, and he felt her warm breath on his sex. "Tell me if I do something wrong."

He moaned in response and Genny, heartened by that sound, caressed him with her mouth.

"It's too much," Alec said after but a few moments and pulled her away. He came over her and into her in a deep, abrupt thrust that made her cry out. He spread her legs wider and pushed deeper, then drew back and pulled her upright and onto his thighs. "Wrap your legs around me, Genny."

She did so and he grinned at her, his hands on her hips, working her against him, and he eased off the bed, standing. "Alec!"

She grabbed him around his neck and he was so deep inside her, filling her, then withdrawing, his hands caressing her fiercely, and it was wonderful and she didn't want it to stop. When he eased onto the bed, this time on his back, settling her atop him, she felt him touching her womb, so deep was he.

"Alec," she said again, leaned down, and kissed him. He stroked her breasts; then his hands were kneading her belly, going lower until he found her. The result was beyond anything he could have imagined. He watched her climax, her back arched, her hair in wild disarray around her shoulders, her breasts thrust outward.

Then he was deeper still inside her, pushing and pounding, and he spewed his seed into her, and he was rocked with the power of his release.

It was very nearly too much. Genny stared down at him, seeing more than his man's perfection. She saw the beauty of his very being, and it moved her as nothing else could.

"I love you," she said, and she knew as surely as she knew the sun would rise on the morrow that there was nothing else in the world more important to her than this man.

He opened his eyes and gave her a bemused smile. "Do you really?"

She nodded, wary now because he didn't know her, didn't know how great a step this was for her, but she didn't want him to doubt her word.

"Did you love me before?"

"I don't know. There was little time, actually."

"Show me," he said, and pulled her down to kiss her.

Alec thought sometime later that he really was two men. The Alec of old and this new Alec. There had to be differences. He knew that. Why had Genny not loved him before? Hadn't he been kind to her? The rawness of his thoughts made his head hurt and he shied away from it, but it was no good. He hated this, hated it more than anything he could dredge up even in a nightmare, and there was nothing he could do about it. The helplessness appalled him. It made him bitter.

He heard Genny groan softly, and kissed her. She was sweet, this unknown wife of his.

Why couldn't he remember?

They'd been aboard the *Night Dancer* for four days when Genny became as certain as she could be that she was with child. She was clutching the chamber pot, her stomach heaving, her body shaking with the effort of retching.

"My God, Genny! What's wrong? You're seasick? *You?*"

She turned her face away, not wanting him to see her like this. "Go away."

"Don't be a fool. Let me help you.'

"Go away, Alec. Please."

He didn't. She saw him wet a cloth and stride over to her. He knelt down beside her and pulled her back against his chest. She felt the wet cloth on her face and it was a blessed relief.

"Do you need to vomit some more?"

"There isn't anything left," she said and wished she could somehow die and be done with it.

"Dry heaves, huh?"

"That sounds charming."

"So do you, love. Charming and quite green in the face. If you have no further need of the chamber pot—" He said no more, picked her up in his arms, and carried her to the bunk. He laid her gently down on her back, then sat down beside her. He placed his palm against her forehead.

"Somehow I can't imagine you—my original sailor—being seasick."

"It isn't that."

"Isn't what? Did you eat something bad?"

"No, it's something you did, Alec, if you would know the truth!"

"Something I did?" He stared down at her, then broke into a huge, very masculine, quite unforgivable grin. "You mean you're pregnant?"

"I don't know. I think so."

He paused, thinking back. "You haven't had your monthly flow, at least since we first made love again—when my memory began again, that is. I'll have Dr. Pruitt take a look, all right?"

"No, I don't want him doing anything to me." She felt a wave of nausea and hugged her belly.

"Oh, Genny, I'm sorry. A sea voyage and pregnancy—"

"I'll survive."

"I know, you're far too stubborn to do anything else. How far along are you, do you think?"

"I think you made me pregnant even before we were married, curse you."

"That potent, am I? I took your virginity—Lord, I wish I could remember that—and planted my seed like an industrious farmer, all in a very short time. Virile and potent. Yes, indeed."

"I would hit you in your stomach if I had the strength."

"You don't do anything except lie there and rest. I'll ask Dr. Pruitt what you should be eating to keep you from being so ill, all right?"

She nodded, feeling too miserable to care.

"Nothing will happen to you because I know exactly what to do when the baby comes." He

359

stopped cold, frowning. "How do I know that I know about birthing a child?"

Genny swallowed. "I think you felt very helpless when your first wife died. I think you learned from an Arab physician all about it. Some part of you, deep down, knows that and it just came out."

"I hate this!" He struck his fist against his thigh.

"Papa."

Alec whipped about to see his small daughter standing in the open doorway of the cabin.

"Papa, what's wrong?"

"Genny isn't feeling well."

"No, I mean with you."

Alec looked at Genny, then beckoned to his daughter. "Come here, Hallie." She regarded him warily and took one step into the cabin. "Come here," Alec said again, and patted his thigh.

She climbed onto his lap and he tucked her against his chest.

"I heard Pippin talking to Mr. Pitts. He said it was really strange the way you didn't remember things, the way you had to ask when you should have known, when it should have been second nature. Then he saw me and got a real funny look on his face."

Alec cursed luridly, then stopped cold, eyeing his attentive daughter.

"It's all right, Papa. If you want to say bad things, I don't mind."

"You're too tolerant, Hallie. It's true. I don't

remember anything. I was hit on the head during the hurricane."

She looked at him, her head cocked to one side. "You don't remember me?"

He wanted to lie to her but knew in just his brief experience with her that it wouldn't work. His daughter was appallingly perceptive. "No, I don't."

"But he will soon, Hallie," Genny said, sitting up against the headboard of the bunk. "He doesn't remember me either. But he remembers little things, more and more every day now, and people from his past. I guess since we're in the present, we'll have to wait a bit longer."

Hallie didn't say a word. She studied her father's face, then slowly raised her hand and patted his cheek. "It's all right, Papa. I'll tell you all about me. And if there's anything you need, you just ask me."

"Thank you," he said, marveling at this small person who had sprung from his loins. "It appears that I'm very lucky with my womenfolk."

Hallie looked past her father to Genny. "I'm sorry you don't feel well, Genny, but Mrs. Swindel was saying to Dr. Pruitt that it was natural and nothing to fret about."

Genny gaped at her.

"I want a little brother, Papa." Without waiting for him to respond, Hallie slipped off his lap and dashed to the door. "I'm going on deck. Pippin will look after me."

And she was gone. Alec simply stared toward the now empty doorway.

"She's incredible."

"More to the point, she listens to everything and everyone."

Alec leaned down, gently kneading her flat belly. "Shall we give her a little brother?"

"What if he looks like me?"

"That could prove embarrassing. Every gentleman in the area would be chasing after him."

Genny giggled and poked his arm. Just as suddenly, a wave of nausea gripped her and she hugged her stomach. "Oh, this is damnable. I doubt I'll ever forgive you!"

Alec didn't leave her until she'd fallen asleep. He went to see Dr. Pruitt.

Then he spent several hours simply thinking. He was aware that his men eyed him askance, with obvious worry, and some with doubts. Who could blame them? A man forgetting everything in his past? It didn't sound too bloody likely. He tried to remember, and indeed, snippets would pop into his mind, then disappear just as quickly. It was frustrating and enraging. Genny had been right for the most part. It was people from his past who came briefly into his mind. Now he saw several women, all of them quite lovely, and he saw not only their faces but their white bodies. He saw himself making love to them, caressing them and thrusting into them. He swallowed. Had he been such a randy goat? Hadn't he cared for any of them save for the sex they'd given him?

And he saw Nesta again. She was dead, lying there against the white sheets, her face pale and waxy. He broke into a sweat. He knew he couldn't bear much more of this.

He took the wheel from Mr. Pitts toward midnight.

"A storm's blowing in," Alec remarked.

"Not a big one, thank the powers."

"You're certain about your decision, Abel? The *Pegasus* would be your ship."

The big man turned to his captain. "Quite sure, my lord. Baltimore is a nice place, and I don't mind the Americans overmuch. But the man you selected is one of them, and it will go better for her ladyship's business with an American in charge. And besides, my place is with you and your family. Particularly—" His voice dropped off like a stone from a cliff.

"Particularly since I can't remember a damned thing and we're going to a country which could be China for all the memory I bear of it."

"Yes, my lord."

And that, Alec supposed, was an end to it.

20

They landed in Southampton during the third week of December. As a true Baltimorean, Genny couldn't quibble about the gray, drizzly skies and a wind that could slice through the warmest of wool cloaks. Still, it wasn't Baltimore; the sky wasn't the same murky gray. The men swarming over the docks were dressed like American sailors and clerks and draymen, but the words that came out of their mouths, and the way they said those words—she'd never heard anything like it before. Welcome to England, she thought, my country's avowed enemy just five short years ago. You, my girl, have certainly made your bed, married to an Englishman.

Made her bed. Indeed, not only had she made it, she'd lain in it numerous times, joyfully, and now there was a child in her womb to attest to the fact.

Genny sighed and pulled her cloak more closely about her. Her stomach was still more flat than not, just a slight swell that was visible only to her and to Alec, but her breasts were heavier and her waist thicker. She thought occasionally that he knew her body as well or better than she did. Sometimes after he'd loved her most thoroughly, he would balance himself on his elbow and simply stare down at her. Sometimes he would span her belly with his splayed fingers, look thoughtful, then nod to himself. Sometimes he'd simply look at her belly and smile like a very arrogant, self-satisfied male, which he was.

Arrogant and remarkably even-tempered, given the fact that most of his life lay in a void of blankness, or in small snips of memories, tantalizing but elusive, always just out of his reach. Only once on the long voyage had she see him truly angry. There was a new man, an American from Florida, Cribbs by name, and he had secreted aboard a stash of liquor. He'd gotten drunker than a eunuch in a harem, seen Genny enjoying a warm evening on deck, become amorous in a bumbling way, and found himself with a broken jaw. Alec didn't suffer fools, and

Genny had discovered that even though he didn't remember her, he would protect her with his life. In this instance, it was nearly Cribbs's life to be forfeit. She saw Cribbs now, sober as a reverend on Sunday morning, tying down the yards and yards of canvas from the mainsail. She wished she could be helping, doing something, anything, but the one time she'd asked Alec if she could learn the finer points of sailing a barkentine, he'd simply given her a bewildered look and a novel to read. It was as if he'd completely forgotten that she'd captained the clipper herself.

She sighed again. She couldn't wait to be on land. Her stomach had been calm now for three weeks, but there were strange currents and strong crosswinds when the *Night Dancer* had come into the Channel, and a few lurches of the barkentine had brought the nausea back. She concentrated on memories, pleasant ones with her father. At least she had memories. What did Alec do when he was troubled and wanted to escape the present? She wondered what her life would be like if Alec hadn't come to Baltimore. Her father would still have died and she would have the shipyard, for all that would have been worth now. Would she have fallen into destitution? Knowing the men of Baltimore, she decided that the answer was probably affirmative. Then they would have probably felt it their duty to see that one of them married her to keep her from starving. Well, that was all to no point now.

Fog shrouded the landscape and she could make little out. The air was filled with the sounds of shrill foghorns. The *Night Dancer* moved at a snail's pace, a pilot boat leading them.

Hallie was standing at Genny's side, Moses beside her. He was muffled to his ears in thick scarlet wool, the scarf a gift from Pippin, of all people. The two of them had become great friends on the voyage from Baltimore.

Hallie was quiet, something that Genny appreciated, then worried about. She was too quiet. Genny took the little girl's hand. "Are you excited, Hallie? You're nearly home now."

As was her wont, Hallie gave the question thought before answering. "Yes, but you know, Genny, I'm kind of young to really feel excited about coming home. I'm worried about Papa. He isn't excited about coming home either. I think he's afraid that he won't know anyone here, and that will make him feel worse. He still doesn't remember us, Genny. Sometimes I see him looking at me and he's trying so hard to *know* me, but he can't."

"I know. He will, though, soon."

"Sometimes I wonder," Hallie said. "He's not happy."

Maybe that's because of the woman he's tied to legally, Genny thought, but didn't say anything aloud.

"This fog is for burying," Moses said, lifting a gloved hand as if to feel his springy gray hair. "Nice and gloomy, fit for a cemetery."

"That's a happy thought," Genny said. She turned, wanting to have just a glimpse of Alec, but he was in conversation with Abel and Minter, and she could see only his back.

"Mama died the same day as my birthday. That's two days from now."

"We will have a party, love, a very nice party with Pippin and Moses and Mrs. Swindel—"

"And don't forget her wonderful father." Alec smiled at his assembled family. He hadn't even thought about a birthday for his daughter, not having remembered the anniversary of his first wife's death. He had two days to come up with a present to make Hallie happy. He'd spent a good deal of time with her during the past weeks, taking part in her lessons, speaking French and Italian with her—which he had no trouble at all remembering, the words coming out of his mouth without conscious thought—performing as the enemy in mock sea battles. He liked his daughter. That, he supposed, was a decent enough beginning. Even when she got tired and whined and carried on, he didn't become overly impatient with her. He discovered that he could simply give her a look and she would subside quickly enough. He said to Genny, who was looking a bit too worn for his liking," Another fifteen minutes and we'll be docking."

"Good," Genny said with fervor. "I want my feet on dry land."

"And your stomach, too, I expect."

"Yes, indeed. Where will we stay this evening, Alec? In Southampton?"

"Yes, at the Chequer's Inn." Alec paused, then added in a deliberate voice," Pippin told me of the inn. He also said that a good friend of mine owns it, a man by the name of Chivers."

Genny squeezed his forearm, an instinctive

gesture to show him that she knew what he felt. To her surprise, he shook off her hand.

"Excuse me now. I must go back." And he left them. Genny stared after him, wondering what was wrong.

Alec was angry. At all of them, including his well-meaning wife, of whom he had no memory at all; at himself for his damnable, endless weakness. If he had more of a brain, wouldn't he have remembered by now? If there were something worthy to remember, wouldn't he have recaptured it by now, what was it, nearly six weeks after his accident? He'd held such hopes that he'd remember upon landing in England. There was nothing as yet. It could have been China for all he knew. He got a grip on himself. None of it was her fault, or anyone else's for that matter. Damnable, damnable thing to have happened.

The Chequer's Inn was over a hundred years old, cozy, filled with blazing fireplaces from its oak-paneled taproom all the way to Moses and Pippin's room on the third floor. "It smells so good," Genny said, doing a twirling circle in the middle of their bedchamber. "So clean and fresh and warm."

"That reminds me of you, wife."

Alec sounded carefree again, and Genny breathed a huge sigh of relief. "No bilge-water smell?"

"Not a whiff," he said, sniffing behind her left ear.

She just grinned at him. "My stomach feels like it's died and gone to heaven."

He saw Nesta at that moment, her belly huge

with child. He shook his head, willing away that particular image because it brought pain with it.

She saw that look in his eyes, knew that whatever he was seeing made him feel bad, and sought to distract him with something to which she knew the answer as well as he did. "What will you do with all the cargo, Alec?"

"My man—his name is George Curzon. No, Genny, don't get your hopes up. I didn't remember him. Even before we left Baltimore, Pippin showed me all my records, all the names of the men I deal with, and the like. In any case, I'll meet with this Mr. Curzon tomorrow. We'll make a fine profit on the tobacco and cotton we've brought from America." He paused, then added in a flat voice," No, I didn't remember what kind of profit the tobacco and cotton would bring. Thank the powers I keep good records. But of course you know that, don't you?"

"Indeed I do." That was something the new Alec didn't seem to mind at all. Genny had slowly begun to take over more and more of the bookkeeping. It was nothing new to her, although Alec's system was a little different from the one she and her father had used. She'd simply changed Alec's a bit. She was quick with numbers and normally accurate. Most important, Alec seemed to enjoy her pleasure in the work. He also seemed to enjoy discussing ideas with her. Sometimes they'd even been hers and he hadn't appeared to mind. He'd said not a thing about her aping men again, at her trying to do a job meant for a man.

369

Genny placed a tentative hand on his arm. "I'm starving."

That startled him and he gave her a slow smile. "Do you always say things so baldly?"

"Always." She didn't look away from him but let her hand glide over his belly. He'd lost weight, she thought. Her hand continued downward, until she lightly touched him. "Always," she said again, and pressed her fingers inward.

Alec responded immediately. He was hard, rising against her hand, pressing into her palm. He pulled her to him with little finesse and kissed her roughly. But Genny, who hadn't experienced abstinence since knowing Alec, had endured that miserable state for the past three nights when Alec hadn't come to their cabin. Now he was moaning into her mouth as her hand fondled him. His response made her equally wild, but when he toppled her backward onto the bed and wildly pulled aside her clothing, she stared up at him, bemused. His eyes were intent, his expression one of near pain.

"Alec," she said as he spread her thighs wide apart.

He came into her with one long, deep thrust, but she was ready for him, and her hips lifted to bring him deeper into her.

He never forgot to be generous, to be knowing, even when he was frantic with need, she thought vaguely as she felt his fingers caressing her between their heaving bodies. His fingers on her swelled woman's flesh—probing her, teasing her, knowing her so very well—made her rear up. She drew him deeper inside her and watched with so much love in her eyes that he must see it as he threw back his head and moaned, thrusting wildly into her until she let herself go and joined him, melding them together, making their need one, making herself one with him.

It was wonderful and she never wanted it to end. Even as his body shuddered and trembled over her, she knew they were building new memories for him. These would be good ones. She would always make it so. "Don't leave me," she said, and knew that she'd said the words silently, deep in her mind, in her very being. She couldn't imagine feelings that now enveloped her—had they always been inside her just waiting to be released? Released by a man who didn't even know who she was. "Don't let it end," she whispered, but even though she'd spoken aloud, he hadn't heard her.

It did end, of course. Alec still lay on top of her, not so deep inside her now. He lifted himself onto his elbows and looked down at her.

"You're a wild woman. Wanton. Abandoned. It is very well done of you."

"You made me that way, Baron. From the very beginning, you made me wild and wanton and . . . no, I refuse to be abandoned. That is going too far."

"Ha! Well, I'm enjoying the results of my handiwork. Doubtless I'm a great initiator of young virgins."

"You called me a long-in-the-tooth virgin."

"Yes, I remember you telling me that. Now you're a long-in-the-tooth wild matron."

She felt him leaving her. He mumbled aside,"

I'm too heavy for you. I don't want to disturb my son."

"Your son doesn't mind."

Still, he rolled onto his side, balanced himself on his elbow, and looked at her thoughtfully. "You have a very stubborn jaw."

"Yes."

"But you've been such a gentle, sweet, giving—"

"Do stop—you make me sound like some sort of virtuous, very boring person."

"But with that jaw . . ." He paused, frowning. "You're not acting completely like yourself, are you? I mean, you feel somehow responsible for me, don't you? You're holding back your cannon fire until I'm whole in mind again?"

"You just said I was gentle, sweet—"

He waved her words aside, then rested his waving hand on her breast. "Somehow I see you more as a woman who doesn't easily tolerate fools."

"Neither do you."

"You weren't always so agreeable to me, though, were you? Did we have dog and cat fights?"

She held her tongue. She didn't want—

"Genny, it's true, isn't it? We fought?"

"More times than even I can remem—count."

"Why? Over what?"

She swallowed. She didn't want to tell him the truth. He just might revert, might lock her out of his business dealings . . . She frowned at his Adam's apple. He hadn't changed, not really, but he had seemed more tolerant, more willing to understand her views. Also, there'd been no reason for him to force upon her any ironclad ideas of what was proper for a lady and what wasn't. It hadn't been necessary for him to even think about it. Even though she was firmly part and parcel of his business affairs, he was still his lordship, Baron Sherard, the master. It was she who had changed, and she'd done it willingly, eagerly. She'd said not a thing to him when he'd refused to let her help sail the barkentine. She'd bowed her head and accepted the novel he'd handed her—*Pride and Prejudice*—with a smile. Indeed, she'd become everything the most demanding of men could want: sweet, gentle, giving; ah, yes, giving so much of herself to him, not reckoning that what she valued would never be given back to her. As for the business side of things, she'd simply inserted herself, not honestly, candidly, but stealthfully, like a thief, a guileful woman who had no power save what she could ferret out for herself. At intimate times like this she hated it. But she feared that candor and honesty would make him look at her with something akin to disgust, and that such a request upon her part would have put up his man's back.

Did it matter? Was anything as important as this man? No; for her, nothing was. It was that simple.

But what was important to him? When he remembered her, would he want nothing more to do with her? Oh, she knew he wouldn't leave her, but would he simply withdraw from her? As he had on the barkentine today?

"Genny, aren't you going to answer me?

You're worlds away from me. Come, what did we argue about?"

"Never anything important." Then she gasped down a frightened breath, flung herself on top of him, and pressed him onto his back. She kissed him, stroked her hand over him until she found him, still free from his breeches. She unfastened his breeches and yanked them down. "Alec," she said soft and warm into his mouth. She lifted her skirts and took him into her, her skirts and petticoats billowing about her, and she rode him, giving him all of her, wishing she could tell him that all she had was his. Until he remembered.

And after he'd climaxed, jarring both of them with the depths of their pleasure, he said in a fervent, very pleased male voice, "Whatever brought that on, don't ever let yourself forget."

She was sprawled on top of him, his sex still inside her, and she burst into tears. She was a liar, a fraud, and she'd do anything else necessary to keep him content with her, to keep him from the awful depressions she'd seen on board the barkentine.

"Genny!"

Her hair had lost its pins and was in wild disarray about her head, and he stroked it, his fingers finding the back of her neck and massaging her gently. "Hush," he said. "Hush, you'll make yourself ill. I don't like to think my lovemaking reduces my lady to tears and sobs. Was it so awful? Did I give you no pleasure, then? Am I to be cast aside like a worn boot? Will you go to Hoby's to find boots more to your liking?"

Her sobs ceased and she gave him a watery smile, just as he'd hoped she would.

"You're starving. For food now?"

Genny was still as a statue over him, staring into his face.

"What is it? Have my eyes crossed?"

"No. Who is Hoby?"

"Why, he's the finest bootmaker in all of London and—" Alec gave her a rueful grin. "I remember my bootmaker. Heaven be praised. A man can't ask for much more than that, can he? My God, my bootmaker!"

"It's another piece. Don't complain. You make progress every day."

Later she wanted desperately to ask him if she could accompany him to see Mr. Curzon. She wanted to see how this part of business was conducted. But in the end, she was too afraid to ask.

As for Alec, it never occurred to him to include his wife. He finalized his business with Mr. George Curzon on Battle Street. He'd indeed turned a fine profit. The two men made plans for the *Night Dancer*'s next voyage. Mr. Curzon never realized that Baron Sherard didn't know him from his next-door neighbor.

The Carrick family and its retainers left Southampton the following day. Abel Pitts remained with the *Night Dancer* and would captain her on her next voyage. They stopped in the afternoon at the Peartree Inn in Guildford. There they celebrated Hallie's birthday. And Alec thought again of his dead first wife, whose face he'd seen a good half-dozen times during the past seven weeks.

He gave his daughter a replica of Cleopatra's famous barge, handmade in Italy and in Mr. George Curzon's back room. Mr. Curzon had most willingly sold it to the baron for a quite reasonable sum.

Genny gave her stepdaughter a sextant.

It was Pippin who brought Hallie a porcelain-faced doll, gowned as a French aristocrat. To the surprise of all of them, Hallie looked at the doll and held it tightly to her chest. "Her name," Hallie announced a while later, "is Harold."

"Harold," Alec repeated slowly. "That's what Nesta wanted to name you had you been a boy."

Hallie, more interested in her doll, merely nodded to her father, then threw her arms about Pippin.

And Alec, getting himself together, had managed to remark in a light-enough voice to Genny, "She's changing so much every day, it doesn't seem to matter that I can't remember the beginning. This, I believe, is her first doll."

It mattered, but Genny merely nodded. They were off to London the following day. Alec hadn't asked where the Carrick town house was, but he unerringly directed his driver to it, saying without hesitation that it was the large Palladian structure on the northeast corner of Portsmouth Square. He was riding, something else Genny hadn't expected. He was a graceful rider and she found, wool-tangle brained female that she'd become, that she would be quite content to simply watch him riding beside the carriage.

Mrs. Swindel didn't try to point out every site of interest to their American colonist, something Genny appreciated.

London was a revelation. It was huge, dirty, and filled with smells and noise and so many people that Genny stared, then stared some more. She was still staring when they arrived at the Carrick town house. Only his town house, she amended silently to herself. And it was a palace. She felt horribly out of place, horribly unsure of herself. She was suddenly being thrust into another world, a world she'd never cared about, indeed, a world that hadn't had any meaning for her. Before now, before today, and before this moment. She was Baroness Sherard. Now everything mattered.

How could she have been so stupid to have married an English nobleman? She'd never thought, never realized . . .

She thought of her home in Baltimore, where Alec had lived for several weeks. He'd said nothing, but the Paxton house must have seemed like a miserable hovel to him. It hadn't occurred to her that he'd been used to something so far above her home as to be in the heavens. She swallowed, allowed Alec to help her from the carriage, and managed to lift her chin a good inch as they walked quickly into the house to avoid the drizzling rain.

"My lord! What a wonderful surprise. We received word only yesterday of your arrival. And your ladyship. Welcome, my lady, welcome!"

This enthusiastic welcome was from a very

gaunt hollow-eyed individual of advanced years who looked like royalty-gone-hungry.

"This is March, my dear," Alec said, and winked at his daughter. Pippin had told him that Hallie adored the wizened old man.

"March!"

The gaunt-eyed individual was quickly clasped about his neck and soundly kissed. At least Alec's daughter was a democrat, Genny thought, looking on. Whilst Hallie was renewing her acquaintance with the Carrick butler, Alec introduced Genny to Mrs. Britt, a comfortably fat lady with tiny gray sausage curls framing her face. It was Mrs. Britt, seeing nothing amiss with his lordship, who hastened to introduce all the house staff to the new baroness.

It was done. Very smoothly, Genny thought. Not one of them would realize that their master didn't recognize them. Worrying about Alec had markedly reduced her terror at meeting his servants. It wasn't until Genny was walking beside her husband up the wide curving staircase that she was again flooded with feelings of absolute worthlessness.

Her voice filled with awe and insecurity, she asked, "Are they all your ancestors?"

"Those folks covering the walls? I haven't the foggiest notion. Probably. They look arrogant enough."

She forced herself to smile, for Mrs. Britt was following behind them.

The baroness's bedchamber adjoined the master suite and it was into this large, darkened room that Mrs. Britt led Genny. It was somewhat eclectic in its furnishings, more feminine than Genny either liked or was used to, the predominant shades of peach and pale blue in the carpeting, in the counterpane, and on all the chairs. The room reeked of disuse. Alec stood beside Genny, aware of the tension that was holding her rigid, and not quite understanding it. He supposed it was simple enough, really. She didn't care for the room. It was, he remembered, quite different from hers back in Baltimore. He said easily, "Come with me into the master suite, my dear. We'll see how you like it. Who knows, perhaps you'll decide to share it with me."

This brought a snort of what seemed to be disapproval from Mrs. Britt, and a look of complete relief from his wife.

For Alec, of course, it was like stepping into a brand-new room, replete with furnishings he'd never before seen, an ambience he'd never felt before. It was disconcerting, to say the least.

There was waist-high wainscoting of a rich mahogany on every wall. The draperies were heavy gold velvet, the furnishings Spanish—heavy and dark and substantial. His first reaction was one of dislike. The room was somber and depressing as the devil. He thought of the books he'd read about the Spanish Inquisition and wondered if his father had been a devotee.

"My God," Genny said, gazing about her in awe," this reminds me of a painting by a Spaniard called Francisco Goya I saw in Mr. Tolliver's house in Baltimore. It's so very gloomy, Alec."

"Then you will simply eliminate all of this and have it refurbished and repainted and whatever

379

else you deem necessary. Your suite as well. Or you can forget about your room and simply share mine."

And that, Alec hoped, seeing her eyes light up with enthusiasm, should get her through her initial period of newness in this house, in London.

To Genny, there seemed to be no end to the opulence, to the deference paid to the master and the mistress. Even though she was a colonial, she was still to be tolerated, and with proper civility. Every servant put his or her best face on it and called her "my lady." Everything reeked of wealth—old wealth—and privilege, and so many generations of an inbred sense of self-worth, that Alec, even with no memory of his surroundings at all, fitted right in, without a pause, all his natural charm and graciousness at one with him and with those who served him. He was admired by every one of his retainers, including the scullery maid, protected by them and given their complete and unquestioned loyalty.

The day after their arrival, Alec left Genny to visit his solicitor. It was upon his return via St. James Street that he was waved down by a lady holding a charming parasol. He wondered if she wasn't freezing. The day was frigid, no wind to speak of, but just a bone-chilling cold that made him shudder—and he was wearing a monstrously warm greatcoat. He'd found the baron's wardrobe to be filled with clothes that he also liked. Something of an irony, that, and it made him smile. One of the very few things that had made him smile.

He pulled his horse to a stop and said, flourishing his beaver hat, "Good afternoon. How are you?"

She was a redhead, tall, deep-bosomed, and her eyes were wild with passionate depths. She would be uninhibited and utterly frenzied in bed. He didn't know how he knew this, but he was certain that it was true. Had he slept with her?

"Alec! You're home at last. It has been far too long, my dear man. Ah, this is wonderful. Do come to my house this evening. It's just a small soiree, but you'll see all your friends."

"He doesn't look like he recognizes you, Eileen."

"Don't be absurd, Cocky!" said Eileen, her voice sharp as she turned on her companion, a veritable tulip, replete with a monstrous cravat that nearly reached his earlobes, a lavender pair of morning breeches, and highly polished Hessians. His greatcoat was of the palest yellow. He was a vision and Alec winced. He recognized the man as a macaroni, but not the man himself.

"Cocky," Alec said and bowed slightly from his saddle.

"Do come, old man. Eileen is still on Clayborn Street, you know, number seven."

"I'll tell everyone you're back in London."

Alec nodded. He'd decide later what excuses to send to Clayborn Street. Right now, he had a great deal on his mind. None of it was pleasant. There were plans to put into motion.

An hour later, Alec faced his wife across the breakfast table in a small circular room that was blessed with privacy, coziness, and a fireplace.

Genny's attention was upon her husband.

381

"What is it, Alec? What did your lawy—solicitor say?"

"His name is Jonathan Rafer. He's known me since I was in leading strings and was a great friend of my father's. His wife will send over some of her chef's popsy cake, a favorite of mine, Mr. Rafer told me."

He sounded angry. He stopped talking and speared a slice of ham on his fork. He chewed on it thoughtfully, taking in the delicate furnishings of this small room. It was well done. He wondered who was responsible.

"You don't care for the main dining room?" he asked Genny.

"It's too cold to use and it's much too large for just the two of us."

He said nothing to that fine logic.

"The solicitor, Mr. Rafer, Alec."

"There appears to be evil at work, according to Mr. Rafer. The local magistrate, a Sir Edward Mortimer, claims it was the work of discontented tenants of mine. He claims the tenants murdered the steward and set fire to the Grange. I'll be leaving in a couple of days for Carrick Grange to get to the bottom of this mess. Unfortunately, Mr. Rafer didn't go to the Grange, merely reported to me what he'd heard from Sir Edward. I don't know how long I'll be gone, but—"

"Hallie and I will go with you, naturally."

"I'm not a invalid, Eugenia!"

"No, you're not, but that isn't the point. Where will you stay in Northumberland? In a gutted bedchamber? Who will see to your meals? Who will see to your people? Who will see to the rebuilding and refurbishing of the Grange?" She stopped, realizing she'd gone too far. It was true that she fully intended to be completely involved in these things, but she wasn't certain how Alec would react to that. More to the point, none of that really mattered. She simply couldn't bear to be apart from him.

"The majority of your list could be accomplished by servants."

That was doubtless true, but it raised her hackles nonetheless. "And who will sleep with you every night? More servants?"

"Who knows? The countryside of England can't be totally bereft of available females."

She gasped, and he said abruptly, "Cut line, Genny. There could be danger. I have no memory of tenants who could have done such a thing, but who knows? You will remain here in London, safe, both you and my daughter."

"Alec, both you and I survived a great deal more danger in that hurricane. I can't imagine why you're getting so excited about a simple jaunt into the English countryside."

The Alec of old spoke in a voice that reeked of centuries of arrogance, control, and dominance. "I've made up my mind, Genny. You're my wife and you'll obey me. You will remain here. I will take no risks with your health or that of my unborn child. Now, please pass me the carrots."

That made her see red. "You will not leave me here, alone, in a strange house, in an equally strange city, surrounded by strangers! It's cruel and you can't do it."

That gave him a moment's pause. There was

some logic to what she said. Well, even that was neatly to be solved, thanks to a woman with very passionate eyes named Eileen. "Tonight we're going to meet some friends. For you. They're mine now, evidently. The woman giving the soiree is Eileen, and the gentleman with her was named Cocky. I don't know who they are, but I do know where the lady lives. We'll go. Perhaps someone's face will jog my lamentable memory. In any case, you will meet some people and hopefully make some friends."

"I don't want to go!"

Alec tossed his napkin down on the table. "I don't care what you wish or don't wish to do. You will accompany me tonight and that's the end to it. Be ready, Eugenia, by eight o'clock."

He strode out of the small breakfast room, leaving Genny to fume at the carrots.

21

Genny didn't want to go out. She didn't want to meet strangers who were also foreigners to her. She didn't want to meet a woman named Eileen who was very probably in love with Alec. The London weather reflected her mood. It was cold and drizzling, the air heavy with fog. She paced the pale blue Aubusson carpet in her bed-chamber, angry with her autocratic husband, telling the empty room all her woes.

She also felt fat. Alec hadn't bothered to

384

concern himself about the fact that his wife had fewer gowns by the day, probably none at all suitable for an evening with London society. She had one gown that fitted her, and that one just barely. It was an old gown from the days before Alec and his shopping expeditions with her. She'd always thought it very pretty, but now, staring in the mirror, she wasn't so certain. She'd gotten so used to seeing herself in gowns that Alec had approved. And there was the matter of her overflowing bosom. Something had to be done.

Genny knew it would be grossly improper to show so much of herself in public. What she didn't know was what to do about it. She remembered suddenly that long-ago evening when she'd sewn lace on her gown, wanting to make herself prettier for Alec. So she wasn't a seamstress of note. She shrugged her shoulders. She would do better this time. She ripped a piece of lace from a gown that was too small and sewed it into the neckline. Her stitches weren't all that even, but neither were they all that crooked. The result wasn't bad, she thought, eyeing her work closely. So there were a few knots, a few spots where the lace was bunched up a bit. She sighed. She'd done the best she could. At least she wasn't half naked anymore.

She remembered the white velvet bows on that gown she'd worn to the Baltimore Assembly room. She remembered how she and Alec had both ripped off those damnable bows until there had been a pile on the floor between them. Well, Alec didn't remember. She was very tempted to track him down and ask him how she looked.

But no, she thought, she was fine, just fine, and besides, she was more than perturbed with him. She imagined that he'd give her the gratuitous brunt of his tongue. And there wasn't one single white velvet bow for anyone to take exception to. She gave herself one last long look in the mirror, felt a moment's insecurity, then squared her shoulders and came away.

Alec was waiting for her. He was dressed like a royal prince, at least to Genny's jaundiced eye, in black evening clothes and a pristine white shirt and cravat. He looked beautiful, but his normally warm eyes were cold as they rested briefly on her. A slight frown drew a line between his brows.

She merely nodded, remembering that she was not on the best of terms with him. She didn't want him to forget it.

"Shall we go?"

She nodded again and swept past him to the carriage. A footman held an umbrella over her head until Alec assisted her inside. She heard him give their driver directions—a man he called Collin—then he joined her in the carriage. He didn't ask her if she was cold, just merely covered her legs with a carriage blanket.

Alec settled back against the swabs. He was still a bit miffed with his wife for her rank stubbornness. He wasn't used to such behavior from her. Ah, but she did look lovely. She hadn't worn that cloak since that one evening aboard the *Night Dancer* some three weeks before. Oddly enough, she'd told him that he'd selected the material, color, and style for the cloak and the matching gown. That had surprised him. He'd loved slipping his hands underneath the cloak and stroking her breasts through the equally lovely gown beneath. He found himself growing randy and supposed it was more healthy than anger. It was certainly more pleasurable.

He grinned in the darkness. It wasn't her fault, not entirely anyway. He had been rather presumptuous, rather domineering. He said easily, "The woman's name is Eileen Blanchard, Lady Ramsey, a widow. I thought I was being the most subtle of intelligent human beings with my sly questions to March, and you know what he said?" Genny didn't pursue an answer, so Alec continued. "He told me that Moses—a fine fellow—had informed him of my small problem, and it was a good thing that he had—fine fellow that he is—and that it would be a matter of the greatest discretion. I wasn't to worry. Everything would be taken care of." Alec grinned toward his silent wife. "He made me feel like I was seven years old. Then he told me he didn't know much about this Eileen, but he recalled that I'd liked her well enough. Thank the Lord he knew her full name."

Genny felt a smile lurking at the corners of her mouth. When he gently picked up her gloved hand and patted it, she sighed and turned to him.

"Hello," he said and kissed her, very gently. "You do look lovely, Genny. I like your hair like that."

"Mrs. Britt insisted. You truly like it braided up in a coronet?"

"Yes, I certainly do, and I like the way the loose tendrils caress your face. I especially like

387

the tendrils that curl down the back of your neck. Very wanton very—"

"Not abandoned, please."

He kissed her again. He touched his fingertips to her warm lips. "Forgive me for my abruptness with you today. I am sorry. I don't want you to worry about this evening. I won't leave you adrift amongst strangers. I am assuming that the people I did know are decent and will thus prove likable."

Genny had to be content with that. He could manipulate her so easily. She knew it, railed against it, but never railed enough.

As for Alec, he kissed her again, loving the taste of her, the feel of her soft mouth. He would like very much to slip his hands beneath that cloak and fondle her breasts, but he held back.

He hoped that the staff were treating her well. He knew that they did—at least in front of him—but she was different, she was American, and she wasn't used to having a servant assist her in dressing. That had brought an appalled cry from Mrs. Britt, who cried again to Pippin, who in turn had informed Alec as he was dressing for the evening, "She thinks Genny has to be something of a savage, Capt'n . . . my lord. She didn't say it in so many words, but I think she thinks that Genny trapped you into marriage after your accident." Pippin had then grinned from ear to ear, disregarding Alec's frown. "Not to worry, my lord. My guinea's on Genny if it comes to a fracas. But Mrs. Britt will come about, you'll see. I just thought you should know the lay of the land."

Well, Mrs. Britt had arranged Genny's hair and most charmingly.

They arrived and were duly assisted from the carriage by a footman holding an umbrella. When they reached the reception line in the main salon, Alec removed his wife's cloak and handed it to a waiting footman. When he turned back again, he sucked in his breath in consternation. He whipped around to catch the footman, but the fellow was gone.

Where had she gotten that god-awful gown? She looked worse than a fright. Her gown, a strange shade of dark green that made her look horribly sallow, was too small, pulling terribly across her shoulders and breasts. The style was beyond anything Alec could have created as a model of bad taste. There were six ruffles, starting below her breast and ending at the hem, each one an even stranger shade of dark green. At her bosom there was a row of white lace sewn in crookedly. Suddenly in his mind's eye he saw Genny wearing another gown with a row of lace sewn into the bodice. He saw himself staring, then chuckling.

Alec shook his head. He swallowed. The image disappeared, followed by an even more unusual one. Genny was standing in front of him, and there was a pile of white velvet bows on the floor between them. He saw her rip one off. Then he ripped one off. What the devil was going on here? He shook his head again and the memory flitted away. He was once more firmly planted in the present. Standing beside her and looking down, he could see her nipples. He hadn't thought, hadn't realized . . . but good Lord, she was a woman, a lady! She'd always dressed in lovely clothes. Where had this awful apparition come from? Was it a punishment? Had she worn it on purpose to embarrass him?

Oh, God, what to do?

He said in a low, furious voice, "Genny, we're leaving now. I will have quite a bit to say to you later." He grabbed her hand, but it was too late.

"Why, good evening, Alec! So wonderful to see you here." Eileen Blanchard held out her hand to him.

Helplessly, Alec took it and raised it to his lips. "Hello, Eileen." There was no hope for it. They were trapped for at least five minutes. Then he would get his wife out of here and home.

"This is my wife, Genny. My dear, this is Eileen Blanchard."

She was lovely, Genny thought, and smiled her friendliest smile. "Hello."

"Your wife!" Eileen took in every inch of Genny in a remarkably short number of seconds and laughed. "Really, Alec, you are far too amusing!" She laughed again, not a nice sound at all, Genny thought, staring at the woman. "Wife!" Eileen repeated, her laughter nearly making her gasp for breath. "A fine joke, my lord, but enough is enough. Do you want to insult your friends? Send the doxy on her way and I will allow you to waltz with me."

Doxy!

Genny felt her breasts heave with fury but managed to hold her temper. The last thing she needed was to fall out of her gown. "I am not a doxy," she said loudly. "I'm Alec's wife."

"You're an American! By all that's marvelous, my lord! Cocky, come here and meet Alec's jest on us for the evening!"

Alec, appalled to his toes, intervened quickly, his voice very quiet, gentle, calm. "Eileen." He clasped her slender wrist between his long fingers. "This is my wife. Do you understand me?"

"No," she said, giggling now, and his fingers tightened, hurting her. She sucked in her breath. "Your wife? But that's absurd . . . you married? You swore you'd never again marry. You swore that you enjoyed women too much to allow only one to hold you, and said that if I really liked you, I would present you with a harem for a Christmas gift. And why her? Just look at her, Alec. Why, that gown and—"

Alec turned to a very interested footman standing behind his mistress. "Fetch her lady-ship's cloak and mine as well. Immediately."

Cocky, Reginald Cockerly by name, resplendent in black and pale pink, gaped at the scene, wisely keeping his mouth shut. Other people, however, were beginning to notice that something was amiss. Conversation died. People craned their necks to see better. Alec wished he could magically disappear, his wife tucked safely under his arm.

He'd wanted a harem for a Christmas gift? Good God, what kind of a man was he?

He looked at Genny. She was pale but seemingly very composed. She was staring straight ahead, her eyes narrowed, her lips thin. Where the devil had she gotten that wretched gown? She had done it on purpose to embarrass him, to infuriate him; there was simply no other explanation.

"But you can't leave now, Alec!"

Alec ignored Eileen, grabbing Genny's cloak from the footman. At least the cloak was beautiful. He bundled her into it quickly, then shrugged on his own.

"Alec, really! That is all too absurd. Cocky, say something, don't just stand there like a stupid buffoon!"

Cocky, wisely, remained silent.

Alec gave Eileen a brief bow, took his wife's arm, and led her from the house, leaving the interesting buzz of conversation behind them. They walked silently down the narrow steps. It had stopped raining. There was even a quarter moon shining through the gray clouds. Odd, the things one noticed, Genny thought, knowing the only way to salvage herself was to remain detached.

Once inside the carriage, she didn't say a word, merely pulled the carriage blanket over her legs. She was vaguely aware that Alec was poking his cane head against the ceiling of the carriage. They rolled forward with a slight lurch. Genny grabbed the leather strap to steady herself.

Alec said in a controlled voice, "Will you tell me why you wore that gown?"

"It was the only one that fitted."

"It doesn't fit. I could see your nipples, for God's sake, And the color and style . . . my God,

Genny, you certainly succeeded in gaining your ends, didn't you?"

That put a stop to her wonderful detachment. "Gaining my . . . what are you talking about?"

"You wore that gown to embarrass me, to humiliate yourself and thus me, so I would have no choice but to take you to Carrick Grange with me."

If she'd had a hammer, she would have coshed him with it. "You're wrong. Completely wrong. Go to your precious Carrick Grange by yourself, I don't care!"

That drew him up short. She sounded impassioned, unquestionably sincere. "You didn't wear that gown on purpose, then? But why? I don't understand. No one would wear that gown unless . . . Tell me. Why?"

"It's one of my old gowns. You don't remember this, but I don't have what you would call very good taste in clothes. All the gowns you've seen me wear are those that you yourself selected."

He could but stare at her in the dim carriage light. If she hadn't done it on purpose, then . . . She had no taste in clothing? "I'm sorry," he said, and reached for her hand. "I'm very sorry for what happened. I told you I didn't know that woman. I thought, nay, I truly believed, that if she had been a friend of mine before, she would be pleasant. But she was a bitch, an unaccountable bitch. I want you to forget the things she said. It was nastiness, all of it."

But Genny wasn't thinking about Eileen and the gown. She was thinking about Alec's harem.

She saw this succession of hopeful-looking, very beautiful women, all waiting for Alec to give himself to them. Had the woman Eileen been one of his mistresses? Or lovers? There was probably a distinction, but she didn't know for certain what it was.

"Genny, please, say something."

She did, in a quite calm voice. "What is the difference between a mistress and a lover?"

He gaped at her, at sea.

"I ask because I was wondering if that woman Eileen had been your mistress or your lover."

"I don't know."

"The difference?"

"No, if I've ever slept with her. I think that I did, more fool I. I suppose she would be a lover, rich and widowed that she is. She would choose the man she wished an *affaire* with." He pronounced it in the French way. "I don't remember."

"I think she and I could become great friends don't you? Both of us doxies. She could show me how to be a doxy on the inside rather than just on the outside. Perhaps you should visit her, Alec. It seems rather likely that she could tell you a great deal about your past."

"Don't be sarcastic. It sits ill on your shoulders, your very *naked* shoulders."

If looks could have killed, Alec would have lain dead on the floor of the carriage.

He sighed. "Oh, the devil! Where did you do your shopping before I came along? From a little old lady in Baltimore who was half blind and sewed for a hobby? Was she paid by the number of ruffles she sewed on each gown? God, then this thing must have cost a bloody fortune. And that lace—who is responsible for that? It isn't even sewn on straight."

She fell as silent as a statue. Alec, furious with himself for his unmeasured words, tried again, in a more measured tone. "You should have come to me. You should have asked my advice, particularly since you've done it before."

Genny gave him a weary look. "I told you, it was the only gown that fitted me. Also, I was very angry with you, if you'll recall. I didn't want to draw any more of your fire." Her chin went up. "I didn't realize I looked so bad."

He could only stare at her. "But the gown isn't in the least flattering, loose or tight. The color is awful, and your breasts—" He broke off, then said slowly "Your breasts are swelled from your pregnancy."

"Surely you didn't think I would become flat-chested instead?"

"You should have said something to me. Angry or not, you should have come to me."

"If you will recall, Baron, it wasn't just on my side. You kept your distance from me until it was time to leave."

"Still, that's no excuse—"

"I told you, I didn't realize it was so bad."

"That's absurd. A blind woman would know that—Oh damn and nonsense. You and I are going shopping tomorrow."

"I wouldn't go back to Cape Hatteras with you!"

"Do be quiet, Genny. You'll come with me and that's that."

She folded her tent. She was tired, depressed, her will flattened. "All right. It's foolish of me to cut off my nose to spite my face. I do have lamentable taste in clothes. As I told you, 'twas I who sewed on that lace myself. I'm not very good. In any case, I made something of a fool of myself at an assembly in Baltimore. You took me shopping and selected some gowns for me. Unfortunately, none of them fit anymore. Only this one, and as you so generously pointed out, it doesn't either, not really."

That was true enough, curse her innocent and guileless hide. Alec closed his eyes. He remembered the snatches of images he'd had over the past weeks, many of them of women, quite naked, and all of them loving him with gratifying fervor.

"Was I a bloody rakehell, then?" he said in a wondering voice.

"I don't know, but it could be true. You're so very beautiful and charming and nice."

He hadn't really meant to say that aloud. And here she was, adding her remarks in a voice that was very nearly devoid of anything but polite indifference. He exploded. "Why do you sound so wonderfully calm about it? Why the devil can't you at least be a bit jealous? You're my wife, dammit, not my bloody sister!"

"All right," she said and turned to face him, her eyes burning. She slapped him hard, on his cheek so hard that his head twisted to the side. "You bastard!"

She slapped him again. Her breasts were heaving, her breath coming in short gasps.

"That's quite enough." He grabbed her wrist and pulled her hand down into her lap. "Quite enough."

He'd finally pushed her over the edge. "You deserve punishment, do you hear me? Perhaps I don't have taste in what is fashionable and what is and isn't good taste—"

"What a wonderful understatement!"

"Very well. I simply don't see things the way you do. But at least I'm loyal and faithful and am not a man-izer—whereas you're an arrogant bounder, a despicable womanizer, and I hope your parts rot off!"

He stared at her for a moment, his eyes widening at her final curse. "Rot off?"

"Yes!"

"What a repellent notion. Dear Lord, what would you do? May I remind you, Eugenia, that you must be the most enthusiastic of all my women. After all do you not hold me faithful to you?"

"We've not been married very long."

"That's true. Nevertheless, it wouldn't do to curse me in that way. Now, whether you like it or not, you and I are going shopping tomorrow—" He broke off, seeing in that instant a small birdlike woman surrounded by bolts of cloth, twittering, giving him approving looks, speaking with a definite American accent. "This seamstress in Baltimore, well, I think I just saw her. It's odd, this remembering. You'd think I'd remember our wedding night, for example, not some practical stranger."

"It must not have been very memorable for you."

"Oh, I doubt that, Eugenia. So I've a wife with no sense of taste or fashion. Well, it's a good thing I do. Never again will you have to sew lace in your bodice to keep your breasts hidden." He started laughing then, deep, full laughter. She wanted to kill him. His laughter grew until he was holding his belly. "My God, that lace! Some of it was hanging off and I could see all of you!"

He was still holding her wrist, so she couldn't hit him.

"I could even see snippets of thread. It wasn't even the same color as the lace or the gown or any of those bloody ruffles!"

He roared.

She let him roar until they reached the Carrick town house. It was raining now, full blast. She didn't wait for Alec to help her. She dashed from the carriage up the narrow steps to the front door.

Even as she picked up her skirts and ran up the stairs, she could hear him chuckling as he came into the entrance hall. Even as she tripped on her skirt, grabbed at the railing, and cried out in surprise, she could hear him, only he wasn't laughing now. "Genny! Are you all right?"

She brushed herself off. She didn't look at him, merely said under her breath, "Wretched, arrogant creature!"

"Am I, now?" And he laughed again.

He wasn't laughing, however, when he came into her bedchamber some thirty minutes later.

He stopped beside her bed. "Why are you sleeping in here? You don't like this room. I offered to share mine with you."

"I wanted to cosh you on the head, which could lead to my arrest for murder, so I decided to sleep in here, by myself."

"I'll sign a special paper saying that if my wife coshes me, she's not to be hung at Tyburn. Now, do you come with me or do I sleep with you in here?"

"Alec," she said, her voice thin, "I don't like you at the moment."

She said nothing more because he swooped down, scooped her up in his arms, covers and all, and carried her back into his bedchamber. "I think I'll have the adjoining door boarded up. You belong with me, wife, and that's an end to it."

He kissed her then, a slow, very deep kiss, and she could think of not a single reason to go against his dictum.

"All right," she said, and kissed him this time.

"Ah," he said, his beautiful eyes glittering as he laid her on her back. She watched him shrug out of his dressing gown. Naked, all of him, and he was so beautiful and strong that she wanted to hold him to her and keep him there, forever. He was grinning down at her. In the next instant he was pulling off her nightgown, then flipping her onto her stomach. "Now," he said, "there's something I want to do, something I think you'll like."

He brought her up on her hands and knees, and came over her, his hands caressing her loose breasts. And when he thrust into her, she arched her back, pressing her hips against his belly, and he moaned as he kissed her ear. Then his hands stroked her belly, going lower to find her and tease her swelled woman's flesh, and it was her turn to moan and cry out as the wonderful sensations flooded through her. "Alec," she said, "oh, please. Alec . . ."

He pumped into her even as his fingers drove her to pleasurable distraction. She met his deep thrusts, wishing only that she could kiss him, feel his tongue in her mouth, his warm breath on her cheek as he exploded in his climax.

"That was rather nice," she said when she at last lay on her side, her head on his shoulder.

"Yes, it was." He sounded abstracted.

"What is it, Alec? What's wrong?"

"We've done that before."

"Yes, in Baltimore."

"I didn't see us doing it—not like the other images that come to me—but I felt it, if you can understand that. It was familiar to me . . . feeling how deeply I was inside you, knowing how your breasts would feel in my hands, so full and soft, and your belly, dear God; how you feel, so wet and swelled and hot; and then you shudder and arch your back and your legs tremble and I'm so deep that you're part of me or me of you or something."

His words were powerfully erotic and she came up on her elbow, leaned down, and kissed him.

"Does that mean you forgive me?"

"Probably." She kissed him again. "I can't stay

angry at you, no matter how much I want to. I'm a weak-willed female."

That didn't sound precisely right, but Alec wasn't certain why it was that he would think that. Certainly she'd been furious with him, but he would have been equally furious if he'd been in her place. Since he'd known her—his mind wiped slate-clean—she'd been nothing but sweet and gentle and wonderfully kind and giving, both to him and to his daughter. But something wasn't quite right. He shook his head, staring up at the smooth white ceiling. He didn't know what it was. He felt her relax against him, heard her soft breathing even into sleep.

The next morning, Pippin came in to build up the fire. He looked toward the bed and smiled to see his master and mistress burrowed under the covers holding each other and sleeping blissfully.

When Alec awoke, the room was warm. He pushed back the covers, easing out of Genny's arms. He looked down at her bare breasts. White and soft and much fuller now. Lightly, his finger touched her nipple.

She shivered and opened her eyes.

"Good morning."

She smiled back, unconsciously offering her breasts more fully to him. He continued to smile, but it was an effort. He covered her quickly.

"Today we shop for you," he said. He consulted the clock on the night stand. "It's very late, Genny. I would like nothing more than to continue our activity of the previous night, but there's too much to do."

So it was that Alec took her to Madame Jordan,

a woman who was truly French but had been married to an Englishman who died in the Battle of Trafalgar. "Iz my name for too many years," she'd explained comfortably. "Iz no need to use anozzer."

It was a repetition of Baltimore, Genny thought, watching her husband and Madame Jordan pour over materials and patterns presented immediately after a snap of the fingers by three assistants. Her pregnancy was discussed fully, as if she weren't present. Styles were selected that could easily be altered as the child grew.

When she was measured, Alec was there, watching. She didn't know whether to be embarrassed or miffed. She decided she was too tired to be either and docilely did as she was bidden. It was Alec who called a halt a half hour later.

"She will wear this gown, then, madame, and this cloak."

Genny eyed the incredibly beautiful sable-lined, pale gray velvet cloak. She'd never owned anything like it in her life. Indeed, in Baltimore she'd never even seen anything like it. As for the gown, it was a high-waisted muslin of soft, pale blue. It flattered her and hid her rounding stomach quite nicely. There were no flounces or bows. It was simplicity itself, something, Alec had said firmly, that was just in her style.

"Very good, milord," said Madame Jordan, all agreement. "You are lucky, my dear," she added, and patted Genny's cheek. "You have ze generous husband. He'll take good care of you."

That sounded nice, but just on the surface of

402

things. Genny didn't want to be taken care of—well, perhaps when it came to a suitable wardrobe, but she could buy that for herself. The shipyard was hers, after all, and all the income from it. Then she remembered that she had decided not to have Alec deed it over to her. It was still in his name. But what did that matter? They were married; the shipyard was theirs; it belonged to both of them. She shrugged her answer to her silent question.

"Day after tomorrow," Alec said as they rode back to Portsmouth Square, "we'll leave for Northumberland. You'll have enough gowns by that time."

"Ah, you've decided that I am worthy to accompany you, then?"

"Don't be snippy. I have no choice." She could tell that he didn't like it.

"And Hallie."

"Yes, and my daughter."

Genny wanted to assure him that she would be of remarkable assistance to him, but the frown that furrowed his brow made her hold her tongue. I have become a weak-willed female, she thought. It was not an observation that pleased her.

22

"Ho! Alec! Good Lord, man, welcome home!"

Alec whipped about, making his stallion, Cairo, whinny in protest, to see a gentleman waving at him from beside the entrance to White's. He was a tall man, black-haired, lean, and well dressed. He had a military bearing. No, it was more than that, Alec thought. It wasn't just his bearing; he *knew* the man had been in the army. He shook his head at himself, knowing that it was true, but again not knowing how he knew.

He smiled and waved, drawing Cairo to a halt. He dismounted and took the other man's outstretched hand.

"I'd heard you'd come home. Arielle and I are in London for a fortnight. We're staying at Drummond House. The boys are with us and would very much like to see their favorite uncle and their cousin. How is Hallie?"

"But I don't have a brother or a sister," Alec said slowly, studying the gentleman's face for a likeness to his own. "At least I don't think so."

"Alec, what's wrong with you? Come into White's and let's have a brandy. I'd heard you were married. Is that true? Arielle can't wait to meet your wife."

Alec nodded, handed Cairo to a waiting postboy, and accompanied the gentleman into White's.

He waited until they were seated in the vast oak wainscoted reading room, a brandy in their hands. Only two very old gentlemen were present, and they appeared uninterested in the two young men. Alec said as he raised his glass, "I'm sorry, but I don't know you. I had an accident nearly two months ago, and my memory . . . well, it's gone."

"Are you jesting?"

"I would give just about anything I own to be jesting. You're not my brother, are you? Nor is your wife my sister. You said I was your boys' uncle."

The look of astonishment remained, but the gentleman's voice was smooth and calm. "My name is Burke Drummond, Earl of Ravensworth. My wife, Arielle, is a half sister of your first wife, Nesta, who died in childbed some five years ago."

"Nesta," Alec said, looking thoughtfully into his brandy snifter. "I've seen her so many times. Just flashes, you know. In some of them she's pregnant, smiling, so very sweet-looking, but in most she's dead, lying there cold and silent and—" Alec broke off. "You're married to her sister."

"Yes," said Burke, "I am. For five and a half years now."

"And you were a military man."

"How did you know that?"

Alec shrugged. "You have the look, and I . . . well, I just know. Were we close friends?"

"Not really, not for many years now. You were living in America, in Boston, for several years. Then you and Nesta voyaged many places together. You came home and stayed with Arielle and me in August of 1814. Then you took Nesta to your estate in Northumberland. She died in December." It was Burke Drummond's turn to come to a halt. This was beyond anything he'd ever encountered. He'd met Alec more than ten years before, when he'd been an incredibly popular young man newly loosed on London

405

society and London ladies. He and Alec had both enjoyed themselves immensely. But as the years passed, their paths had diverged.

"Have you consulted a physician here in London?"

Alec shook his head, then took a sip of his brandy.

"Would you like to tell me how this happened to you?"

"It's a long story," Alec began, then grinned. "No, actually, it's very short. I was hit by a falling mast, and when I regained consciousness, I didn't have the foggiest notion of who I was or who the naked woman lying beside me was."

"Your wife, I presume."

"Yes. Her name is Genny. I would like to meet Arielle. Perhaps seeing her would bring things back."

"You and your wife must come to dinner this evening. Tomorrow Arielle and I can bring the boys to your house and see Hallie. Is the child all right?"

"You mean with her father a stranger? Unfortunately, there was no way to keep it from her. She worries more about me than she worries about herself. She's a very precocious little girl."

"She always has been," said Burke, rising. "When the boys are older, I don't have a doubt who will be the one to lead them into mischief." Burke paused a moment, then added matter-of-factly, "My children's names are Dane and Jason. Dane is fast becoming a little boy, but Jason is still a baby." He took Alec's hand. "It will be all right."

"That's what Hallie says, after she pats my hand."

Burke laughed.

Nesta's sister, Genny thought. Now she would learn more about her husband. Genny was gowned appropriately, since Alec was once again selecting what she would wear and what jewelry should adorn each gown. When he'd discovered she didn't own any jewels, he immediately went to his solicitor, learned of his family's vault in the Bank of England, and fetched jewels that had been in the Carrick family for more than two hundred years. He dumped the bundle in Genny's lap as she sat trying to make sense of a roman à clef written by Caroline Lamb three years previously.

"Goodness! What is this? A come-to-life fairy tale?" Diamonds, rubies, and emeralds shimmered through her fingers.

"The lot looks as though it's been sitting in that vault for years and years. Do you like any of the pieces?"

Genny, who was frankly staring at gem after gem, could only continue to stare. She said, laughter lurking, "If I look hard enough, perhaps, just perhaps I shall see something that merits a second look."

Together they selected the jewelry that didn't need to be reset. There was a magnificent ruby, set simply, hung on a gold chain. Alec picked it up, then dropped it as if it were hot. "It belonged to Nesta," he said, staring at it.

"It's beautiful. How do you know?"

"I just do. I was saving it for Hallie."

"Then we'll continue to save it for Hallie," Genny said calmly. "The ruby is the largest I believe I've ever seen. Do you know where you got it?"

"I haven't the foggiest notion."

"Well, in that case, how about this string of pearls? I like the pinkish cast. What do you think?"

Alec approved. That evening they went to the Drummond town house with Genny wearing a pale pink silk gown deeply scalloped at the hem, pearls around her throat, and pearl studs in her ears. Her long gloves and slippers were the same soft, pale pink shades. She looked exquisite and Alec told her so. "And do you now like having someone help you to dress?"

Genny giggled. "Mrs. Britt finally just told me that she would do it. She didn't allow me to say anything."

"You will hire a lady's maid. Mrs. Britt has too many responsibilities to be worrying about you as well as the house."

"Perhaps after we've settled matters at Carrick Grange."

He started to protest, then decided he wouldn't at all mind being her lady's maid at Carrick Grange.

Genny liked the Earl and Countess of Ravensworth. They put her at ease immediately. They did not make her feel like an interloper or a foreign oddity. Genny smiled at a jest made by Arielle Drummond, a charming young lady with the most glorious red hair she'd ever seen. Thick and curling, untamed, her hair framed a piquant face that held a good deal of character and sweetness.

Dinner was spent providing Alec with a life before two months ago. The name Knight Winthrop came into the conversation. Alec saw him so clearly that he choked on his julienne soup. "He's got gold eyes, doesn't he? Fox's eyes? He's tall and an athlete? And he's so funny you clutch your stomach from laughing so hard?"

"That's Knight," said Arielle. "Five years ago he was London's most loudly self-proclaimed bachelor. He claimed equally loudly that he would follow his sire's philosophy to the letter."

"What was his father's philosophy?" Genny asked.

"Not to marry until he was forty, and then to wed an eighteen-year-old girl who was malleable as a sheep and a good breeder. And after he'd bred an heir, he was to leave his son to grow up without any of his sire's opinions or faults or failings. As philosophies go, it was no more absurd than many others." Arielle shook her head and giggled. "Poor Knight."

Genny sat forward, seeing the vivid humor in Arielle's eyes. "Do tell us what happened."

"Knight married. He now has seven children!" The words out of Arielle's mouth, she burst into merry laughter. "It's a wonderful story. He married the most beautiful woman I've ever seen in my life, and she already had three children— well, they weren't really hers, but they were Knight's cousin's children. The cousin had been murdered. That's all very confusing, isn't it?

Well, they married, and then Lily, Knight's wife, birthed two sets of twins."

"Does this Knight still adhere to his father's philosophy?" Genny asked.

"Goodness, no," Burke said with a grin. "Dear Knight can easily make you slip into nausea in his devotion to his family.

"It's true," Arielle added. "You never see him without at least three of his children clutching his hands, his legs, his ears."

Burke smiled at his wife. "Knight is a very happy man."

"And Lily is so beautiful men simply stop and stare after her. Even when she has all seven children in tow. It's most amusing to see Knight act the disinterested, oh-so-tolerant fellow when the poor nodcocks gawk at his wife."

"Do you stare, Burke?" Alec asked, raising an eyebrow.

"Every once in a while, just to make my wife sit up and growl."

"Conceited oaf," said Arielle in high good humor.

The evening continued in an amusing vein. It wasn't until Burke Drummond spoke of Lannie, his former sister-in-law, that Alec got another glimpse of someone in his past. He saw this Lannie very clearly in his mind. And she was chattering, her small hand on his sleeve. He forgot the wild duck on his fork. He described her perfectly.

Genny smiled at the table at large. "He's remembering more every day. I think when we go to Carrick Grange it will all come back to him."

"You're not staying in London for a while, then?" asked Burke.

"No," Alec said. "There's been trouble at the Grange. The house has been burned, I'm told, and my steward murdered."

"Good God!"

"How awful!" Arielle said. "The Grange is a huge house, over two hundred years old. There were many fine furnishings there. I hope some of them have been salvaged. Perhaps seeing your childhood home will bring back your memory, Alec."

"I think I need another coshing on my head. My wife occasionally offers to act as the cosh."

"Do tell us how you two met," Arielle said.

"I can't," Alec said.

Genny told them, an abbreviated edition, to be sure, with no mention of any brothel or her in trousers. Alec showed no sign of recognizing anything. It was disheartening that he would recall Burke's former sister-in-law and not his own wife.

"You're increasing," Arielle said without preamble to Genny after they'd left the gentlemen to their port and cheroots.

"Yes, I am. I'm rarely ill anymore, but the voyage to England was something I'd just as soon forget. I wanted to murder Alec for what he'd done and at the same time cock up my toes."

"Yes, isn't it true! And gentlemen just smile in that odiously superior fashion at us and pat our stomachs. Burke did."

"Alec much enjoys sleeping with his hands on my stomach. It makes him feel God-like, he tells me."

"It's been very difficult for you, hasn't it?"

To Genny's utter chagrin and surprise, Arielle's kind words made her want to burst into tears. She swallowed and looked away.

"I can't begin to imagine how you feel, married to a man who doesn't remember you, but it must be very trying. Just know this, Genny. Alec is a good man. Nesta's death hit him very hard. He didn't love her, not as a man should love his wife, but he was immensely fond of her and he felt guilty when she died. He didn't want Hallie, not at first, because he saw her as the instrument of Nesta's death. When Burke and I arrived after Nesta had died, we offered to take Hallie. It was then that he realized what he was doing. He kept her with him. Her upbringing to date has been most unusual, but Alec loves her so much that I can't believe it will matter. Now Hallie has you, and you, Genny, seem to be a very sensible woman. Do you get along well with your new stepdaughter?"

"Very well. I think that if Hallie hadn't liked me her father would never have considered marriage. She doesn't really manipulate him, it's just that they have great empathy. Now Hallie has taken me under her wing as well."

"I'm relieved she isn't jealous of you."

"Oh, no. She requested a little brother or sister even before we were married. Perhaps she saw me as her means to an end."

412

"More to the point, Hallie saw you as the woman to make her father happy."

Genny raised an eyebrow at that observation, then said in a wistful voice, "Sometimes I wish I were as beautiful as this Lily you spoke about. Is she as beautiful a woman as Alec is a man?"

"Just about, I should say. The two of them together would bring everyone to staring silence. It's much better for the progress of civilization that they aren't together. But you know, Genny, Alec is remarkably oblivious of his handsomeness, just as is Lily of her incredible beauty. He is also strong-willed, obstinate as a mule, and loyal as a tick."

"You should also add that he has very strong notions about a woman's role in things."

"What do you mean? What role?"

"My father was a master shipbuilder. I was raised to design and build ships. I have learned that men won't tolerate women who know the same things they do. I don't understand it, but it's true. If Alec hadn't come along, I would now own a shipyard that would be bankrupt because no self-respecting gentleman would conduct business with me, a woman."

"Alec didn't approve either?"

"Good heavens, no! We had colorful disagreements, I can tell you! Then he had his accident and I folded my proverbial tent and buried all my visions deep away. He needed me, you see. He still does. There can be no one more important than Alec."

"I see," Arielle said slowly, and indeed she did see. This very vulnerable young woman was much in love with Alec Carrick. Arielle suspected also that Genny was as strong-willed as her husband. And just as obstinate. "You are carrying his child as well now. You are his daughter's stepmama. You are, in short, doing everything a woman should do as a proper wife. Is that the gist of it?"

"Yes, it is."

"You know, my sister, Nesta, would have killed for Alec. Never, as far as I can remember, did she ever disagree with him. He, in turn, was quite gentle with her, tolerant, amused, but always the master, always the one in charge, in control. He was the protector. I can't recall ever hearing them argue, but then again, I wasn't with them very much during their marriage. It is possible he became something of a domestic tyrant." Arielle shrugged and smiled. "I shouldn't sound so very definite about Alec's character. But Nesta wrote me many letters during the years we were separated. She loved him to distraction and beyond. He could do no wrong in her eyes. She, in turn, would willing have lain down and let him tread on her, like a rug."

"That could turn a saint into a tyrant, and the good Lord knows that Alec wasn't ever a saint. I don't think I've become quite a rug"—she smiled thinking about the previous evening and their yelling match—"but if a woman weren't careful, it could happen."

"Things will turn around once Alec is himself again. But back to Nesta. Don't get me wrong, Genny. He did make her very happy. Whenever

414

I think of Nesta now, I think of how very happy she was for those five years with Alec."

"I don't believe Alec ever thought to remarry." Genny looked at Arielle, saw the interest and concern in the countess's lovely eyes, and yielded without a whimper. She told her all about the hideous experience with a woman named Eileen Blanchard.

". . . and that's what Eileen said. That Alec never wanted to be remarried."

"How very unpleasant for you! This woman sounds like a disappointed mistress—"

"Or lover. I think money makes the difference."

Arielle stared at her, then broke into laughter. "I shall ask Burke. He will know for certain. Now, the stories that got back to me—as you say, Alec is a lovely man. Women much enjoy him. You, if you don't mind me saying so, Genny, don't seem at all as malleable as Knight's mythical wife/sheep."

"No, I'm not, but as I told you, Alec doesn't realize it. He believes I'm sweet and giving and yielding, and dammit, that's all I've shown him since his wretched accident. It isn't fair!"

"What isn't fair?"

Alec was smiling at her from the drawing room doorway.

She said without missing a beat, "That you gentlemen get to remain in isolated splendor drinking that expensive French brandy and no doubt gossiping."

"When we get home, I'll share some with you.

415

Perhaps I can even make you tipsy. Soften you up a bit."

As if he ever needed to do that, she thought. All Alec had to do was simply look at her and she was soft as honey.

An hour later, they did drink a bit of brandy, Genny seated on his lap in front of their bedchamber fireplace. His hands were lightly stroking her belly, as was his habit. "You're still too thin," he said.

"Ha! I begin to think you preferred women who were plump as spring partridges."

"No," he said thoughtfully, "I don't think that's true. Kiss me, Genny. I've missed making love to you."

"It's just been since this morning."

"That long ago? You're cruel, woman, to deny me so."

"I'd never deny you." She thought of Nesta and wondered in that moment if she had thought the same thing.

He came into her as she sat facing him on his lap, her legs around his flanks. He was deep inside her and he looked into her face as his fingers brought her to shattering pleasure. And then she watched him when he moaned deeply and spilled his seed inside her.

It was exquisite. She was sitting on his lap, his member deep inside her and her head nestled in the crook of his shoulder. She didn't want to move. She wasn't surprised when he filled her again, his sex hard and throbbing. She cupped his face between her hands and kissed him as he lifted her, then eased her again over him. It

416

quickly became too much and Genny moaned into his mouth. Her yielding to him, her absolute surrender, drove him over the edge. But he took her with him, as he always did, for they were together in lovemaking.

She fell asleep still with him inside her, her head on his shoulder.

The next morning the Earl and Countess of Ravensworth brought their two small boys to see Hallie, and Genny observed her five-year-old stepdaughter play the sweet but no-nonsense mother to the little boys. When Arielle asked if Hallie could remain with her while Alec and Genny traveled to Carrick Grange, Alec immediately turned to his daughter.

"Would you like to, Hallie? You could doubtless give your aunt pointers on raising the boys correctly."

Hallie gave her father a long, very assessing look; then she smiled, a beautiful smile, and Genny caught her breath, not realizing that the child hadn't smiled very much of late. She was suddenly a little girl again. "I think I will, Papa, if it is all right with Uncle Burke and Aunt Arielle."

"We would love to have you with us," Burke said.

"All right, then," Hallie said. She looked at Genny. "You'll be fine without me?"

"I will, but I'll miss you dreadfully."

Late that afternoon Genny found Alec in the library, poring over papers at his desk.

"Whatever are you doing?"

He rubbed an abstracted hand over his jaw.

417

"More accounts for the *Night Dancer*'s last voyage."

"Shouldn't I be doing that?"

Alec looked at her like she was his savior. "You wouldn't mind, truly?"

"Of course not. I—I don't want to be a useless appendage to you, Alec."

He tossed his pen onto the desktop, leaned back in his chair, and gave her a big smile. "An appendage, huh? That sounds rather absurd to me. You're my wife, Genny. You're carrying my child. If this gives you pleasure, by all means do it."

Genny wondered as she totaled a column of numbers if Alec would have relinquished this task to her if he remembered. She couldn't imagine him doing so, not the Alec who'd come to Baltimore in October.

The Carricks didn't leave London until after Christmas. On January seventh, their carriage turned neatly through sturdy iron gates to bowl down the long tree-lined drive to Carrick Grange. An old, toothless man waved at them and Alec tipped his hat. The gatekeeper, he supposed. He kept waiting for memory to stroke, full and complete, and make him whole again. He immediately recognized certain things, like the incredibly thick-trunked oak tree just off the drive. He knew his initials were carved deep into the bark. When the Grange came into view, he sucked in his breath. It looked like an unlikely combination of a medieval castle and an Elizabethan manor house with its three soaring stories, two circular turrets on each end, scores of chimney pots, mullioned windows, and huge, carved front doors. A good deal of the fine, mellowed red brick was blackened by the fire, but only the east wing appeared to be severely damaged. His home, he thought, the place where he'd spent his boyhood. Images bombarded him, filling him. Quick, crystal-clear images that rolled in single, split-second pictures through his mind. He saw himself looking up at a very beautiful woman whose hair seemed as soft as melted gold, and he knew it was his mother and that he was very small and was hiding something behind his back, something he didn't want her to see. Unfortunately, he couldn't remember what it was. Then there was a tall man, magnificent on a black Barb, laughing and speaking to him, and he was again small, still a child. Then, just as suddenly, the man was gone and he was alone and his mother was there and she was crying. "Oh, God," Alec whispered. He shook his head. He was feeling the pain from the images, pain that he hadn't experienced in decades.

"Alec? Are you all right?"

Genny speaking to him, bringing him back. Genny's hand firmly on his coat sleeve, shaking him. He didn't want to remember any more. It hurt too badly. His heart was pounding, his breathing harsh and raw.

An old man stood on the front steps, staring at him. Who the hell was he?

"My lord! Thank the powers you're home!"

This must be Smythe, the Carrick butler since

Alec's childhood. His solicitor had told him of Smythe and of Mrs. MacGraff, his housekeeper.

Raw, wild feelings, not memories, swept through Alec the moment he stepped through the wide front doors. The huge entrance hall that soared upward two stories was smoke-blackened but undamaged. He felt rampant, wildly intense emotions—some deliriously happy, others so tragic that his eyes teared. And he knew those feelings were his, although they'd been felt very long ago. He'd come home to find memories, but instead those long-ago feelings from those memories had found him. He cursed, fluently and loudly, to rid himself of them. Genny stared at him. Smythe stared at him.

Mrs. MacGraff said, "My Lord! Whatever is wrong?"

Genny stepped quickly forward. "His lordship has been ill. He will be better now that he is home."

"You're alone?" Smythe asked as he led them up the winding staircase to the upper floor.

"Is that a problem?" Alec asked.

"The men who murdered your steward, my lord are still at large. They could be dangerous."

"Yet you're living here, Smythe. How many other servants?"

Smythe spoke about the servants, the damage to the Grange, the machinations of the local magistrate, Sir Edward Mortimer. He flung open the master-suite doors.

"Oh, dear," Genny said, eyeing the impossibly grand apartment. It was a huge room designed and furnished for a king, all heavy gold brocade

420

draperies, heavy, dark chairs and sofas, the most lush and rich of Aubusson carpets on the polished wooden floors. The fireplace was of rich Danish brick, and a warm blaze was burning. Genny walked toward it to warm her hands. She watched Alec from the corner of her eye. He was standing in the middle of the room, not moving, as if he were waiting for something. He looked tense and very wary.

Fortunately for Alec, there were no lurking feelings or emotions to accost him. He continued to stand there, rigid, but nothing came to his mind.

"Thank the good Lord," he said.

It was nearly midnight before Genny and Alec were ensconced in a large, deep armchair before the fireplace, Genny on his lap.

"Thank God most of the damage was limited to the east wing. That was where my steward, Arnold Cruisk, lived. Whoever killed him surely wanted him dead. I've spoken to many of the servants. They don't believe the murderer, or murderers, set the fire. They think it must have been an accident. They say that everyone on this estate loves the Grange too much to damage it." Alec sighed, leaned his head back, and closed his eyes.

"You're safe in this room, aren't you?"

That brought him back to full attention and his eyes snapped open. "You know?"

"Yes. The memories were hurting you dreadfully, but in here they leave you alone."

He eyed his wife. It was a bit frightening to realize that she knew him so well, was able to discern what was happening to him. She'd dealt adequately with Smythe and Mrs. MacGraff and the half-dozen other servants currently in residence at the Grange. They didn't seem to mind that she was an American. He didn't realize that it was his wife's obvious worry for him that made his servants ready to do anything she asked.

"You're pretty smart, aren't you?"

"More than you know, my lord." She nuzzled his throat. "Tell me if I'm wrong. You've seen images, but the difference is you're feeling the emotions you felt at the time each incident occurred. It must be awful for you. Pain can be borne when it must be, but to be bombarded with it—out of context, as it were—I shouldn't like that at all."

"You're perfectly right. It's disturbing."

"Oh, Alec, you're the master of understatement! I think you're the most wonderful man in the world and I love you so very much."

The instant the words were out, Genny clamped her hand over her mouth, but the words had been spoken and couldn't be retracted. She stared at him, wary, frightened, her heart pounding.

He smiled, very slowly. Then he set her away from him a bit, cupped her face between his hands, and kissed her. His breath was warm and tasted of the sweet claret he'd drunk at dinner. His tongue touched her lips and she parted them. She yielded her mouth, her body, all of her. Fire licked through her when his tongue touched hers, its heat concentrating between her thighs, making her ache, making her hot.

"Alec," she said into his mouth.

"Did you never before tell me you loved me?"

"No. I didn't realize that I did. And then I was afraid to tell you."

His hands were caressing her breasts even as he nipped the corner of her mouth, touched his tongue to hers. "How could you ever be afraid to tell me that? You're my wife."

"Because you don't love me. You never loved me. I think you found me something of an oddity—a woman who had no sense of taste or style, who needed you to do her shopping for her."

"You didn't tell me that before," he said, disregarding her attempt at humor. "Afraid to tell me you loved me? Why, that fills me with all kinds of wonderful feelings, Lady Sherard. A man wants to be loved, he wants his lady to yield herself to him completely."

And that, Genny thought, she certainly had done.

"You know something else, Genny Carrick? You're not an oddity, you're a very sweet, loving, pregnant lady. You fascinate me, Genny. Right now, do you know what I want to do to you?"

Her heart pounded, loud, deep strokes.

"Ah, are you thinking what you want to do to me?"

She nodded, looking at his mouth, unable to find words to tell him of her feelings for him.

"I want to kiss your belly, Genny . . . then I want to caress you with my mouth between your beautiful legs. I want you to tug at my hair and

423

shoulders and arch your back and yell when I bring you your release."

She was quivering and he knew it, and she knew that he knew, and thus pulled herself together. She gave him a siren's smile. "And I want to kiss your belly, Alec, then take you into my mouth. I want to hold you when you moan your pleasure."

"God, woman," he said, obviously pleased, startled, and excited at the same time. "I proclaim you the victor. Or rather, both of us will win, won't we?"

Genny agreed completely. They took each other and the pleasure they gave rivaled the pleasure each received. And Genny told him again that she loved him, as her body convulsed in its release. And again he smiled at her and kissed her. Heat for him quickly flooded through her and again he took her, thrusting deep as he told her how she felt to him and how beautiful she was when she climaxed. And his fingers caressed her until she cried out, a broken, raw sound, and it was immensely erotic to Alec.

He didn't love her, she thought, on the edge of sleep. How could he? He didn't remember who she was.

But he was remembering so much now. It would be soon. She knew it.

23

Alec's memory did flood back, in an instant of time, but neither of them dreamed Genny would be the catalyst.

She was intently searching through old papers and ledgers in Arnold Cruisk's estate office in the devastated east wing. She'd studied piles of scorched pages dealing with household accounts for a period of five years, but had found nothing she believed important, nothing that provided a clue to why the steward had been murdered. Because it was filthy in here, she'd dressed in men's clothes, the same ones she'd worn when she'd worked at the shipyard in Baltimore.

She'd just given further instructions to Giles, a Carrick footman, and was standing on her tiptoes trying to reach a bound folder that sat precariously on a burned top shelf when she heard someone coming. She turned and smiled as Alec gingerly stepped into the gutted room.

She bade him good-afternoon and started to ask him how his visit with Sir Edward Mortimer had gone when Giles asked her a question. After she had answered him and then turned back to Alec, she saw that he was staring fixedly at her. Genny cocked her head to one side in question as she wiped her dirty hands on her trouser legs. She smiled. "Yes, Baron?"

Alec didn't move. He doubted he could even

if he wanted to, which he didn't. Feelings, images, more memories than he could imagine a single person having, were swimming madly about in his brain, stirring up chaos and mental pandemonium. Then, just as suddenly, everything righted. He saw Genny for the first time, dressed in her men's clothes, standing on the deck of the *Pegasus*. He remembered what he'd felt that moment when he'd first seen her. She'd been giving orders to one of her men just as she had now with Giles. Merciful heavens, he thought somewhat blankly, he was whole again.

"Alec? Are you all right?"

"I think so," he said, but didn't move. He'd thought upon occasion that his head would burst with too much information when his memory did return. But it didn't. Everything was in place now. Genny was in place now.

As for Genny, she knew something was different. Quickly she said to Giles, "That will be all for the moment. Thank you for your assistance."

Alec watched the footman leave. He remembered Giles, of course. He'd hired him himself some five years ago, just before Nesta had birthed Hallie and died. He looked at his wife now. His incredible American wife who'd run a shipyard. He said very pleasantly, very precisely, "May I ask just what the devil you're doing aping a man again?"

His cold, distant voice froze her to the spot. This wasn't the man who'd awakened her early this morning, his hand already stroking between her thighs, his mouth already suckling at her breast, telling her how sweet she was, how soft and enticing. This was another Alec. This was the Alec she'd married, she realized with a start. She dismissed his words. They weren't important. Dear heavens, he'd remembered. Finally, he'd remembered.

"You remember," she yelled, trembling with excitement for him, for her, for both of them.

"Yes, everything, including the first time I saw you. You were dressed then as you are now. You were giving orders to a man then just as you were now."

She ignored his words again, relief and pleasure for him flooding through her. She was happy, deliriously happy. She ran to him joyously and he caught her against his chest. "Alec, oh, Alec, you've come back to me and to yourself. It's wonderful! Oh, my dear, you must be feeling ready to slay dragons!"

She kissed his chin, his mouth, his jaw, all the while chattering like a berserk magpie.

He smiled. At last he smiled.

"It's over," he said, looking down into her eyes. "How odd that seeing you jarred everything back into place. You in your men's clothes. As I said, that was as I'd first seen you. The tilt of your head, perhaps, as you spoke to Giles. But the clothes helped, they definitely did."

"Then we shall have to frame them and display them in a place of honor!"

He didn't know what to say to that, for in that moment the past merged as it should with the present and he realized how different he'd been before and after the accident. He caught himself.

427

No, it was Genny who had changed, not he. Now she would revert back to her old ways. He felt mired in confusion. Where everything had been simple and straightforward but five minutes before, now he was beset by mental confusion. He set her away from him.

"Alec?" Her smile faltered just a bit. She stroked his cheek with her fingertips. "Are you all right? Does your head hurt?"

Gentle, giving, soft, submissive to him—she'd been all those things since his accident. She'd yielded to him, surrendered so very sweetly to him, to all his wishes, all his desires. And he'd wondered at it occasionally, he remembered now, had asked her about it, teased her about that stubborn jaw of hers. The Alec without memories would doubtless have simply laughed to see her in breeches poking about the ruins. The old Alec, the one she had married, the Alec whom he was now, the one who'd left no doubts about what he thought of females aping men, had been manipulated very expertly and very cleverly. He felt betrayed, he, Alec Carrick, who had always been contemptuous of men who allowed themselves to be deceived by a woman. She'd done him up quite nicely.

He looked her over, his fingertips stroking his jaw. "One thing that's difficult about wearing a man's pants, Genny," he said finally. "I have to pull them completely off you to take you. That's why a female should wear skirts, my dear. Then a man can toss them up and enjoy a woman whenever he wishes."

She stepped back, surprise and hurt washing

through her, making her pale. But her voice remained calm. "I'm wearing pants simply because it's so dirty in here. My old gowns are too small to wear now, and I don't wish to ruin the new ones you bought for me."

"As I recall, you always sounded so very reasoned when you wished to continue playing the man, playing at something you could never be. Have you always envied men, Genny?"

She stared at him, anger roiling up from her belly at his indifferent cruelty. She held onto her control. "No, I've never envied men. I don't like them a great deal, however, when they feel it necessary to look down upon women who happen to know the same things they do."

"But, Genny, you wouldn't know a damned thing about designing or building vessels if your father hadn't treated you like a male and taught you."

"A man wouldn't know a thing about building vessels either unless someone taught him. Doesn't that tell you something?"

"It tells me that you had no mother to teach you how to be a woman. Thus you can ape a man but you can't even select appropriate women's clothes. That's what it tells me."

She slapped him, hard, and his head snapped to the side. Breath hissed out between his teeth. He grabbed her arms, shook her, then dropped his hold. He stepped back. "Get out of those damned ridiculous clothes or I'll tear them off you. Do you understand me? Never do I want to see you playing the man again."

She ran from the room without another word,

without a backward glance at him. She feared what she would say, what she would do, if she remained.

Alec stared silently after her. He drew a deep breath. She'd manipulated him royally, he thought again. So neatly. He'd been willing to give her anything, to allow her to pursue whatever absurd desire she had. He'd allowed her to take over the bookkeeping for the *Night Dancer*. All because he'd loved her, all because he'd thought it would give her pleasure. No, it was the blank-brained Alec who'd fallen in love with her. Not the old Alec. The old Alec had kept women in their place, using them, enjoying them when he wished to, but not allowing them to become part of him, deeply part of him. The old Alec had slept several times with Eileen Blanchard. The old Alec had jested that she could give him a harem for a Christmas present.

Alec sighed. He'd liked Genny very much, cared for her enough to marry her. And now he'd been unfair. He'd seen her in those damned clothes, gained his memory, and lost his head. The good Lord knew that he should be calling for champagne and celebrating. He was whole again. He was also married to a woman who'd managed to make him into a weak-willed ass who would accept and encourage her in anything she wanted to do. It wasn't to be borne.

Acting like a man, and at the same time she was carrying his child. He wanted to shout at himself to stop it. For God's sake, he was himself again. There wasn't a single blank spot. He saw Burke and Arielle Drummond and he saw Knight

430

Winthrop, heard him pontificating in the most cynically amusing way about his sire's philosophies. Knight was now married with seven children. And he, Alec, a man who'd never intended to remarry, was tied to a female whose motives left his mind taut with uncertainty, who made his body randy with lust and reduced him to an anger-monger, something he'd always abhorred before.

He was whole again. Despite everything else, he was as he had been. He saw Hallie, *knew* her, and wished that she were here right now so he could hug her close and tell her how much her father loved her. He saw the little boy again—himself twenty years before—helplessly watch his mother cry because his father was dead. He didn't feel the awful wrenching pain now. The memory was simply there and he knew of the loss, but all the pain was faded into the past, years and years into the past, where it belonged.

And Genny was looking up at him with trust and sweetness and wonder. It was their wedding night, and he'd loved her until she'd trembled and he'd trembled, and he'd held her and stroked her beautiful hair until they'd both slept, close in each other's arms. And he'd wakened her in the dark hours of the night and loved her again, and her beautiful cries had filled the night, and him.

Alec glanced around the smoke-blackened, devastated room and wondered what Genny had really been doing in here. He saw piles of scorched papers on the remains of his steward's desk and wondered cynically if she'd been trying to figure out the worth of Carrick Grange.

Genny dressed carefully in the other set of men's clothes she owned. She stepped back and gazed at her figure in the cheval glass. She still looked trim enough with the leather vest hiding her thickened waist. Even as she stared at herself in the mirror, she raised her chin a good half inch.

He wouldn't order her about.

If he wanted to be an autocrat, he could go to the devil. She wouldn't let him play the tyrant, with her his dutiful and obedient slave. She wouldn't put up with his ill temper, with his absurd conclusion that she was envious of men and, unable to be one, therefore aped them. For heaven's sake, she carried a child in her womb. That should be a sure sign even to the meanest intelligence that she was every inch a woman.

What had set him off? She'd made him remember with these silly clothes. He should be thankful to her. But no, he'd turned into a man even the old Alec hadn't approached. His attitude surprised her, hurt her, and eluded her attempts to understand it.

Genny looked over at the gown Mrs. MacGraff had laid out on the bed for her. It was one of the new gowns that Alec had selected, a pale lavender silk with a deeply cut bodice tightly banded beneath the breasts and a full, flowing skirt. It made her look like a quite delicious confection of womanhood, a delicate creature worthy of a man's protection and approbation.

She slapped her breeched thighs. She wouldn't wear the bloody gown. When he apologized, when he ceased behaving like an arrogant lout, she would willingly don any gown he wished her to. But she wouldn't be treated like a calculating creature who had purposefully deceived him.

He'd acted as if that was exactly what he thought she was.

He'd acted as if he not only disapproved of her but held her in contempt. She remembered each of his cruel words. She doubted she would ever forget them.

Did he honestly expect her to simply lie down at his feet and let him put his spurs into her? She had been soft and loving and submissive during his illness; she'd felt he'd needed all her support, all her understanding, her love and absolute acceptance. If she continued in that way now, she knew deep down that he would indeed become the tyrant. It wasn't in her character to be an insignificant, whimpering little female, dependent on her husband for her every need. She couldn't, she wouldn't, do it. Not for any man.

Genny straightened her shoulders and marched from her bedchamber down the long corridor to the central staircase. She gave a nasty grin to the particularly obnoxious ancestor whose full-length portrait hung on the wall beside the stairs. She strode into the drawing room, came to a stop, and stayed still until Alec, who had his back to her, turned slowly upon hearing her enter.

He stared at her, his fingers tightening about

the stem of his wineglass until his knuckles showed white.

If she'd been wearing a cap she'd look like a boy.

She looked exactly as she had the first time he saw her on board the *Pegasus*. No, that wasn't quite true. Her breasts were larger, swelled with her pregnancy. Even her loose jacket couldn't hide that fact. She didn't look at all like a boy.

"Good evening," she said, and her voice was strident, a goad to raise his hackles.

Alec said very calmly, "You will return to your bedchamber and remove those clothes, at once."

Her chin went up another quarter of an inch. "No."

His eyes glittered; his jaw tightened. "I told you what I would do if I saw you wearing men's clothes again. Did you choose to forget my words? Or did you believe that you could continue to manipulate me? Treat me like a weak-willed fool?"

"Manipulate you? What are you talking about?"

"You know quite well what I'm saying. Soft and submissive, all of it was a lie, down to the last moan from your pretty mouth when I made love to you. Your days of ruling me with your velvet glove are over, madam. Now, either you will take off those clothes yourself or I will do it for you."

It was true, she had been soft and submissive, but . . . "It wasn't a lie, Alec. You needed me and I simply adjusted to what you needed. I wouldn't

434

manipulate you. I doubt it would be possible, even if your memory never returned."

He sneered, and the expression nearly took away his handsomeness. She hated it. "Why, I wonder," he mused aloud, "did I marry you? Did I see you as a challenge, a nitwit female who needed to be shown her place? Somehow I can't reconstruct my reasons."

"I daresay you thought you lo—cared for me."

He laughed, shaking his head. He tossed down the rest of his sherry. "As I recall now, I reacted like a chivalrous fool. As I further recall, I also felt protective of you, pity for your situation. You had such adamant complaints about the unfairness of life. Yes, I felt sorry for you, particularly after your father died. You were alone and helpless."

"I wasn't helpless!"

"Oh? The shipyard would have gone bankrupt, and if you were as intelligent as you think you are you would have admitted it to yourself and—"

"And married a big, important man?"

"You weren't at all stupid, were you? You were quite realistic. You did marry a big, important man, a man to take care of you, to give you as many gowns as you wished. Of course, you haven't the taste to pick out any gown that doesn't look like a Cit's castoff—but that's neither here nor there, since I do—have good taste, that is."

"I didn't want your pity, Alec. Nor did I need your protection. Your fashion sense, however, has been a good thing."

"Well, you got both my pity and my protection,

for I am a man, Genny, who was raised to be honorable."

"You can be at once honorable and cruel? An odd juxtaposition, I think."

"Cruel? You truly think so? I disagree. For the first time since my accident, I think I'm seeing things clearly. Oh, yes, I should add that I also wanted to deflower you, truth be told. You were quite a virgin, Eugenia, and that appealed to me, though I would have denied it even to myself at the time. I thought I much preferred women who knew how to please me, who knew how they wished themselves to be pleased. But it didn't matter, for you had all that passion just waiting to be released. A sleeping beauty in men's clothing. And I wanted your passion, Genny. It was a powerful aphrodisiac to come into you and feel you arch up and hold me as close to you as you could, to hear you moaning against my shoulder, to feel your fingers digging into my back. I felt all-powerful. You were very responsive, Genny. Yes, that was probably my primary reason for marrying you."

"But you appear to still enjoy making love to me."

"Yes. It's something of a puzzle, isn't it? I do believe it's true. I was wrong to doubt your sexual eagerness—you were and are quite passionate. That's why I married you, that and the fact that Hallie seemed to approve of you."

"You'd made love to ladies before and hadn't married any of them. Why me?"

"Because you were so damned pathetic."

She reeled back as if he'd struck her.

"Now, my dear wife, go remove those absurd clothes. I won't sit down to my dinner with such a creature."

"No. No, I won't. I won't take orders from you, Alec. You're my husband, not my jailer."

"I'm everything to you, Genny. It is I who will choose what it is you deserve and need at any given time. You will obey me."

She held to her temper by a thread. "I don't understand you. I was simply searching about in that room to try and discover anything I could about your steward's murder. What difference does it make what I was wearing? Who cares, for God's sake? Why are you behaving so horribly to me?"

"I didn't ask you to become a detective. It isn't a woman's place to take chances like that. You could have hurt yourself in that room and—"

She couldn't bear any more. "Stop it! I can't believe you're saying these things. Alec, I'm your wife and I want to help both you and me because Carrick Grange is my home as well. The murder of your steward affects me as much as it does you."

He strode over to her. She held herself steady. His expression was unreadable to her. She remained perfectly still. He clasped his large hands around her shoulders. "Listen to me, Lady Sherard. You are my wife and you are carrying my child. I want you safe. It is my responsibility to keep you safe. Don't you understand some-thing as simple as that?" He shook her slightly.

"You're a fool," she said, her voice flat. "A damned fool. Let me go."

"Will you take off those clothes?"

She looked up into his beautiful, stern face. "Go to the devil," she said.

Alec released her suddenly and shoved her onto a sofa. He strode to the drawing room door, pulled it tightly closed, and locked it.

"Now," he said, turning.

She scrambled up and ran behind the sofa. The small distance gave her the courage to fuel her rage at him.

"You try to touch me, Alec, and I shall make you very sorry."

"I imagine that you would try," he replied without much interest. "But it doesn't matter. Again, if you would but recognize the fact, you're a woman. You have half my strength—"

"But more than enough determination. I mean it, Alec. Stop this nonsense and unlock that door."

He paused as if struck by her words, then nodded. "You're right. This isn't at all a good idea." He matched action to words and within seconds the drawing room door was open and he was standing beside her, proffering her a mock bow.

Genny said nothing more. She forced herself not to run, but her step quickened as she passed him. Suddenly she felt his arm go around her waist. He lifted her under his arm as if she were a sack of flour. Then, as if remembering the babe in her womb, he quickly shifted her until she lay over his shoulder.

She threatened him with every bodily harm she could imagine. He laughed. When she threatened to yell for the servants, he laughed harder. She smashed her fists against his back but knew she did him no harm. She looked up to see the butler, Smythe, the footman Giles, and Mrs. MacGraff. They said nothing. She saw, in fact, that Giles was doing his best not to laugh. This infuriated her and she struck her husband's back again.

"Stop it, Alec!"

He merely shook his head and quickened his pace. When he reached the master suite, he entered, then kicked the door closed with his bootheel. He dumped her onto the bed, then locked not only the bedchamber door but also the adjoining room door.

Genny rose quickly to stand by the far side of the bed. She was watching him, following his every move, wondering what he was thinking, what he planned to do. Rip the men's clothes off her, most likely, she knew, and moved closer to the wall. She turned to look out the window. She couldn't jump; it was a good thirty-foot drop.

"Don't even consider it," he said from behind her. "I know you're a woman and thus endowed with only a modicum of sense, but it is December and you are pregnant. Because of your delicate condition, I shall content myself with tearing those clothes off you. I would prefer thrashing you, but I am a reasonable man and I embrace compromise. Come here, Genny."

Her chin went up and her body went still. "Go to the devil."

"You're becoming repetitive. That sounds so very American of you. Come here. I shan't tell you again."

"Good, because you're boring me, Alec."

He strode toward her, and Genny, seeing that he was as enraged as she was, dashed toward the adjoining room door. She prayed he'd left the key in the lock but he hadn't. She felt his large hands close about her upper arms. He jerked her back hard against him.

"Now," he said, and ripped her shirt from her throat to her waist. Buttons flew across the floor. He grasped her vest and pulled it from her despite her flailing arms.

"Let's see what we have here." He twisted her about to face him. Genny freed her arm and drove her fist into his belly. He grunted and she saw the anger blaze brightly in his eyes.

"Let me go, Alec. Unlock this door and leave me alone. If you wish me to leave, I shall do so. In the morning. You'll never have to bear with my company again. Let me go."

He said nothing. He moved quickly, giving her no warning. In the next moment, the shirt was in shreds on the floor and her chemise was ripped down the front. He pulled it off her, leaving her naked to the waist. Genny tried to calm her deep, heaving breaths. She knew he was looking at her, and that made her furious and at the same time made her feel helpless. It was awful. "I'll never forgive you for this, Alec. Damn you, let me go now!"

He remained silent, staring down at her. Then he said, "Your breasts are larger." He lifted his hand and gently cupped her breast. "And heavier. And extremely beautiful." She flinched, but he held her still, his other arm behind her back.

"Let me go."

"All right," he said agreeably. And he stripped off her breeches, boots, and woolen stockings. When she was completely naked, he smiled down at her. "Very nice, my dear wife. Very nice indeed."

His hand was on her breast again, fondling her gently. She felt a stirring of desire but firmly ignored it. He picked her up in his arms and carried her to the bed. He didn't toss her onto the bed but laid her quite carefully in the center, on her back.

He sat down beside her. "Now," he said, his tone as light as a conversation about the weather, "let's talk, wife. You want to leave me?"

"Yes. I won't stay with you and be humiliated and insulted."

"How about lying on your beautiful back, quite naked, with me, fully clothed, looking at you? Will you accept that?"

She sucked in her breath, raised her hand to strike him, but he blocked her fist and bore it down to the bed. "Oh, no, you don't. Now, I want to look at my son."

"It's a daughter!"

He lightly ran his palm over her belly. He closed his eyes and held his hand still. He said quietly, not moving, "You aren't going anywhere. You are my wife and you will agree to do just as I tell you."

Genny's stomach growled loudly at that moment.

Alec's eyes flew open. He laughed. "I'll feed

you, but not just yet. No, now I want to enjoy looking at you."

He leaned down and kissed her stomach, nipping, light kisses. When he straightened, his eyes had darkened. She knew he wanted her. She saw the pulse throbbing in his throat.

"You don't like me," she said. "How can you want to make love to me?"

"Perverse of me, I suppose. You have a lovely body, Genny. I will much enjoy watching your belly swell. And your breasts."

"I'm cold, Alec." She followed action to words and shivered.

He stripped quickly, flinging his clothes about the floor, something that was very unlike him, for Alec was normally painfully neat with his belongings. He slipped beneath the covers and pulled her under him. He settled her against him, kissed her forehead, and said in the gentlest voice, "Now, Miss Eugenia, I'm going to come inside you. Should you like that?"

Her body would very much like that, but she, Eugenia Paxton Carrick, wouldn't. He'd said he was a reasonable man; well, she would try. She pulled away far enough to look into his face. "Alec, why are you doing this? Why are you treating me like this? I've done nothing to hurt you. I've wanted only to help you, to be with you, to make you feel less alone."

He didn't answer. Suddenly he was over her, his hands pulling her legs apart. He eased between them, and she felt his strength, the heat of him. "You are mine. If ever you say something so stupid again,, I will lock you up.

She stared at him, mute.

"You'll never leave me, Genny." He reared back, lifted her hips in his hands, and thrust forward, deep and hard, filling her. She was hot and ready for him and he smiled, a triumphant smile that made her want to kill him and scream with pleasure at the same time. But her hips were lifting to draw him deeper and his belly was pressing against hers and all her feelings were centered deep and low and she was sobbing softly, wanting him so much. The pain of his words and actions coalesced with the intense sensations he was making her feel, and it was too much. He was stroking inside her, so deep, then pulling back, making her moan with the intense pleasure and moan again with frustration. He knew her body so very well. She'd thought he'd also known *her,* but she'd been wrong. Even as she saddened at the truth of the thought, she was crying out, arching upward, clasping him close against her, and he was thrusting into her again and again until she was wild with wanting him and wanting her pleasure, and then it was upon her and she was trembling and convulsing, her legs stiffening, her body awash with such strong feelings that she couldn't separate herself as an individual from him. She was part of him and she accepted him into her at that moment.

"You're mine," she whispered against his throat. "I love you and you're mine."

Alec heard her words even as his body exploded into mad climax, ripping through him, tearing at him yet making him whole, blending the two of them together, inseparable, and it wouldn't end, ever.

"Yes," he said, kissing her breasts. "Yes."

She shuddered and held him even closer.

But five minutes later she was staring at him with bleak eyes.

24

"I mean it, Genny. Give your instructions to Mrs. MacGraff. It's your right and your responsibility, but stay out of the other. We don't know who is involved in this mess. There could be danger and I won't have you involved."

He was still deep inside her, still a part of her, and he'd said he would never leave her, ever. It was a lie, words spoken by a man in the throes of his own mad desire, but nonetheless a lie.

She said nothing for many minutes, looking over his left shoulder.

"Can't you be content to be my wife?"

Soft and inveigling, that was Alec's voice. The voice of a reasonable man to his unreasoning wife.

"Would you sign over the deed to me now?"

He became very still. She felt him leave her and he rolled onto his back, staring up at the ceiling. She felt bereft. She felt the stickiness of him between her thighs. She said nothing more, for after all, what else was there to say?

"Why now? As I recall, you told me not to— you even insisted that I not do it. You had faith in me then and I wasn't even a whole man, just a blankwitted fool. Now I am once more the man you tied yourself to, and you no longer trust me to care for you."

"The shipyard belongs to me. I want it in my name. I don't want to be dependent on your . . . whims for my keep."

He turned on his side toward her, his face suddenly taut with anger. "I was certainly dependent upon your good graces, upon your arbitrary female whims, after my accident!"

"Very true, and I didn't disappoint you, did I? I stuck close, gave you everything I could. I trusted you, and now look what I have gained for my efforts—another man who disapproves of me more than the man I originally married."

"I shouldn't say that my disapproval of your ridiculous male-aping habits has anything to do with you trusting me. I haven't slept with other women. I haven't beaten you. I haven't given you cause to doubt my honor or accuse me of shirking my responsibilities toward you. Now, madam wife, I will say it but once more. I will deed nothing to you. Nothing. You will learn trust for me, and that's an end to it."

She sat up and struck his shoulder with her fist. "It's mine! I demand that you give it back to me. That's what is fair."

He grabbed her wrist and bore it down to her side. "I determine what is fair and what isn't. Now let's feed you. I don't want my son to know hunger."

"It's a bloody daughter!"

"No," he said slowly as he jerked the covers

445

back to look at her belly. "It's a son. I know it. I can't tell you how I do, but I know it's true. Would you like your dinner up here? No, don't answer. I would."

He rose, naked and long-limbed and beautiful, and pulled the bell cord. He built up the fire, and she watched the play of muscles across his shoulders, across his back, and the long thick muscles in his legs. He stretched then, knowing she was watching him, his body silhouetted by the flames. At last he shrugged on a dressing gown, one of thick black velvet with gold velvet cuffs. He looked magnificent. She watched him stride to the bedchamber door, open it, and give servants orders for their dinner.

Genny felt numb. Why had she married him? She'd known that he didn't approve of her. The past two months were outside reality, outside anything that could have been predicted. The months were gone now, as if they'd never existed. And this Alec was different. He was more strident, more forceful in his opinions, than the Alec she'd married. It was as if he were afraid to give an inch, afraid that he would lose her, or perhaps himself again.

It didn't matter, and she was simply making excuses for him. She said slowly, "I was a fool to trust you. I should have had you sign that deed over to me immediately. You were willing then. You might not have remembered a thing, but you were a reasonable man, a kind and generous man. Well, it was my own fault, for at that point I insisted that you shouldn't. Now I haven't any money at all. I have nothing."

"I'll provide you with an ample allowance."

She said not a word. When she remained silent, Alec asked a bit sharply, "Don't you want to know how much I shall give you?"

Her hand fisted in her lap, but he didn't see it.

Alec looked at her bowed head. He knew she'd spoken more to herself than to him. He realized he hated that defeated voice from her. What had she done, after all? She'd given herself to him, kept all the strain she could from him, comforted him as best she could. And he'd turned on her. But she was a woman, she was his wife . . .

She's not at all like Nesta. She wasn't like any woman he'd ever known before. He sighed and opened the bedchamber door to the two footmen carrying their dinner. He said nothing, watching them pull a low table in front of the fire, arrange the dinner, settle the chairs, then look to him for further instructions.

He thanked them and nodded dismissal.

"Would you like a dressing gown or would you prefer to be naked?"

Genny sighed, then felt her chin go up. She stepped off the dais and walked languidly toward the set table. She sat in a chair, feeling the heat from the fire warm her bare flesh.

Alec stared at her, then smiled. He hadn't expected this. She liked a challenge, his wife. Odd, how her gentle, sweet behavior had masked that from him. He shrugged out of his dressing gown and, naked, joined his wife for dinner.

They feasted on roast hare, gravy, and currant jelly, followed by rump steak and oyster sauce.

447

The carrots and parsnips were crisp and fresh, the Spanish onions stewed and spicy. Alec poured her a glass of sweet French wine.

"I would like to say something, Alec."

"You wish to go to work in a shipyard in Liverpool? A pregnant lady climbing the rigging?"

"No."

"It's difficult to pay attention to your words since your breasts are so very enticing, but I shall endeavor. Go ahead, wife."

"It's not about our situation, our personal situation, that is, but rather about your steward's murder. I'm beginning to believe that it wasn't one or several of your tenants—murdering rabble, I think you said Sir Edward called them—who are the villains in this. I think your steward is the one we should look to."

"My steward is quite dead. I don't believe it's likely that he did away with himself."

"The theory is, if I understand it aright, that Arnold Cruisk discovered that some of your tenants were dishonest and had threatened to have them transported, and thus they killed him. I think the answer lies rather in the direction of Mr. Cruisk's dishonesty."

"I hired the man myself some five and a half years ago. He always sent me detailed accounting records. He always kept me informed. He religiously deposited quarterly sums into my bank. He'd been the steward for Sir William Wolverton before he came to me. Sir William wrote that he was an excellent man who knew his job and could be trusted."

"Where is Sir William now?"

"Good heavens, Genny, why do you want to know that? Oh, very well, he lives in Dorset, near to Chipping Marsh, if he's still alive. The reason my steward left his employ was because his son had taken over the estate management."

"I think we should write to him. Perhaps, just perhaps, Mr. Cruisk forged a letter from Sir William. You've never met this Sir William Wolverton, have you?"

Alec stared at her a moment, then said, "I thought I told you it wasn't your place to play detective. It isn't something I want you to do."

Genny ignored him, saying, "That's why I was searching through the papers in his office this afternoon. There must be something, Alec, to prove he was a scoundrel. His papers to you could have been pure fiction. I've also spoken at length to Mrs. MacGraff, to Giles, and to Smythe. There are several hotheaded tenants, but vicious? Murderers? They don't think so. On the other hand, Arnold Cruisk wasn't one of their favorites. He swaggered, so Smythe told me. He treated the Grange as if he were the owner, not you."

Smythe had told Alec much the same thing even as he'd exclaimed again and again how happy he was that Alec was home.

"Of course, their perceptions can't be considered proof. I also spoke to an upstairs maid. Her name is Margie."

Alec placed the very pretty, young upstairs maid. He studiously chewed on a parsnip and swallowed it. "So?"

"I can't be sure as yet. I found her crying as

if her heart would break. She seemed quite distraught. But she didn't really say anything. Still, it was the air of desperation about her when I asked her questions that made me wonder. That and what she didn't say. I think—no, I am *certain* she knows something but is afraid to tell."

Alec played with his fork. It was heavy and it was gold and his family crest was displayed elegantly: an eagle's head behind a gold shield, the shield supported on either side by a winged sable, its throat encircled with a gemmed collar. The Carrick motto below the shield was: *Fidei Tenax,* or Firm to My Trust.

The one thing he couldn't seem to capture from his wife—trust.

Odd, how her reasoning paralleled his own. He, however, hadn't yet thought to write to Sir William. He would now. He knew every one of his tenants, had known them since his birth. There were a couple of bullies, several greedy louts, but most of them were honest, hardworking people. Even the bullies wouldn't murder. Besides, he'd asked himself again and again what sort of dishonesty they could have done. Could they have stolen and sold an estate plowshare? It was a rather ridiculous theory when closely examined.

He'd not known anything about this upstairs maid. He looked up to see his wife gazing at him. At his mouth. He smiled, a very male smile. It was nice to be wanted by one's wife. Very nice indeed. He would write the bloody letter tomorrow.

He wanted his wife now.

He took her with all the intensity that was within him, and she was his in those long minutes, but at the same time, he thought on the verge of sleep, she'd captured him, completely, irrevocably. He heard a sound and turned his head slowly on the pillow toward her. Another sound. It was a sob. He stilled. He didn't know what to do. He raised his hand to caress her shoulder, then slowly lowered it to his side again.

Why couldn't she be as he wished her to be? Was it so very much to ask of her?

The sobs trailed off. Alec listened to her erratic breathing soften and even off into sleep.

He stared upward into the darkness for a very long time. He realized just as he was dozing off that Genny never bored him. She enraged, infuriated, and beguiled him, but she never bored him. She'd been a mystery to him at the very beginning and she still was.

He remembered his cruel words to her, that he'd married her because she'd been so pathetic.

He was a fool and a cheat and a coward. He'd married her because he didn't want to live without her. And that was the truth. A truth that should be said. Perhaps trust was gained by complete acceptance of the one loved. And respect. She had both from him. It was time he told her that.

Late the following morning Alec forgot his vow to tell Genny the truth—that he loved her, that he respected her. She was poking about in his steward's office again. She wasn't wearing her men's clothing—he'd shredded each and every

451

garment. She was, however, wearing one of the new gowns he'd selected for her in London, a pale peach silk. And she'd ruined it in the filthy, smoke-blackened room.

"I haven't found a thing," she said as she looked up to see him watching her. If she noticed his stern visage, she chose to ignore it. She shook ashes and burned paper off a bound pamphlet, looked through it quickly, then tossed it aside. "Nothing. It is most depressing not to be able to prove one's theory. Have you written that letter yet to your Sir William?"

"Yes. I even sent it by special messenger. We should, hopefully, hear back within three days."

"I understand from Mrs. MacGraff that we are to have Sir Edward dine with us this evening."

"Yes. I trust you will change your gown. I would dislike Sir Edward believing I keep my wife on such an abjectly short string."

"A short string," Genny repeated slowly, smiling. "I've never heard that before. It's terribly English, I suppose."

She'd defused him. His lips thinned. "What do American men say when they wish to express that they're not at all niggardly toward their wives?"

"Perhaps they say that they love them, and that's all that's necessary."

He stared at her, remembering his vow, seeing the surge of hope in her expressive eyes. As he remained silent, he saw the hope drain away, to be replaced by pain and wariness. She was waiting for him to speak, and in speaking, to wound her.

"Damnation," he said very quietly, strode to

her, and hauled her into his arms. "Forgive me," he said against her hair. "Forgive me, Genny. I'm a damnable beast and I'm sorry for it."

She remained tense, and he felt the depths of the pain he'd given her, heaped upon her so gratuitously. He kissed her temple, her ear. "Forgive me," he said again.

"My lord . . . oh! Do forgive me, that is—"

Alec slowly released his wife and turned slowly. "It's all right, Mrs. MacGraff. What is it?"

"I, ah, that is, I wished to speak to her ladyship, but—"

Alec heard Genny's harsh breathing from behind him. He said mildly, "Her ladyship is a bit short of breath at the moment. She will fetch you in fifteen minutes."

"No, no," Genny said, quickly coming around from behind her husband. "What is it, Mrs. MacGraff?"

"I'm not quite certain, my lady. 'Tis Margie. She's crying and carrying on and she begged me to let her see you. I don't understand it."

Genny didn't want to leave Alec, not yet, not when he seemed to be . . . but there was no hope for it. "Take Margie to the small yellow room. I'll be there shortly."

Alec was frowning. He was full to bursting with words and feelings and vows and apologies and declarations. But now wasn't the time. "Can I come with you?" he said instead.

Genny didn't think that would be such a good idea. "Wait here, Alec, over there in the shadows. I'll bring Margie back with me. I spoke to her again earlier. Pressed her as far as I could. It's about what she knows of Mr. Cruisk's murder, I'm sure of it."

In five minutes Genny was back, Margie in tow. It was obvious that the girl didn't want to come into the burned-out room. But Genny urged her forward and pulled shut what remained of the door.

Alec stood quietly, out of sight, and watched his wife. She was gentle but firm. He watched Margie burst into tears and Genny comfort her. But she brought her back again and again. And he listened openmouthed when Margie burst out with:

"He raped me, milady. My Gawd, he forced me and told me if I said a word to either Mr. Smythe or Mrs. MacGraff, he'd make sure me ma and me little sisters would starve in a ditch. He said he could do anything when the baron wasn't here, that he was the master and he could do just as he pleased with me, with everyone."

Genny drew the girl to her, cradling her head on her shoulder even though Margie was much larger and taller. "Oh, Margie, I'm so sorry, so very sorry, but it's over now, truly over, and there's nothing more for you to fear. Baron Sherard is a fair man. He'll understand, I promise you. All you must do is tell the truth. You've nothing to fear, truly."

Margie drew back, her dark eyes filled with more tears and her mouth filled with confession. "Ye don't understand, milady! He tried to rape me again, here, in his office. I fought him and I picked up the candle branch and struck him with it, and the candles went flying and they were lit

454

and they caught the draperies on fire, and I tried, truly I did, but I couldn't stop it and I ran and it was awful . . . horrible!"

"I know. I know."

Alec wanted to emerge but he waited. Genny would handle it just fine. "And then Sir Edward came and you were more frightened, weren't you?"

"Oh, Gawd, I was never more afraid in all my life."

"I know. You did right to tell me, Margie. I'll speak to his lordship and to Sir Edward. You acted in self-defense. Everything is all right now. Don't be frightened anymore. Now, why don't you go up to your room and have a nice sleep. You're very tired, aren't you?"

The girl was exhausted. She nodded numbly. After she'd left, Genny turned to face her husband. He stepped out of the shadows.

"The bastard," he said. "None of us realized or suspected or anything. . . ."

"Odd, isn't it? What shall we tell Sir Edward?"

"Not the truth," Alec said thoughtfully. "He has an inflexible mind. He'd believe the girl a slut, no doubt, and want to deport her. No, I'll think of something to tell him. Margie will be safe enough now."

And he did, over dinner that evening. It was a wonderful tale about how Mr. Cruisk was dishonest and he had been afraid that he, Alec, would discover his perfidy and send him, Arnold Cruisk, to Newgate. It appeared to Alec that the steward, in attempting to flee, had accidentally knocked over the candle branch and died in the resulting fire.

Sir Edward, no fool, wanted to applaud the baron's melodrama, but he had just finished his third glass of excellent port and thus really didn't care if the truth of the matter matched the baron's tale. It would do, he thought, and nodded benignly.

Alec was told the following morning that the baroness was, at last sight, going toward the stables. It was cold, the sky overcast and bloated with snow. Alec quickened his step. He paused in front of the slate-roofed stables. Some of the slate tiles were loose, others missing entirely. The older section of the building sagged. The wood looked rotted and some of the windows hung precariously in their casings. Alec frowned. There was much to be done here at Carrick Grange. He entered the tackroom at the back of the stables.

"Hello," he said to Genny. "Sir Edward was here again, his head free of the effects of my excellent port. Doubtless he wasn't certain he'd heard aright last night and wanted to see my performance again in full daylight. I trod the boards once more for him, a born actor, I daresay, and now he is again on his way, content, hopefully, because Baron Sherard is content."

Genny lowered the rag she was using to polish the stirrups on Alec's Spanish saddle. She looked at him, remembering his words spoken the day before. She'd finally fallen asleep waiting for him the previous evening. Sir Edward had held him in three rubbers of piques until very late. Alec hadn't awakened her.

"We make a fairly decent team, I think," Alec said, closing the tackroom door. The room smelled of leather, linseed, and the comforting odor of horse.

"Perhaps."

He raised an eyebrow.

"You handled Margie very well. You got the truth out of her. I'm really quite proud of you."

Genny stared at his cravat. "Are you really?" she said, and she sounded both wary and defensive.

Alec frowned, seeing again what he'd brought her to. How he'd wished that Sir Edward would have left the previous evening, but the man hadn't budged away from the deck of cards. Alec had thus lost ground. "Come here," he said and drew her into his arms again. "Now where was I? Ah, yes, I recall that I was waiting like a martyr pleading divine intervention. Will you forgive me?"

She searched his face. "Forgive you what exactly?"

He grinned and she felt her heart turn over. She would probably forgive him anything, he made her feel so besotted.

He traced his fingertip over her cheekbone, down her nose to the small dimple in her chin. "For forbidding you the joys of being a detective, for forbidding your men's clothes—"

"You've already destroyed all of them!"

"I'll buy you twenty pairs of trousers. Boots? Ten pairs at least, white leather with tassels. And—"

She sent her fist lightly into his arm. "No more, please." Her head was lowered, her voice tight.

"But most of all, forgive me for forbidding you to be you. The you that you are is the you I fell in love with, Genny. I like the sweet, submissive creature who cared for me when I was a blank slate, but I married the wench with all the vinegar. She drives me to bedlam and to ecstasy as well. She makes me furious and blissful. She makes me want to howl at her stubbornness and moan with desire. Say you'll forgive this stupid man, Genny. Be my love and my wife and my partner."

She stared up at him, mute.

"Why have I changed so suddenly? I can see you wanting to ask, but I've made you so wary of me, haven't I? What should I expect? The truth is that I discovered what a bloody fool I've been to you. But, Genny, in all fairness, it took me less than twenty-four hours to come to reason. That's progress, wouldn't you say? I realized there shouldn't be pain or distrust or anger between us, at least not for more than a ten-minute stretch. We've a marriage that's matched two very strong, very stubborn people, and I doubt not that we'll roar and yell and make people tremble around us, but it will be for our ultimate amusement, Genny, for we're bound together, you know. For always, and I am more than ready to accept it. I want you to accept it and believe me and try your best to forgive me. What do you say?"

"You'll not try to be a domestic tyrant?"

He gave her a slow smile. "Is that what I was being? I'm not certain I understand. You mean just because I was telling you what to do, ordering you about, and sneering away all your ideas and opinions, you believe me a domestic tyrant? Good heavens, what a lowering concept. Yes, I very probably will try. It's in my man's makeup, I suppose. What about you? Won't you try to rule me? Make me your lapdog?"

"Very probably. I think I should like you lying at my feet, with a meaty bone in your mouth." Her own smile faded and she shook her head. "I don't know what's to be done. It's a difficult situation, Alec."

"Isn't that splendid? I thrive on difficulties. Difficulties make me randy as the devil. In fact, you know what I should like to do right this minute? Well, I'd like to do it just as soon as you tell me you love me more than the stirrups on that Spanish saddle."

"I love you more than any stirrup ever made, regardless of its nationality."

"And I you, Genny. And I you."

He turned and locked the tackroom door. He turned back and smiled at his wife, raising his hand to her.

"Can we begin again?"

She smiled and placed her hand in his. "Yes," she said. "I should like that."

EPILOGUE

Carrick Grange, Northumberland, England
July 1820

Alec had never been more scared in his life. He knew he'd never forget that day as long as he lived. Now he felt drained, unutterably weary, and wonderfully contented because it was over and Genny was safe and his small son was alive and healthy and wailing. If he listened closely, he could hear him through the adjoining door. Then it was abruptly quiet and Alec smiled. His son was doubtless at his wet nurse's breast, suckling like a little stoat.

He sat down in a chair beside the bed and leaned back, closing his eyes. Dear Lord, the messes one got oneself into. He and Genny had decided to picnic the previous morning and had taken the dogcart and a huge basket filled with every delight Cook could concoct to Mortimer's Glen, a beautiful, quite primitive and quite private place complete with a cold mountain stream, scores of oak trees, and soft moss-covered ground.

He'd made Genny forget her aching back and her swollen belly for a little while. He'd told her tales that made her laugh and groan, and they'd had such joy together until the damnable rain

460

had begun abruptly, without warning, a thunderstorm that had turned the glen into a quagmire.

And the dogcart had broken a wheel and turned over. And Genny had gone into labor a week early and they were miles away from the Grange.

Alec opened his eyes and looked over at his sleeping wife as if he feared she wasn't really there, that she'd died as Nesta had died and he'd failed her and was alone. But there was color in her cheeks her breath rhythmic, her hair brushed and shining. Looking at her now, Alec found it impossible to tell that she'd been in agony twenty-four hours before.

He winced, his belly muscles tightening at the thought of it. No one should have to bear such pain. He'd never before stayed with a woman birthing a child. It wasn't allowed. Gentlemen were banished. Although he'd heard Nesta's cries, they hadn't pierced his soul, for he'd been so far away from her.

But Genny had stared up at him, her eyes filled with agony, and she'd grasped his hand and squeezed, moaning when she couldn't bear it anymore. He'd been an abject fool, dithering and frightened, he thought now, until he'd realized that what he'd learned from that Muslim physician was no longer just an intellectual exercise. He would deliver his own child. He would save his wife. There was, after all, no one else.

Thank God for the small dilapidated cottage he'd remembered that was but a quarter of a mile from the glen. He'd carried her there, stopping to hold her close when the contractions hit her.

461

He'd stripped her, laid a fire, and begun to act like a man who knew what he was doing.

And when she'd screamed and screamed, apart from him, the pain imprisoning her into her body, he'd finally pushed down on her belly, then slipped his hand inside her, easing his child further into the birth canal. His son had slid into his cupped hands and he'd stared for a moment, not really believing the miracle before his eyes. "Genny," he'd whispered, looking at his wife's white face. "We've a son, love. It's over now and you've given me a son."

And Genny, nearly unconscious with fatigue, had rallied and croaked in her hoarse voice, "Nay, Alec, it must be a daughter. You're wrong I promised you a daughter."

He'd laughed and cut his son's cord and wrapped him in his own now dry shirt. "Hallie will be pleased, and you, madam wife, will come about. Now let's rid you of the afterbirth."

He and Genny and their wizened little babe had been found three hours later, just as the sun was setting, by a contingent of servants sent by Smythe to search for them.

Alec dozed off. He didn't know how long he slept, but when he awakened he saw his daughter staring at him, her serious little face filled with worry.

"Papa? You're awake? Genny is all right? My brother is all right as well? His nanny treats me like a little girl and won't tell me anything. I slipped in here when no one was looking."

"Yes to everything, pumpkin." Alec lifted

Hallie onto his lap. "Everything is wonderfully fine."

"Mama looks awfully tired, Papa."

I would, too, if I'd gone through what she had, Alec thought but didn't voice it aloud. "She'll be right as rain in a couple of days."

"What's his name?"

"Your mother and I haven't decided yet. What do you think, Hallie?"

"Ernest or Clarence."

"Why such pious names?"

"Nanny said he's so beautiful he'll be a terror when he grows up and he should be kept on the straight and narrow, and religion and a series of good works would be good for his character. I thought a dull name would help."

"Goodness, and here I thought he looked like a wizened little monkey. Just like you did when you were his size."

"Papa! I'm not beautiful!"

"No," Alec said dryly, staring at his daughter's upturned face, "not at all. You're naught but passable-looking. Doubtless you'll be a spinster and take care of me and your mother in our old age. What do you think of a life of good works for yourself ?"

"Papa, we must name the baby. He'll feel strange if we don't."

Alec suddenly remembered that it had been many days before Hallie had been named. He hadn't wanted to think about her, he— He shook his head. "All right. We'll ask Genny when she wakes up."

"I'm awake, I think."

"Mama, do you feel all right?" Hallie had scooted off her father's lap and gone to the side of the bed. Her small hand lightly stroked Genny's cheek.

"I'm just fine, love. Now, your father has already picked out a name, Hallie. We discussed it thoroughly when I was in labor at that cottage. Tell her, Alec."

"James Devenish Nicholas St. John Carrick." Hallie stared.

Genny laughed and took the little girl's hand. "He'll grow into it, Hallie. And your papa is adamant. We'll simply humor him, I think, and call your little brother Dev."

"Dev," Hallie said slowly. "I like that. Can I go see him now?"

"Of course you can," Alec said. "But if you love me, don't wake him up. His lungs are too powerful for my sanity at present."

Once alone again, Alec eased down beside his wife. "No protruding stomach," he said thoughtfully.

"Thank goodness for that." Genny yawned.

"You feel just the thing?"

"Yes. You're quite the handy man to have about, Alec, particularly when a lady is having a baby."

She saw his throat constrict.

"I was scared out of my wits, what few I had left."

"It was only temporary. Mrs. MacGraff told me that Arielle and Burke are due to arrive in a couple of days."

"Yes, Arielle wanted to be here in good time for your lying-in."

Genny giggled or tried to, but what emerged from her throat was a raspy creak.

"Hush, madam." He pulled a blanket over himself and eased Genny against his side. "Let's nap. The good Lord knows that I deserve it, and since you're but a weak female, the good Lord will understand when you fall asleep without good reason."

"You're a lovely man, Alec, even when I want to cosh you."

"I know." He kissed her cheek.

"I made a lot of money the last quarter. My design for the clipper is marvelous. I shall become quite rich."

He grinned against her temple. "Whatever brought that on?"

"I just wanted to remind you what an excellent woman of business I am. And now I'm a mother. Behold a very talented—"

"Wench. Abandoned wench—at least you used to be. Do you think you will be again?"

She wanted to laugh but she was too tired. She felt warm and comforted and sublimely happy. Life was sweet.

"Probably," she said against his shoulder. "Very probably."

"I'll be counting the days," Alec said. "But I shan't complain. I'll care for my son and daughter and see that the stables are properly finished and I'll even learn to be a better horseman, though I'll never ride like Knight or Burke."

"No, let's go traveling, Alec. Let's take the

Night Dancer and sail away. I want to see the monkeys on Gibraltar. And meet the governor. What was his name?"

He felt his blood stir as she spoke. The sea. Yes, he wanted to feel the deck rolling beneath his feet. He could forgo the damned monkeys, but if Genny wanted to see them, well . . .

She was asleep.

He kissed her temple and closed his eyes. He pictured the four of them aboard his barkentine. Bound for Gibraltar. And he could show her Italy and northern Africa, and perhaps they could sail to Greece. Ah, Santorini in the summer; there was no more beautiful a spot on the face of the earth. . . .